Praise for

The Winds of Fate Reviews:

"…captivating romance that takes us to the world of seventeenth-century London…Sexual tension and legal and familial intrigue ensue with the reader cheering on the lovely pair." – *Publishers Weekly*

"has everything…full of passion, betrayal, mystery and all the good stuff readers love." – *ABNA Reviewer*

"Original…strong-willed heroine…I love all of it…the unlikely premise of a female member of the aristocracy visiting a man who is condemned to die and asking him to marry her."– *ABNA Reviewer*

Surrender the Wind Reviews:

"The lush descriptions of the southern countryside, the witty repartee between the characters, the factual descriptions of battles woven into the storylines, and the rich characters kept me glued to the pages." – *Alwyztrouble's Romance Reviews*

Surrender the Wind received the "Crowned Heart" and National "RONE AWARD" finalist for excellence. "With twists and turns…and several related subplots woven in, no emotional stone is left unturned in this romance." – *InD'tale Magazine*

Sweet Vengeance: Duke of Rutland Series I Reviews:

"A historical romantic masterpiece…sizzling sensuality, touching emotions, and great historical detail. – *International Book Award*

Embark on a new adventure!

Lord of the Wilderness

Duke of Rutland Series IV

Elizabeth St. Michel

Elizabeth St. Michel

ISBN: 9781950016006
ISBN: 1950016005
Library of Congress Control Number: 2019904319

For Michael James

You make me laugh.

"Smiles the earth, and smile the waters,
Smile the cloudless skies above us,
But I lose the way of smiling
When thou art no longer near me!

~Song of Hiawatha: XI.
Hiawatha's Wedding-Feast: Henry Wadsworth Longfellow

Chapter 1

New York Frontier, 1779

*L*ady Juliet Faulkner finished chopping and stacking the wood on the porch, her breath crystallizing in white puffs. Feathery flakes scattered widely through the air and hovered downward with uncertain flight. New snow piled on the mountains, bathing the land and, for a moment, in its silent beauty cleansed the horror that had brought her from England to this place. *America.* On a far-flung farmstead, the frontier…a murky, misty wild land of savages…had left an indefinable impression in Juliet's mind.

Lady? She was far from that title now as it had been stripped from her at the time of her seizure. No one had come to her aid. No one, not even the judge who turned a blind eye to her pleadings, transporting them directly to a ship riding anchor in the Thames, and then dispatching them across the stormy Atlantic. Sold into indenture, Juliet had no rights. No freedom. Seven years of bondage. Seven years of hell.

The door opened and closed and Mary, her best friend, joined her smelling faintly of warm bread the girls had kneaded before the break of dawn. "Mistress Orpha is in a fury. She will beat you raw and turn you out into the snow to freeze if you don't answer her summons."

Juliet dove her hands in the layers of her tattered skirts. "Oh, come Mary. Surely, a little rest won't be a problem."

"You know better," said Mary. "Remember how the mistress doused Eldon with water, then thrust him outside when temperatures were so cold rocks exploded? She shrieked the same punishment for anyone who dared to help him. He would have frozen if you'd not risked letting him in when everyone was asleep."

Wolves howled in the distance, looking for food, closer now with the long cold winter upon them.

"I fear Indians attacking us." Mary shuddered and not from the freezing temperatures.

"They never leave their longhouses in the winter," Juliet said to allay her friend's fears, her neck prickling in anticipation of the sting of a razor-edged knife. Since they had come to this new land they had seen few Indians. Unusual for the staggering population and number of villages purported to be near, according to their Master, Horace Hayes.

Mary clutched her shawl. "They will tear the skin from our face and head and disembowel us while we are still alive."

Mary, like her vicar father, was given to the dramatic. In England, he had sermonized about the savages, where civilized people in an unimaginable wilderness were fated to struggle with pitiless agents of Satan. Too many nights Juliet had to calm Mary's night terrors, sprung from the vicar's graphic descriptions of horns and hooves and devouring creatures. Oh, how he preached his fear with fire and damnation, ending amid a flourish of redemption and forgiveness.

Except he had showed no mercy to his only child, expunging the record of her existence for a single lapse.

Juliet's throat tightened. She met Mary's suffering with soul-shattering sorrow. For Mary's pain mirrored a wound in Juliet, buried so deep…all those years pretending her father, Baron John Faulkner's scorn didn't exist.

Her father had loved her mother deeply. She'd died bringing Juliet into the world, an unforgiveable act that precipitated his hateful condemnation of the child. To be blamed for the death of her mother? Juliet's survival had served as a constant reminder of the sin of her birth.

Four small crosses shadowed the white-cloaked yard, grim reminders of the frailties of life on the frontier. The Hayes' children had all succumbed to disease before any reached four years.

Mary followed her gaze. "Mistress Orpha's evil is rewarded with their deaths. They are the lucky ones. At least they will be spared of an attack."

"Quick, change your thoughts and you'll change our future." She had to keep Mary's hope alive, her own hope alive. Most indentured servants did not last a year. "We have survived a terrible ocean crossing when I thought the ship would sink and we'd all perish. We will survive this." Her voice startled a bird hiding in the treetops. Panicked, it flew to another tree in a flurry of frantic wings.

Were they being watched? Indians? She peered through the veil of snow. Nonsense. "Mary, go in before you catch your death of cold. I'll collect the eggs for you after I attend Orpha."

3

Mary had been so ill aboard the ship and had been slow to recover. If anything happened to her dear friend…

Juliet followed Mary inside, and moved through the house, no less surprised at the size of the mansion in the middle of the wilderness. Wood paneled walls, Chippendale furniture, silver, crystal, china, wines, the finest of linens rivaled the best of middle-class homes in England and stood testament to Master Hayes' success as a prominent trader.

In the dining room, she paused at a tapestry dominating a wall and the one ornamentation that fascinated her. In the fine weaving, a story unfolded of a splendid half-clothed warrior on his chariot pulled by two white horses, his spear pitched high and victorious over the melee.

She tapped her lip. Achilles, wasn't he?

What touched her was the swarming endlessness of colors, the tangle of textures that went into each strand of that infinite, complex tapestry…each one vibrated under the crush of battle, pulsating and sending echoes of courage, or bloodlust, or fear, or flash of swords. The theater of death filled up with keening and caterwauling as the sodden earth became oily with gore.

The creativeness of a weft of doves carried the powerful hero across a celestial vault where the air scattered hues of brilliant blue sun rays and deposited him to a peaceful firmament. There he basked in the light of a half-clad beauty who bestowed him her hand, and linked to the heavy, sultry strand was the glow of the hero's adoration. Toward the bottom, the fibers stretched taut and bonded themselves solidly, its silk made from the slants of playful stags, a unicorn, and squirrels, embedded in a magical forest.

Her breath hitched. How she loved the hero and imagined his heroic feats.

Without beginning or end, the tapestry existed as a work of such great beauty, her soul wept, and her mind numb to—

"Juliet!" Orpha's shriek rang throughout the house.

Almost everything. Juliet hurried upstairs, knocked, and entered Mistress Hayes' lair.

"You're late," Orpha snapped. Perched at her dressing table, she primped her velvet night robe over folds of ponderous girth. "I hate to be kept waiting. I paid a fortune for you lazy, blasphemous, and treacherous girls."

"Yes, Mistress." Juliet grabbed the silver brush before Orpha struck her. Too often, she had endured the beatings and accepted the indignities the same way she abided the stench of the privy.

She brushed the wispy strands of hair, at least what remained of it. Orpha leaned her head back, her lips parted in the beginnings of a smile and her watery eyes closed in ecstasy. Gaps showed where she had sacrificed a tooth for every child she had borne.

Due to her reigning vanity, Orpha allowed only Juliet and Mary to attend her. Bright, unforgiving light streamed in from the window, illuminating what scarlet fever had wrought, a receding hairline withdrawing to the last third of her scalp. How ironic—Orpha was Hebrew for skull.

Two years before, Juliet sat at her dressing table at her ancestral home, Faulkner Manor, her hair brushed by her nurse, Moira O'Neill.

Sometimes the bad things that happen to us in our lives put

us directly on the path to the best things that will ever happen to us.

Moira had pounded the thought into her young charge's head. Moira, the closest substitute for a mother, yielded a love for a child desperate to be loved. Her heart squeezed at the thought. Moira had long since gone to Heaven.

After that, Juliet's life had been a series of horrors. They had been herded off a ship in Philadelphia, scrubbed of lice in a freezing river, and then paraded on a platform for the sale of their indenture. She shivered at the thought.

While standing on the block, the captain had bowed to her, swinging his arm above the masses, and mocked her, saying, "Her Majesty here, has grandiose illusions. Thinks she's nobility." The men hooted and shouted, the women tittered.

He had bent close to her ear. "I have the power to make ye disappear if ye don't keep yer mouth shut." He was part of the prosperous business in white slavery where huge profits were gained. Juliet shuddered. The leering looks of men who checked her teeth and touched her in intimate places had her fearing for not only her future, but her life. Juliet's heartbeat raced faster with each stroke of the brush.

Mary's beauty attracted even worse behavior, men laughing and joking with crude innuendo, outbidding each other as they fondled her under her dress and pressed themselves against her. She and Mary were both sold on the auction block to a hideous woman and her husband, yet Juliet thanked providence for the miracle of being sold to the same master.

"What did you say?" Orpha narrowed her gaze at Juliet, hauling her from the ugly memories.

"Nothing, Mistress." Best to work hard and keep her mouth shut.

Mary backed in, laden with a heavy tray of oatmeal, fresh baked bread, layers of smoked bacon, steak and eggs. Juliet's stomach rumbled. She had not eaten since the morning before. Their master gave the servants barely enough food to exist, parceling out each morsel as if it were gold. While she'd gotten used to eating less, her boney body evidenced their cruelty.

"Master Hayes is due home today. I want the house cleaned top to bottom."

"Yes, Madam."

Horace had cut into the trade routes, carving out the middlemen by buying furs directly from the Indians, and then supplying traders with goods who traveled north. As a King's man, he had learned the Mohawk language and combined his personal business with diplomacy, acquiring thousands of acres of Native land and becoming very wealthy.

He was gone most of the time, leaving the running of the farm to his wife, who lived to beat, starve and confuse her servants. Orpha relished telling tales of Indian atrocities in case any of the servants thought to escape—as if they required her divination. The whipping post in the front yard stood a grim reminder of the punishment those who had attempted escape received.

Carrying two heaping buckets of fireplace ash, Mary staggered to the door. Juliet nodded to her, a silent assent of the ordeal to come. Master Hayes had a taste for the serving girls and provided a constant struggle with his cat and mouse games.

Juliet placed a glosser cap over Orpha's bald pate. "Will that be all, Mistress?"

Orpha watched her in the mirror, locking her gaze on Juliet, and then rose with a self-important swirling of her heavy robe. She lowered herself against the pillows on her bed, picked up a hunk of bread and lathered it with warm butter. She popped the whole thing in her mouth and smacked her lips. Juliet's mouth watered and she turned to depart.

"I did not give you leave. Plump my pillows." Orpha tucked a finger up under her cap and gave her bald head an idle scratch. How Orpha delighted in making Juliet stand and watch her eat.

While Juliet rearranged the pillows, Orpha took a hunk of bacon and chewed, grease trickling down her chins. "Stick that abominable red hair in your cap. You should be ashamed to have it seen."

Juliet clenched her teeth. All her life she'd been ridiculed for the color of her hair. Her father's sister possessed a rabid contempt for Juliet's Gaelic ancestry and browbeat her into believing she was the devil's agent and induced to criminality because of her red hair.

To counteract the hurt enacted by her cruel aunt, Moira had wiped Juliet's tears. "Your Irish mother had the same color hair when she was young, and later it deepened into a beautiful shade of red."

Juliet tidied the well-appointed room, Orpha's fanciful frontier imitation of Versailles with blue-colored silk peacock wallpaper, cupids painted on the ceiling, and matching draperies.

"You may go. Don't forget to heat the water for my bath."

Juliet bobbed a curtsy and closed the door.

The blast of heat from the kitchen warmed her. Mary cut slices of bread and ham and shoved them across the table. "Hurry up, the cook has gone to the privy."

The girls stuffed their mouths with warm bread and butter as Mary peered through the window. "A half-moon is carved in the top of the door for the witch to escape."

How many times had Mary made the superstitious comment over the year of their indenture? "She will not slither through the crescent." With her fingers, Juliet scooped up jam from the compote and closed her eyes over the rare feast.

Outside the cook stamped her feet on the porch to rid them of snow. Juliet wiped the crumbs off Mary's face, and jammed slices of ham and bread into her pocket.

The cook swooped in, glanced at the table, her unblinking eyes focused on the girls. "You haven't taken any of the Master's food, have ye? The wolves are howling in the daytime. Wouldn't take too long to find ye tied to the whipping post."

Juliet tensed. Orpha's round-bellied, lick-spittle cook kept a tight grip on the food supplies and reported if any were missing.

"The mistress wants you to warm water for her bath," Juliet said to divert the cook's attention from the missing fare.

Juliet patted her pocket with the food for Eldon. The poor boy's ribs stuck out like slats on a corncrib. How long would he last from the hard work, lack of nourishment and Orpha's floggings?

She lifted her chin, picked up the basket. "I'll collect the eggs."

Juliet cut a new path through deep snow. A rooster called out, lazy with the late morning light. She swung open the door to the coop. Her nose twitched with the dust motes flying through the air. The hens clucked and scolded as she reached beneath them to get their eggs, fanning their feathers out from the indignity.

Light filtered between the planks, giving a church-like glow and a momentary sanctuary to crawl into the despondency burrowing into her soul.

She felt like she'd swallowed yeast, and whatever loneliness was festering inside had doubled in size. Oh, to be loved by someone without being judged and thought inferior. That would truly be heaven. Living in the middle of the wilderness prevented her from meeting anyone of worth. Spinsterhood loomed with the near decade she must serve for her indenture. She sighed, viewing the glory of the sun with a vacant eye.

"I don't need someone perfect. I just need someone to make me feel I'm the only one," Juliet whispered to the chickens, hoping her mother and Moira in Heaven had heard her plea. Her hand closed around the precious golden cross Moira had saved for her from her mother's jewelry case. To be seen by someone and be loved, bordered on the miraculous.

A shadow crossed over her. Juliet swung around and dropped her basket. Eggs cracked. A tall, lean man stood shadowed in the doorway. Embarrassed, Juliet flinched, tearing her finger across a jagged wood shard. She pressed her hands to her cheeks.

He leaned a long thin rifle against the wall and took a step toward her. Juliet winced and examined her throbbing finger. The man muttered something and grabbed her hand. She tugged, a useless activity since he refused to release her.

He crouched and reached into his deer hide bag. Juliet stared down at her hand in his. A tiny rivulet of blood seeped out from the narrow slice, winding around her finger and onto his like a slender ribbon linking them together. Remarkable that such large, work-callused hands could feel so warm and gentle without losing their sense of strength. She gazed at his bent head, so near she could smell the scent of leather, wood smoke and winter air. So near her breath stirred his dark hair. So near she could press her lips to his brow without stirring much at all.

He smeared a poultice and wrapped her finger with a dried leaf. His face was caught in the gloom. Was he an Indian? He stood again, towered over her. She was tall for a woman and annoyingly she had to tilt her head back. The sun coming through the slats illuminated his face. Her breath caught in her throat.

He was devilishly handsome, with dark brown hair falling just beneath his broad snow-covered shoulders. His visage of classic Greek perfection possessed a distinct patrician nose, a wide full-lipped mouth, and a face, stark with chiseled angles that spoke strength—and intimidating power. My God, if he wasn't dressed in a deerskin shirt and leggings, he might pass for an English lord!

"You must bandage your injury with a fresh cloth." He smiled broadly, his clean white teeth lighting up his smile.

Her blood rushed. "The eggs," she said, heat rising to her cheeks as she kneeled to pick up the ones that were not broken. "Mistress will be angry." She cast her gaze to the whipping post.

He frowned. "Don't worry about Orpha. I'll tell her the

chickens don't lay well in the shorter days. She believes everything I tell her."

He took her hand, lifted her to her feet and wiped the blood from her cheek with his forefinger. Like two souls caught in an artist's frieze they studied one another. His eyes were blue, dark as lapis, like the pools among the marshes, drawing the beholder down into their depths.

He removed her cap and she gasped. Her *abominable* hair fell down her back. He reached out and took one of her curls in his hand, holding it as if it were a precious ruby.

"From watching you, I never would have guessed."

"You've been watching me?"

"I'm careful before stepping from the woods. I'm fierce to keep my scalp."

She remembered herself, swatted his hand away and reached for her cap. No doubt he thought her the spawn of Satan with such red hair, and an easy conquest. "Tis improper to touch my hair."

"Tis beautiful." The deep resonance of his firm rough-hewn voice reverberated through her like a lingering caress.

"Beautiful?"

He pulled a knife from his belt. Juliet froze. Was he going to kill her for her red hair?

The knife whizzed past her ear, sailing end over end and pitched into the darkness behind. She spun around just as a dark striped-headed creature squealed its last breath.

"A badger. Cornered like that, the animal would tear apart your leg or worse. A badger will kill all the chickens, merely for the fun of killing."

His wide shoulders brushed past her. He yanked up his knife and threw the carcass outside. Then, knife still in his hand, he turned to look at her. "Sometimes there are men like that. You must constantly be aware."

Juliet did a quick intake of breath. Was he talking of himself?

Chapter 2

*L*ord Joshua Rutland, third inheritor of the fourth Duke of Rutland, had long divested his title, emerging as Joshua Hansford, fur trader on the frontier; a convenient front to fool the masses. He whistled, slowing his stride through Horace Hayes' home.

He couldn't get the stunning girl out of his mind and hoped to catch another glimpse of her. Her tattered clothing did not diminish her serene loveliness, and her face, delicate of feature, owned a sweetness to which he was powerfully drawn.

It was a safe bet he'd frightened her by admitting he'd observed her. Why had he disclosed that truth? When mending her hand, she had trembled, and he'd resisted the urge to let her go.

His whistle collapsed in rapid decrescendo. It wasn't the color of her eyes that were so breathtaking. It was how bright they were, like a meadow of cornflowers, or a perfect spring sky, swirling in a whirlpool of apprehension.

Joshua scrubbed a hand over his jaw and the two-day growth of wiry beard. With certainty, she was dangerous. She possessed the kind of beauty that paralyzed a man, edged under his muscles and made his blood surge. That lush waterfall of red hair tumbling down her back had been made for a man's hands to explore.

He'd been in the wilderness too long.

Yet, so taken with her, he'd not asked her name. It made no difference. There was no time for a woman in his life. He had a mission to keep.

He dug down deep in his pocket, fingered the lace-edged handkerchief and the note that authored a senseless act of violence. A familiar shiver crawled down his spine. How much Sarah must have suffered.

He didn't know her killer or the motive. Not yet. Revenge rioted through his veins and he wouldn't rest until he identified the murderer and killed him.

After a year of agony and heartache, one thing was clear. It was better not to love anyone than to have them taken from you.

Outside Horace Hayes' study, Joshua raised his hand to knock on the door and heard a female gasp from the other side. Regardless of Orpha's vigilant eye, Horace was known for tupping his servant girls.

Horace, a prominent King's man and Loyalist in the Colonies remained unsuspecting of Joshua's intrigues. He massaged his trades with Horace, tantalizing him with a fine array of furs, to tease out a transaction that preyed upon the merchant's tight dealing. Allowing a parsimoniousness man to make a big profit tended to loosen his lips and unwittingly, Horace had provided a font of information, unknowingly aiding the Patriot cause over the course of the war. No need to disturb or anger him.

Joshua had used the ruse as a trapper to keep his spying activities covert. He worked hard cultivating Indians and colonials to gain seeds of information under the alias of Joshua Hansford. The fervor of the Patriot cause had caught fire in him, and he fought for the idea of a free country, a place where he could build upon his own lands.

He turned to leave.

"No. Please don't." The woman's voice rang out from behind the door.

The pleading in the woman's voice stopped him. *Vulnerable.* No one to protect her. No one to thwart Horace's unwanted advances. There was a difference between willing and unwilling.

Raised in a household where a hands-off rule applied to female servants, Joshua possessed a deep sense of honor and fiercely protected those who were unable to protect themselves.

If he intruded, the consequences of alienating Horace could be disastrous, losing a valuable source of information for General Washington. Yet, wasn't silence the true crime against humanity?

Damn!

Joshua knocked once, then swept open the door. He ducked just in time as a pewter candlestick sailed over his head, banged against a wall and thumped to the floor. "Have the Patriot's set their cannons to fire?"

Horace crouched behind his desk. Above the man stood a beautifully enraged she-dragon goddess, with her glorious red hair falling over her shoulders, her mob cap flung on the floor. She lifted her chin and narrowed a cold, hard look at Joshua, daring him to speak against her. No need for him to worry about the unwilling maid. She had everything under control.

Joshua swaggered into the room, folded his arms and let the scene play out. She was no more than a slave. Many indentured servants were cruelly treated by their masters especially young girls as beautiful as she and who were helpless against the assault. When they became pregnant, the sin of adultery lay at their feet and added years of indenture as punishment.

Red-faced, Horace fixed his gaze on the red-haired warrior who raised another candlestick high over her head. "Not only an instrument of the devil but a lunatic, too."

She lowered the candlestick, seemed to collect her words in her hand, gnash them together and hurl them over the desk. "Not only a libertine, but a braying ass, too," she spat out.

"What is all the noise?" Orpha screeched from upstairs.

The she-dragon paled.

Fire hardened Joshua's muscles and licked through his veins. The hairless Orpha would accuse and punish the innocent girl for enticing her lecherous husband. Joshua strode into the hall. "Your husband spanned his hands to emphasize a point and knocked over a candlestick," Joshua answered, his voice raised so she could hear him.

"Tell Horace to be more careful," Orpha snapped, and then in a gentler tone, said, "Cook is preparing you a wonderful dinner, Mr. Hansford."

Joshua angled his head. "Thank you, Mistress Orpha. I look forward to it and to your charming company."

He stepped back in the room and kicked the door shut. Through clenched teeth, he said, "I would think, Horace, it would be incumbent upon you to treat all the ladies in your employ with respect."

The strip of white hair across the center of Horace's head bounced sunbeams in the light. A half-tankard full of rum fortified his mettle. "Juliet's my property and will do what I bid."

Juliet. *Melodic and lovely.* Appropriate.

"Get the girl," Horace gruffed out. The trader moved his head from side to side anticipating when the girl would launch her missile.

Joshua's hands fisted. Oh, what he would like to do to…could do…

At the age of seven, Joshua always tagged along with his older brothers, Nicholas and Anthony, who had developed a taste for boxing. Early on, Joshua had acquired the same lust for the sport, sparring with the tenants on his father's estate, enormous farm boys molded from hard-bitten work, excited to take on the duke's son with no concern for his station. The fighting was dirty, and he liked it that way.

Horace stooped and pressed his palms against the scalloped carved molding, bordering his desk. "Help me and when I'm done with the girl, you can have her."

Within seconds, Joshua shot across the room, grabbed Horace up by his frock coat and bent the smaller man over the desk. "You owe Miss Juliet an apology." A chill hung on the edge of his threat.

"I-I apologize," Horace choked out, appealing to Juliet who he'd a moment ago attempted to molest, then glanced at the rough frontiersman.

She snatched up her mob cap and tucked her hair beneath. Juliet moved beside Joshua and put her hand on his sleeve. "I can take care of myself."

Not good enough. Not when he was gone and she couldn't guard against Horace.

"I could give you the whipping of your life, Horace. As a consequence, I wouldn't have a trading partner to trade my excellent furs."

Horace flinched, but with his usual aplomb said, "The furs you carry are superior and of good price?"

Joshua's message apparently didn't turn the wheels in Horace's brain, and it was conceivable he didn't possess the mechanism. He tightened his grip on the Loyalist's lapels. "We could encourage Orpha's attendance on this conversation. I'm sure she'd have an opinion."

Horace's eyes widened in horror. Joshua tamped down a grin.

"No, no. It is not necessary to inform my wife of anything. If it makes you feel better, I'll offer you a bonus for your furs."

The swine thought to buy him off?

"You look deadly," hiccupped Horace.

"This is my nice face. You haven't seen deadly."

Joshua shoved Horace away in disgust. The man tumbled head over heels, struggled to finally stand, and then hitched up his pants over his hefty girth.

Horace cleared his throat. "At dinner tonight, you won't mention—"

Blood shot to Joshua's brain. Men like Horace ranked the lowest part of humanity. "You realize my reputation with the long rifle and my lethal aim. In the future, if I hear of anything happening to the ladies in your household...I promise, I won't miss."

Chapter 3

*J*uliet put the final touches on the place settings for dinner while Mary freshened the guest room for the buckskinned frontiersman. Strangely warm and energized, thoughts of the man ran through Juliet's mind and her eyes fixed on the tapestry. Oh, how he was like her Achilles. Who was he? Where was he from?

To think he had championed her. Master Hayes was an important man in the Colonies and with all the ferocity of a winter squall, Joshua had dared to quarrel with him and—at risk to his trade.

Juliet laughed. How easily he had tossed Horace over his desk. No need to worry with regard to Horace's advances in the future. She'd threaten the scoundrel with the frontiersman.

He was so sure of himself, he even charmed Orpha. No one performed that manipulation. And then she remembered the hard flex of muscle beneath the buttery soft hide when she had placed her hand on his arm.

Eldon brushed past her, his arms loaded with firewood for the fireplace. She hauled him back by the collar and kept a watchful eye on anyone who might enter the dining room, stuffing the food she had pilfered into his pocket. He nodded his head in gratitude and hurried on his way.

She dusted the spindles on the chairs to a new sheen and sighed. From beneath her mob cap, she pulled out a lock of hair and examined it. Had he truly called her hair beautiful?

When he'd bandaged her injury, the strength of his hands and the gentleness of his touch had surprised her. A complex man under the rough exterior, a man who had the strength of character to stand up for the lowly household servants.

She was being fanciful and pushed her hair back in the mob cap. With certainty, he'd said she was beautiful to keep her talking and to distract her from the dangerous badger.

With a rag in hand, she picked up a pewter tankard and buffed. No amount of rubbing removed a spot of tarnish. She swallowed feelings of unworthiness and forced herself not to yearn for what she could never have. Locked into indenture, no man of any value would want her.

Mary screamed. Juliet dropped the mug. Wasn't Mary upstairs? Mary's cries came from outside. Juliet tore out the front door and plunged through the snow, her heart rushing to her throat. If anything happened to Mary she'd by no means forgive herself.

Juliet burst through the dark mouth of the barn. On the hay-strewn floor, Mary lay motionless, her bucket overturned and milk pooled to the side. A large Indian stood with a razor-sharp knife in his hand, Mary's silky hair in his palm.

Juliet picked up a pitchfork and rammed it at the Indian. He dodged, a cat's whisker away from the spiky tines piercing his abdomen. He prowled, his muscled frame moving soundlessly, a dance of sorts around Mary's unconscious body.

Juliet circled her friend, holding tight to her weapon, drew back and shoved. Again, and again she thrust the pointed tines. Still the Indian came at her, dodging each lunge, his eyes as hard as agates, and his arrogance, with a confidence bred on past victories, crushed the assumption of her defense.

The fork lay heavy and Juliet's arms trembled. Horses in their stalls reared their heads, blowing loudly into the chill air. Sheep bleated their cries.

In one sudden move, the Indian leapt over Mary. Juliet backed away, thrusting the sharp tines at him again and again. He dodged the tines, then spun around, ripped her weapon from her hands and tossed it high into the loft. Juliet screamed.

He glared at her.

"Be damned to hell!" Joshua's voice rang out.

Juliet glanced to the door where he stood. Her body trembling, she wanted to fall to her knees and shout to the Catholic saints her deliverance. Joshua would take care of the savage.

But he didn't move. Instead he spoke in a guttural tongue she didn't understand.

There was the flash of a blade as the savage bent over Mary.

Juliet screamed, took a step toward the savage. Joshua yanked her back, held her against his chest. She kicked and clawed to get free. Was he going to allow the Indian to kill Mary?

Juliet's heart pummeled against her ribs as she watched the Indian cut a lock of Mary's hair, then slip it in his deerskin pouch.

Laughter rumbled through Joshua's chest, and he released her. "He would never hurt your friend."

Juliet kept her eyes glued to the savage as she rushed to Mary's side. What lunacy was Joshua speaking? She sank to the uneven plank floor, patted her friend's hand She scowled at the Indian, then back to Joshua. "Would you mind telling me the meaning of this?"

"This is my friend, Two Eagles."

"Friend?" She sent them both a withering glare.

"He meant no harm. He has never seen hair the color of corn tassel and wanted a good luck charm to protect him."

Like the bitter wind, comprehension swept over Juliet. Savages held peculiar habits and traditions far from her realm of experience. "He could have asked."

Joshua laughed and her esteem for him slipped a notch. "He probably did and she didn't understand him. He does not like English nor speak it."

Mary woke. Eyes wide, she stared at the Indian. He proudly wore a fine doeskin blouse, and breeches, and calf-high moccasins, and covering his wide shoulders was a broadcloth blanket distinctive with deep red borders. His black hair was shoulder length, not the adopted style of a Mohawk warrior Juliet had seen once who had shaved his head except for a brush-like tuft of hair from pate to nape.

Two Eagles gave an impatient grunt from their rude inspection.

"He scared the death out of me," said Mary, rising to her feet and bringing Juliet up with her. "He is the biggest savage I've ever seen."

23

Juliet forced her limbs to relax, saying a brief frantic prayer of thanks for her friend's safety, and then elbowed Mary to quit gawking. "You've barely seen a handful of Indians."

"Two Eagles has just arrived. He accompanies me on my trapping business and is harmless," said Joshua.

Harmless? Juliet had seen a bear less fearsome.

The cook yelled from the back porch. "Mary, Juliet what is all the commotion?"

Joshua chuckled and waved to the cook from the door. "The girls have been introduced to Two Eagles."

"Tell those worthless twits to get inside. They've work to do, not spending their time cultivating savages."

Juliet grabbed Mary's hand, skirted around the two men, and hurried along the sheep's stalls where the sheep piled on one another to escape.

Her cheeks burned from the cook's rebuke especially in front of Joshua who seemed nice. Maybe he could suggest how she could escape and get back to England. To bring Baron Bearsted to justice.

Chapter 4

*O*rpha put out her best when business customers visited, but that night she exceeded her standard welcome for the handsome frontiersman. Under a chandelier lit with a myriad of beeswax candles, gleamed a fine cherry dining table set with Orpha's polished silver, linen napkins and delicate rose china.

Juliet finished serving Orpha a plate of roast pheasant, roast beef, braised cabbage, carrots and potatoes. With Horace's plate in hand, she looked up at Joshua and caught him studying her intently. His perusal scrambled her thoughts and caused her skin to go up in flames.

She dropped Horace's plate on the table.

Orpha glanced at her sharply. "Cease your clumsiness, Juliet." Orpha pouted and leaned over to Joshua. "You can't get good help these days."

The frontiersman ignored Orpha, and Juliet's chest expanded with gratitude.

Orpha pulled her shawl around her. "Juliet, stir the fire, I feel a chill and you know how I hate to be cold."

While stirring the embers, Juliet darted a glance at Joshua again. He was as elemental as the changing seasons, unrestrained power, with naught lagging or degenerated about him—no softness at all to his rock-solid and daunting frame, honed from living on the frontier.

"The great surprise was when the principal chief of the Onondagas, Rozinoghyata chose Thayendanegea over Gucinge to fill the most important office over the Six Nations," said Joshua.

The discussion carried a surreal nature. So businesslike as if there had been no altercation between him and the master that afternoon. Horace had tried to punish her for throwing the candlestick by giving her more chores to perform. Juliet reminded him of Joshua's aim. She smiled, thinking of the horror on her master's face.

Horace thumped his fist on the table, using his innate sense of drama to call attention to himself. "Gucinge's bravery is unquestioned, his leadership qualities are considerable, his experience exceptional and his sagacity is consistent. But…his flaw is his impetuousness."

"I can understand Thayendanegea's appointment. He has great knowledge of the whites, their ways, language and written word. The Indians who have aligned themselves with the King also required someone with more restraint." Joshua sipped his wine.

Juliet fidgeted with the dishes on the sideboard, paying attention to how the frontiersman shifted from casual conversation to pointed statements. *Too nonchalant.*

Horace cut his beef, sticking a large piece in his mouth. He sucked at the juices and said, "I understand Colonel Butler has recruited and armed the Senecas and other Indians of the lower Great Lakes region and is assembling them at Fort Niagara to receive their presents and instructions." He took a letter from his pocket and slid it across the table to Joshua. "This arrived for you a couple days ago."

Juliet pressed her back to the wall, waiting to be called upon. As a servant, she was almost invisible except for those hawk-like blue orbs of the frontiersman watching, but not watching her.

She studied her tapestry, struck how every goal, motivation, conflict, every color, every figure, every feat and consequence, every part of earthly realism and the judgements it created, every bond made, every subtle moment of history and probability, every sword thrust and bush, every passion and birth and promise, every potential entity ever was intertwined into that infinite, expansive web.

She inhaled, feeling the smolders in the whorls of the weaver's fingers, and then caught the frontiersman slanting his head where her attention had been gathered. He nodded. Heat rose to her cheeks.

Was he in agreement with her sentiments? No. Far from the sophistication of England, she found colonials smugly narrow, possessing an indifference to cultural and aesthetic values. To own was all they deemed necessary.

"Bribes the Rangers and Tory militia use to cultivate the Indians against the colonials," said Joshua.

The frontiersman's fingers curled around his fork. *Anger?* She straightened, weighing the information bandied at the table.

Horace threw back his head and snorted. "In addition, Thayendanegea had been taken to England to be inspired by royal munificence with assurances after certain British victory, the Empire would help see to all Indian tribes in North America subjugated to the Iroquois."

"A tremendous carrot to dangle in front of the War Chief," said Joshua.

Orpha waved her crystal goblet and Juliet refilled it with wine. No doubt, the trader was intelligent and had been educated. But his accent intrigued her. How he cultivated the colonial inflection. A bit of a drawl, sometimes a burr.

"Butler and his followers were the ones responsible for the attacks on Forts Fifty and Summermute along with several settlements in Pennsylvania, south of here," said Joshua. "I should remind you, Horace, the Indians are on the move. No mercy will be allowed."

The news of a potential Indian attack sent shivers down Juliet's spine.

Nonplussed, Horace smoothed his velvet waistcoat. "You want us to bleat like sheep? We are Loyalists and protected by the King. Alliances have been made with the Indians swayed to suppress the rabble creating the insurrection."

Juliet studied Joshua to see his reaction to Horace's bravado. He turned his eyes on her, his expression neutral. *Difficult to read him.*

"You will not be immune. Many of the tribes you speak of, the Senecas, Onondagas, the Cayugas, and most Mohawks agreed to fight the Americans on behalf of the English," said Joshua. "Plying my trade across the frontier, I am aware of the hostilities."

Horace slapped his wine glass down on the table. "Juliet, bring me more wine," he ordered. "How you render a heated impression of apocalyptic danger, Joshua. I have no proviso to worry," he said, allaying his wife's growing alarm.

A subtle tightening came to Joshua's jaw. "It is the most unprepossessing declaration of war ever made by the Six Nation Iroquois. But others have rejected the alliance with the King and remain neutral or fight for the Patriots who they have lived peaceably with for years."

There it was again. He had slipped without realizing his vernacular mirrored a higher station. Definitely English born. Nobility? No. Surely, a highborn wouldn't wear buckskins nor would he risk his neck in a wilderness that offered him nothing. The son of a professor? A merchant? A bastard? The pieces didn't fit.

Juliet's fingers came up to toy with her necklace. What was he really doing here?

He tilted back his chair on two legs. Was it a departure of ingrained manners vital to hide his secrets?

Horace remained silent for a long while and when he continued it was with unmistakable hardness. "In the present dispute with the mother country and the Colonies, I'd sooner have my head cut off than lift my hand against the King or sign any association."

Horace closed his fist over Juliet's hand and rubbed his thumb over her fingers. "You will find the elderberry wine here to be the sweetest and most lush, Joshua."

Juliet shook and pulled back. His flaccid fist held fast. To throw his wine in his face had appeal but, as a result, Orpha would delight in punishing her.

Joshua tossed back the contents of his glass. He frowned, staring at the bottom as if the wine were too bitter for his liking.

Joshua glared at Horace. "As I mentioned in the library this afternoon, I can trek through the forests with no sign of my presence. My prey has no idea when I will strike and—with precision."

Horace choked on his food and Juliet wished he'd keep on choking. She jerked from his hold.

Orpha clapped her hands. "Oh, Joshua, your excellent marksmanship is extolled over the frontier, conceivably the entire Colonies. I'd love to see a demonstration of your skill."

Juliet hid a smile.

Horace blanched the color of a yellow-hued cadaver. "Point well taken."

Joshua cut his beef in exact pieces. "From a Royal Grant, I see you have amassed four thousand acres, twenty-five horses, sixty black cattle. The times have been good and well-disposed to you. A quid pro quo for favorable services to the Crown?"

Like a cat licking its paws of salmon paste, Horace gave a hint of a smile, all thoughts of his indiscretion to Juliet forgotten. "Petitions not sweetened with gold are but unsavory and often refused. The King needed a man of integrity and honor and has rewarded him well, as with others who are dedicated to his cause."

"Juliet, give our guest more wine and bring out the dessert," said Orpha.

When she returned from the kitchen, she served Joshua his pie and poured his wine. He leaned into her, his shoulder next to hers. She inhaled sharply and dropped a china plate. Joshua scooped it up before it hit the floor and handed it to her.

"Thank you," she whispered. If the precious china had broken…he had saved her from a beating.

"Of course, there is a Patriot rascal busy moving through the New York wilderness offering many Indians money, blankets, tomahawks, paints and anything else there was to help fight the King's troops," said Joshua.

"Bah! A lot of good it did him. Most refused, others agreed to fight, took his presents and disappeared."

Horace's grunt showed the depth of his contempt for the Patriots. Juliet herself had always shown her allegiance to King and country. Other than Horace's and Orpha's conversations, the conflict in the Colonies had been remote. Juliet's concern was not to get swept up in anything that would make it difficult for her to return to England. She hadn't worked out how she'd have Baron Bearsted punished for his crimes. Not yet, but she burned with a fever to make it happen.

She stifled a yawn, counting off the many chores to perform before retiring. The night was cloudless and she yearned to snuggle beneath the quilts high in their attic bedroom and gaze on the heavens. Mary was busy in the kitchen and she loved sharing with Mary everything she had learned viewing the constellations with Moira. And then memories of assisting Moira, a midwife with the joy of bringing babies in the world brought a pang to her heart. Not a typical upbringing for a girl of nobility, but then she did not have a normal life.

Juliet removed the dishes and wrinkled her nose. What were the frontiersman's true political inclinations? She was going to ask if anyone required anything else, then stopped short when a pair of blue eyes from across the table questioned her. She couldn't look away.

Orpha sat up, heaved her great shoulders like a crow would

lift its wings delighted with fresh carrion to pick. "Juliet, the cook has gone to bed with a cold. Our guest seeks a bath. So while you are cleaning the kitchen, you can prepare his bath."

"But Mistress—"

"I order you to stay in the kitchen and see to *all* of his wishes."

Joshua drummed his fingers on the table. Juliet had proven to be a delightful diversion, and to his disappointment, Orpha's crassness had caused her to scurry into the kitchen.

When Horace had put his hand on Juliet, his gut blazed with the indignities the girl suffered. When Orpha offered Juliet's body to him, his blood raged through his veins. He debated how long it would take to geld and hang Horace. One hour? Two hours?

How long would it take to hang the fat crow, Orpha? He'd string her up next to her husband. Of course, he'd require a thicker rope and Two Eagles' assistance.

He pushed the crust around his plate, and contemplated the evening's discussion while Orpha prattled, cringing at the rasping sound of her voice every time she opened her mouth. He glanced at the tapestry he had seen Juliet regarding and wondered why. The weaving was a unique piece. In Belvoir Castle hung a superior version that would hold her in greater awe.

He was quite taken with how Juliet flushed under his perusal. Her mouth was both generous and beautiful; the lips had color and warmth, possessing none of the narrowness he'd witnessed in many women's faces, where jealousy or avarice flourished— like Orpha holding court at the end of the table.

How easy it had been to manipulate Horace and gather crucial information. Joshua had to scout out Colonel Butler, the head of the hydra of the infamous British Rangers and what was occurring at Fort Niagara. He turned back to Horace, struck again by the unusual nature of his hair, a white patch roving down his scalp, the remainder black.

He had heard of the Patriots' failure to woo the Indians. There had been conversations with his commanders and General Washington over the vulnerability of the Patriots on the frontier, especially with the menfolk far away in Washington's army and unable to protect their families. The exposure on the frontier grew more alarming each day.

Joshua bit back a string of curses. "The Iroquois are natural allies of the British as the swamps and forests. The Haudenosaunee or peoples of the Longhouse have fought in each war in America during the previous century. To have expected them to remain neutral in this war was beyond the power of man."

Horace clanged his fork on his plate and grabbed at the tray of apple pie and gingerbread cake, piling many slices on his plate. "What a great mistake the Oneidas made, turning their backs on those advocating to raise their hatchets on behalf of the King."

A King on the other side of the ocean who cared nothing for his subjects except for what tribute could be exacted from them. Joshua opened his mouth to criticize, then stopped.

Horace steepled his flabby fingers. "They are a bunch of spiders the lion will crush with his foot."

Palms up, Joshua spanned his hands. "Such are the wages of war." *When the spiders unite, their webs will tie up the lion.*

Joshua stood. "The evening is late. I bid you goodnight." He didn't care one whit for Horace or Orpha or his rudeness by ending the conversation abruptly. His mind was occupied with Juliet. By now, she'd have the bath filled and left the kitchen. Or maybe she'd still be there.

He hoped so.

Before Juliet had departed, her eyes had been cast downward. Of course, he'd at no time take advantage of the maid. His fondest wish was to wipe away her miseries. Still, he'd caught a hint of defiance, glimmerings of the proud fire-breathing she-dragon hovering over Horace that afternoon, not a girl beaten into submission. The devil in him looked forward to rekindling her temper. He hoped he didn't earn a bucket of scalding water dumped on him in return.

Chapter 5

He entered the kitchen and stepped back in shadow to observe the two women undetected. With her back to him, Juliet had planted herself in the path of her friend, Mary who struggled with an armload of blankets. Side by side, he was struck by the contrast of the two and perceived where Horace's greed won out. Juliet didn't possess her friend's angelic beauty and temperament. Mary fainted at the slightest provocation where Juliet would impale him on tines and make the act more harrowing. Where Mary was lovely, Juliet personified stunning sensuality.

"Can you open the door for me?" Mary shifted, straining from the burdensome load. A blanket slid off the pile and fell to the floor.

Juliet refused to budge from her position. "Where are you going?"

"The heathen is sleeping in the barn."

"I thought you were scared of him."

"Mistress Orpha ordered it."

"And going out there alone makes it right? I don't trust him. He's dangerous."

"I'm not afraid."

"Humph." Juliet picked up the blanket, plopped it on the top of the pile and swung open the door. "I'll be done cleaning the kitchen soon. Every nerve in my body is shrieking to finish the dishes, fill the tub and leave before the counterfeit rascal finishes talking to Horace."

Counterfeit rascal? Joshua arched a brow. She was far too discerning. With certainty, she had listened closely to him…far too closely. He mulled over the evening's conversation. Nothing she could glean from what he'd said. He was a spy and still alive thanks to his exact attention to detail. What were her political leanings? He would provoke her thoughts and understand her position.

His gaze fell to where she stepped out onto the porch. A triangle of light spilled on her. "It is a clear night…if you must have help—" she called to Mary. She stayed glued to the spot despite the freezing temperature, and then exhaled, her breath frosting on the night air. "If you need me—"

Her friend slogged through the snow, commandeering the bundle of blankets, her lantern sashaying in the wind then dimming when she closed the door to the barn. An emaciated servant boy carried buckets of water drawn from the well. Joshua frowned. All the servants in the Hayes' employ were thin and starved.

Juliet followed the boy inside, rubbing her hands up and down her arms. "Put the buckets next to the fire, Eldon. On the table is a plate of food for you. Go to bed. You're exhausted. I'll collect the plate in the morning and no one will know."

Juliet was clearly the boy's protector. A trait Joshua admired.

"Thank you, Juliet." Eldon hugged her and picked up his plate. "Goodnight, sir."

"Sir?" She whirled, a dainty hand flew to her chest. "How long have you been standing there?"

"Enough to understand I'm a counterfeit rascal."

Her mouth dropped open. "You should have made your presence known."

Back was his she-dragon.

She lifted the heavy iron kettle off the fire.

He moved to her. "Let me help you."

She put her hand up and stopped him. His skin burned and her gaze dropped from his eyes to where her palm lay on his chest. She snatched her hand back...lifted her chin so high he could see the dark hollow in her slim white throat.

"No, thank you." She filled the tub with hot water and it steamed upward.

From one of the ice-cold buckets Eldon had drawn from the well, she refilled the kettle over the fire and then turned to him, her fists plunked on her hips. "If you think Orpha's implication means more than drawing your bath, you've a lesson to learn."

"I've looked forward to a hot bath for a long time. Promise not to look?"

"Ha! I've more important things to do with my time. Take your clothes off. I'll launder them when you're finished. On the table, there are linens for your use."

She turned her back to him and dried dishes, dismissing him like a queen would a minor peasant. Joshua chuckled and tore off his clothes, laid them in a pile and eased into the copper tub, letting the warmth soak his exhausted muscles. Water sloshed to the floor. The she-dragon would not be happy. "A cake of soap?"

From over her shoulder, she tossed him the bar where it plunked into the bath, splashing his face. She must have practiced the trick.

"It's the master's precious bay rum soap. Now I have to add mopping the floor to my chores tonight," she said gruffly.

He wanted to know her. Had she thought she signed up for a better life in the Colonies like so many people were fooled into doing? "Why are you here?"

"I'm not expected to explain the entirety of it to you." Her tone betrayed her unwillingness to do so.

With the sponge, Joshua scrubbed his arms and neck. At Belvoir, he'd have his bath in his chambers attended by several footmen and his valet. Here in the Colonies, he'd settled for the less civilized and lovely view of her backside. He imagined a shapely bottom and long lithe legs. "Trying to make pleasant conversation is all."

"No, you are not. You want to know if I was a thief or some other vile character transported to the Colonies. I should ask *you*, why you are really here?"

Tread *carefully*, his inklings regarding her were correct. If she were a Loyalist she might report her suspicions.

She pressed her palms into her back, as if to rub away a pain, and her rounded bosom strained against the linen of her threadbare gown. His throat went dry.

"You didn't answer my question. What are you running away from?"

Did she grow more ethereal in the candlelight? A feast for his eyes and torment for his body. Her question taunted him, reminding him how he had arrived at this miserable point in his life.

Images of his dead fiancée, like an old dream, and all the living and dying and heartbreak that went on continuously in his head. In those flashes of sudden remembrance, the inability to protect his Sarah plagued him. His hands shook...damp and helpless.

He shoved away the memory and resented Juliet for making him dredge up the past. Yet it wasn't her fault. He decided to make light of the present awkward situation. "I'm trying to place what animal Horace's hair reminds me of."

Juliet burst out laughing. "A skunk."

She hurried to complete her tasks, anything to get out of his proximity. Gently reared, she had not once seen a naked man and being forced into this position irked her.

Silence as thick as mud fell over them. She glanced at the door, waiting for Mary to reappear so she wouldn't have to endure the frontiersman's company alone. What was taking her so long?

"You're ignoring of me is so loud, it's deafening."

His amusement rankled her. "Perhaps your dim-wittedness has left you deaf."

A deep boisterous rumble echoed through the room. "You are not used to bathing a man?"

He wanted to know if this was part of her duties with all invited male guests. Let him think what he wanted. "Done with the same pleasure of handling a sack of cats I want to drown."

"I thank you for your high praise," he said.

39

"It wasn't meant to praise."

"Neither is getting clobbered senseless by a candlestick."

A smile tugged at her lips.

He shifted, drumming his fingers on the side of the tub. "Red hair, in my opinion is dangerous."

Juliet dried a knife overlong, rubbing the towel up and down the blade. "Marked by the fires of Hell and like the Scythians, prone to convert the skulls of their enemies into drinking cups."

"Do I have much to fear?"

With the tip of her finger she touched the sharp point. "Do not test me."

Water splashed. "My, what a sour temperament. With what remaining time I have, why should I long for such shrewish companionship?"

Her breath burned in her throat. "I am not slow to understand." She jammed the tip of the blade into the cutting block, the knife vibrating. If he wanted a challenge, she would give it to him. "I have been chased around the dining room table by Master Horace countless times, warding off his advances, and I refuse to be bullied by an ill-bred colonial and sink to his level of lewdness."

"The endeavor could be illuminating." His voice dropped lower, aloof and confident.

Juliet shivered at the rich, masculine tone of his depraved proposal. The intimation swept over her like a caress. Outrageous. "There are some things best not learned."

She tripped on his clothes. Plates clanking, she scrambled to right them, kicking his garments free from her feet. "You don't have lice, do you?"

She placed the clean platters in the sideboard, and then darted a glance at him. She widened her eyes in admiration of his male beauty. He was like the warrior, Achilles, whose nymph mother dipped him into the River Styx to make him invulnerable to battle. Broad shoulders and chest, muscles rippled to a narrow waist. The tub hugged his long legs and muscular thighs and farther…

"Nothing but trouble there—" A faint note of cynical amusement rose in his voice.

With fire in her cheeks, she snapped her gaze to his face. Oh, the infuriating man.

"And following her, fawning, went both gray wolves and fierce-eyed lions, bears and swift leopards insatiable for deer."

His voice lowered, pleasant, potent, tempered and muted by his English accent. For a moment, Juliet was back in her cozy cottage in England, set against downy pillows and reading her favorite ancient Greek verses. "Seeing them, she rejoiced inwardly in her heart, and in their breasts, she threw desire, and they all lay down together in pairs in their shady dwellings."

Juliet pressed her hands to her face. Damn him. She had finished the most salacious part of the Homeric hymn to Aphrodite.

He leaned over to retrieve the letter that had fallen out of a pocket of his clothing and placed it on the table beside him. So casual, in control, but not as cavalier as he attempted to appear. What was he hiding?

When she traversed the room he grabbed her hand, pulling her back to meet his roguish regard. Juliet truly wished he'd go away, his presence wreaking havoc on the peace she so desperately desired. Sleet smacked against the windows, drops as big as farthings.

"You have the universal power of Aphrodite, over all living beings, divine and human, who live on land, in the sea, and in the air, and most of all me."

She kept her gaze averted to the naked man in the tub and tugged her fingers loose. Had he referred to her as the goddess of seduction and lovemaking? She would have none of it. "Carry your charms elsewhere, Mr. Hansford. I have no need for empty flatterers."

"Here, scrub my back—" He tossed her the sponge, and it plopped at her feet, soaking the frayed hems of her skirts. She glared at him and just stood there, mouth pinched, hands on her hips.

"Orpha ordered you to attend me."

Of course, he'd remind her of Orpha's crude commands and underneath, she had an inkling he was diverting himself with her. But just in case he wasn't, she'd be at risk for a beating if she refused.

Her eyes dipped to the lean muscles of his back. "Impossible—" she faltered.

"Impossible?"

She dumped a bucket of ice-cold water over his head leaving him sputtering, and then huffed from the room in the wake of his echoing laughter.

Chapter 6

*W*ind whistled along the mountain slopes and rustled through the naked trees while the first fingers of the rising sun burned off the surrounding mist. Water trickled from roofing shingles with a midwinter snowmelt and ensconced in Horace's study, Joshua sat warm before the fire as he put the final touches of his carefully coded letter for General Washington.

His carved powder horn was slung on his shoulder and hanging from his belt were a pouch of bullets, and a sheathed knife. Light danced off his long gun where it lay against a wall of bookcases. Two Eagles packed the rest of their gear and waited in the barn. They had many miles to cover to get to West Point where he knew the missive would be delivered to the colonial commander.

He placed the quill in the bottle, stretched his legs in front of him, and waited for the ink to dry. Juliet swept in, her tattered skirts brushed against the cherry floors. He frowned. She deserved so much more.

With a finger held to her mouth, she closed the door and

rushed around the desk. The scent of roses and biscuits curled through the air. Her eyes were huge and intense and for a moment, held him prisoner.

"You are leaving?"

Her voice trembled as she spoke. A knot grew in his belly that someone so good like her should suffer. He cursed Horace and Orpha, and the wickedness of her indenture, wished he could take her away, but he could not. If he helped her, he risked exposure which would put his mission at risk…and his life in danger. He couldn't help anyone then. But all the rationalization in the world did not make him less of a coward.

An unruly curl poked from beneath her mob cap. He could not resist touching the lock of spun sunbeam, the whorl like fire in his palm. "You must be wary, sweet Juliet. Horace's hubris will be his downfall. The Mohawk War Chief, Onontio, is ruthless and plans to settle his ax into many white skulls. Horace may not be immune. Have a care." He dropped his hand.

"I will."

"You've heard stories of Indian torture? Until you see it, until you hear the screams and know when your turn comes…" He stood and placed his hands on her thin shoulders and squeezed. "If you see any hint of an attack…escape. Get Mary and run far away from here."

Juliet looked at him in disbelief, and momentarily stared out the window at the whipping post where punishment was meted out to servants caught escaping. "Where would we go?"

His chest tightened at her desperation. The Indians were not the only thing causing her fear. She begged to get away from Orpha's madness. Was the fool girl planning to flee on her own?

Joshua peered at the craggy cliffs covered with snow, and then back to her. "To escape during the winter is irrational. Wildcats, cougars, wolves are a problem, but no more than falling through snow and ice into a crevasse. Winter isn't a time to escape."

She swallowed hard and glanced around. Indecision crossed her lovely face, as if uneasy with a secret she held and was hesitant to share with him.

"Do you know Colonel Thomas Faulkner? He has been commissioned to the Colonies—"

The man's name caused him to curl his lip in disgust. He had met Colonel Thomas Faulkner in Boston before the Battle at Lexington and Concord. "The British commander at Fort Oswego on the edge of Lake Ontario? What is your connection to him?"

Was she his paramour?

Blood surged in his veins.

"He is a-a friend. I need to get to him."

"A friend?" he taunted with a nasty laugh. Juliet and the loutish colonel?

"He is family. He is my cousin."

Her cousin was the haughty British Colonel Faulkner? He'd be walking into a den of snakes taking her there.

"Can you take us with you? Please."

"Snow can fall three feet a day. You'd not survive the journey." He was a Patriot agent. The frontier was the left flank of the Continental generals' battlefront and way too dangerous for two women.

She cast her eyes downward. Joshua stood close enough to

see the pulse leap at her temple. He wanted to turn, to shield his eyes from her. He did not want to see her courage or her desperation nor did he—may God forgive him—want to pity her.

She placed her finger on his letter and lifted her gaze to him. "Your words might be considered treasonous."

Joshua paused, his face tight. His muscles tensed. She could read? Could she decipher what he wrote? *Damn her.* "Don't be silly. A letter to an old friend."

"What about the letter Horace gave you at dinner last night? I wonder what it said. So clandestine."

She referred to the letter that ordered him to West Point. "You have an inquisitive mind, Miss Juliet."

She lifted a brow. "Let's not insult either of our intelligences by lying to each other."

"Of course." He backed her up against the wall, trapping her between his arms. "What do you plan to do about a letter that means nothing?"

"I could report you to Horace."

"You won't."

"Are you sure?"

He inclined his head in an exaggerated bow. "There is nothing to divulge, and then Horace might learn you are blackmailing me in order to help you escape."

Her mouth dropped opened. "You blackguard."

"Thank you for the compliment."

A violent gust cracked against the house. She narrowed her eyes on him. "Consider that a most flattering dedication."

He chuckled. "Checkmate."

He lingered and awareness filled his every pore, even the air he breathed. She pushed at him. He didn't budge.

"Get away from me." She shoved with all her might. "I'm sure you make all of your colonial women swoon with glib flattery by hailing your exploits, and then settling on them like a rattlesnake. Pray save your amorous attentions for your lamentable frontier women."

"Do I detect a wholehearted spurning? Or jealousy?" He ran his knuckles down her cheek. "So soft."

"You are perhaps the lowest specimen of a man that I've ever met."

"And you talk too much."

Her breath sped and the lacy fringe of her eyelashes lifted in question.

Heat from the fireplace washed over them and allowed a drowsy warmth. A spell was woven and he thought, for one moment, he might kiss her. How would that feel? Her soft generous lips beckoning him…

He was a man who took what he wanted. He was by no means blind to his attraction, for the woman radiated strength and fire, drawing him like a magnet.

Why not take her with him? Because, if he took Horace's servants, he'd be hunted down. He didn't fancy a noose laid over his head. His mission demanded he remain invisible. He and Two Eagles had been ordered to move among the Indians and Loyalists on the frontier to spy for General Washington. He had to report soon to Colonel Rufus Putman.

But his reconnaissance was not the real reason.

The revulsion he held for himself, the sleepless nights, pushing himself beyond exhaustion over the death of one woman he had cherished was enough to last him a thousand lifetimes. No. He could not take her.

"I'm sorry."

He wanted her. Wanted to silence her with his lips, cover himself with the soft strands of her hair, and see it blazing red against his skin. He grew fascinated with the swift fury and intelligence he saw in her blue eyes.

He had meant just to brush her mouth with his, a whim, a slight memory to take with him. He felt her heart beating rapidly against his chest, felt her fingers burn upon his neck. But the instant their lips touched, a surge of possessiveness churned in his mind, merging with the memory of her blood trailed across their fingers, pulsing with the beating wind. He dragged her into his arms, marveling at her rounded body, and crushed his mouth down upon hers, opening his and letting his tongue search, taste, seek a treasure he couldn't name.

She tasted like some heady, indescribable pureness and her lips were soft, so unbearably soft. An explosion of feelings burst inside him, like a man too long confined and then too, abruptly unchained.

She made a small sound in the back of her throat—a helpless whimper, an entreaty for him to stop.

"Someone is coming," she begged.

He stepped back, arms to his sides. Juliet wore a bewildered expression; her lips were moist and bruised by his.

He cleared his throat.

To hell with Horace. Joshua would return for her and take

her friend, too. He didn't know what he'd do with them but by damn, he'd get her away from this vile place.

He folded the letter, placed the missive in his pocket and picked up his long gun. "If I'm still alive, I'll be back in the spring. I promise."

Chapter 7

*J*anuary stormed into February, snowing into March, and now into the birth and death of April. And still no sign of Joshua Hansford. Juliet's shoulders sank with the depressing thought he'd been killed or was a wanderlust character who made careless promises.

Juliet finished churning the butter, then picked up a knife to cut bacon from the slab she had lifted from the smoke house for breakfast, laying the final pieces in the skillet where it crackled and popped.

There was double duty of chores today, filling in for Eldon and the cook who had taken sick. The latter she felt was faking her illness for a day off. In the attic they shared, Juliet had knelt next to Eldon's pallet alarmed by his pallor and burning fever. Juliet and Mary gave him drink and food, careful of the cook who watched their every movement as they passed her comfortable bedroom on the second floor and reported back to Orpha.

She feared for his survival.

Orpha's madness grew with vigor, and so did her abuse, targeting the servant boy with her cruelty, cutting his rations and increasing his workload. Juliet knew it was a twisted punishment for Eldon who survived when Orpha's own children had not.

"Where is my breakfast?" screamed Orpha from up above.

Juliet gazed out the window as she had many times since Joshua warned her of a potential Indian attack. Perhaps with the late winter snows, there would be less inclination by the savages.

The wood pile was low and had to be replaced. Her back ached from the endless chores performed since morn. She pulled her skirts away from the fire and lifted the baked bread from the hearth and set the warm loaf on the table. With the cook in her bed, Juliet sliced off large pieces for Mary and Eldon and swathed them with strawberry jam. She hummed a tune, cutting off extra portions of bacon. They would eat well today.

She touched her fingers to her lips, remembering Joshua's golden kiss. She had certainly not been kissed before and he had fulfilled everything for a young girl's dreams.

Inadvertent bits of information with reference to Joshua came from the Hayes. A neighbor had visited and Orpha bragged she had hosted the legendary frontiersman.

Joshua's reputation stretched across the frontier. Sorting out the fanciful from truth was easy, and she dismissed most of it as fact. No doubt, there was his fabled marksmanship, but with a long rifle flung backward on his shoulder and shooting ten deer with a single ball?

She blew a tendril of hair out of her eyes. From the ludicrous to the sublime, tales touted the killing of a colossus mythical bear that ate people whole, tied up the ornery wind with a grapevine, and in deep water lakes, jousted with serpents the size of a house. He possessed the ability to disappear in the wilderness with no hint of his existence. Her favorite being how mountains knelt before him.

Her thoughts went back to Eldon.

An impatient knocking spurred her attention.

Was it Joshua come to take them away?

Her heart leapt. She dropped her knife and flew to the door. Her shoulders slumped when a red-coated soldier entered, stamping snow from his boots on the floor where Juliet had worked hard to polish that morn.

"I'm Captain Milburn Snapes, in His Majesty's service. Is Master Hayes home? I have urgent business with him." His high-pitched voice came as a sneering insult and so did the smack on her behind when she had turned.

Juliet raised her hand to slap his face and stopped. No sense earning a beating. She had to stay in good health to escape.

He laughed, and his closely-spaced, blood-shot eyes flicked from side to side like a boar inspecting a trough. His piggish mouth with a sloping chin jutted from bulging cheeks. He lacked only a ring through his nose.

"I'm in a hurry, girl, but wouldn't mind a tup or two with you warming my bed."

She was sick of being bullied and Joshua's threats to Horace emboldened her. With certainty, she would not allow a soldier to intimidate her. "Master Hayes has some goats you can make yourself available to."

He touched the pair of silver-mounted pistols stuck handily in his belt, and then moved a hand on the hilt of a long-sheathed knife that hung on his side.

Juliet pivoted and made her way down the hall, pointing to a room on the right. "You can rest in Master Hayes' office while I get him."

"I remember a slight," he said behind her. "You're an uppity servant who wants a lesson."

He didn't enter Horace's study. She didn't need to look behind. The stamp of his boots told her he followed close on her heels.

She skimmed a hand in front of her nose to eradicate his rancid smell. "Even the goats wouldn't have you," she said over her shoulder.

Into the kitchen she fled. Mary had returned and was cracking eggs. "Go get Master Hayes. He has a visitor," Juliet ordered.

Mary hesitated, looking to Juliet, and then to the man who had burst rudely into the kitchen.

"Hurry," Juliet mouthed.

Mary flew up the back stairs.

The man burst into the room and slammed her against the wood block, his guns and sheathed knife pressing into her belly. He lifted her skirts and she tugged them down. His hands were everywhere.

"I always wanted to sink my quid into a redhead," he laughed.

She pushed at him, but he held her drawn between his legs. Up close, he reeked even more. Her stomach roiled. His face leered above her as he ripped at her skirts.

"So much boldness. I don't think you're as confident as you pretend."

A sickening terror crawled up her belly. His hands clawed up her legs, forcing her thighs to open.

"I won't let you—"

He knocked off her cap and coiled a mass of her hair tight to his fingers and yanked her face inches before his own. "You will learn obedience like the bitch you are."

When she squirmed, he laughed, and mauled her breasts in a punishing grip, pinching her nipples. She wanted to scratch his disgusting sneer off his swine face. She bit his hand. He slapped her, and then grabbed at her nether regions.

Heart pounding in her ears, she reached back, stretched out and arm flailing for something to grab. The basket of eggs crashed to the floor. She stretched harder…felt the hilt of the knife she had used earlier. She grasped it and whipped it to his throat…pushed it into his flesh. A trickle of blood dripped from his neck onto her chest. "Get away from me before I slit your throat."

He backed away just as the cook came into the kitchen, then took a step back, eyes wide. Juliet threw down her skirts and moved around the cook, thankful this one time for her presence. Out of breath, Mary burst in behind her.

"Get yerself upstairs, Juliet. I'll report yer whoring to Mistress Hayes later."

Her body trembling, Juliet straightened. Visions of the whipping post loomed. "I've done nothing to encourage—"

"She's a slut," sneered Snapes, wiping the blood from his neck. "Would spread her legs for anyone."

"I know her kind," the cook scoffed. "Saw her lusting after Joshua Hansford."

Snapes froze. "Joshua Hansford was here? When? What was he about?"

What was Snapes' interest in Joshua? Juliet's stomach beat a wild tattoo. She sensed whatever his interest, it did not bode well for Joshua.

"Months ago," said the cook.

The cook moved her bulk round the kitchen, inspecting the broken eggs on the floor. "I'm sure Juliet will earn a whipping for her sins, but the Mistress is in a terrible temper over Eldon. He goes first."

"What? The poor boy is sick, cannot lift his head from the bed." It was a moot point how the cook was obviously hale and healthy and derelict in her duties.

"Mistress has to teach him a lesson."

The punishment was madness and they were helpless to stop the lunacy. "There is no need for this cruelty." Juliet said. "Mary and I are doing his chores."

Juliet caught the English captain's malevolent stare directed at her. "Tell Mistress Hayes, I'll do the honors."

Amidst moans, the boy was dragged down the stairs and in such a feverish state, Juliet prayed he did not know what was happening to him. Orpha, in her dressing gown, commanded her position from the porch. The servants were aligned around the post for optimal viewing and the consequent lesson to be learned. Snapes had secured Eldon, his hands tied above his head, his toes barely touching the ground.

Barely conscious, his chin slumped to his chest.

Like a showman, Snapes smiled, taking great delight in teasing out the macabre moment before administering the lash. One. Two. Three…the whip cracked.

Juliet lost count and held back the bile in her throat.

"Dear God," said Mary. She leaned against Juliet, gasping. The other servants stayed rooted and trembled, too afraid to speak up against the horror unless they wanted to be next. The cook lifted her chin in approval. Orpha clapped and cheered with each blow.

Over and over again, Snapes cracked powerful, punishing blows on Eldon's back. Blood streamed in rivers off his emaciated body.

Juliet put her hands over her ears. "Stop! Stop it!"

His arm lowered to his side, Snapes regarded Orpha. His questioning gaze seemed to beg for more lashings.

One of the servants put his fingers to Eldon's throat. "The boy's dead."

A maniacal gleam grew in Orpha's eyes. "No more than he deserved. Enough excitement for today. For her whoring, Juliet's turn will take place tomorrow."

"Why not today?" suggested Snapes.

She wanted to claw the sneer off Snape's face. No doubt, the cook and Snapes conspired against her. Protesting her innocence was as futile as holding water through wide-spread fingers.

Knees buckling, she righted herself, refusing to show weakness. Somehow, she had to keep up this dangerous game, faking a bravado she didn't have and holding her breath waiting for Orpha's whim.

"Not today. I like my entertainment parceled." Like a vulture, Orpha's wrapper flapped about her as she turned to go inside the house.

Juliet breathed a sigh of relief and cast her gaze on the distant mountains rolling onward with infinite depth. There was no sign of Joshua. To expect him to return was a useless venture. She leaned to Mary and whispered, "We leave early morn."

Chapter 8

$\mathcal{J}$oshua and Two Eagles entered the fort at West Point, a crucial military location guarding the Hudson River and critical for the transportation of food and supplies. A blue-coated soldier escorted them to a crowded office.

"Joshua, Two Eagles, it's a pleasure. You have news of the frontier?" Colonel Rufus Putman gestured for them to sit. "This is General Anthony Wayne. He is also interested."

Joshua spent the next half-hour over maps, detailing the movements of Indians and the British.

General Anthony Wayne leaned forward. "I'll make sure General Washington receives it posthaste."

"There is an indentured servant at Horace Hayes' farm, claiming she is Colonel Faulkner's cousin and wants to escape to England."

General Wayne cleared his throat. "And you want to help her escape and return her to her cousin," he said matter-of-fact.

"I do." Joshua nodded.

"Well then. While you are at Fort Oswego, you can do intelligence gathering for us."

"Agreed. I'll stay one night to rest and resupply, and then be on my way."

"Good," said Putman. "Take from the quartermaster whatever you need."

Joshua shook hands and left with Two Eagles.

Outside the commander's office, Joshua fell in with Ghost, a renowned trapper. He shook his shaggy head. "Just came from the south and barely missed a huge party of Onontio's moving north."

Joshua froze. *Juliet.* She'd be vulnerable. "Where?"

In a milky haze, snow fell, lacing the dawn, rendering everything silent. Still hanging on to its ragged coattails, winter seemed to spite the advent of spring.

Eldon. She had cared for the servant boy so much, she felt she might bleed to death with his passing. She and Mary had wept silently through the night, grieving the poor boy's horrid fate, wishing him well into a far better world. Eldon's death and the imminent threat of Juliet's lashing cemented their departure.

The horrid Captain Snapes slept upstairs after spending half the night in deep conference with Horace.

The first few streaks of dawn swathed the house when they tiptoed down the stairs, gathering foodstuffs and a knife from the kitchen while everyone slept. Juliet purloined a coat from Horace and one from Orpha made of heavier wool for their travels. The labors they had performed for the Hayes' more than paid for the items pilfered.

Juliet and Mary crossed themselves when they passed a fresh dug grave where the servant boy had been laid to rest. They hurried past the whipping post, a lone bloody sentinel in the yard, a grim reminder of what would happen to them if caught. Entering the barn, they crossed to the back. They pulled aside a loose board and stepped through the cow pasture where huge bovines snorted out short puffs from their nostrils, unconcerned with the interlopers.

Nerves dancing in her stomach, Juliet turned to see if anyone from the house was watching. She exhaled and the air became frozen lace. Satisfied no one could see them, and that the barn blocked any view of their passage, they climbed through a split rail fence, slogged up a meadow and into the barrier of the woods. Their footprints were left in the snow, but Juliet couldn't do anything about that.

So quiet. Unearthly quiet as if the world quit breathing, imprisoning her in a glare-white silence. Up the mountain, trees seemed to leer at her, grabbing at her with their long branches, talons scratching her. Yet nothing sounded, nothing stirred, nothing sang.

Gooseflesh rippled up her back.

We will escape. We will escape. She puffed the promise with every footfall. Why did nervous sweat slick her body?

"We must keep going, Mary. To put as much distance between us and the farm is vital."

From atop a sharp treeless precipice, they paused to catch their breaths. The inordinate number of coyotes howling in the distance lifted the hair off the back of her neck. Unusual. Mating season didn't start until later in the spring. With rough woolen mittens, she rubbed her forehead. How would they defend themselves against a pack of coyotes?

Below lay a pastoral view of the Hayes farm. Quiet. Serene. She had loved the peaceful hours before the other servants rose. Sheltered from the elements, warmth, and food beckoned from the uncertain fate ahead.

"Where will we go?" asked Mary.

"My goal is to reach my cousin, Colonel Thomas Faulkner. Joshua had informed me he was stationed at Fort Oswego. I pored over and copied a map of the New York frontier in Horace's office while he entertained Captain Snapes in the dining room last night." She breathed a little prayer to Moira who had imparted her knowledge of the stars. She'd use the skill to forge north.

All of a sudden came horrendous cries rattling the nerves up her spine. Numerous warriors, their heads plucked clean except for a strip of hair an inch wide, cut short and brush-like, running from above the brow to the nape, scattered from the forests and surrounded the house. She and Mary froze. *An attack.*

You will not be immune. Joshua's words came back to haunt her.

Juliet gripped the hood of Mary's cloak, hauled back, and the sudden motion caused her friend's feet to fly out from under her. Both girls hit the ground with a muffled thud. With shaking hands, she pushed a ledge of snow blocking their view in front of them apart. Icy cold cut into her chin as she peered over the outcrop.

Shock robbed Juliet of speech. She lay as motionless as an iron anvil.

Servants were herded outside. The cook ran from her grotesque-painted captor.

One of the warriors directed the charge. Juliet stared at him. From the distance, his facial features were obscured. He stood a mountain of a man, a sordid creature from *Dante's Inferno*. Despite the frigid temperatures, he was shirtless, wearing only moccasins and a loincloth. Blood-curdling screams rose from him. Juliet pressed her mittened hands over her ears to drown out the terrible cries of his warriors.

As the cook fled past the whipping post, her nightgown flailing like a sail, the enormous Indian threw his tomahawk. She half-turned, then fell.

Captain Snapes, fully dressed walked out onto the grounds. No one touched him.

Crammed between two warriors, Master Hayes was wrestled to the porch. "You bastards. I'm the King's man. Snapes do something."

Snapes laughed. With certainty, he'd known of the attack.

Impatient, the leader of the Indians yanked his tomahawk from the cook's skull, shifted to Horace, and raised it again. The blow glanced off the side of Horace's head, right above the ear, opening a wide scarlet gash. Master Hayes took a step forward, his mouth open in an empty cry. The giant Indian plunged his tomahawk into Horace's skull, then raised his foot to Hayes' back and yanked it out. Horace plummeted face first from the porch.

Mary moaned and leaned into Juliet, covering her eyes at the grisly scene.

Orpha, still in her sleeping clothes screeched and clawed as the savages dragged her across the porch, and then tied her spread-eagle across the woodpile. Like parting the sea, the leader moved through his warriors. He lifted his breechclout and straddled Orpha. Her free hand flailed, searching for her nonexistent cap to cover her baldness. When he finished, one warrior after another took their turn with her.

"Dear God," whispered Mary.

Orpha, raped repeatedly by a number of Indians was left to the leader. He jerked a wicked knife from his waistband and cut a deep circle in her scalp from the receding hairline back from her forehead to the crown. With a tremendous jerk on the hair, he pulled the scalp off and shook it high above his head.

Juliet's mouth opened in a voiceless scream. Unable to look away, her hand closed convulsively around her gold cross as another Indian knelt on Horace's back and cutting his scalp free, picking up his tomahawk.

There seemed to be a dispute about the cook's scalp with one Indian holding up his tomahawk over the other. He pushed his competitor off the cook, completed removing her scalp and shoved it into a pouch attached to his waistband.

The house was torched and the flames grew brighter, fed by the winter wind, roaring like tongues from the windows and casting blood-red outlines on the ground. The snap and hiss of the flames invaded the snow-insulated quiet of the day.

Two warriors shouted from behind the barn, and squinting, Juliet saw them pointing to footsteps printed in the snow. Through a drumbeat of shock, she heard the leader and Snapes shout to follow.

"Hurry, Mary." Juliet helped her friend to her feet. Slipping and sliding on a deer trail, they disappeared among the thick woods, fleeing up the mountain.

At the apex, fragile snow gave way and buckled beneath them. Arms flailing in the air, everything sailed past. Juliet plummeted down a steep embankment, grabbing at rocks, branches, clawing at icy roots to break her fall. She slammed into a mucky embankment, her breath whooshing out of her as Mary crashed into her.

Bruised and sore, Juliet crawled to her feet. "Mary, are you all right?" If there were any bone breaks, they'd be doomed.

Mary stood on shaky legs. "I'm fine."

A creek burbled, the first indication of a winter thaw. "We have no choice. We have to travel downstream. Wait here."

Juliet tossed her bundle on her back and hiked up her skirts. The icy water took her breath away and soaked through her boots.

She held out her hand to Mary, the cold numbing her feet. For a mile, they scrambled on slippery rocks. Mary's teeth chattered, and Juliet worried over her friend's well-being.

On a steep embankment, Juliet climbed up on rocks, turned around and hauled Mary up beside her. They rubbed the circulation back in their legs. No way could they rest, not here in the open and not with the Indians tracking them. She stumbled onto an animal path and disappeared beneath the hulking branches of hemlock.

They traveled north. At least, Juliet, believed they were heading in that direction, as they ambled into an open meadow looking for the North Star to guide them.

"I'm so cold," Mary coughed. "Couldn't we light a little fire?"

"It would be so easy yet we dare not. You saw what happened to Orpha. If they observe the glow from our fire, they will find us."

Sleet bit at their faces and the girls huddled beneath an outcropping of rock, shivering, their feet wooden from traveling through the creek. Juliet pulled her coat tight around her, stepped away and scanned the horizon. She cocked her head to the side and perceived no sound except the click of sleet on branches. No thud of foot or sway of branch. Even the animals had hunkered in their dens.

Surely the Indians would have discovered them by now? Perhaps content with their prizes from the Hayes' farm and conceivably settled before warm fires in their lodges. A wind rattled through the bare trees, a portent in a world of ice and darkness.

Mary coughed behind her. The unending cold, the enemy.

Juliet returned to Mary and unsheathed the long knife from her waistband and cut pieces of beef and bread. She insisted they put on dry socks. Not much good that would do since their boots were soaked. Mary slumped on her shoulder and Juliet eased her friend to the ground and lay beside her, her muscles stiff from the cold.

"Juliet!"

Mary clawed Juliet's arm as an Indian dragged her across the snow by her long golden hair.

Gripped with terror, Juliet shot from deep sleep to wakefulness, throwing her body across her friend. The warrior's eyes, veiled pools of sinister black revealed the monster that lurked beneath. Never before had she witnessed a more frightening figure. This was the leader who had hacked Master Hayes to death, raped Orpha, and scalped the cook. Like a bizarre raccoon, his head and face congealed with red-blood paint, and a black mask daubed around his eyes with detailed black lines descending across his cheeks. A black line of lightning brushed across his forehead. Secured to his tuft of hair dangled a lone eagle feather.

She would fight him. Juliet sprang. She scratched, digging her nails into his neck, his ears, anywhere she could reach. She kicked with her booted foot against the savage's shins.

Her head jerked back. She felt a tearing pain. He had ahold of her long braid. Her hand tightened on the hilt of her knife. On a low, throaty scream she yanked it loose and slashed the Indian's face. His hand swept up to the gash she made, his blood now dripping on her.

He reared, dropping her suddenly to the ground, and leapt away as if touching her had reduced his strength. He pointed to her hair. Was it fear she now saw in his eyes? Did it have something to do with the color of her hair?

The painted warriors launched into a discussion with each other, gesticulating wildly and espousing deep guttural tones directed at her hair. Unbidden, a flock of crows lifted from their roosts, circling and cawing, adding their voices to a howl of sudden wind. Owls hooted. She couldn't see the creatures but the savages pricked their ears to the sound, scanning the heavens, their harshly whispered words hanging in the air like little frozen clouds.

"What are they going to do with us?" cried Mary, scooting from beneath her.

"Quiet." Juliet placed her arm protectively round Mary's shoulder and stared at the number of scalps looped on their belts—proud trophies. Sick fear coiled in the pit of her stomach. Black hair with a white tip at the crown congealed with blood. Master Hayes.

The leader with the red and black stripes painted on his face, returned his gaze to her and gestured roughly. Juliet held back a scream, rose to her full height and craned her head back looking at this mountain of a man and his crazed, inhuman eyes. *Do not show weakness.*

From his side, one of his warriors, spoke harshly, "Onontio."

Onontio. Joshua had warned her of the War Chief, his posture stiff as an arrow, his downturned lips, spoke of cruelty.

Knees shaking, she stood on stiff legs while they argued. A tattooed warrior with many nose rings wanted them dead, she surmised. Onontio pushed him to the ground, glanced at her and grunted.

A warrior with a string of bear claws around his neck and a red jacket fondled and blew upon Mary's golden locks. He shouted in angry tones to others of the group who dared to come near. Had he claimed ownership of Mary?

"Joggo!" The gorget of silver on his neck and wide bands made of the same material around his upper arms vibrated with his command.

Juliet interpreted "joggo" to follow. She stumbled on her skirts and reached a hand down to pull Mary up. The tattooed warrior on the ground stood up and tied their hands, angry with the menial task. He jerked their leashes, yanking Juliet and Mary forward, following Onontio.

Half of the group preceded them and the remainder tracked behind. The Indians had one idea in mind. Speed. They rushed the two of them forward, ever forward.

Were they being followed? Did they desire to put as many miles as possible between them and Master Hayes' home? Might a handful of staunch neighbors follow to avenge the massacre? Fueled with the hope, she dragged her feet often to slow their progress.

Onontio ordered a short and stocky Indian with bowed legs and gripping a hickory sapling in his hand to walk behind them. When Juliet lagged for a moment to catch her breath, Bow-Legs lashed the whip around her legs. The Indians farther to the rear picked up grass and weeds broken down by their feet to blot out signs of their passing.

Where were they going? There were herded along, through a clearing, marching through ice cold waters of a stream for some distance, then pushed through a thicket and into a meadow. Up and down mountains they marched, blue ranges looming high up on the skyline. Blinding snow drove in their eyes and the wind lashed their clothing tight about them. Her toes and fingers stung from the cold, her calves burned with steep uphill climbs. Each step was torture, her feet blistered, and heels scraped raw by the wet leather of her boots. Her lungs seared from frigid breaths and the piercing stitch in her side stayed a constant companion. At the top of the mountain, the snows were deep, the arduous task of lifting one foot high and then the next nearly breaking them.

They traveled day and night with little sustenance, stopping little to rest. The frigid temperatures gave way to torrid heat as winter vanished and seemingly skipped spring, emerging to summer. Mary whimpered and leaned on her. Juliet neither knew nor cared where they went. Keep moving, walking and running as fast as she could. No rest. No time to catch her breath. She stumbled and suffered the sharp blows from Bow-Legs' hickory stick.

Northward they made their weary way over the mountains, climbing steep heights and running down abrupt slopes, wading through rocky brooks and waist-deep streams. At no time did Juliet see a road. How did the leader, Onontio know where he was going? Her gown caught on branches and brambles. Her legs were lashed and scratched by thorns. Her red hair hung tangled and uncombed. She tripped and picked up a piece of jagged flint, concealing it in her pocket.

Her stomach had shrunk into a hard, little fist, gnawing with unbearable hunger. The hunger eventually passed and, with it, all other sensations. Keep going. No pause. No rest.

Images of the savages burning their prisoners alive as told by Orpha caused her to panic. Juliet curved her arm around Mary's shoulders and pressed her chin onto her silky head. "We will escape tonight, when they sleep."

"But what of the forest? Won't it be our demise?"

"Better than what they have planned for us. We will live on roots and berries."

"They are cannibals. My father preached how they savor devouring white people."

Juliet had not heard the sermon and wondered of the truth. Her eyelids grew heavy. She fought sleep, cutting through their bonds with the sharp flint and waiting for the snoring rhythms of the warriors. She rubbed her wrists and poked Mary awake.

With the light of the moon, they skirted the circle of men and moved through the forest. A cold wind stirred like a whisper through ancient hemlocks, a wolf howled in the distance, answered by the baying of other wolves and drawing shivers up her spine. She pressed through the woodlands not knowing where they were going, hoping to get far enough away before their captors were alerted to their escape.

The jerk of a cruel hand threw her prostrate and the lash of a whip stung her legs. Bow-Legs stood over her, his face twisted like a goblin. Behind him stood Onontio, sneering. Mary cried as they were herded back to the camp and tied to a tree.

The next morning food was handed out but not for the captives. Onontio picked up the pace. His way of punishment.

"We will survive," she whispered.

"Water," Mary rasped through parched and cracked lips. "I want to die."

Bleak and lifeless, the sound in her voice struck terror in Juliet's heart. Bow-Legs whipped them for talking. Fierce rage swelled up in Juliet. No more did she care what happened to her. No more would she tolerate Bow-Legs' whipping. She swiveled, grabbing the whip and cracked the cane on him over and over again. He lifted his arms to ward off her blows. "You can kill us right here. We won't move again until you give us food, drink and rest."

At first shocked, the Indians now laughed to see Bow-Legs dodge her blows. They teased and humiliated him. A shadow crossed over her. Onontio yanked the whip from her, his face twisted like a gargoyle. Her legs shaking, Juliet pulled a length of her hair forward and thrust it in his face. He stepped back. Juliet laughed. Madness bubbled up from her throat. He feared her.

Days passed one after another until Juliet lost count. The land leaned down to rolling hills, and still they pushed their way through tangled brush and deep forest that led to a river. Now, two braves paddled them upriver, avoiding floating logs and rocks.

When the sun reached its zenith, she viewed smoke spiraling up beyond a bend in the river. Juliet curled her hands around the gunnels, sweat trickling down her back as the Indians paddled to a village. A group of scattered lodges stood in an open meadow, constructed on pole frameworks, with sides and roofs covered with great sheets of tree bark. Open platforms for storing hides and meat loomed up close by, and piles of firewood lay near doorways.

A white dog barked alerting the villagers of their arrival. So many people were coming and going, hollering, laughing, and merrymaking. The bloody scalps were displayed and rejoiced over by everyone from grizzled grandfathers to naked toddlers.

Many women walked toed-in, bent forward, with shuffling gaits to greet them. They wore deerskin leggings and embroidered moccasins on their feet. Silver earrings adorned their ears, silver bracelets were cuffed upon their arms and strings of beads hung round their necks. Their hair was parted in the middle with a streak of scarlet paint on the part, and fastened behind in single braids, doubled back upon themselves and tied. Onontio pointed to Juliet and growled a long narrative to the women.

"Juliet," Mary said moments before she was ripped away and dragged into a longhouse. Were they going to be burned alive?

There was nothing Juliet could do. Women grabbed hold of her and tied a leather thong around her neck and secured her with a two-foot leash to a stake in the center of the village. They poked her with pointed sticks. She ducked her head when they threw rotten vegetables and jeered. No mercy would come to a white captive in this godforsaken wilderness. She did not cry out or whimper and stared boldly at them. She hated all of them and refused them their joy by not making her fear known. Juliet grabbed her hair, thrusting it forward, and shouted curses. The women backed away as if looking at a strange animal and pointing to her hair. They quickly disbanded and left for the longhouses.

Her lips were parched and her skin red and swollen where she'd fallen against sharp rocks. Her hair, a mass of knots flew about her face and shoulders. Her tether tied tight rendered sleep impossible. She slumped against the post and sobbed, her heart bursting under the crushing weight of grief, of years and days of suffering. What sin have I done other than be born into this world to deserve this punishment? *Oh, God, please help me.*

A blanket was placed over her, shielding her from the torrid sun, and through tear-stained eyes, she peered at a dark-clad figure. He lay his hand on her shoulder. "Do not weep, my child."

Through her tears, a man with one arm appeared. He wore priest's clothing and spoke to her in a thick French accent. "I am Father Isaac Devereux."

He placed a bowl of food in Juliet's lap, the skirts of his ankle-length cassock brushed against her. She held the gruel in her hands, savoring the warmth, but suddenly the smell of food made her feel faint. She pressed a hand to her stomach to ease the pain of hunger.

She picked up the wooden spoon and dipped into the watery substance, holding the spoon aloft as she first eyed the large crucifix hanging from Father Devereux's neck and then at her uncertain food.

"It is a mixture of corn and meat, not poison." His voice was soft, yet somehow reassuring. "You must eat to gain strength, but eat slow so you won't lose what you have consumed." He hiked up his cassock and sat in the dirt beside her.

Slowly she sipped the odd and tasteless food that rolled grainy over her tongue. "Strength for what? So they can torture me?"

Father Isaac's good arm dropped to his side and, immediately, his hand rose to steady his broad hat. "No, my daughter. Onontio plans to marry you."

A sharp spasm in her stomach pulled her gaze from the Jesuit to Onontio, cheered and admired by many of the village maidens. Their eager enticing had him disappearing into a longhouse.

To be married to the monster would be a life of hell. She shivered with images of the warrior's coarse fingers rough against her skin. His ghoulish painted face hovering over her, and flat black eyes possessing the penetrating cold of a serpent she'd seen under the statue of the Blessed Virgin. To go to bed each night with a beast like that?

The priest tilted his head down to her, his great black hat with a rounded crown and wide, circular brim shadowed her shoulder. "You will endure. Onontio believes you have great power. Two of his young wives have died giving birth. To remove the curse and bear powerful sons, he demands a union to you. The Mohawks are a superstitious group who believe your red hair possesses the same potency of a demi-god."

The priest's remarks reinforced her conjecture of Onontio's fear of her hair.

"Where is Mary?"

"She is with Red Jacket's wife, learning what work she must perform. Mary will be her slave."

"Are you not afraid of reprisal from Onontio for giving me succor?"

The priest shrugged, the stump of his left arm raised. "Onontio and I respect each other. He is the one who removed my arm."

She dropped her spoon in her bowl. "How do you know he will not remove your other arm?"

A young boy with a huge tooth suspended from his neck brought Juliet a vessel of water. "Thank you," she said, marveling at the unbidden kindness of the boy.

The priest ruffled the boy's hair. "Onontio's ruthlessness was my reward. By removing my arm, the Indians know I cannot hold a bow to hunt for food to survive. As a result of my sacrifice, I grew in esteem and was able to convert the chief's wife and this boy, Garakonthie, or Moving Sun. I remain under their protection and they let me live in peace among them. They even protect me from the British who remain resolute in running off the French, especially the Jesuits."

He waved to an old woman who shuffled across the grounds. "She is Ojistah, a Mohawk medicine woman and the boy's grandmother. She is greatly revered for her skills as a healer. When Onontio cut off my arm, she took pity and nursed me back to health. She is sensitive and compassionate, capable of soul-stirring energy, and possesses special intuitive abilities."

"I could plead my case to Ojistah?"

Father Devereux shook his head. "The Mohawk medicine woman wields great power, but even she would not go up against the War Chief."

Moving Sun, the boy with the single bear tooth ran off as Milburn Snapes marched through the Indian village. Her hands curled into fists and she tore at her tether to get free. She hated the British captain for he epitomized the worst kind of betrayal. He had wined and dined with Horace and Orpha though knowing of their fate at the hands of the Indians.

"He was at the attack on the Hayes' farm and condoned it, Father Devereux. As a British officer, his first responsibility was to protect loyal subjects of the Crown, but he did nothing. The slaughter was terrible. No one deserved to die that way—even the hideous Orpha."

Juliet gave the priest an abbreviated version of what had happened, how she and Mary had left the farm early only to be caught by Onontio and the agonizing journey they endured to the village. Not once did Snapes look in her direction. Did he know she was in the village? He spoke quickly in Iroquois tongue to an Indian woman. Juliet heard the name, "Onontio".

Just then, the War Chief thrust aside a deerskin flap, and

exited the longhouse, his mouth tight from being disturbed. A half-naked woman giggled behind him. Onontio's breechclout was raised from his swollen manhood probably from the woman's continued stroking. He shrugged her off.

Milburn Snapes squatted before a campfire, staring at the licking flames. A dozen Iroquois, large, well-muscled men wearing deer hide breechclouts, leggings and moccasins crouched around the fire close to him. They had adopted European long shirts decorated with porcupine quills.

This must have been an important occasion. The red-jacketed leader with the bear-claw necklace who had taken Mary dipped his fingers into the paint pots, and with the other warriors, reapplied hideous designs upon their faces. Onontio, to demonstrate his supremacy wore additional gorgets of silver and wide bands around his upper arms.

Captain Snapes lifted his eyes from the fire and let them pass slowly over the ten warriors, and then come to rest on their two leaders. Snapes launched into a long speech, his hand gesturing upon the attending crowd.

"What is he saying?" Juliet asked. Captain Snapes and Baron Bearsted were cut of the same cloth and she wished them to perdition. For as long as she breathed, she would do everything in her power to make sure they were both brought to justice.

"I'm versed in most of the language but not all so bear with me. He wants to remind Onontio and his faithful Mohawks of the friendship of the King and his Loyalist brethren. Onontio has asked him how many prisoners he wants from the raids of other settlements that will arrive shortly."

"Not many," Snapes shrugged. His close-spaced eyes darted

over Juliet and she drew back into Father Devereux. He'd been aware of her presence the whole time.

"How many scalps?" The leader with the bear-tooth necklace asked, and they joined him in laughter.

"As many as you can take without losing your own. Not that you have much to lose, Red Jacket," Snapes pointed to the bald Indian. The men laughed again.

"These prisoners," Onontio went on, "you can have them except the red-haired woman. There is a power round her. She will bear me sons."

Snapes glanced to Juliet. "I know her quite well."

Onontio drew his finger along the bright red scar she'd cut on his cheek and spat. "Like a dog, she needs to learn obedience."

"Be careful she doesn't take your balls," Snapes said and they all hooted.

Red Jacket pounded a fist on his chest. "The light-haired woman will be my wife's slave."

Juliet inhaled with the Jesuit's rapid translations.

"What will your wife say when you take the light-haired woman to bed?" Snapes snickered. The men laughed but Red Jacket did not find it amusing.

Snapes beat his chest. "General Carlton has late intelligence Fort Stanich is no real obstacle. There are poor picketed defense works with no more than sixty men. Maybe he is right. Maybe not. Scout it out and see what you think. Capture some of the garrison and bring them to me. They'll tell us what we need to know." Snapes looked at every one of them. "When the moon passes full many times, Colonel Butler from Fort Niagara will gather forces for raids south of the Mohawk Valley. Many scalps, prisoners and plunder are assured."

Onontio stood and clasped hands with the British officer. "Captain Snapes, you be witness to my wedding."

Snapes nodded at the War Chief's hospitality. "It is an honor. But I must beg leave and do reconnaissance for our Great White Father."

Onontio spoke loudly for the assembled braves, his furious speech climbing to a crescendo. Clenching his fists to the heavens, he said, "Next full moon we will strike out. Maybe capture the fort. We will sharpen our hatchets and bring back many scalps."

When he finished, the Indians jumped from the ground and roared their approval.

Snapes nodded with the War Chief's declaration. "Ten pounds per scalp. You will be a wealthy man before this war ends, Onontio."

Snapes swaggered to where Juliet sat with the priest. "You are not so brave now."

Juliet glared at him. "You ordered the massacre against the Hayes' household."

"Yes, I did. Horace had taken land from me and I paid my debt. Such are the spoils of war. Enjoy your life as Onontio's wife." With an Indian, he took to a canoe and disappeared down the river.

Chapter 9

Joshua paddled hard, his first thoughts—to get to Juliet. Two Eagles matched his grueling pace across the mountains, and then stealing a canoe, they made their way to Onontio's Mohawk home where, with certainty, the War Chief would return and declare his greatness, displaying his scalps and parading his captives.

Damn the orders from Albany that took him from the Hayes' farm. The charred ruins gone cold for a week. He shook his head, still unable to get the gruesome massacre out of his mind. He had braced himself for his worst fears, turning the scalped and mutilated corpses over, thankful Juliet and Mary were not among them.

Two Eagles had been adamant it was the work of Onontio, and then followed the tracks of warriors, leading to the capture of the women. It was his best hope the tracks were Mary and Juliet's and they complied with the War Chief, their deaths fated if they dared to complain or slow the war party's progress.

They pulled up the canoe against the sandy bank on the village of Tionnontigo. Children squealed a series of whoops to announce their arrival. Out from the lodges, men, women and children poured. The Indians fawned and eager women loitered with flirtatious smiles, none of which Joshua cared the least bit about.

Parting the crowd was Ojistah, the medicine woman and Two Eagles' aunt. "Too long you have been gone, my sons." There was censure in her tone.

Joshua scanned the village. Ojistah threaded her arm through Joshua's, passing several longhouses, the council house and to the center of the village. His heart pounded.

His gaze fell on Juliet and a black crow Jesuit sitting beside her. She was beaten, bruised and her clothes were torn, and her hair spilled in wild abandon down to her hips. His heart pounded.

She was alive.

Their gazes locked. Her dreadful misery was mirrored in her face, but it was the entreaty in her tear-stained eyes that came as sure as if she'd shouted the words.

You've come to save me!

Despite the indignities he was sure she had endured, she held her head high. She carried herself like a queen and, for that, he was proud.

He clenched his hands into fists. The dark circles beneath her eyes, pale skin and loss of weight showed her ill-use where she'd likely been pushed beyond endurance on their travels through the forests. Bred in his nature was the protection of women. He cursed Onontio and his band. They would pay for their abuse of Juliet.

He strode to her. Ojistah jerked him back.

"I know who you have come for. Be patient, my son."

But Joshua didn't hear her. He ignored the fact he was a guest in the village, bound by custom not to intervene. He ignored everything except the fact that Juliet needed his help and he'd come for her.

He shook off the medicine woman's hand and started for Juliet. Two Eagles stepped in front of him. "If you want to save her, stay where you are and let my aunt scheme. This is not my village where I could allow you to go to her. Juliet is a captive and will be difficult if not impossible to free. Onontio has been ordered to appear along with the chief."

Joshua swore, forcing himself to stay rooted and let the matter play out. Helpless. Rage burned in his belly.

Onontio, a mountain of a warrior, his hideous face painted black and red, wormed his way through the crowd. "What do you want, Ojistah?"

"A problem has occurred. You have taken our brother, Joshua's woman."

Onontio pounded his chest with his fist. "She is my captive. She will not be taken from me."

The chief intervened. "Joshua is our brother in blood and to be respected, but Onontio is our War Chief and through great heroism and trial has returned with his prize. He will not be cheated of his conquest."

Ojistah pulled herself up to full height, her grandson next to her. "Joshua is a brave warrior. His magic is far more powerful than Onontio and cannot be contested." She raised the giant bear tooth suspended from Morning Sun's neck to remind them of the bear with evil orenda Joshua had destroyed.

The villagers murmured, pointing at the venerated amulet.

With the unblinking gaze of a hawk, Ojistah cast her gaze over the crowd. "He has done far more to protect the village than—"

"No!" Onontio spat. "I will not let this dog of a white man usurp what is mine."

The chief nodded his head, considering the medicine woman's words. "There is much force in what you say, Ojistah. The only way to determine who gets the woman is for Joshua to run the gauntlet. If he survives, he gets the woman."

Before the echoes of warriors' shouts, Joshua was pressed to the precipice of two lines. On their guard, warriors eyed him and shuffled close, yet Ojistah's play on their superstition of his magic made them wary. Because of their fear of his suggested supernatural power, he sincerely hoped he'd have the upper hand.

Still, there were hardened warriors out to make a name for themselves. He inspected the motley group, restless, angry, armed with clubs, tomahawks, sticks, any sort of weapon they could find. Like a pack of curs, they were ready to hunt and tear apart their prey. One warrior with a red jacket possessed a particularly monstrous war club made from the burl of a tree and might crack a man's skull like a scythe through wheat. Joshua flexed his arms. He had no intentions of falling under any of the weapons.

"Run fast, with your head down," said Two Eagles.

Joshua danced in place on the ground to loosen up. "Remember when I rescued you from ten armed trappers?"

"There were twenty." Two Eagles smiled.

"Ten ran away. They didn't count. I don't think these seasoned warriors will run."

"Did you see the fresh bruise on Juliet's face?" asked Two Eagles.

His blood raged through his veins. Joshua knew what his friend was doing. He faced the ghastly collection of painted faces. They might have scared most men but to Joshua, they were laughable. The War Chief waited at the end of the gauntlet with a particularly nasty war club. The warrior stood two hands taller and broader than Joshua. It'd be like cutting down an oak tree.

Get ready, Onontio. I'm coming for you.

It was a question of force and speed. Joshua was bigger than ninety percent of them and faster, too. And like a roaring wind he came, breaking between the lines of stick-wielding Indians with the fleetness of a hunted animal.

The warriors shrieked and screamed. They pelted him on all sides with cruel cuts and blows. With great force, he used his knees, heels and elbows adroitly, simultaneously swinging his head with great force, that his opponents were knocked violently on both sides. He kept his head down, powerful strikes descended on him. He swerved into the line using his body to unbalance them and at the same time deliver cross punches.

He got his right hand to the back of a warrior's neck and helped him along with a vicious back hand that shoved him into the next five warriors, the inertia causing them to collapse like a row of dominoes.

Before the opposite line knew what happened, he elbowed one in the throat, sending him sprawling in the dust. A tattooed warrior came at him. Joshua kneed him in the groin and he went down, too. A short bow-legged warrior to his right swung his club in a mighty arc. The swing, too high, took too long. Joshua gave him a right hook to the jaw. Bow-Legs lifted two feet off the ground, teeth went flying and the warrior hit face first in the dust.

He jabbed another in the throat because jabbing was quicker and afterward, breathing became an impossibility. He swung out his leg, tripping several of his competitors, and then kicked them to make sure they stayed there. Some braver warriors closed in. These warriors were at a disadvantage for they had no idea of his pugilist skills as well as his impulse for brawling.

The warrior with the red jacket came at him, his club a great curve which would crush his skull. Like a boxer, his lithe dancing helped him dodge the blow and with a powerful upper cut, knocked Red Jacket out cold.

A tomahawk grazed his ear, he twisted his head, kicked his assailant in the stomach with enough power to cause him to fly backward. The tomahawk wheeled back on his opponent and sliced off part of his ear.

He came to the end of the line and laughed. Warriors drew near and shouted angrily. They had been cheated of their prize. Silence pulsed in the air.

Joshua placed his hands on his knees, breathing, keeping an eye on Onontio. The War Chief drew himself up, his eyes blazing, a knife palmed between his hands. He was ugly, the fresh scar slashed down his sagging cheek made him uglier.

Joshua stumbled forward, glanced over at Juliet, sitting majestic and beautiful. He saw how the tether whipsawed against her tender flesh. The agony she must be enduring choked him and fueled the violent fury within him. "Onontio, you may quit now, saving yourself a humiliation and—your life."

Onontio saw where his regard lay. "My cock will be rammed into the red-haired witch many nights."

Cold fire burned in Joshua. He held himself in firm check until his rage cooled.

Cheered by a chorus of Indian shrieks, Onontio said, "Beg for mercy like the dog you are. I promise a slow death."

They strutted a bizarre dance like two hell-roosters circling each other. Onontio was twice his size; his arms, like an ape, a longer reach. The knife flashed in his hand. Of course, the War Chief's skill with a knife was as brutal as it was legendary. He would not play fair. Unarmed, Joshua crouched.

Onontio advanced with a slash to the right. His movement came high and Joshua jumped to the side. Without a weapon, the odds were not good leaving him useless to Juliet.

Onontio rushed him, flicked at Joshua's shoulder amidst the cheers of their audience. "Your death awaits you. You would be wise to rest content with it. But fight if you like. My friends are amused."

A knife tipped into the earth at Joshua's feet. He glanced to Two Eagles, his benefactor. Joshua's hand closed over the hilt and, in an instant, Onontio ran his knife down Joshua's thigh. Joshua leapt to the side, pain rocketed through him. He numbed the ache in his mind, too busy with survival. Blood poured from his wound.

He pivoted as Onontio circled him, deadly intent glittered in his black eyes. The Indians hooted, tossing their comments; the fight made for their entertainment.

"You seek to fight with me? With your injury, you are like the coyote who sings while he is castrated. You will lose," said Onontio.

Joshua's leg tired from loss of blood. Fatigue set in from their frantic journey to Tionnontigo. He strained to stave off the soreness from running the gauntlet, aching in every part of his body. How much longer could he last? He had to end this fight soon.

He smiled, his eyes as hard as granite. "I promise you will learn defeat and crawl into a cave to suck at the tit of an old woman."

Shivers of laughter ran through the observers.

The jibe riled Onontio. His teeth bared, the Mohawk attacked then drew back with a savage thrust. With a swift, sudden unexpected counter, Joshua drove Onontio back, slicing him on the wrist.

The Indian lunged to take Joshua's bicep. With a poise and calm born of instinct, he ducked but not quite enough. The knife glanced off his forehead and blood poured down. It burned like hell.

Joshua went down, splayed in the dirt. Someone had tripped him. Onontio advanced. Joshua crouched. At the last possible moment, he thrust himself off the ground, his speed and strength surprising Onontio. With a potent upper cut, he hit the War Chief in the triangle of flesh, dead-on beneath the ribs. Stunned, the giant Mohawk could not get his breath.

With the speed of a cobra, Joshua feinted with his right hand, and with a left hook powerful enough to disembowel a bull, he smashed his fist into Onontio's face, knocking him out cold. Disgusted, he stepped over Onontio's lifeless form and didn't look back. Perhaps he should have killed the War Chief. It would be tiresome to have to fight him all over again.

A nose-ringed brave and his companions gathered around Joshua, menacing in their numbers. He and Two Eagles might do damage on a number of them.

Ojistah shoved through the crowd and stood in front of Joshua.

"You will not touch him. He has shown great bravery surviving the gauntlet. Onontio shamed our people and dared to show his cowardice to take it further, and now he lays punished. Joshua has won the day and we will respect his victory."

Joshua's strength flowed away from him like water down a river as he gazed at Juliet. He had saved her from Onontio.

Juliet didn't realize she was wringing Father Isaac's good arm until all eyes turned to her. "What did the old woman say? What will they do with my friend, Joshua?"

"You have made Joshua's acquaintance?" the priest said surprised. "I have met him during his visits to the village. In answer to your question, I could not hear everything over the crowd's shouting, but from what I have gleaned, Joshua is under the protection of Ojistah and will be in good hands with her healing skills," Father Devereux said.

Unable to understand why Joshua had to run the violent gauntlet, she scanned the crowd, screaming inside for everyone to leave so she might get a glimpse of him. At last the horde thinned. Two Eagles slung Joshua's arm over his shoulder, and her heart stopped at the amount of blood pouring from his wounds. She yanked at her bond. "Free me to help him."

A shadow covered her, and she jerked her head up. Ojistah's dark eyes grew darker, unfocussed and distant, as she appeared to slip away, deep into a mysterious domain, searching and discerning.

Many women swarmed behind the old woman. Was Juliet to be beaten again? Would she have to endure the gauntlet? Nothing made sense in this world turned upside down.

Ojistah's eyes cleared, and placing a leathery palm beneath Juliet's chin, she smiled. An unfathomable lightness emanated from the medicine woman, swirling, brushing against Juliet and catching her in its net. She widened her eyes, basking in the medicine woman's approval. She could not explain the thin tenuous ribbon binding them, comforting as a hug from Moira.

Ojistah handed a knife to the priest, and then spoke rapidly in her tongue to the women.

Father Devereux cut Juliet's bonds free. "Ojistah has ordered these women to take you to the river. Afterward, you will be returned to her lodge."

"Why to the river? Take me to Joshua."

When the priest perceived her alarm, he helped her rise. "You have nothing to fear."

Her pleas fell on deaf ears. Pulling her along, the women were cheerful, speaking in their language and smiling. Juliet was mystified at their friendly treatment, a remarkable departure from their earlier conduct.

Up close, she noticed the women's many ear piercings and necklaces carved from the nacre of fresh water mollusks and shining like rainbows. Where giant oak trees extended their branches like great arms over the sun-dappled river, they removed their clothes. Wading into the water, they motioned for her to follow.

Juliet's cheeks burned with their lack of modesty. She had been brought up with a certain mode of dress and deportment and possessed highly instilled values not to exhibit any skin. As a midwife, she had been exposed to women during childbirth but they were under sheets and were clothed in a dressing gown.

To be so open and free?

They motioned for her to disrobe. Juliet shook her head and clapped her hands on her tattered skirts and dug her boots into the squishy mud along the river bank. They emerged from the water and surrounded her, their breasts jiggled and dark nipples unnerved her, their long dark hair wet and plastered upon their skins. Unable to understand them, she looked at the sky, the sun beating down on them, anything to avoid their nakedness. They pushed her down into the mud, tugged off her boots and yanked her into the water, splashing and frolicking.

A great blue heron, unhappy with the uproar, lifted from its rookery, beat its great wings and vanished down the river in a thin gray line. Laughing the women took hold of her and tore at her garments.

"No!" said Juliet, pushing away their hands. "Stop it."

But the women were too many. When one of the women produced a knife, Juliet backed away. Was this a sacrificial ceremony?

Juliet dodged one woman and with her weight upended another. She picked up her skirts, and rushed to the opposite embankment, her sodden clothing like an anchor around her legs. Smiling and chattering, they grabbed hold of her again and guided her to the middle of the river.

The woman with the knife cut away her garments. Her chemise floated on an eddy, her petticoats snared on an upended log, and what was left of her shredded dress caught in the current and drifted downstream. She crossed her arms in front of her breasts to hide her nakedness. What would she wear?

If only she could swim away and hide in the reeds.

Squeezing her eyes tight, she conceded as hands rubbed, starting with her neck, down her back and arms, removing the accumulated dirt and grime. Her nerves danced, her brain raced, and her stomach somersaulted.

She opened her eyes.

The sand was abrasive and reddened her skin. The women reached to the river bottom, scooping up more grit and scrubbing her clean. She pushed their hands away, a worthless endeavor. They were resolved to bathe her.

Juliet stared at a young beautiful pregnant woman, her stomach enormously protracted. She gracefully sat beneath a willow, the branches swayed as if paying her homage. Two women attended her. No doubt the woman was near her time and they planned to assist her if necessary.

An old woman smashed a tuber against a rock and rubbed with her palms vigorously until bubbles appeared, and then nodded her head to the women to hold each of Juliet's arms at right angles from her body. Trapped, they splayed her legs, allowing the woman to lather the foam over her. As they cared for her, their hands gentle on her bruises, and voices comforting, Juliet felt herself begin to relax, banishing some of her fear.

Hands moved about her waist, and neck and back, and they commenced to sing, a melodious tune that seduced her into its sinuous rhythm. Hands swirled around her breasts, the startling sensation causing her to inhale sharply.

"You must stop. It isn't proper." She tried to jerk her arms free but they laughed and held her all the more, the silky soap gliding over her sensitive nipples, her face a hotbed of shame.

The women oohed and aahed, spanning their hands, making note of her hips and nodding their heads in approval of what she supposed was her contrasting white skin and ability to bear children.

They pressed her under the ice-cold water and held her there. Were they trying to drown her? She fought to the top, sputtering and wiped her hair from her eyes. The woman lathered foam through her hair, massaging her scalp.

Oh, to be clean again. They pushed her under again to rinse and ushered her to shore. A blanket was wrapped around her and she was led through the village. Warriors gaped at her as she clutched the blanket to hide her nakedness. She was escorted to a small lodge where they left her.

She pressed aside a deerskin tarp and let her eyes adjust to the dim interior. Heat fired to the roots of her hair. Father Devereux gazed heavenward. Two Eagles grunted. Joshua, laying against furs, stared.

She cleared her throat and pulled her damp hair out. She managed the blanket as much as possible to conceal her state of undress and knelt next to Joshua, smoothing her hand across his brow when all she wanted to do was pull him into her arms and soothe him.

His paleness and loss of blood distressed her. The gash in his head and congealed blood beneath the legging of his thigh alarmed her. The actions of the Indians, Father Devereux's frustrating translations revealing little, and the day's events remained a mystery. "Is it a tribal ritual for a white man entering the village to run a gauntlet?"

"Go and guard the lodge, Father Devereux. Tell me if trouble brews," Ojistah ordered.

His cassock swishing, and cross banging against his chest, the priest clasped his hat and bent his head to exit.

Juliet looked to Two Eagles and pleaded with her eyes. "Mary."

Ojistah rattled her language and Two Eagles swept out of the lodge. "I have told him to go and get your friend. To tell Red Jacket, I have ordered it."

Would he be able to rescue Mary?

Her nerves pulled tight. Joshua eyed her strangely, as if trying to gather a sense of time and place. Did he have a head injury? Would he linger in a fog for the rest of his life?

Juliet remained, mesmerized, fascinated, and drawn into those blue orbs.

Beneath the filth and dark beard, a rugged flesh and blood man radiated strength, masculinity and power. Even with his leanness, he dwarfed her.

He raised his hand to touch her and she held his palm against her cheek, felt tears prick her eyes at seeing him like this. "I'm so sorry this has happened to you."

He swallowed hard, searching to form words, and rasped out, "There is still an ordeal ahead, if you accept—"

"Accept?"

His hand went limp in hers and his head rolled to the side. No answer there.

Suspended from the rafters were lengths of corn braids. Strange face masks adorned the walls, looking inward. Shelves were filled with earthen pots, woven baskets, wooden implements and furs. To have her own lodge spelled Ojistah's importance.

The medicine woman, heedless of Juliet's inquiry, sprinkled herbs in two earthen pots, set them on the fire, and then removed a kettle to cool. Rising, Ojistah snatched more herbs from the rafters and added them to the pots.

Joshua's mud-caked clothing was sopped with black-crusted and fresh red blood. She reached out, then drew her hand away. In her entire existence, nothing had prepared her for this and she cursed Onontio, his warriors and their horrid practices.

To survive, Joshua needed a miracle.

His blue eyes flashed in her mind, wounded eyes, like those of a child stretching out to her for comfort, shadowed with sincerity. Her heart lurched.

"His wounds are many but not dangerous. He is a strong man," said Ojistah.

Juliet rubbed her eyes from the stinging smoke swirling up to a hole in the roof. "You speak English?"

"The black robe has taught me." Ojistah stirred her pungent concoction using a wooden spoon with a wolf's head carving. "I have given Joshua herbs in a sleeping draught which takes a long time to set in and explains his lack of responsiveness. I have also brewed restorative teas of sassafras and witch hazel to heal and give him strength. He will be affected by a deep nourishing sleep and be awake by the evening's events."

With a knife, Ojistah cut off his buckskins, revealing an angry gash across his thigh. Ojistah handed her a cloth. Juliet's blanket dropped. Her face flaming, she pushed aside her modesty and washed away the clotted blood; the coppery smell of fresh blood wafted. Her stomach roiled and whirled. She swallowed down the oncoming waves.

"Is there any other way I can help?"

"Hand me the basket in the corner." Ojistah boiled balsam and juniper bark, taking out smooth pieces and allowing them to cool.

She filled the gash along Joshua's thigh with powdered red punk wood. "Hold his shoulders down," Ojistah commanded.

Juliet pressed her knees into his shoulders, anchoring him with her weight. She tried not to wince as a fiery ember was touched to the punk wood. Light flashed across the angry laceration. Joshua soared off the furs, knocking the two women aside. Ojistah and Juliet pushed him back on the furs where he fell to sleep again.

"The burning stops any bleeding. Now help me bind the wounds. The bark has healing properties and soothes bruises and burns."

There were no bandages, but the balsam and juniper bark served as a substitute. Ojistah demonstrated and Juliet followed.

Why did she feel a connection with the woman?

"We are both medicine women," said Ojistah without looking up.

Juliet jerked her head and stared. There it was again, an incomprehensible force Ojistah aroused, a strange *knowing* that rattled her like it had when Ojistah had clasped her ancient hand beneath Juliet's chin.

Ojistah raised an eyebrow, the action furrowing wrinkles in her forehead. "Are you not a healer?"

"I am a midwife. How do you know?"

Ojistah smiled. "I know many things. You have great powers breathed by the Great Fire Dragon. Your appearance in this land is nearly as sacred as Sky Woman who fell upon the Great Turtle's back. Be not afraid, push aside your confusion and accept what gifts come to you with humility and hone them to your best ability."

Juliet attempted to grasp Ojistah's obscure message and fumbled with the smooth balsam and juniper bark.

Warm hands were placed upon hers, patiently instructing as they applied the bandages to Joshua until Juliet understood what to do. Ojistah's touch instilled a baffling, burning light of confidence.

"He will sleep for now. Tonight, he will be strong as an ox." Ojistah's voice ministrations mirrored those of a mother for her child, her reassurance, soothing.

"You care for Joshua?" Juliet asked.

With Joshua between them, Ojistah sat cross-legged, and readjusted her silver armbands. "A monster bear, carrying evil orenda and consuming human flesh, terrorized the village for many moons. Numerous attempts by our warriors to hunt and kill the bear were met with death. Foolishly, my young grandson decided to kill the bear.

"The bear trapped him. Joshua happened to have been visiting the village, heard his cries, ran at the bear and killed him with his knife, a single blow to the heart. The bear toppled on both of them. Two Eagles and other braves rolled the massive bear over. My grandson was huddled under Joshua and the two were alive and unharmed."

Ojistah paused. "Killing the bear when no one else was able, garnered great respect, and made Joshua immortal. My grandson keeps the tooth of the great bear around his neck," Ojistah smiled. "Saving my grandson made Joshua close to my heart."

The bear story was true? Not a whimsical yarn?

Ojistah poured an infusion into a wooden bowl. "Brewed willow bark will tamp down any fever and ease his pain." She lifted Joshua's head and Juliet spooned in a portion, stroking his throat for him to swallow so he'd not choke.

"Joshua is blood brother to Two Eagles."

Two Eagles' blood brother?

"Now for you. I will not take no for an answer."

Ojistah bathed Juliet's blistered feet and bruises in a brew of red oak, wild cherry bark and dewberry roots. With a deer bone comb, she untangled Juliet's long red hair until it shone in bright copper waves. Juliet closed her eyes, feeling the tension leave, marveling at her gentleness.

Suddenly, Ojistah stilled, dropped the bear comb. Juliet glanced behind her, her hair caught in a hard grip. The medicine woman's eyes rolled back, only milky-white remained. *"Behold my vision. I see many villages destroyed, hunger pinching the bellies of our children, the crying of women and children, diseases and the losing of wisdom of our elders for they will die."*

Outside a flock of ravens circled and cawed in a ghastly flapping of wings. Dogs howled, a zephyr gusted, shaking the wigwam. Juliet sat motionless, the harshly whispered words hung, suspended like the coiling smoke. Ojistah's head dropped then lifted, her chocolate eyes returned to normal yet seized with great fear.

Questions crowded in Juliet's throat, but before she could speak, a hawk pitched a horrific cry above the smoke hole.

Juliet whispered, "You have had a vision."

"Very bad. I must think on it."

A woman entered with a beautiful white doeskin dress decorated with beads and porcupine quills.

"For you," said Ojistah, discarding any hint of her revelation.

Juliet stood and looked to where Joshua tossed and turned. He was sleeping, wasn't he? Satisfied his eyes were closed, she dropped the blanket and allowed the woman to place the dress over her head. She gasped at the softness of the dress, and her eyes welled with tears at Ojistah's generosity. Smooth moccasins were placed on her feet.

With lingering touches, Juliet fidgeted with the beads, obsessed with what Joshua had said before he went into an induced sleep. "What did Joshua mean by my acceptance and why did he have to run the gauntlet?"

"He had to win his bride."

"His bride?" Was Joshua to marry an Indian woman?

Bracelets clinking, Ojistah touched Juliet's hair. "He fought for the white captive with hair of fire."

Chapter 10

$\mathcal{J}$uliet reeled from Ojistah's admission, unable to fathom Joshua had fought for her, and at risk to his life. To marry Joshua? She liked him, but to be connected for a lifetime to a man who was a complete stranger?

Certainly, it was an Indian ceremony and held no obligation. She would not hold him to the vows. They would marry to put on a front. Once away from the village, they would separate and no one would know the better of it.

Angry voices drew their attention. Father Devereux ducked his head into the lodge. "You ought to make an appearance, Ojistah."

The medicine woman rose and Juliet followed. Mary stood behind Two Eagles, wringing her hands. When she beheld Juliet, she tried to run to her. Two Eagles shook his head, staying her with his powerful arm.

Red Jacket's face was mottled with rage but far more incensed was Onontio who spoke rapidly.

Father Devereux moved to Juliet's side and translated. "Onontio has claimed the light-haired woman from Red Jacket since he cannot have the red-haired captive. However, Two Eagles argues corn-tassel is his woman."

Onontio grabbed Mary's arm, and then found a knife stuck at his throat.

"One more step…one more motion…in this direction," Two Eagles grunted in his tongue without taking his eyes from Onontio, "…and I will cut your throat."

"Ganösá," swore Onontio, his expression beyond astonishment. "I made the raids. She is my prisoner. You are lucky I allow you to live."

With nervous fingers, Juliet clutched her bodice watching the tableau. Onontio was not the kind of warrior to yield and he might win Mary.

The Mohawk medicine woman stepped forward and lifted her hand for all who had assembled. "Two Eagles says she is his woman. He speaks the truth. I've seen it in a vision."

A pregnant hush fell upon the villagers and a moment of indecision stretched interminably. Some of the Indians stepped back, venerating Ojistah. Her gift of sight was not to be dishonored.

Onontio's lips curled, his teeth bared. "One day I will kill you, Two Eagles."

Two Eagles smiled at the War Chief, a distinctly vulpine curve to his lips. "Only if you come at me or what is mine, like the coward you are…it is you who will die."

For a long moment, Onontio glared at Two Eagles, and then turned, shouldering his way through a ring of spectators and knocking a number to the ground.

Mary flew into Juliet's arms. "I've been so frightened. Now I'm Two Eagles' woman. Which is worse?"

Juliet glimpsed the disgust on Two Eagles' face before his formidable control was back in place.

Ojistah placed her hand on Mary. "You must walk with Two Eagles to reinforce my prediction. If not, you will be returned to Onontio."

Juliet hugged her friend and pushed her away. "Do what Ojistah has said. I sent Two Eagles to get you, and now you have insulted him."

"The savage does not know what I said. He does not speak English." She rubbed her hands up and down her arms, glancing uncertainly at Two Eagles. Two Eagles had departed and Mary hurriedly followed him round the village, leaving Juliet wondering if Ojistah's vision had been a ruse or not.

Chapter 11

Evening mantled the village. Joshua inhaled fragrant wood smoke from several lit fires that illuminated the smiling faces of the villagers. The marriage of their blood brother was an occasion.

Women surrounded Juliet, jabbering together in excitement, pushing her ahead. Joshua craned his neck to catch sight of her. She stood tall, carrying herself with dignity and grace with each step forward. His chest expanded, admiration and respect for her growing. She wore a white doeskin dress that clung to her feminine curves, curves he'd a glimpse of when he stirred from sleep while she had dressed for the wedding. The tantalizing image sizzled through his brain, dazzling as the first glow of the world as she lit his bleak existence. Tall, her hair, shining like ethereal fire, and tumbling down her back, covering her rounded hips…set a man to dreaming.

She stopped in front of him. He limped a step closer.

She raised her head, her gaze roving over him. Her eyes shone as she looked at him, then just as quickly, she glanced away, a blush reddening her cheeks.

"You approve?"

She lifted a brow. "I see you are hale and healthy. It is like you have never been injured."

His thigh throbbed where Ojistah had burned him, but another part of him burned even more. He nodded, fought a compelling urge to bury his fingers in her hair. "Thanks to you and Ojistah. Of course, my immortality adds to my legend."

She fingered a long, pointed porcupine quill on her dress, its point poking her fingertip. She suffered for what to say and he pitied her. He was a stranger to her, a caprice of fate that would make him her husband.

He captured her trembling hand and held it in his larger one. Her hand lay innocently on his. He wondered at this strange new sensation, her hand feeling so at home in his, like it was meant to be.

He placed his mouth by her ear. A strand of her hair caressed his cheek. His gut clenched. "Are you frightened?"

"Am I not supposed to be?"

Her warm breath touched his cold skin, light and soft as a feather.

"I have won you, but you have nothing to fear from me."

She glanced around at the women stepping in time to a beating drum. "You are gallant for sure, but you don't have to go through with this ceremony," she whispered. "Surely the vows will not be considered sacrosanct?"

"Ah, but we must go through this ceremony. I might be able to fight my way out, but I could not guarantee your safety. Let us get through the least of our problems at the moment. Afterward, we can discuss our futures."

Onontio pushed through the revelers, bobbing and weaving, whacking people out of his way. The broken nose Joshua gave him swelled as big as a pound of raw hasenpfeffer and with the scar down his cheek, served as an improvement.

"This marriage will not hold. They do not worship the same gods and I demand to see the marriage consummated," spat Onontio.

A nighthawk shrieked above in a moonlit sky, his sight on certain prey. The chill of a breeze settled over Joshua. Hushed murmurings rang through the Indians. Some nodded their heads in agreement, others pulled back slightly.

Someone asked the medicine woman for direction.

"You will demand nothing, Onontio." Her face lit with the dancing firelight. "And I will see the marriage is consummated."

Father Devereux stepped forward. "For any doubt one might have, The Longhouse ceremony and the Code of Handsome Lake allows me to perform the marriage ceremony of my God at the same time. The marriage will be consecrated."

The crowd roared their approval, eager to celebrate with the roasted venison, wild turkey, smoked fish, and corn cakes cooked the entire day.

The chief stood before them and presented the tribe's valuable wampum. Joshua took hold of them and lifted Juliet's shaking fingers on the sacred beads. Father Devereux translated.

"Are you prepared to be the wife of the warrior, Joshua for the rest of your life? Will you care for Joshua if he becomes ill? Will you prepare food for your husband and children?"

She sought out his gaze, her vulnerability tugging at him.

He gave her a reassuring smile and he saw the relief in her face.

The promise of each vow was supported from her sweet lips. He wanted to cradle her close and tell her everything was fine. The chief turned to Joshua with the same questions, and concluded. "Marriage is a partnership and no one has authority above the other; you do not dominate your husband, and he does not dominate you. Today you have become members of a fine and loving extended family of Tionnontigo."

The chief allowed Father Devereux, Bible in hand to begin.

Juliet sensed Joshua was extremely serious about the vow he was about to speak. The look of resolute and unwavering determination manifested on his face assured a rare kind of promise Joshua straightened and with intense and complete profoundness said, "I do."

Beneath the stares of villagers, curious about the foreign rite, Juliet's nerves went taut as a drawn bow. She said yes, to every lifelong pledge, not actually hearing the words until Father Devereux closed his book. "Those whom God hath joined together let no man put asunder."

In one forward motion, Joshua caressed her face with his big hands, his lips stirred against hers, gentle at first, then persistent. The cheers of villagers caused her to remain stiff and awkward. But the gentle massage of his kiss sent currents of desire though her. Blood pounded in her brain, leapt from her heart and made her pulses race like quicksilver. And in that moment, the fires, the noise, the world seemed to melt away, leaving only her and Joshua.

He finally broke apart, but his blue eyes riveted her to the spot. Suddenly looking confused, he turned away to a series of backslapping and knowing winks.

Ojistah produced a wheel made of a wooden branch and decorated with white deerskin strips and a burnt feather design. "This wedding wheel is a symbolic gesture, guaranteeing your hopes and dreams for a happy future."

Juliet was again touched by the medicine woman's generosity and held the wheel against her heart.

"Go now to my lodge, you will not be disturbed."

Juliet colored from the innuendo, yet happy with Ojistah's assurance that a consummation would not be investigated.

Pulsing drums beat, gourd rattles clattered, while villagers danced to the Feather Song, swishing a mesmerizing array of white plumes. Joshua pressed his hand to her back, guiding her away from well-wishers, but some pulled at them to stay, apparently disappointed the newly wedded couple was leaving so soon.

"I should carry you over the threshold but, at this moment, my leg will not allow it," Joshua held open the flap for her to enter. "I'm sure this is far from the wedding ceremony you have ever dreamed."

Inside, a feast had been laid out on platters for the married couple. Her stomach flip-flopped as Joshua's large shape filled Ojistah's lodge. She doubted she could eat a thing.

They were alone for the first time. In light of the fact this was a sham marriage, in England, such a contact with a man, particularly one of his station, would have been scandalous. But that life was far behind her, for here in America, the rules were very different.

"How did you happen to come here?" Her head had spun at his sudden appearance at Tionnontigo and part of her sought to hear he'd remembered his promise to return for her.

He positioned himself on the floor and tore off a piece of roasted venison. "I swore to come back for you. When we came upon the Hayes' farm, I feared we were too late."

Her blood quickened. *He had come back for her. He had not forgotten his promise.*

She drew a long thankful breath. "We might have been slaughtered, too, but the night before…" she said. "Orpha ordered Eldon to be whipped. She had a British captain by the name of Snapes whip him to death." She drew a quivering breath, remembering the horror. "I was to be next. So, Mary and I escaped at dawn. We were on the hill when…the screams…the attack…the butchery…" Her throat clogged. Tears welled.

Joshua waved his hand for her to come join him. "No softly-bred woman should ever witness that, and with certainty, Onontio proved his ruthlessness. When we didn't find your bodies, Two Eagles searched, picked up a faint trail, suggesting you heeded my instructions and left before the attack. Later, my worst fears arose when we discovered the spot Onontio captured you."

Sitting beside him, she stole a glance. Firelight played on his recklessly handsome features, the mean cut on his forehead, and the ridges and valleys of his muscles. What words had been on her tongue disappeared as quickly as snow on the desert. She twisted her fingers together. She did not know this man at all nor what he expected. He had saved her and she owed him a great debt. Her mind spun like a bewildered child as their marital night loomed.

Certainly, she was attracted to Joshua, and she came from a country where arranged marriages happened all the time. Couples managed through the years, sometimes barely, and some spouses cheated while the other looked the other way, accepting of their unhappy states.

Images of her father loomed, horrid old wounds surfaced, disallowing her peace. Exhausted from being undesirable and unloved, she wanted more...to break free of the chains of feeling unwanted. To marry for love. Was there such a thing?

She looked at the splintery rafters scored with thorny herbs. He was destined for a life far from what she was accustomed to, and faraway from England. But her new life was not what she was accustomed to either. "The last days have frightened me beyond anything I've ever encountered, and I pray never to go through the experience again."

Her chest panged. Her marital declarations lay fervent upon her heart. To her, marriage, an act consecrated before God, lay indissoluble. The handsome Achilles sprawled next to her. To know his kisses, to feel his warm embrace...wasn't that what she desired? No.

Joshua had been noble protecting her and his honorable gesture precipitated him to be forced into marriage. But to feel yoked to her? To be miserable in a relationship he never wanted? She couldn't do that. "I will not hold you to your vows, Joshua."

In the flickering shadows of the fire, he raised a dark brow. "You mean by way of an annulment?"

Had it been a trick of the light, his earnestness when the vows were spoken? Of course, he had to put on a show for their audience. Why should she expect anything more?

She straightened. "Of course. I'm sure under the circumstances, you—"

"It is just a business arrangement. I went along with the ceremony to save our lives."

Juliet swallowed. "We are not expected to—"

He tore off another piece of venison. "Eat. It would be a great insult to our hosts." He ignored her question on completing the marriage. He seemed to be studying the hot coals of the fire, but she felt his full attention on her.

"You will return to England and be dissolved of all ties to me."

"To England?"

"I can make it happen."

"How can I repay you?" She dipped her gaze to the furs strewn on the floor. Instinct warned her to flee. There was danger here, close to her, a whisper away.

He saw where her gaze lay and shrugged his shoulders. "I will take you to your cousin at Fort Oswego. I have no need of a wife."

Her chest squeezed. Her cheeks burned. What had she expected? That he'd been so taken with her that he'd want a real marriage? That for once in this life she'd feel wanted? Her gown grew scratchy as if it were wool chafing her skin instead of soft doeskin. She dragged her palms over her dress. "Do you already have a wife?" The thought of him being a bigamist repulsed her. Yet she was to blame. He'd married her to save her life.

Black laughter stirred his broad shoulders. He leaned close, his breath warm upon her cheek. "Those dreams are long gone."

A wave of relief washed over her. A strange silence grew between them and she nibbled a piece of cornbread sweetened with honey, nuts and berries, yet bitter upon her tongue. For a moment, she could have sworn she'd seen a flash of remorse cross his face. Guilt? "Has something happened to someone special in your life?"

"My affairs are not your concern."

He sat in silence, saying nothing at all. Instead of the pain she sensed in him a moment ago, now there was cool detachment. "I wouldn't want to burden you with a wife. I was just thinking that maybe you and I...might possibly suit."

"Juliet, this is just a business arrangement, and like you said, you are terrified in the wilderness. I'm gone long days trapping. I couldn't protect you during my absences."

She pressed her lips together. "I see. I will not provoke your sensitivities any longer than is necessary nor have you saddled with my company. How do you plan to get me back to England?"

"My first plan is to leave as soon as possible without offending our hosts. There are many braves who are Onontio's friends determined to make our leave-taking—difficult."

He did not say he and Two Eagles could dissolve into the forests, yet with two women? To escape with the added burden might bring them to great peril.

Juliet pushed her hair behind her, anxious to be gone from this place.

"You mentioned Captain Snapes?" A vein pulsed in Joshua's neck.

Images of Snapes' leering face, his filthy probing fingers…what could have happened…what almost happened. A ping of caution erupted in her chest. What if Joshua and Snapes were friends? A year of indentured servitude had taught her to keep silent or earn a beating.

His face was set in a grim line and she straightened with the ferocity of his inquiry, prompting her to risk telling him the truth. "He was at the Hayes' farm at the time of the attack. He was in Tionnontigo recently and made a point to inform me he ordered the attack on the Hayes' as retribution for Horace stealing land from him."

Joshua's head snapped around. "I can't imagine a British officer going against a loyal King's man. When was he here?"

"Would you do something to Captain Snapes for his crimes?" She wanted the man brought to justice. Patriot or Loyalist, no one deserved that kind of slaughter.

He bowed his dark head which gleamed in the meager light, the muscles in his body tightening. "I want to catch the bastard for his raids—"

"He left shortly before you arrived. Snapes ordered Onontio to raid forts to the south and leave when the moon turns full. He is to meet up with Colonel Butler and Captain Snapes with many warriors. Snapes promises ten pounds for each scalp. To know that others will suffer what I saw at the Hayes' farm. He must be stopped."

A woman's frantic voice called to them from outside the lodge. They both rose, Joshua translating the woman's rapid-fire words. "Ojistah must have Woman with Hair of Fire to help Princess Evening Dove."

As Juliet moved to follow the woman, Joshua hauled her back against his chest. "You must refuse. What knowledge do you have of such things?"

She tossed her hair back over her shoulders. "I am a trained midwife."

He jerked his head back with that revelation, and then narrowed his eyes on her. "Even so, this is not England. If anything happens to the chief's wife or child, you will be blamed and our lives will be forfeit."

"My mother died in childbirth and if my father had allowed someone with ability to tend her, she might have survived. I cannot fail Princess Evening Dove, not when I have the skills to help her."

She wrenched free and trailed the woman to the birthing lodge. The chief shook his head, refusing to let her pass. Ojistah spoke impatiently with heated argument.

Joshua limped beside her. "Ojistah told the chief you have great power."

"Tell the chief, I have great skills. If I bring his child into the world, then he must set us free."

Joshua translated. "The chief says if the child and the mother die, we will all die."

"I am not afraid." The lie came out smoothly.

The chief stepped aside. Juliet ducked beneath the flap. Princess Evening Dove, her hands tied at the wrists above her head, squatted from a center pole. Naked, her black hair lay plastered to her dark skin. In Europe, Juliet had heard of similar practices where women were held beneath their arms and made to walk to expel the baby.

"Could the chief come in and help us lay Evening Dove on the furs?"

A look of horror crossed Ojistah's face. "Men cannot tread the same path as a pregnant woman. They lose their power."

Ridiculous. "Untie Evening Dove and lay her on the furs."

Ojistah translated. The three women helpers glared at her, and then glanced to Ojistah for orders. Juliet gazed at the heavens through the smoke hole, saw the stars, wishing Moira was with her. Memories of the many childbirths she'd helped Moira perform came back to her in a rush. She returned her gaze to the medicine woman.

"Excuse them," said Ojistah. "They are the chief's sisters and heavy with suspicion." Her silver braids swung as she roughly rebuked them for their hesitation. The women shifted and laid the chief's wife upon the furs.

Juliet dropped to her knees, moving her hands across Morning Dove's swollen belly. She was young and pale. In the forefront of Juliet's mind was how the chief had lost two of his previous wives. Juliet squared her shoulders, fully dedicated to using everything in her power to keep Evening Dove alive.

In an even tone, Ojistah said, "I have given her a tea of squaw root to speed the delivery. You will see the baby is bottom first."

Juliet concurred as she, too, observed the breech presentation. Moira had told her breech babies were ten times more likely to cause both the infant's and mother's death.

The child had dropped, making outside manipulation impossible. In England, a doctor might have been called—if there was time. Only twice had she witnessed Moira's interior maneuvering of an unborn baby. Furthermore, Princess Evening Dove had been given an herb to speed the contractions. Not good. She glanced over her shoulder to the door flap. Too late to leave.

Juliet grabbed a strap of sinew and knotted her hair on top of her head, trying to remember everything Moira had instructed her concerning the practice. Observing and performing were two different things.

The princess moaned and panted with the savagery of one contraction after another—a child impossibly positioned to bring safely into the world. Her lip bled and swelled where she bit too hard. How long could the woman last with the rapidity and intensity of contractions? Not long. "Ojistah, I'm going to reach inside and move the baby."

The old woman, always calm, nodded her head. "You know of such practice?"

Juliet did not answer. Not when her nerves prickled up her spine, and screamed for her to run, not when she prayed to have as much faith placed in her as possible. She searched the lodge and washed her hands in a vessel of cool water.

"Oil?"

Ojistah produced a clay pot. "Sunflower."

While the medicine woman poured, Juliet lifted her hands, palms up, and slicked the greasy substance over her hands and wrists. She spoke to Evening Dove as Ojistah translated.

"Princess Evening Dove, I know you are in much pain but what I'm going to do will bring more pain if I'm to bring your child into the world. You may scream all you want."

The princess' eyes widened. She shook her head viciously, uttering obscure words Juliet did not understand.

"No!" said Ojistah. "It is a disgrace to show pain and fear and shame her husband."

This world of theirs was mad.

"Give her that stick to bite," Juliet ordered.

Juliet gritted her teeth and with one hand on the upper belly, she reached up toward Evening Dove's womb. With her other hand, she probed around the membrane, praying she'd not injure the baby. Her fingers slid stickily. Her heart pounded in her ears.

She exhaled when she identified the foot. The foot slipped from her grasp. Juliet scrunched her eyes shut, seized the foot and flexed and grasped, and gently pulled. The membrane broke and the musk of Evening Dove's water gushed out. One foot emerged. Good. Juliet used the next contraction to pull and turn until the buttocks appeared. She reached up and grabbed the other knee, straightened the leg and pulled out.

Evening Dove thrashed and moaned, clamping hard on the bite stick. She did not yell or scream. Juliet knew she hurt her terribly and marveled at the Indian woman's dignity compared to the hundreds of births she'd assisted of European women.

Juliet turned the baby back, the shoulders presented and she removed one arm, and next rotated the baby again to allow the other arm to be pulled out. Beads of sweat dripped down her forehead. She twisted the baby again until it was face down. Placing her hand under the baby's slippery body, she held her other hand securely on the infant's neck.

When the next contraction came, Juliet shouted, "Push."

She lifted the baby up and the head was freed.

When the infant burst through with angry wails, demanding the world to know of its arrival, all the pain and violence of childbirth lay forgotten. Juliet cried out with wonder and the other women did, too. Joy swirled, whirling and weaving like threads of a great tapestry around them, ending enmity and uniting them in an overwhelming ocean of affection.

Juliet wiped the newborn's eyes and nose clear, and Ojistah cut and bound the cord. She gently laid the infant on Evening Dove's chest and basked in the love between mother and child meeting for the first time.

When the afterbirth was delivered, Ojistah explained to the women the use of herbs and packing Morning Dove with moss to stem the bleeding. Ojistah wrapped the babe in doeskin and nodded for Juliet to follow her. They emerged from the tent, as the first fingers of dawn shone in a brilliant display across the morning sky. Breathing a sigh of relief, Two Eagles, Mary, and Joshua stared in disbelief at the infant.

"You have a son," said Ojistah.

Worn and ragged, the chief smiled proudly, tears in his eyes as he lifted the child into his arms. "Thank you, Ojistah."

"Thank White Woman with Hair of Fire. Her medicine is stronger than mine. It was she who brought your child onto this earth and saved your wife."

He stood in awe of Juliet, and pulling the blanket from his raging son, touched the infant's soft black hair, his little fingers and toes. The chief said, "You will be under my protection. You may go."

But it was the undisguised pride in Joshua's blue eyes that caused Juliet's heart to skip. He put his arm around her, pulling her close, the brush of his evening beard against her cheek, and comforting. His deep voice vibrated through her soul. "You are magnificent."

The chief's sisters ducked out of the lodge, pointing and exclaiming to the east where it rained across the distant hills. A beautiful rainbow arched across the valley.

Ojistah whispered in reverence, "A great sign given by our Creator, one that has not been seen for many generations…this child…what greatness will he bring?"

One of the sisters took the baby and returned to the birthing lodge. At the nod of the chief, his other sister led Ojistah, Juliet, Joshua, Two Eagles, and Mary to the river.

Ojistah pushed a hemlock branch back, allowing Juliet to pass, and then took her arm in hers. "In my life, I have had a series of visions, ranging from sadness to inspiring. I have seen the pale-faced people arrive in gigantic canoes with spreading white wings. Motivated by insatiable avarice, these pale-faced people have rapidly grown in strength and power and without remorse continue to encroach on the land of the red men, who are weakened by disease, firewater, and extended warfare against British, and the "long knives" of Americans. There will be no peace for the Mohawk."

Juliet stopped. "Ojistah, I am a woman of peace."

Ojistah's hand, large and heavy and smelling faintly of bear grease, cradled Juliet's cheek with a gentleness reminiscent of Moira. How she craved that long-ago warmth. "The deep part of your spirit resonates."

Juliet was about to speak when Ojistah shushed her. Motionless now, her eyes glazed over and once more she appeared to slip away, deep into a secret realm of intuition and vision.

A flock of crows lifted in the air and a great powerful wind swept down from the top of the mountains, blowing up and over them, swirling treetops and spewing the scent of leaf mold and pine. Juliet stayed rooted. The rest of the world melted away, leaving her and Ojistah swaying.

"I see blood and fire, loss and reunion, and a love so great neither time nor death can destroy it."

The harshly whispered words streamed hot like the sun's rays upon a forest floor.

"You are a woman of great love and the power of that love will conquer every single opponent, and again through your daughter, and her daughter."

Ojistah's callused thumb rasped in a circle on Juliet's cheek. Deep inside Juliet, something stirred and shifted, grew warm like an ember fueled by the breath of a zephyr. She sensed a bright mystery in Ojistah's words, and for all that they were but ambiguous prophecies, they fixed themselves in her heart.

Ojistah glanced over her shoulder to Joshua, trailing behind, and then her dark eyes, clearer at the moment, locked with Juliet's, veiled pools of black confronting deep blue eyes. "I know—" Lifting her head, she glanced to the rainbow, and said, "This is an unusual time. My visions come one after another. You should know Two Eagles' mother, Waneek, is my twin. She is expecting you."

Juliet stared at Ojistah. A twin? But Juliet was on her way to her cousin and through him, on to England. "I'm going to Fort Oswego."

The medicine woman's blunt finger slid across the curved line of Juliet's cheek, edging along until it encountered her chin. The gleam in her eyes held an inner light. She padded down a slender trail, her moccasins rendering no sound on a moss-covered path. "You will give my sister my best wishes."

"I don't understand," Juliet ran to keep up, mystified by the medicine woman's confidence she'd meet her twin. Two Eagles drew up beside her and grunted as if her words were no great feat.

At the river's edge, a lightweight canoe fashioned of birch bark and light of weight had been loaded with fur packs and foodstuffs.

"Onontio and his friends are going to cause trouble. I put medicine in their cups to make them sleep. This is our fleetest canoe, swifter than the clunky dugout," said Ojistah.

"I thank you for the gifts," said Joshua.

The chief's sister held the craft while they boarded. Ojistah pushed the other canoes belonging to tribal members out into the river where they floated away with the current. "No one will follow you."

"You are at risk, Ojistah," said Juliet.

She shook her head. "The chief has ordered your safe travels."

Chapter 12

His arms ached, his thigh smarted with his movement, and so did every bruised muscle in his body. He required sleep but that was not to happen. His loaded long rifle and two dragoon pistols rested on the bottom of the canoe along with his powder horn, ammunition bag and tomahawk. Thanks to Ojistah there was plenty of shot and tinder. His knife was sheathed in his belt.

With an early start granted by the chief, he had to put as much distance as possible from Onontio's threat. Twice the War Chief lost and would not forget the great insult. He'd follow their trail and exact retribution. Still weak from his wounds, Joshua had no intention of meeting up with Onontio and his following. Outnumbered for sure, the results would be bleak. Yet, if there was trouble, he and Two Eagles would fight to the death.

What concerned him was Snapes, Butler and the build-up of hostile forces against the settlers. By the waning of last night's moon, he had four weeks, but therein lay the conundrum—running south to warn the forts and settlers or take the two women to Fort Oswego in the opposite direction. His greatest hope was running across a Patriot committed to forwarding the significant intelligence.

The scent of woman assailed his senses, and he sucked it in as if it would cure the pounding in his head. Juliet was braver than any woman of his acquaintance. The English women he'd known strove for male attention, driven to make a good match at their debut. Like so many colorful flowers, if confronted with an Indian, they would have fainted dead away. Juliet personified strength, reliability and loyalty. She had survived the Hayes' insufferable treatment, and humiliation at the hands of Onontio and the Mohawks. She went up against him and delivered the chief's son, despite the danger and his warnings.

She was gentle and kind and not meant for this godforsaken patch of earth that reaped violence and bloodshed. Her journey through life and his dedication to the Patriot cause were diametrically opposed.

Yet in a small way, by saving Juliet, he had made up for not protecting Sarah. To live his life without the lodestone of guilt? His jaw hurt from clamping his teeth. If only that remorse could be purged.

There was nothing left to remember Sarah now except her handkerchief and a crass letter left by her murderer. His life since her death a year before still left him feeling as if she were nothing but a dream. For him, what happened in the past expanded over the present, and understanding the past defined the future. Who was he fooling anyway? He could not allow Juliet into his heart. With his mission, he could not protect her.

Yet Juliet was like the river he dipped his paddle into—clear and pure, yet the depths, mysterious and impenetrable. The culture of her speech and mannerisms could pass for nobility in any well-established family in England. Why would a woman of noble birth be slaving away in the wilderness? Was she bastard born? The pieces didn't fit.

"So the laughter-loving, sweet-smiling Aphrodite dared to mingle her goddess nature with a mortal man and ventured to America," he said because he was in the mood to provoke the she-dragon and learn more of her.

She turned to him, nostrils flaring. "You think it was by choice? I was kidnapped and expedited by a corrupt judge with illicit warrants, and sold into indenture. Mary and I were forcibly herded onto a ship, crowded into horrible conditions below deck with unemployed, criminals, rootless dissidents, troublesome youths swept up from the slums, and children sold by their parents for a seemingly better life."

Given that her emotions were running high with the Indian village and the birth, Joshua let her vent.

"Our shipmates told us there were gangs of kidnappers, working to supply colonial hunger for labor, even so low as to discuss their targets in St. Paul's Cathedral. Operating their flourishing business, these gangs had accomplices, strong-armed men and fences, dealers in stolen goods, ships' captains, merchants in England and America with corrupt officials and magistrates. Once caught, there was no going back, stuck like the tar on the keels of the ships that brought us here."

Juliet continued her explanation. "Exiled and sold for seven years, we learned absolute obedience. Defiance was rewarded with whippings, branding and chaining. We became chattels, objects of personal property with few or no rights."

Caught between the giant arms of oaks stretching across the water, leaf-dappled sunlight slashed across her face. He knew of these practices and felt sorry Juliet had been trapped in the scheme. General Washington had also been concerned and desired to have indentured servitude abolished. "Slavery is a weed growing in every soil. The man who is the property of another, is his mere chattel, though he continues a man."

"You know Aristotle?"

He shrugged. "A smattering of the philosophers."

Juliet turned and narrowed her eyes on him. "How is it you are so knowledgeable growing up in the wilderness?

Careful Joshua. She is bright and discerning. "Books are my friends, my sweet Juliet. Erudition is the reward of reading."

How little he knew her. From sitting behind her, he identified every gesture, look, habit—each hair on her head, this woman, his wife he did not claim. Yet he knew nothing of her or her family and past. They had many days of canoeing and overland portages to get to Fort Oswego where her cousin commanded. A slow smile began to build with the lingering satisfaction that time would allow to know more regarding her.

"Are we in danger?" She caught him scanning their surroundings.

They were in danger. He kept a keen eye behind him and appreciated Two Eagles did as well. Not necessary to alarm her.

"Tell me of your life in England."

Juliet sighed. "After Moira died, I had a hard time coping. To grasp that I and the mice in the walls of my little cottage were the only ones still breathing. I had no one else. I tried to tell myself life doesn't stop because you lose someone you love.

Even if it's another part of you. Told myself time has a way of obliterating old hurts, and one day I'd wake up and I'd be happy again. Only it never happened."

Juliet an orphan? She had said her mother died during childbirth and there had been no mention of her father. "Who is Moira?"

Juliet eased against the fur packs Joshua had positioned for her comfort. Despite her turmoil, the river was fair to look upon, so fine and broad, quiet and peaceful, giving no hint of storm or perilous wave. "My nanny who was like a mother to me." She shifted. "After Moira's death, Mary disappeared, and no one knew where. She had been my one solid friend from when we were very young. Being alone was darkness for me."

Mary had abandoned her death-grip to the gunnels and fallen asleep in the bottom of the canoe behind Two Eagles. Every once in a while, the normally stoic Indian would turn his gaze on Mary.

The hills were ablaze with the showy pink and white crown of dogwood. From the heavily wooded banks great bass trees bloomed with blinding snowy blossoms, promising a tantalizing bid for honey bees and the assurance of sweet nectar. As they skimmed along the water's surface, a calmness settled over her, traveling farther from Tionnontigo and the warmth of the late spring sun on her face.

"How did you and Mary become friends?"

Ducks scattered among the reeds growing near the bank's edge. Juliet weighed telling him. Since her friend was sleeping, and because she had long kept secrets trapped inside, she said,

"Mary and I have been friends from when were very young. One day, I went to Mary's home. Her father, Vicar Abram slammed the door in my face, shutting me out, and would say nothing. Upset and confused I knocked every day for a month. He refused to answer the door."

"I would have broken down the door to get answers," said Joshua.

She smiled, picturing him doing just that. "Vicar Abram wore his own righteousness as an impregnable suit of armor. Devout in his conversations with the Almighty, he met his congregation with evangelical fervor and piousness, stressing God was at his elbow. Yet, his forceful preaching on love and forgiveness were hypocritical when it came to his lone child. He had turned his back on her when she needed him the most. For that act of hypocrisy and cruelty, I can never forgive him."

She liked how Joshua listened to her. He was a man of contradictions…tenacious, principled and honorable. He was also self-righteous and relentless.

"I worried of Mary's whereabouts, and her father's strange behavior. Months eclipsed and a carriage pulled up to my cottage. A man begged me to assist a woman in childbirth. Since this was my trade, I agreed. I traveled a great distance, and I grew alarmed. Despite my relentless insistence to our destination, the men remained determined not to give me any information."

"At last, I arrived at a manor where I was rushed inside. A frantic, middle-aged gentleman, Baron Bearsted begged me to save the baby, which I thought was strange because he didn't include the mother's safety. He whisked me into a room. To my shock, I found a very pregnant Mary in desperate labor. For hours, I used my skills to save her and the baby. The child emerged into the world a stillborn, and I cried not saving Mary's child."

Juliet glanced again to Mary. "Then to my complete horror, Baron Bearsted flipped his anxious concern to cruel taunts and his scheming. How he relished Mary's father throwing her out of the house so he could enjoy nights of sexual pleasure from her young body—and since his wife had supplied him with daughters, he required an heir."

He bragged how he seduced Mary, to supply him a son with designs to steal her child and present it as his own. How he gloated over Mary's baby, glad the child she gave birth to was dead. He had no use of a bastard daughter and the dead baby saved him from having the child meet a fatal accident."

At her words, Joshua stroked deeper and harder. She could almost feel the furious power in Joshua's shoulders as they moved ever faster through the water. "Then Baron Bearsted ordered his men to move Mary to a wagon. Her hemorrhaging was terrible, and fearing her death, I threatened to go to his wife and reveal his brutality."

She heard a grunt from the bow. Did Two Eagles grip his paddle tighter? "My threats were hollow. For coin, there would be no witnesses, and my pleadings as to who I was and the truth of Baron Bearsted's treachery fell on deaf ears. I believe Mary's father and my uncle were never contacted, and no doubt if they were, they'd never help. With illicit warrants, a dishonest magistrate accelerated out voyage to America and slavery was determined."

Two Eagles darted a glance at the sleeping Mary. For a second, warmth, tenderness and protectiveness showed on his passive face. He covered Mary with a piece of cloth so her fair skin would not burn from the sun. He knew Juliet watched him but did not acknowledge her. He didn't turn away either, which was as close to proper etiquette as the Indian ever allowed.

The sun reached its zenith and descended, casting long, late afternoon shadows. Joshua stuck his paddle in the murky depths to avoid a rock. Like layers of a river bottom, Juliet kept parts of herself secret. Before Joshua entered a British stronghold, he intended to know her political leanings. "What is your opinion of the war?"

She sat quiet, gathering her thoughts, twisting her opinions in her hands. "War is terrible. Is there not an answer to stop it? Put a gun in the hands of men and they will use them. Give them mottos and they'll turn them into a reality. Sing the battle hymns to glorify them. The beating of the war drum surges the blood of men to a maniacal fervor. Maiming and killing ensue. When it is over, and if they have survived, it is the widows and orphans who are left to pick up the pieces."

He steered the canoe up onto a sandy bank. Two Eagles covered the canoe with hemlock boughs. Joshua heaved packs on his shoulder and proceeded up a deer path through the forest.

She sighed from behind him. "I've seen and heard glimpses of both sides. There is persecution of Loyalists, men stripped, tarred and feathered. Some hanged. The taking of their lands. Women and children taken hostages, some women raped and scandalous depredations committed."

"Patriots are not all murderers."

"Neither are they all Sir Galahads, but with the atrocities at the Hayes' farm, I can imagine what Loyalists have done to unsuspecting and peaceful settlers…and as I fear what Captain Snapes has ordered Onontio to do to unsuspecting farmers and the forts to the south."

Joshua tensed, worried, too.

"Is there any way we can warn them, Joshua?"

"You are starting to sound like a Patriot."

"I only care for defenseless people. Patriot or Loyalist."

"I need to find an outpost to relay a message." To someone he could trust.

At a clearing, hidden from the river, he tossed the packs to the ground and waited while the women traveled into the shrubs to relieve their needs. No fire would be laid tonight. No need to alert Onontio to their presence if he had followed them.

Juliet returned. "If the Patriots win which seems impossible against the most powerful country in the world, I wonder what future generations will say about England."

He signaled to Juliet to follow him, picked up his long gun and trudged to the river, confident when he heard her soft footsteps padding behind him. "The defenders of a destroyed old regime have to wait before history does them justice. Their conquerors write the accepted history books. As a consequence, the defenders will be credited with many infamies and encrusted with the mud of prejudice."

"As always, the logic exposes no blemishes credited to the one side and few virtues to the other."

He stopped, and she collided into his back nearly plummeting him headlong into the river.

She grabbed his arm to haul him back and her touch burned through his shirt. "Sorry," she said, dropping her hand, and a blush stole up her cheeks. "I wasn't looking where I was going."

"Not to worry."

She smiled with his absolution and her face took on a mesmerizing radiance, and then he followed her searching gaze over the river. Loons ducked beneath the water and emerged several feet away.

"Two Eagles and I remain neutral, merely fur traders trying to eke out a living and staying out of the fray." He didn't dare tell her he was to scrutinize Fort Oswego's defenses. Too dangerous of a weapon to put in her hands.

She drew up beside him, her shoulder brushing his. He tried not to look at how her dress stuck to her like a second skin, tried not to look at her breasts pushed impudently against the doeskin.

Side by side they stood in companionable silence, peace descending with the setting sun, and he wondered momentarily how it would be to have this woman by him for the rest of his life. He shook the notion aside. A dragonfly skittered across the water. A bass jumped, caught it in its jaws and disappeared forever in the murky depths. "Living in the wilderness during this war, you live or die. There is no middle ground."

Juliet harrumphed. "Such is the madness of men. Now why have you brought me to the river?"

"I want to teach you how to load and unload a gun without alarming Mary."

"You expect trouble?"

"We must be prepared and having one more person to help wont' hurt." He positioned the butt end of his long gun to the ground and gave her the powder horn. "Pour a little down the muzzle, and then press the ball straight down the barrel with the ramrod." He moved behind her, anchoring his feet beside hers, and then placed his hands over hers, close enough to smell her scent.

Juliet's heart hammered with his strong arms about her, finding an incredible consolation in the gentleness of his grasp. *He's teaching you to protect yourself.*

He lifted the gun. "Pull back on the hammer and put a little powder in the pan."

His hand curled beneath the gun. She hesitated, studying his long, strong fingers, hands of a man of the forests, callused by hard work and hard weather—a frontierman's hand, one that held a tomahawk and a long gun and killed people. How could it be the same hand that patiently taught her to load a gun?

Do not read any more than what is there.

Hadn't he told her the fake marriage was the only way he could ensure her safety?

She stepped away and faced him. "Do you think you'll ever return to England?"

Joshua stared at her, and she savored the progression of expressions that transformed his face: surprise, scorn, and finally shuttered blankness.

"What makes you think I come from England?"

He surprised her by reaching out and gently tracing his finger along her cheek. "Soft," he said with a wolfish grin.

She was not sidetracked and relished his uneasiness. "Your accent comes through despite your effort to conceal it."

"I come from Boston."

She cast her gaze farther into the dimmed and flickering shadows, the lofty, straight trunks of hickory, walnut and maple rose to touch the sky, topped by a canopy of meandering fox grape. She regarded him critically. "You may have come from Boston but you are not from Boston. You can't hide your midlands English accent from me."

"You are an authority?"

From a hole in a floating log, a slippery muskrat swam out, sat up to inspect them, and then slid into the water. Joshua's sarcastic tone confirmed he was evading something and she smiled inwardly. Her probing, inflamed an acerbic response. She'd ferret out what he was concealing soon enough.

"I'm from Leicestershire near Lincolnshire. There is a distinct intonation. You can't change those clipped vowels. Have you been in the Colonies long, Mr. Hansford?"

"Long enough."

He might deflect with his authoritative tone but she wasn't fooled for a second. She burst out laughing with her small victory. Oh, to push through that veneer of his.

He took the gun from her and sighted. What magnificent skill he must have to have earned him his reputation. "I will not shoot. The sound might invite trouble. When you get to be an expert, you'll be able to load the gun four times a minute. In time, I'll teach you to shoot."

"What do you do when you are not trapping? Do you have a place to call home?"

"I have a little patch of earth up in the Mohawk Valley with a small cabin. Eventually, I want to farm. The soil is fat and lusty and everywhere a man spits, plants grow. Cherry trees that fruit like clusters of grapes. All sorts of fowls, to take at our pleasure. Nuts as big as eggs. The river flows with lush green grass within the shelter of a mountain."

Such eloquent descriptions for a fur trapper. And he had the most extraordinary profile she'd ever seen. If she were a portrait artist, she'd define the contours and sharp angles, and capture the light and shadow that made his visage even more handsome. His eyes caught an errant gleam of waxing light, and for a hair's breadth of a second, she glimpsed pain and stark wrenching anguish before it vanished.

Lies and secrets, they were like a cancer to the soul. They ate away what was good and left destruction. She should know. She was the greatest practitioner of keeping secrets.

She dragged her palms against her gown, trying to scrub away the painful emotions of her past, realizing not once had he answered her question regarding his origins. She had liked the way his voice deepened, telling her of his home in the Mohawk Valley, and it was as if she were seeing what he described. The cabin, snug and warm in the winter, with smoke curling from the chimney. Or cool in the summer, with the door open to catch a breeze. Tall grass waving in the meadow along with dazzling colored wildflowers and a bubbling river to swim through on hot summer days.

"Sounds like paradise," Juliet whispered. A blue jay darted

out from the leafy shore, a flying flash of the sharpest blue, and passed so close Juliet might have reached out her hands to touch it. A place called home elusive as the blue jay. Where did she belong?

Her cousin, a British officer had the power to return her to England. What was there for her? Loneliness? Her heart seized, split amid two domains and at the mercy of fate.

Joshua skirted the boundaries of their encampment, making sure they were safe although he was assured Two Eagles had already performed the task. Juliet stifled a yawn as they entered their camp. He imagined her craving a month of sleep from her ordeal.

"Where have you been?" said Mary, her manner accusing Juliet of desertion. "I was alone with—"

"He won't eat you if that is what you think, Mary." Joshua chuckled and set down his gun while Two Eagles unwound the sinews binding the fur packs, snapped out a large bearskin, and made a bed on the ground. Joshua was weary, his leg ached, but he'd not get a wink of sleep with two skittish females and the sleeping arrangements. "Juliet, tell me more of your life in England."

"Why?"

She placed her hand on her gold cross. A movement he'd come to realize as a defensive gesture. "There's nothing interesting."

"Try me." He narrowed his eyes on her and she turned away,

removing corn cakes and salty deer jerky, setting the meal on a stump for everyone to sup. She offered him a piece of jerky, and he refused to release her hand.

Mary gave a disgusted snort. "Since she won't speak, I'll speak for her. She is really Lady Juliet Faulkner. Her father was Baron John Faulkner."

Juliet glared at her friend.

"Lady Juliet Faulkner?" He dropped her hand. She had said her full name during the wedding ceremony and he'd paid no special attention, yet it was beyond his wildest imagination, she was the daughter of Baron Faulkner.

"And you were going to tell me this fact, when?" His father had purchased an obsidian-black Arabian from Baron Faulkner, a lesser baron from the northeast of Derby County and renowned for his horses.

Juliet lifted her shoulders. "My title certainly makes no difference. My father died. My uncle took over the baronetcy."

Mary plunked her fists on her hips. "What she didn't tell you was when her father died, his younger brother was quick to seize the baronetcy, appropriating all tenements, lands, monies, rents, freehold profits and manor. Except for a small broken-down cottage, nothing had been provided for her by her father. Not that that was any surprise."

"I'm warning you, Mary."

Joshua was getting a vague idea of Juliet, yet there was more to her story. "How does a gently-reared noblewoman learn midwife skills?"

"I learned from Moira. She was a midwife."

His sister, Abigail on no occasion would be allowed to dabble in any kind of trade. For a woman of nobility to get her hands dirty was considered scandalous. "Your father encouraged this activity?"

There was a catch in her voice, a sadness and he presumed it had something to do with her father. Why would Baron Faulkner allow his daughter to perform inferior tasks with common people? And why would he leave his only child a tumbled down shack to live in for the rest of her life?

Juliet plunked down next to a tree, her arms wrapped around her drawn up knees, the hem of her doeskin dress tugged down to cover her shapely ankles and a picture of misery. "Moira wasn't just my nanny. She had been trained as a midwife in Ireland and later became my mother's lady's maid. Because of her special talents, Moira was called upon in the local villages to assist mothers in labor. No one cared what I did with my time. At thirteen summers, I followed her, and she trained me."

Joshua stretched the thigh Onontio had sliced open, then grimaced. "Still doesn't answer my question. How did your father allow you to practice the trade?"

When she seemed disinclined to talk, Mary said, "Her father knew nothing of it."

"Shush, Mary. Not one more word."

"You will not shush me. It is nigh time you faced the truth concerning your horrid—

Juliet rose, placed her hand over Mary's mouth. "Not one more word."

134

Juliet's body ached and her eyes grew blurred staring at the cold hard ground and then at the soft warm fur. Two Eagles and Joshua lay down on the furs, leaving a place in the middle for the women. She didn't even ask. She tiptoed to the edge and lay down in the center of the furs.

"There is no way I'm going to sleep next to a savage." Mary stood with her back plastered against a hickory, interrupting the quiet babble of the river as it beat upon a nearby sandbar. "No doubt the heathen's skill with a knife is celebrated. I'll never turn my back on him. He'll cut my heart out and hold it before my eyes, a second before I die."

Two Eagles glared at her and turned his back.

Joshua gave an exaggerated sigh. "Be my guest, Mistress Mary. Sleep wherever you like. If a wolf carries you off or Onontio secrets you away, it will not disturb my sleep. However, if you wish to be protected you will sleep in between us. Your virtue will be safe. We are both honorable men. Two Eagles has many Indian maidens who vie for his attention. He does not thirst for an unwilling maid."

Mary lifted her chin. She ripped off shaggy bark from the tree behind her and flung it to the ground. "Indian maidens! I'll take my chances."

Two Eagles spoke quickly in his native tongue.

Mary shot daggers at him. "What did he say?"

Joshua punched a fur into a pillow. "He said to be careful of rattlers. They love to cozy up to a warm body at night."

"Snakes." She flew to the blanket and cuddled next to Juliet, distancing herself from Two Eagles.

Juliet heard the deep rumble of Joshua's chuckle as he rose to check the river, she presumed to guarantee they were not followed. She waited until he was out of earshot and whispered to Mary. "You should be more appreciative of what these brave men are offering."

"He probably lives in one of those silly wigwams that blows over with the first wind."

Two Eagles grunted.

"The savage can't even speak English. He simply grunts. Imagine the King's language denigrated. Nothing near this world is civilized." She flounced around to get comfortable. "It's terribly cold."

Two Eagles settled a fur over the two girls.

"I thought you said he wasn't civilized," Juliet said.

Mary sniffed. "He's quiet and aloof, observing things around him with a detached curiosity as one might observe ants on an anthill struggling to carry off a crumb of bread."

"I think he watches you."

The croaking frogs filled the silence.

Mary ran her hands through her hair. "At the very least, I could offer him a friendship yet he has shown not the slightest interest other than to point and growl and order me around. In fact, rarely does he look my way if he can avoid it. But I'll admit he is quite comely in his savage way. If I were to compare him to an ancient, it would be Alexander the Great, lithe, muscular, graceful."

Juliet coughed. "You call Two Eagles graceful?"

"Dear Lord, the man moves like a panther. Sneaks up on me and gives my heart a shake. Maybe it is the forbidden nature of a white woman attracted to a savage. I've yet to sort it out. Thank

God, he doesn't understand me. Not ever would I fan his vanity with all those Indian maidens chasing him."

"You sound jealous."

"Ridiculous." She flounced over, her back to Juliet. "Onontio and his band proved crueler in their crimes, atrocities and outrages than what my father preached in his sermons. Men savages, what is the difference? Every single one of them is the scourge of nature, much like rats, fleas, lice or the plague. I'll never trust any man again."

Juliet sighed. "You are referring to Baron Bearsted who represented the worst kind of betrayal. Your young heart was tricked by a deviant man who lied, promising an impressionable girl a life way beyond her strictures, and—promising marriage when he already had a wife. He seduced you with sweet words and luxuries to gain a son who he'd keep, and then threw you out."

"My trust was forever broken. The lies Baron Bearsted cast were enough to cement disbelief in any truth expressed by any man."

"In time, you will heal your skepticism, Mary. There are good men out there. Haven't Joshua and Two Eagles shown us sacrifice and protection when we needed it the most? Are they not good men?"

Soon, Mary's soft snores came from the side of her. Juliet threw back the fur and walked to the river. Tired as she was she could not sleep. Joshua drew out of the shadows and startled her.

"I thought you'd be asleep."

He pulled her to sit by him on a fallen tree. "We can rest

here, and you can unload on me or not say a word. Sometimes the silence of the night is enough."

He knew what was bothering her.

An owl hooted, and an animal scrambled beneath the bushes. He scooted closer, his knee touching hers.

Was it the darkness, or the gentleness in his voice that prompted her to acknowledge her shame?

"Form early on, I absorbed loneliness and scorn. I should have died instead of my mother. My father may not have ever come out and said it, but his actions betrayed his bitterness toward me."

"Go on," he encouraged, but his voice hardened. Then he spoke more temperately, and she shoved away the self-protective caution she hid behind.

"My father loved my Irish mother deeply and never forgave me for her death. He refused to have anything to do with me. Forbidden to be in his presence, I was hidden in the kitchen to take my meals with the servants. As a child of four summers, I played in the stables. My father appeared with his paramour. The woman laughed at me, asking where I had come from. My father told her I was the stablemaster's daughter. As young as I was, I understood the flagrant rejection and cried in the haymow the whole day.

"Do you know how it feels to thirst for a father's love, and no matter what you do to try and please him it is all completely for naught because he couldn't abide the sight of me.

"The worst of it was when my father placed me in the care of his sister. My matronly aunt was quick to remind me I caused the death of my mother, and my father had to hide me because of my abominable red hair. The same red hair reminding everyone of the misfortune of my birth and that I should have been drowned."

"I'm sorry," he said, his voice hoarse.

I'm sorry. She was sorry, too, but that didn't change the facts. "Don't feel sorry for me. I don't want anyone's pity."

Chapter 13

*D*uring the night, Joshua took turns with Two Eagles keeping watch. The women were still asleep and not made for hardship and the elements. Especially Lady Faulkner. He was still reeling over how a gently-reared woman had come to be a slave in the Colonies, and the cruelty committed by her father.

"It's time to wake, Lady Faulkner." He stroked her soft cheek, pinkened by the sun. She did not heed his voice and snuggled closer to him. He rather liked her sighs and the way she had thrown her arm over his chest.

He lay back again, thinking of her extraordinary story. The men in her life had not seen fit to protect her and she had suffered gravely. With certainty, her father had left her scarred, and her uncle, as a senior family member should have arranged to have her live in her ancestral home, not let her live alone in a cottage, plying a common trade to survive. He'd like to have called the bastard out.

He hoped the cousin he was taking her to at Fort Oswego would take her under his guardianship, but he had reservations. Before the siege of Boston, and before hostilities had risen to a fevered pitch between England and the Colonies, he had chanced upon meeting Colonel Thomas Faulkner.

The opinionated colonel was a fourth son of an earl with no prospects other than serving His Majesty and possessing a rabid and sworn allegiance to his cause. He had distinguished himself in the *Seven Years War* but if truth be known, it was by his underling's resourcefulness and savvy that had won the day while Faulkner lay inebriated in his tent.

Appointed by Lord North to assist in enforcing the Intolerable Acts upon the people of Boston, Colonel Thomas Faulkner listened to no advice, asked no questions, and painfully meted out unfair justice to colonials.

Faulkner's policies had extended to the Thorne family of Boston. Joshua's sister, Abigail had married the famous American privateer, Captain Jacob Thorne. Under the Articles of Impressment, British soldiers had taken up residence in the Thorne home. One officer maintained a keen eye for Rachel Thorne, Jacob's cousin. When she thwarted his advances, he had attacked her, killed her younger brother, Thomas, who had attempted to stop the rape.

Every single misdeed perpetrated by the British officer was swept under the rug with Captain Jacob Thorne accused of the heinous crimes and to be hanged. Colonel Thomas Faulkner had served as judge and jury on the case, refusing to entertain the truth. Fortunately, with the help of friends, Thorne had escaped his execution, taking up privateering.

Mary's story, just as devastating, had affected his normally impassive friend. Two Eagles had been taken with Mary from the first time he'd laid eyes on her and had pushed as hard as

Joshua to get to Onontio's village. Joshua smiled. His friend had fallen hard for the vicar's spoiled daughter. When Ojistah had spoken her vision of Two Eagles and Mary, Joshua dismissed the uniting of an unlikely pair. Now he wasn't so sure.

There was not a crack of a twig to signal Two Eagles behind him. Without looking, he knew the warrior gazed at the sleeping Mary.

"Kind of pointless to fight for what you want when what you want scorns you," whispered Joshua in the Haudenosaunee tongue.

"I will start by doing what is necessary; then do what's possible; and suddenly I'll be doing the impossible."

"You quote St. Francis. What do you think Mary will say when you tell her you are Christian and an educated man?"

"She must accept me the way I am first."

"Perhaps the maidens in your village will be sighing and longing for your wicked ways?"

"They will no longer keep me warm on a long winter's night. I have designs for corn tassel. She will warm my bed for the rest of my days and bear me many sons."

"You think you can convince her?"

"She is overindulged but will soon learn the ways of my ancestors. Of this, I am most sincere."

He caught Two Eagles with a smile on his face, watching longingly over Mary. "You are a long-suffering man Two Eagles. I think it will take the moons of six lifetimes to accomplish that feat."

"The two most powerful warriors are patience and time."

Joshua stretched, his muscles sore. "I wonder what would happen if you ever came face to face with Baron Bearsted?"

"His scalp and body parts would be removed."

"If it is any consolation, I'll pen a letter to my father reporting Bearsted's crimes. The baron must be stopped before more innocent girls fall under his schemes."

A tendril of Juliet's hair tickled his chin and he watched her sleep. Thoughts of his mother and happy days with his brothers and sister at Belvoir Castle surfaced. For a few moments, he pictured the Rutland ancestral home. Stately English oak trees lined a meandering road that led to a giant stone edifice complete with turrets and mullioned windows that dazzled, reflecting rays of a golden sun. Manicured lawns, formal gardens, mazes, and a lake dotted with snowy white swans. Across the green valley were vineyards, fields of golden grain and verdant pastures. He could almost hear the clatter of hooves as he and his brothers raced through the village.

He preferred to think of Belvoir as his childhood playground where they had all pretended to be knights with clanking armor setting off for Canterbury to save a maiden in distress. It was at times like these, he remembered and his soul ached with homesickness.

To have a family of his own?

His gut churned. The war cut two ways…the supremacy of England and the throng in the Colonies in their bid for freedom. Thousands of men had died, leaving a void in people's lives.

Yet, this was a new experience—sleeping with a woman and not doing what came to mind. She shifted, her movements a faint whisper of doeskin against doeskin, her breath coming out against his neck in a feather-like caress.

Juliet stirred and exhaled. She had slept well, given to dreams of better days with Moira. Life had soared with simplicity and happiness. But Moira was gone. She opened her eyes and stared straight into extraordinary, compelling blue eyes. A slow smile greeted her. With a gasp, she hurtled back to earth to find herself pressed against Joshua, her fingers clasping the soft hairs of his chest.

"Oh." Fingers burning, she jerked her arm from his chest and sat up.

"Good morning," he drawled.

Heat rose from her toes to the roots of her hair, and she was loath to know how long he'd been awake. "What you must think—"

He grinned. "Not at all." He thrust aside the bearskin and rose. He reached down and helped her to her feet, his hand warm, awareness skipping up her arm.

A pink glow marked the horizon, heralding the dawn. She glanced around and spotted Two Eagles behind them, his gaze fixed on Mary who shifted and stretched beneath the fur.

"Must we leave already?"

Two Eagles' shadow covered Mary and her friend looked up wary. He held out moccasins but she lifted her nose and looked the other way.

Two Eagles dropped the pair of deerskin moccasins and pointed to Mary's feet.

"I am not putting those on. You will not be turning me into a heathen."

Bending over, he took off her shoes and stockings and hiked the moccasins up her leg.

Mary pushed his hands away. "How dare you."

"Oh, Mary stop it. He is giving you a gift," said Juliet.

Two Eagles articulated rapidly. His tone not happy.

Mary huffed. "What did he say?"

"A fledgling that stays in the nest has not yet the strength to fly, and your backbone is of soft willow and must be stiffened to oak."

"So, the heathen insults me. I am strong. What does he know?"

Juliet gave an impatient snort. "Mary, you are being childish. Two Eagles has showed nothing but kindness."

Mary brushed her hair back over her shoulder and stood. "I do admit they are softer. "Thank you," she said tersely. She took a step, slipped on cold, damp leaves. Two Eagles scooped her up and placed her back on her feet. Mary held his arm…overlong, gazing at the proud Indian.

He urged her on, taking her hand, and leading her to the river. Juliet raised an eyebrow, mystified by her friend's response and followed.

Days passed, the earth swollen and pregnant with the finale of spring. They traveled north on the lake to another river, and then east onto the Oswego River, crooked and winding, possessing many curves and at various points, tributaries rushed in. Snowy white blossoms of trillium and bloodroot rioted up the hills. Here and there a newly budded green island rose up in the middle to cut the broad river in two. The current rose strong, and a contrary gust of wind shook the canoe. They had seen no one, and threats of Onontio vanished with each passing day, presenting a surreal notion of security.

Two Eagles and Joshua's arms rose and fell as if commanding the elements with their paddles. Indeed, both men were hardened woodsman and knew the way through the trackless wilderness.

"How did you meet Two Eagles?" asked Juliet.

"Two Eagles was set against a couple dozen trappers determined to steal his furs. I balanced out the odds and convinced them it was in their best interest to leave him alone, of course, after a good fight. Afterward, we became friends, Two Eagles teaching me the art of trapping and trading as a profitable living."

"What they say concerning your legendary feats are true?"

"What legendary feats?"

"Killing a mythical bear, how you can catch sunbeams in your hand and hurl them across the firmament, part the lakes with your staff, walk on water," she laughed.

"All that."

"I like your story. I was forever the kind of child who was convinced elves lived in the parks, trees were flesh and blood, and gaps in the floorboards housed fairies rather than rodents."

"I'm just a man."

And what a man. With the warmth of the day, like most days, Joshua had removed his shirt, his skin bronzed from the sun, his broad shoulders seeming broader and his lean stomach muscles rippled with his movements. Awareness of him filled every pore of her being, admiring his male beauty, savage like the wilderness. He matched this world, thrived in its untamed ferocity.

146

She pictured him in a ballroom in London, vying for her hand to dance. Other women swarmed like locusts, pushing her away from this rugged, vital man who had a monopoly on virility. To tear their dresses, to claw their eyes. Oh, how she put the notion to flight.

With him conscious of her scrutiny, her thoughts clouded and erased. Staving off the tingling in the pit of her stomach grew impossible. Twice her hand dropped in the water. What did she say? She swallowed and managed a feeble reply long held in her mind.

"You make me feel safe."

He choked with a rough laugh of disbelief and her heart floundered. Why?

In these beautiful surroundings, it was like looking through a window into this soul—and seeing the enchanted Achilles trapped inside his gruff exterior. In that moment, she had forgotten to breathe. Her mind filled with the image before her: Joshua, her magnificent husband who was always so full of swaggering confidence, hunched like a defeated man. The real question was—by whom?

The breeze ruffled his hair, more brown than black in the rippling sunlight. He kept his own counsel and since the day yielded bright and beautiful, and because she thirsted to learn more regarding this land, she said, "I remain confused on the Iroquois and Two Eagles' tribe."

"There are Six Nations, representing the Iroquois. The Senecas, the Cayugas, the Onondagas, the Oneidas, the Tuscaroras and the Mohawks Clans represent earth, air and water. They are like families living together in one great longhouse with a door at each end. The Mohawks are fierce and are the Keepers of the Eastern Door while the Senecas, the most formidable, are the Keepers of the Western Door. The Cayugas and the Oneidas are in the center, and the Onondagas keep the council fire continuously burning. These tribes look upon each other as brothers and in time of war fight side by side. Except with this war, there has been a schism cast between them.

"Two Eagles belongs to the Oneida Clan, or Ohkwani, Keepers of Medicine and Knowledge and are the peacemakers. His Bear Clan means strong, courageous, wise, disciplined and devoted."

Mary snorted. She was not going to give one inch to the handsome warrior.

On sun-warmed rocks turtles basked. Otters played happily. Juliet trailed her fingers through the cool waters, beaming with their antics. Ojistah had compared her to the Sky Woman.

"Joshua, who is Sky Woman?"

"The Iroquois believe in dreams. The origin of the universe began with a dream which could only be fulfilled by uprooting the Sacred Tree of Life in the Sky World. The act of uprooting the tree caused chaos. An entrance to another world opened."

They entered a deep lake and, at last, Juliet let a breath pass between her lips, the unparalleled shimmering sapphire waters bloomed beneath the sun. And like every cloud in the azure sky with its own story to share, she listened to Joshua's impassioned voice.

"The Sky Woman peered down through the hole to see vast waters. Pregnant, Sky Woman's husband raged and shoved her through the hole. In the freefall, animals rushed to save her, ducks and muskrat cushioned her fall and placed her on the turtle. The animals determined to help the woman dove deep beneath the waters, scraping up mud and placing it on the turtle's back. The creatures sacrificed this for the Sky Woman to exist."

Humming a tune, Juliet braided her hair, and then leaned over to see her image, the sky reflected behind her, and a half-dreaming mood arose in which she naturally floated away in the mirror of the river. To have her life compared to the fantastic Sky Woman? What did Ojistah's confusing predictions mean? She'd give birth to a daughter, and her daughter would give birth to a daughter, a long line of umbilical cords connecting and binding.

How could it be? He pulled back from any kind of attachment. She touched her lips and her face heated remembering his kiss on their wedding day. A longing manifested itself in the pit of her stomach and she stared off into the distant lonely forests.

Why should she be surprised? Had not her father taught her how selfish and faithless men could be? Because her mother had died, he'd abandoned her at birth. Every day was to be a remembrance of her crime and punishment. No matter how hard she tried to please her father at accomplishing her studies, riding, languages, pianoforte, he'd not take any interest in her. He tossed her aside and her hurt and loneliness left her feeling unlovable and unworthy.

She straightened. No matter how painful, it was better to forget Joshua and move on. He was committed to his trapping and trading, a man destined for the uncivilized wilds. There was no sense questioning a relationship that failed to exist.

"What do you think of Ojistah? Do you think her visions are real?"

"She is much the same as Two Eagles' mother, her twin and despite their distances they have an uncanny exchange of each other's thoughts and feelings. Both are esteemed medicine women, eminently skillful in the preparation of specifics believed to be of great efficacy, but whose extraordinary virtues are attributed to their powerful incantations and influence with the good spirits, with whom they profess to have daily communication."

"Superstition, fear, mingled with awe?"

"At one time, I might have scoffed at their supernatural capabilities. But I've seen firsthand what they have prophesized come to light."

He was foreign to her, this man who had taken vows to be her husband in a hasty marriage ceremony in a remote Indian village.

Those whom God hath joined together let no man put asunder.

Did Father Devereux's divine words still ring in his ears as they did hers?

"I want you to learn how to paddle," said Joshua, navigating to the side of the lake to switch places.

The paddling looked easy enough. Juliet climbed in the front of the canoe with Joshua immediately behind her, then Mary. Two Eagles shoved their wobbly vessel off the bank and hopped into the stern.

Joshua leaned over her, guiding her hands and pulling with her. "Move with the rhythm," he spoke huskily into her ear. She colored fiercely and stiffened with the near naked man pressed up against her. A band closed around her chest, held her lungs in a viselike grip and refused her breath.

She responded to Joshua's slow, steady instruction, her body throbbing.

She couldn't see where his eyes traveled but rather felt his heated appraisal. When she stretched the paddle farther, his biceps stroked her arms like a second sinuous skin. When his lips touched the lobe of her ear, she closed her eyes on a moan.

Heat encased her hand. She looked down at Joshua's hand covering hers and his warm breath tickled a frond of hair on her cheek. A warning voice in her head told her to pay attention.

"Steady, Juliet. Remember, we're in this together."

Soon she adapted, keeping the canoe from wobbling, and working in tandem with Two Eagles, guiding with his paddle to correct any mistakes she caused.

Every so often, they spotted Indian villages a little inland. The fields were not plowed, yet rich black earth was piled up on hills two feet high, placed a long step apart. The hills were in rows and the women advanced, planting in the top of hills and singing. Not like the fields planted in England with horse and plow.

"They are planting the three sisters," Joshua said to her.

"Three sisters?"

"Corn, beans and squash. It will see them through the winter starving period when game is scarce."

"What are they singing?"

"They are singing to both the Great Spirit, Hä-wen-ne-yu and to Grandfather Hé-no, the Thunder God. They thank the Great Spirit from the world and all that is good. He made the corn and the plants of the earth to grow, to blossom, and bear fruit. To the Thunder God, they ask for rain to wash the earth, and to slake the thirst of the corn, beans and squash."

"Life is so simple and meaningful," Juliet said. Joshua chuckled, and she turned to look behind her. He reclined against the pile of furs "What is so humorous?"

His hands were folded behind his head. "The days hum sweetly when I have enough bees to do my work."

Juliet back-paddled, flinging up a spray of frigid water over him and offsetting Two Eagles. "How is that for the sting of a bee?"

He sputtered from the icy water, and she glanced again over her shoulder. He smiled at her, his whole smile, wiping away every bit of seriousness, a blatant male smile, sensual, confident and devastating. Her breath caught, and for one heart-stopping moment, she couldn't breathe. She'd never experienced such a force. She inhaled sharply, her insides quickening deep in her belly.

She swung around to face the front of the canoe, her body suddenly a white-hot, pulsating blaze rivaling the sun in intensity. Maybe it was the leftover exhilaration from the heat generated between them when he pressed his body behind her in teaching her how to paddle. Or maybe it was her mind playing cruel tricks on her. After everything she'd been through with the massacre, captivity, and the escape, her mind had turned to mush.

She ought to think of her future. Secretly, while an indentured servant, she'd endeavored to send her cousin, Colonel Faulkner, a letter through a trapper. The man wasn't the most reliable, and she wondered if her cousin ever received her message. For now, getting to Fort Oswego and meeting up with her cousin was paramount. He'd return her to England with Mary, to civilization and sanity.

But what would her cousin say about her indenture? Would he give her the support she needed or turn his back on her like her uncle in England? Without resources, money or power, or family backing her, who was to say they might fall prey to someone like Baron Bearsted again?

Juliet quit paddling to give her aching arms a rest, allowing the current to move them forward, her thoughts grim with the uncertainties of her future. Was what she had gone through in England not more brutal than the honest savagery of this new world?

Chapter 14

The squealing yips coyotes came from the hills. Two Eagles sat at attention. Joshua scanned the shore. His first thoughts were of Juliet and Mary's safety. The smell of smoke and burnt flesh fouled the air.

"Strange, coyotes are only heard at night," Juliet said. Joshua could see she was tenser than she wanted to reveal and with good reason. When she turned to look at him, he gave her a reassuring smile.

Two Indians in breechclouts and a white man emerged from a line of trees, waved at them. A kastoweh was bound round their foreheads, two eagle feathers up and one down. *Oneida.* Two Eagles lifted his paddle in greeting, and Joshua maneuvered the canoe to the shore. The Indians stepped into the water and pulled their bow up on the banks. A dugout to the left of them was packed.

Joshua and Two Eagles clasped the men's hands. "Good to see you, Hadawako and Sheauga."

The white-haired man, in filthy homespun hobbled toward them, his face, crinkled like parchment and his eyes, bloodshot from crying. "Damn those Tory troops and damn those Mohawks. They wiped out my family. My dear Bessie of twenty years. They took my grain, plundered my house, destroyed my furniture, killed my livestock. I was working over the mountain at my mill when Hadawako came to warn me. I saw the smoke and ran, but by the time I arrived everything was gone."

He spat. "My beautiful Bessie, violated and scalped by those savages. My oldest son tried to defend the family but they pushed a lance through him, scalped him. No one deserves to die that way."

Juliet gasped.

"I'm sorry for your loss," said Joshua. "I wish there was something I could have done. What will you do now?"

"There's nothing left for me here other than their graves. This was her favorite view of the river. Now she will have it eternally." He pointed to the nine crosses on mounded patches of earth. "I'm traveling to Albany to live with my brother."

Joshua slipped easily into the Oneida tongue, spoke rapidly to Hadawako and Sheauga. "You must warn the forts and settlers to the south. Captain Snapes and Colonel Butler are gathering for a big battle. What happened here," he angled his head to the graves, "is a sample."

Hadawako and Sheauga pivoted and melted into the forests.

Joshua exhaled. His message would get through and hopefully in time. "We must leave this place."

The old man pushed his canoe into the river and vanished ahead of them.

Juliet had observed the back and forth exchange, of flying hand gestures, anger and determination. Whatever had been discussed, Joshua seemed pleased with the results.

She gazed at the forest that had swallowed up Hadawako and Sheauga. Then she asked, "What did you say to them that they left so quickly?"

He tensed for a second. "I sent a message."

"To whom?"

"Get in the canoe."

She sat purposely facing him.

He pushed them into the river, hopped in the stern, his answer too long in coming.

"It is insignificant."

He held the paddle too tight like when he curled his hand around the fork at Hayes' dinner party. "What did you them?"

He rearranged the gear and stretched out his long legs, sandwiching hers. "Winter might come early this year."

She snorted with his falsehood, his strong thighs holding her hostage. "To resign an intense conversation to seasonal predictions is laughable. What are you hiding? At the very least, I'd hoped you'd have them warn the Colonists of Captain Snapes and Onontio's planned attacks."

Joshua's movements were slow, cautious. "Your cousin, Colonel Faulkner would consider the caution treasonous. What would he have to say concerning your Patriot loyalties?"

His question came with a deeper meaning, approaching her in a roundabout fashion like a trout circling bait. "After what I witnessed on the Hayes' farm…I want no one to suffer violence, Patriot or Loyalist."

He probed her with his gaze. "What kind of man is your cousin?"

Again, another inquiry loaded with innuendo. "I've met him once when he was home from the Colonies. He stayed for two weeks and went back, spending years away from home and his family. I can tell you of his son, Edmund. He was the one relative who was ever kind to me. As children, we played hunt the hare for hours in the garden. If Colonel Faulkner is anything like his son, he is of good temperament."

The nine fresh graves and the man's loss of his family triggered a jarring memory of Edmund. When his mother called, he wanted to remain hidden, becoming fearful. *Strange.* If her mother was alive, she'd want to be with her.

Not to forget Joshua's ambiguousness, she leaned back, at ease and in control, and laughed aloud, her laughter echoing over the river. "I am going to learn the language so I won't have to hear of wintry predictions."

Chapter 15

Two Eagles spoke to them patiently in his language, pointing out objects and repeating their Indian names over and over. He gestures were meaningful, marking each word with a specific tonal melody. What Juliet found frustrating was changing the melody changed the word. Mastering the rising and falling pitch proved maddening whereas Mary followed his words closely, picking up the language with ease.

"Odéka', eñgade´gat," said Juliet, practicing some of the Iroquoian words. "I said, spoon, I make a spoon."

Joshua shook his head and laughed. "You said, 'fire. I make a fire.'"

"It is all for naught. Attempting the words is like running through a patch of thorn trees and catching unpronounceable syllables on every barb."

Juliet heard the roar first. They arrived into a basin, carved between two forests, framed by jagged escarpments of slate. Crystal cold water streamed over a mountain shelf, creating the most magnificent waterfall she had ever seen. A silver mist rose with a rainbow half the size of the falls and she inhaled the damp woodland scent of ferns, mosses and wild mint.

Joshua steered the canoe to shore. "We'll make camp."

Julie wondered if they would ever make it to Fort Oswego. She was anxious to get there and seek help from her cousin. England yawned and the so quiet saneness of her little cottage called to her. Foxglove and lilies growing by a stone fence, and bread pudding, and her books. She blew a tendril of hair from her eyes. Was he delaying their arrival?

"You are to learn how to shoot a gun, and I hope with a fair degree at accuracy."

She loaded the gun as he had instructed her before.

"Good."

He stood behind her. A solid wall of muscle and sinew pressed against her back. She sucked in a shallow breath as he helped her lift the rifle.

"You must have the butt end pressed to your arm or the recoil will give you a heck of a bruise." He pulled her closer as he pushed the gun into her shoulder. When he leaned over and sighted down the barrel with her, pleasant shivers traveled up her spine with the brush of his beard against the softness of her cheek. His hand came to rest at her waist.

"Fire."

She sighted and pulled the trigger the recoil causing her to fall backward. He caught her and steadied the gun in her arms. His heartbreaking grin and the sultry heat radiating from his body made her mouth dry.

"What did I shoot?" she said, breathless.

Joshua threw back his head and laughed. "A leaf."

Her shoulders sank. "A leaf?"

"We'll spend some time practicing. You'll learn quickly."

After firing several more rounds and improving, he pulled her through the woods, identifying plants he learned from Two Eagles. "This is willow bark. Boil a tea. It is good to reduce fevers. Over there is knitbone, good for broken bones. Elderberry juice made from crushed elderberries is good for stomach complaint."

"When walking as you are now, you are a clear giveaway for men tracking you. Walk on stones to leave no footprint." He broke off a branch and swept it over the area they had tread. "This will hide your trail."

"You are very experienced."

"You never know when such knowledge will save your life." He smoothed the hair back from her face, and she leaned into him. He dropped his hand and gestured back to camp.

How long could she keep up the charade? Day by day her attraction to Joshua grew. To pretend she did not have feelings for him was torture. How many times had she cautioned herself to stop staring at him? He'd only dismiss her affection.

The intimacy of sleeping side by side had her thinking the impossible and a curl of desire grew inside her. They had brushed shoulders from time to time when putting up and taking down the camp. Other than that, they had kept their relationship familial. But it did not keep her from wishing things were different.

Two Eagles had snared two rabbits, and one hung from a tree. He took some dried leaves from a deerskin pouch, lit them and, waving his hands with an upward motion, ushered the smoke to the rabbit.

Her mouth watered and her stomach gnawed. Delaying a meal of roasted rabbit when she was starving? "What is he doing?" said Juliet.

Joshua threw stacks wood down. "Animals have souls that are alike in their nature to the soul of human beings, yet they are more powerful. The hunter prays to the soul of the animal he kills and explains why he killed it. The souls of friendly animals help man, if man has been courteous, and he prays to the deceased animal's spirit to enter him. The animal is taken for the body and is not stripped of the soul."

"Oh." Juliet found the culture strange yet what Two Eagles performed was beautiful.

"I was brought up to believe animals are beasts of burden for our use," said Mary.

Joshua angled his head. "I will translate your belief to Two Eagles."

While Joshua translated, Two Eagles narrowed his eyes on Mary, speaking rapidly while Joshua translated.

"Animals assist us and act as potent spirit guides. One time my enemy wished to kill me. They blistered my feet with hot coals and forced me to run a great distance. When I tired, they tied me up. I called upon my brothers, the toad, the bat, the mouse and the nighthawk. The toad applied a salve to my feet and I was cured. The bat distracted my enemy by flying round. The mouse climbed the tree and gnawed off the cords. The nighthawk reported my enemy's whereabouts as I made my escape."

Mary flopped on the ground, arranging her skirts around her. "Absurd."

"Two Eagles says nothing more ridiculous than Jonah being swallowed by a whale," said Joshua.

Mary rolled her eyes and snapped sticks in a pile to build a fire. Two Eagles broke out laughing, and Mary twisted her head around. "That is the first time I've heard you laugh. It's rather nice."

He pointed for Mary to clean the rabbit. She shook her head no. He folded his arms in front of him and spoke quickly. Mary stared at him mutinously, refusing to budge. Clearly his manner spoke he would not start the fire until Mary cleaned the rabbit.

"What did Two Eagles say?" said Juliet, puzzling over Mary's antagonistic attitude toward Two Eagles, especially when her friend cuddled up to the one she called "savage" every night. Two Eagles' tolerance was admirable.

Joshua said, "'When one has worked hard and is hungry, the food will lie well on the tongue.' It is a war of wills."

Mary's hunger overcame her and, soon she was gutting and skinning the rabbit with Two Eagles' gestures. Mary, ever wary of the Indian, watched Two Eagles arrange a circle of stones, scooping out a piece of earth, making a hole in the middle. Over the hole he laid thin, dry grasses and twigs, arranging them in neat order.

He picked up a fire-drill and placed the lower point of the shaft upon a piece of dry wood. He drew the bow against the drill numerous times until a spark lit the dry grasses. He blew it into a flame and fed it with additional tinder, following with larger branches. He thrust a sharp stick through the rabbit's body to roast, and then stared at Mary with a thirst of a man who had found a nugget of gold and knew he had found a mountain of the treasure. "I ·sé uni stelist owískla u ·kwé atnutolyaé óshes onúhkwis. I•se haw• akwa•wʌ́ khále⁷ ya⁷táute⁷ ⁷nikuhlatsatste haw• akwa•wʌ́." *You make me laugh white woman with hair of gold honey. You belong to me and always will belong to me.*

"I'm going to collect Indian turnips growing downstream to add to our meal," said Joshua.

"Wait. What did Two Eagles say?" said Mary.

Joshua whipped aside a maple branch, plunged down a path to the river, and said over his shoulder, "He is hungry."

"Men only think of their stomachs," Mary huffed, and, at that moment, gazed longingly at Two Eagles. "I've never met such a man. All the bogey man stories I've been told are ridiculous."

"Am I hearing you might like him?" said Juliet.

"He stands very straight and tall. His nose is long, his forehead high, his mouth wide. His eyes are bright and piercing. I'm struck by his noble appearance."

Juliet gaped. Trying to begin to identify the nuances of her friend's contrary mind was like scraping her shoe on a star and hanging upside down from the moon.

"It's—I at no time was aware an Indian could look so fine, so wise and so good. He certainly is a fine specimen of a man." Mary stood, practically swooned on her feet, and then departed into the forests.

Juliet snapped her gaze to Two Eagles and captured a hint of a smile. Did Two Eagles understand more than he let on?

Mary screamed. Juliet jumped to her feet and dashed down a slender animal path. Two Eagles swept past her, leaping over fallen trees, thickets of bush engulfing him, and disappearing far ahead of her. Were there other Indians? Bear? If anything happened to her friend…

A stitch stabbed her side, and she staggered to catch her breath. How many times had she told Mary not to travel far from the campsite? She tunneled through the overgrowth, scampered over rocks, slipped on mosses, falling, her hands scraped across slate.

Beyond the framing of trees, she saw Two Eagles poised, signaling Mary to cease her shrieks. A seven-foot diamond patterned reptile with keeled rough scales, coiled on a rock, hissing at Mary, its head up, blue tongue darting in and out. The tail rattled a lethal warning. The jaws opened revealing long white fangs ready to strike.

Juliet stopped. With certainty, her movement might provoke the reptile. If the rattlesnake bit Mary, she'd die a painful death.

Two Eagles moved stealthily forward, bobbing and weaving, as if casting some kind of spell, mesmerizing the snake and distracting the rattler away from Mary He slowly drew his knife and threw. Juliet's hand sailed to her chest. The blade traveled end over end and severed the snake from its head, the body uncoiling, and writhing with its last breath.

Juliet could not move if she wanted to.

Mary fell into his embrace, weeping.

Two Eagles held her at arm's length, and spoke angrily. "An Indian woman will learn to be as brave and uncomplaining as his brothers in the forest. The wounded wolf or bear, the dying deer never cries out in pain. The beasts bear their pain in silence, giving no outward sign. They go forward to meet danger. They shrink not from pain or suffering, sickness or death."

Two Eagles gathered her in his arms, rubbing his hand up and down her back.

"An Indian child is taught never to cry. Loud sounds of grief will attract a wolf or panther or an enemy of the Oneidas. You must learn to bear your pain and give no sign."

Juliet opened and closed her mouth, no more shocked than Mary who tilted her head up and stared at Two Eagles. "You speak English? Joshua said you didn't—"

"Joshua was correct. I don't like to speak English. I prefer my own tongue."

Mary's hands flew to her cheeks. "All this time…and you let me think…what a fool you must think of me…all the things I said about you."

Two Eagles smiled and placed her palms on his chest. "I like how your heart spoke."

She pushed away from him but his arms held her head to his chest, touching her hair. "I've not once seen hair this color before. It is like the gold of corn tassel."

"I like your strong heartbeat beneath my fingers," Mary said tentatively.

"You don't need to fear when I'm with you, Mary. I'm a warrior and will protect you."

"I have many fears. I am alone and the wilderness is frightening."

Two Eagles held up her chin and gazed into her eyes. "There is no shame in fear. What matters is how we face it."

"I have been wounded—"

"I know of the baby and the man. I listened to Juliet speak when you were asleep in the canoe and she did not know I understood English. Baron Bearsted is a coiling rattlesnake, whose bite is like the sting of bad arrows."

"You do not judge me?"

"I would kill him. Death would be his atonement. An Indian man would never abandon his woman or his child. Nor will I ever abandon you." Then…he kissed her.

Juliet's eyes widened, her mouth fell open. A second later, she shook her head and not keen to be caught as a voyeur, she retraced her steps to the camp. Mary and a savage? No.

Chapter 16

_J_uliet strode down to the river to confront Joshua regarding his deception with Two Eagles. He sat on a rock, his hair tied back with a leather thong, fingering a letter, absently lifting a lace-edged handkerchief to his nose. But it was the way he clutched the letter, grief ravaging his face. When he noticed her, he secreted the items in his pack, burying his despair, and then cast his gaze over the waterfall.

"What is it?" His tone was gruff.

She pulled herself up to full posture. "I have a matter to discuss with you. Two Eagles can speak English. Why did you mislead me?"

He rubbed the back of his neck and that devilish smile of his came back. "Oh that—"

"You let Mary think and say those things about him."

"What did she say?"

Juliet clamped her mouth shut. He'd not been around when Mary was mooning over Two Eagles like an infatuated schoolgirl. His innocent expression gave him away. No doubt, Two Eagles told him. Never in a million years would she give

Joshua the satisfaction of repeating what Mary said.

"You let me struggle trying to understand him, knowing full well he could speak English?"

"At no time did I say, he couldn't speak English. I said he didn't like to speak English."

"A dance of words, Joshua, making me a fool."

He towered over her. "I could say of course to that notion, if you consider yourself foolish, but I know you wouldn't find that agreeable."

Oh, he called her foolish! Juliet pushed him. Arms flailing, he splashed into the water. He stood up roaring with laughter, and combing loose wisps of his dark hair off his face, the water dripping from his face down to his chest.

"I remember the last time you surprised me by dumping a bucket of cold water on my head. This time there will be retribution."

"Ha!" She turned to go back to camp. "Is a cougar troubled by a mouse?"

Water sloshed behind as she took a step. Arms of steel wrapped around her and dragged into the water. He drew her up to him, holding her tight in his embrace, as if shielding her with his body against the world, against all the torments, fears and loneliness.

Cocooned within Joshua's arms, Juliet drank it all in—the man, the millions of ways he moved her. God, he was warm. And strong. Too strong. His dark lashes swept down veiling a mischievous glint in his eyes. She pushed a finger in his chest. "You are a son of a motherless goat."

He laughed, pretended to slip and she grabbed around his neck. "Where is Lady Faulkner?"

Juliet pushed away from him, swam a few strokes, keeping out of his reach, the water cool and soothing.

She looked behind, transfixed by the droplets dribbling down, down, down. She raised her eyes to Joshua's face. For an infinite moment their eyes locked, and Juliet forgot her fears, forgot England, forgot to breathe.

But what lingered in her mind was what had damaged him. She wanted to understand his secrets. "What is written in the letter?"

"There will be no discussion—" His voice was low, his tone firm. Ominous.

His moods were like the winds, ever shifting. "I do not judge," she said softly.

"I was to be married to the love of my life."

He was to be married? He had a sweetheart? At Tionnontigo, he had told her did not have a wife and she wondered of his anger at the time when she'd mentioned the subject. Had the woman jilted him? Found him wanting? "Why did you not marry?"

The ensuing silence punctuated only by the thundering of the falls seemed to go on forever. He simply stood there, eyes glazed with chilling hate. His big hands flexed and fisted as if he wished to twist someone's neck.

Juliet took a step toward him. "Oh, Joshua. I'm guessing for whatever reason, she called off the wedding. I cannot begin to fathom your grief."

Her voice seemed to snap the cord of his patience. A foul oath burst from him and he waded from the water.

She ran up the steep bank, grabbed his arm and swung him

to face her. The lines in his face hardened and, without warning, he reached out to touch her cheek. Juliet stood her ground. His hand lingered, lightly traced the line of her jaw.

"So many words get lost. They stay in my throat…lose their courage. I want to ignore it, but how can I hide from something that will never go away?"

"I assumed there'd be one great love in my life. Sarah. For ages, I reasoned she was the only one, yet a flame-haired beauty with her omnipresent smiles makes me crawl out from beneath a fog of guilt and forces me to come alive, makes me want more of which I have no right."

Sarah? Juliet gasped. What nightmarish agony had the woman put him through?

"She is dead."

Joshua suddenly hauled her close against his pounding heart. His emotions were out of control despite his efforts to grapple them into submission. He didn't tell her Sarah had been murdered by some sick bastard…couldn't say the words. Not yet.

Juliet, whose face had shone like the sparkling sun, and whose laugh, like the happy sound of falling waters, looked at him questioningly.

Unable to quell the urge, he reached out and gently touched her flaming red hair, like he did every night when he had held her in his arms, when she was asleep and did not know he gazed upon her.

"Stay with me. Do not go away."

Joshua put his finger on her chin and lifted her face, studying her as if a rare butterfly had landed on his fingertip. She was a threat to his necessary isolation, yet she stole into his soul. He would hold her, and that would be all.

Even as he touched his lips to hers, he told himself to resist. Yet his thirst for her dominated all rational thought and caution winged upward, vanishing like embers in the sky.

She brought her arms around his neck and sighed against his mouth. His wild hunger whetted, he slid the tip of his tongue along the crease of her lips, seeking entrance, insisting that they part, and when finally they did, his tongue plunged into the sweetness of her mouth, and then slowly withdrew, then plunged again in flagrant imitation of the act he craved.

He picked her up and lay her down on the soft sweet grass, pulling her next to him. She came willingly, seeming to melt in warm submission, as if she had been anticipating this instant.

"You set me on fire," he breathed against her, tormenting himself with the shape and softness of her mouth, and drawing small urgent whimpers from the back of her throat. The admission came effortlessly. He kissed her again, fiercer, and they sank further onto the grass, pungent with the scent of wildflowers. No bed of feathers could have felt more opulent.

Joshua reveled in the warmth radiating through him, causing the tension in his chest to ease. His tongue probed her soft mouth as if the intimate search would yield the key to her essence. He sought to venerate her, to treasure her, to give her satisfaction.

She clung to him, and her desperate intensity captivated him. She was a woman of many aspects, and at her center dwelt a cache of wild passion he wanted to explore. He stroked her hair, like silk it was, fine as gossamer and spilling like warm liquid through his outspread fingers.

"Your hair is like the sun setting into the sea." He drew a wavy lock across his cheek and cursed the aunt who said contrary.

Her head fell back and sunlight showered the curve of her throat. He moved his lips to the pulse leaping there, tasted the saltiness of her skin. He lifted her deerskin dress over her head, her breasts bathed in bright sunlight.

Joshua felt a jolt of surprise touched with a lusciously forbidden edge of a dream, for no woman had ever appeared so lovely to him. His hand trembled as he cupped it first over one breast and then the other. "Never hide yourself from me," he said huskily.

The satiny weight of her breast in his hand resurrected an alien and exotic sensation for a man accustomed to keeping himself numb to all feeling.

Beneath his palm, her nipple rose up proudly, and he bent his head, brushing his lips back and forth against the brazen tip, feeling the delicate, velvety texture. He felt her gasp of shocked delight against his mouth as her fingers dug convulsively into his shoulder, and she kissed him deeply, as if trying to return the pleasure he gave her.

Stunned by the tormenting sweetness of her response, Joshua lifted his mouth from hers, gazing down at her flushed, intoxicating face while he continued to caress her breast, telling himself that in a moment he would let her go.

Her back arched, and in the brilliant sunbeams she looked like a princess, lovely, delectable, irresistible. Desire burned white-hot at his core.

Slowly, Joshua took his hand from her swollen breast, commanding himself to end what he had begun and end it *now*. No doubt, tomorrow, he'd regret taking things this far with his in-name only wife.

His gaze drifted downward, riveted on the enticing banquet bared before him. Exquisite breasts, round and full, tipped with pink nipples hardened into tight buds of desire, quivered beneath his gaze. Her skin was as smooth as cream, glowing in the sun as untouched as new-fallen snow. And therein lay the problem. Juliet was untouched.

Yet he ignored the judgement that warned him, and the control he had schooled into himself. To bring a new power of Juliet to life, the power that had been slumbering for a lifetime: the bright passion, the sexual thirsting, the womanly appeal she had kept at a distance…until he had met her.

And with some half-formed idea of allowing them both a little more of the pleasure they seemed to be finding together, he bent his head, taking the bud of her breast into his mouth and whisked it with his tongue.

"Joshua?" Hands gripped his shoulders and pushed him back. "What are you…"

He exhaled, unable to speak; his throat aching.

She clasped his cheek. "It's—I don't know my own feelings… you make me feel things…but when we part, then what?"

"Not now," he said, not wanting to hear his own icy logic hurled back in his face. He dragged his gaze from her breasts to her lips and then to her mesmerizing eyes, while his hand rested on her hip. "I can give you pleasure without taking from you what can't be undone. Do you understand?"

"But how?" She touched her finger to his lower lip.

"I can teach your body to experience womanly desires without your loss of innocence. I *need* to touch you," he confessed.

All the days and weeks since he had met her had been building a tension between them, and it was time to release that strain. "I'm thinking of you, Juliet. There is one more night until you are returned to your cousin."

She widened her eyes. "Only one night?"

She accepted what he offered, his brave, sensual Juliet. She turned her head to kiss him, and she was so sweet and pliant that he erased his vow from his mind. Erased the war, erased the dangers of the frontier, erased what had brought them together and what would ultimately tear them apart.

For now, she was the woman in his arms, his Juliet, and he yielded to his impulse to provide her pleasure. His mouth began a slow, erotic seduction that soon had Juliet moaning low in her throat. He forced her lips to open wider until he captured her tongue, drawing it delicately into his mouth as if to sip from its nectar, and then he gave her his...until Juliet matched his movements and when she did the kiss went wild. His hands shoved into her hair, and Julie twined her arms around his neck, lost in the earth-shattering kiss.

His lower body lifted, his legs nudging hers apart, and he forced her into the vibrant awareness of his rigid desire taut beneath his buckskins. Her breasts pushed into his chest, and she stifled a cry when he pulled his mouth from hers, then gasping with surprise as he lowered his mouth to her breasts. His lips closed on her nipple, tugging gently, then tightening, drawing hard on it until her back arched and her legs stirred restlessly with that elusive hunger. He moved his hand lower, over her knee and sliding it over the soft firm flesh of her thigh, always laving her breast, while she ran fingers through his hair, and mindlessly held his head pressed to her.

She writhed and sighed, music to his ears. Right now, she was a woman who desperately wanted the sweet release he could give her.

He pressed her thighs apart and caressed damp, downy curls, the flesh there tender with her wanting. A smile tugged at his mouth, knowing he'd pushed her past maidenly inhibitions, beyond learned taboos, past caring about why she was here and what the future would hold, and possessing no idea where his touch would take her.

Oh, but he knew and he craved it for her. He pressed down the need of his throbbing cock, knew he was being selfish, ending her innocence to bring the dazzling silky path of erotic pleasure; to make her glorious sun set simply to rise again in a boundless instant of exquisite and intoxicating pleasure.

Slicked with her moisture, his fingers moved, knowing intuitively where to please her, manipulating the pressure and maintaining the slow rhythmic in and out motion of his finger and where to apply it. Drawn taut as a bow-string, quivering from his onslaught. Breathing hard, he watched her, luscious, sensual, gauging her response, and waiting for her rapture, his fingers stroking in time with her thrusts.

In that instant, he felt her thighs tremble, her belly shudder, and heard her keening cries as her hips rocked and her womanhood tightened in a convulsive movement, the heady perfume of her feminine essence washing over his hand. Letting out a breath, Joshua held her close, reveling in the feel of her as he cradled her yielding body with his. He dropped a soft kiss on her forehead, cherishing the rapid beat of her heart against his chest, and closing his eyes to the searing agony of self-denial.

"Joshua?" she asked, her voice filled with wonder yet tentative.

"Hmm?"

She took a deep breath. "Did you?"

He nudged his chin into her silky hair. "What do you think?"

She pulled her doeskin dress to cover her and nestled closer to him. Cradled above in the boughs of an oak came the rich and low song of an Indigo bunting called to its mate. "This is new...I had no idea. I believe you made love to me. But it seemed a bit...one-sided. Perhaps I should—"

"Oh, Juliet. What you have experienced is a sample of desire." He played idly with the beads on her dress, telling himself to quit touching her. That it could go no further.

"I am curious why a trained midwife did not know what occurred between a man and a woman."

"I have led a sheltered life, protected fiercely by Moira and not privy to intimacies. Do I—" He could see her holding her breath, waiting for him to declare his feelings, silently begging him not to hurt her.

"Juliet, I gave you a little taste of what it is meant to be a woman. The rest will be supplied by your real husband when you marry."

She turned to her side and stared straight into his eyes,

searching so deeply, he felt certain she could grasp the shaking soul he concealed beneath his sham veneer.

"I don't believe what you are saying. I know you have feelings for me."

He looked away, down the infinite river and beyond, anything to escape her accusatory gaze. *When I see you, I smile. When I touch you, I feel. I love you, Juliet.* "No, Juliet. You are wrong. I have a fondness for you, but do not mistake—"

She struck him on the chest, forcing his gaze back to hers. "Damn you. Damn you to hell a thousand times. You mislead the truth to cover—"

He thrust her aside and jumped to his feet. "You make much when this was a trifling undertaking."

"Trifling?" She sat up and drew her knees to her chest.

"Insignificant," he said, shifting and attempting not to scowl at the mocking throbbing in his loins. "Inconsequential."

She angled her head, glaring holes in him. "After what happened just now, I will never look at you again—at myself in anyway unaffected. You call that trifling?"

"Yes," he snapped. He snatched his sack and slung it with his powder horn over his shoulder. In truth, he wanted her so much that his blood was aflame. He was so hard that it created a burning pain in every nerve and fiber of his being. "You have to go to England. The frontier is no place for a woman. The vows we took were a means to an end. I have no interest in making the kind of promises you require."

"What is it you hide so neatly?"

His nostrils flared. "That is none of your affair."

Oh, it is my affair. After what we just did, I am owed an explanation."

"Damn you, *Lady* Faulkner. Damn you for seeking meaning where none was intended." He would not look at her as he stalked from the river, yet he slowed on the path until he perceived her behind him. He did not want to see her face, for he knew she would read the lies in his own.

She stepped on his heels, struck him on the shoulder. He pivoted and swore. She raised a hefty branch, her arc high, ready to do more damage. Before she struck him again, he ripped her weapon from her hands, and threw it against the trunk of an oak where it broke apart.

"There is a war going on in case you haven't noticed. I could not protect her. I cannot protect you."

Chapter 17

Back on the river, Juliet stared at Joshua's back as he paddled, each stroke deep and purposeful. There'd been a change in him. Now his eyes held neither hunger nor hostility when he looked at her. Those emotions had been replaced by a distant courtesy. She swallowed past an unexpected heat in her throat. He was living the memory of a deceased loved one.

Tears? Where did they come from? She wiped them away; committed not to shed one more. No sense wasting time thinking of a man who neither wanted her nor had a place in her life.

Yet deep in her heart, she grasped he had lied to her concerning his feelings. No man could bring a woman so close to the stars and feel nothing himself.

For three more hours, they traveled north on the Oswego River that pursued its way through rich, green and gently undulating country, until it reached a natural terrace from which it tumbled, and then glided to the deep water of the Great Lake of Ontario. High on a precipice, Fort Oswego loomed with ominous high stockade walls, guarding the mouth of the watercourse like Cerberus, the many headed hound, guarding the gates of Hell.

Juliet's heart raced. Would her cousin help her? Had he received her letter? Did he know anything of what happened to her? A cloud passed over, shadowing them and she craved the warmth of the sun to take away the chill of foreboding that grew in her.

Joshua hailed a sentry up on a parapet. She kept her attention fixed on her husband, helpless to stay the memory of that moment on the riverbank, helpless against a warm shudder of unforgettable pleasure. And her heart ached at his callous dismissal.

With no idea she observed him, Joshua had let down his guard, talking to the soldiers and explaining their presence. What she glimpsed was the ache of loss, possibly the deep contrition and sacredness of grief he embraced, tinged with winter hues of hopelessness. Oh, the somberness he concealed, keeping himself separate from others even when he stood in their midst. That great wall he'd built—impenetrable and unbreachable.

When the gates yawned open, they were bid to pass, and Juliet stepped through. Maybe that's what made her care for him, what compelled her to absolve him for his callous words. Not merely the fervor of his kisses, the tenderness of his caresses, the fiery ecstasy he had shown her. Those made her hunger for him. But the other virtues stirred her compassion—the challenge of his unhappiness, the aura of his remoteness.

The mystery of his secrets.

Under sneering eyes of onlookers, they followed an escort of soldiers with bright red coats, and off-white breeches. A white woman in an Indian dress? She, the poor creature, had been a victim of both white men and Indian's crimes, could imagine what they were speculating. Flung once again in a very moral society, its chin in the air, deciding with swift determination she was unacceptable, she leaned into Joshua, looped her hand on his arm. The tenseness of his muscles flexed beneath her fingers, brought a sense of security…and a wave of remembrance.

A dark lock of his hair fell over his brow, making him appear more wickedly handsome than she could bear. His mouth curved in a humorless smile. "Are you afraid?"

She caught his gaze then glanced away, lest he spot the havoc he had created in her soul. A parade of marching soldiers thumped past them, kicking up clouds of dust. "Very."

He patted her hand. "Where is the fearless Aphrodite who brandishes her candlestick, compelling mere mortals like Horace Hayes to tremble before her?"

Though he tried to make her smile, she could not. His desertion reared its ugly head, speeding her to that howling darkness of childhood, that constant, roaring state of loneliness, where neglect and abandonment were the landscape of her life.

Distantly, a hammer banged on an anvil, officers barked out orders, sentries strutted upon the parapets. None of these Juliet noticed as they passed by several barracks. Outside the commandant's office, they were greeted by a handsome officer.

"I am Captain Sunderland." He dipped an appreciative and curious glance over her, then motioned to Two Eagles wait in an anteroom with Mary.

Juliet stopped. "Joshua," she spoke his name quietly.

Startled, he looked away from the sentries at the door. For a second, pleasure flickered in his eyes, but then he fixed a polite expression on his face and gave a courteous nod. "My lady."

My lady. How formal he was. How cold and distant. As if he'd never hauled her from a river and kissed her. As if he had never lain with her on sweet grass and brought her to a state of wild completion.

With the use of her title, Captain Sunderland raised an eyebrow. The intimacy of the wilderness was no longer. Like an actress on a stage, she must be mindful of her audience.

Her cheeks heated. "I wanted to thank you again for rescuing me, Mr. Hansford."

"I merely helped my fellow countrymen."

"Of course." She searched his face for any sign of the man who had held her the day before. The man who had looked at her with his heart in his eyes.

Instead she saw a cold stranger. "Mr. Hansford, yesterday—"

"Is best forgotten." The muscles in his neck corded and his callous tone set the hairs on the back of her neck on end. He stared straight ahead waiting for the door to open. "You must trust the uncertainty of a new beginning."

She touched her throat. Parting with Joshua created a loneliness and a longing as great as an ocean.

The door swept open and her cousin stood blinking. "Lady Juliet! I did not believe the guard when he told it was you. How is it you are here?" His eyes narrowed, scanning over her from head to toe.

Joshua's entry was barred by a guard barely out of his nappies and who had pushed a bayonet across the doorway. Abandoning

Juliet did not put him in the mood for idle pleasantries. He gave the guard a deadly look that spoke the words as loudly as if he had said them, *"Keep clear."* How many seconds to skewer the pimple-faced guard with his bayonet?

Juliet glanced between her cousin and Joshua, then said, "Mr. Hansford is a trader and at peril to his own life has helped me to get to you."

Colonel Thomas Faulkner sat back, his pudgy hand smacked down on the carved lions on the arms of his chair and nodded.

Joshua smirked at the guard, pushed the bayonet away, and swaggered into the room behind Juliet. He didn't know who he disliked more, the British colonel or Captain Sunderland who stood to the side unable to take his smitten gaze from Juliet.

The colonel's lips twisted with revulsion upon Joshua whom he likely considered an unkempt colonial dressed in dirty deerskin.

"Are you looking for a reward for the return of my cousin?"

Joshua steeled his reserves, flexed his arm muscles. "My reward is knowing the lady is safe and with family. I'll be on my way in a few days and beg respite and practice of my commerce, if you will allow."

Years in the wilderness, years of drinking rum, had degraded Colonel Faulkner's face to the likeness of a tragic reproduction made of unleavened bread left out in the rain, bloated yet sodden, the features flaccid and blurred. The war and the colonel's time in the Colonies had not altered his hubris and, thankfully, he did not remember meeting Joshua in Boston.

The colonel lifted an eyebrow, sneering at Juliet in her doeskin dress. Apparently, he could not see past the tattered gown, the tangled hair, the smudges of dirt on her face.

"The lady remains untouched?" The colonel glared, his eyes like dried blueberries stuck in dough, each with a red rim as though reposing in a ringlet of bacon.

Juliet gasped.

The colonel wanted to know if she'd been raped by the Indians. Joshua clenched his hands, swallowed his need to punch the lout, and he plunged in before her buffoon of a cousin made an opinion and cast her aside. "I arrived in the village of the War Chief Onontio before any harm had befallen the lady and took great care to rush her to the safety of her *loving* family where her person and reputation would be respected, that is," Joshua dared, "if the family matches her innocence and her good character."

Joshua admired the way Juliet bore up under the humiliating disparagement of her cousin. Faulkner's scowl had taken down fiercer officers than a gently-bred girl, yet she met his stare with unwavering ferocity.

Captain Sunderland bowed to Juliet and glanced disapprovingly at his superior. "We thank you for the lady's safe deliverance and obvious good character. She has been through much difficulty and should be heralded for her courage."

"How is it you were in an Indian village in the first place, Lady Juliet?" asked the colonel. "Where had you been taken from?"

A muscle jerked in Joshua's jaw. The pompous bastard. Joshua gave a brief summary. She has been neglected by family who should have protected her. I assume you are honorable and will hold up to the task?"

The colonel narrowed his eyes. "You arrogant colonial. No one questions me about my honor."

Captain Sunderland interjected. "Rest and comforts will be provided to a subject of the Crown. May I recommend bringing her dresses from officers' wives who have returned to England, and a seamstress in the fort to make any adjustments—and, of course, our hospitality can be extended to the trader, right, Colonel?"

"Be my guest for a *few* days." The colonel glared at Joshua and pressed an airy hand through the air. "Make available to Lady Faulkner whatever she requires. Captain Sunderland, you may escort my cousin to a room and make comfortable the other lady." As an afterthought, he said, "Find whatever arrangement for the colonial that space allows."

Chapter 18

*D*espite the remote and primitive surroundings, everything spoke of royal munificence and splendor. The white linen shone around the burnished reflections of pewter and sparkling crystal wine glasses placed in precise arrangements along the table. From the suspended chandelier, candles had been lit against the late hour, and cast their yellow glows on an oily cracked portrait of the colonel. The gleaming patina of muskets and swords, dangling with menace on the wall. Since Joshua was in the belly of the beast, the collection of weapons might prove useful.

He drummed his fingers on his thigh, while waiting for Juliet, the guest of honor. Who seemed to be taking her time. He didn't know why he had accepted the dinner invitation, suffering the snobbery of his countryman. Perhaps it was a chance to see Juliet one last time that had prompted him, to make sure she was safe and would be well-cared for. He'd seen her only once since he'd escorted her to the fort and in the attendance of Captain Sunderland.

Two officers had attached themselves to him. A jaundiced-colored scarecrow of a sergeant, his temples deeply sunken as if a hammer had struck them and frail as a fledgling's belly continued to boast of his high intellect.

"Since you are a common colonial, you will profit from my greater experience and civilization," said one man at his side.

Joshua raised a brow. Wouldn't the sergeant be surprised to learn he was the third heir to the Dukedom of Rutland, an unbroken line for a thousand years, and was educated in the finest schools in England and could wipe the floor with him academically? "Enlighten my ignorant state."

"Did you know, a tea made from horse manure is an effective treatment of Pemphigus?" Joshua took another look at the sergeant whose hand rose to itch large pustules erupting on his face. Joshua took a step back. By the smell of his breath, the sergeant had imbibed liberal doses. Was the prescription more fatal than the cure?

A lieutenant flanked his other side. He had deep-set black eyes beneath bushy eyebrows that marvelously knitted together in the center of his forehead, and possessed a particularly annoying habit: hands moving constantly in competition with his conversation. He, too, was a self-proclaimed physician.

The lieutenant rolled up to the balls of his feet. "Did you know there is a treatment for difficult breathing and excessive spitting? One makes small pills of dried and powdered toad, and consumes the prescriptions until the convulsion fails."

Or until you breathed your last breath. Joshua diverted the delay to review his last two days of reconnaissance.

Fort Oswego projected a primary, two-story structure, loop-holed for musket fire and surrounded by a crenellated parapet which, in turn, was surrounded by a U-shaped stone wall and two integral blockhouses. Overall, it was an eight-pointed star-shaped fort, including a three-bastioned square fort and several four-bastioned forts, an irregular field fortification, three masked coastal batteries, a number of redoubts, retrenched batteries, and other minor works. Such fortification concentrations demonstrated outstanding tactical and strategic importance and a great link to the interior.

The fort was impassable and well-guarded, supplied by British ships across the lake from Canada and replenished with new recruits and regiments. The barracks were packed, even the officers' quarters were crammed, the commandant's quarters, the most lavish and spacious. Of particular note was the northwest bastion housing the munitions beneath. The fort would be a prize for General Washington to capture.

While his attention was focused on what the scarecrow sergeant was saying to him, a hushed murmur rose, growing into a crescendo. Everyone had shifted their gazes. Joshua glanced to his left. The lieutenant possessed the same sappy rapture as the rest of the men in the room. Turning his head, he looked for the source of everyone's interest…toward the doorway…and froze.

"Lady Juliet Faulkner," a soldier announced.

She entered the room like an immortal goddess, Aphrodite, granting divinity to miserable souls. The men stood at attention awed by her beauty and transformation, and so did Joshua.

Gone was her Indian doeskin dress, replaced by an emerald green gown made of stiff silk, the square neck cut low to enhance the deep valley of her swelling breasts, and edged with a fine white lace matching her long cuffs. The front of the dress was drawn back in the current fashion and well-served to show her tiny waist. Beneath flowed a finely embroidered petticoat that hid her shapely ankles. Her flaming red hair was pulled atop her head in an elegant style, leaving long ringlets that spiraled to her creamy white shoulders pinkened by the sun. A breathtaking vision of beauty and breeding.

Captured as every hale and lusty man in the room, he couldn't pull his gaze away. A knot of jealousy churned in his belly. How he wanted to wipe off the stares and ogling of every man.

"It is a lovely occasion to dine with you gentlemen this evening," Juliet said, her spell binding every man in the room with her radiance.

She laughed and said, "Where shall I sit?"

Her voice came as the most amorous sound he knew, more rousing than the rustle of silk on bare skin. She looked to him. But he could not move. No. He could not perform that role any more.

From her clamoring legion of admirers, Captain Sunderland raced to her side. No doubt, she'd find her favor in his handsome ceremonial dress, his pride, authority and rank displayed in the ornamental fringe sewed on his shoulder. He leaned into her, touching her hair.

"You are lovely as a rising sun," Sunderland said and she laughed at his remark.

Then he clasped her hand and brought it to his lips.

She lifted her chin, and her smile brightened. Joshua regarded the spectacle through a scarlet mist, and watched as she directed her courtesies from one male to another, always smiling and nodding.

"Where is Mistress Mary?" asked the colonel. He was not to be disregarded. Dressed in his full regalia, a bright red uniform with shiny gold buttons and dripping with gold epaulets lionizing his rank, and a testament to his soldier-valet to make him appear intact.

Juliet smiled, the kind of smile that wove spells and caused men to run upon hot coals. "Mary has the megrims and begged to stay in bed. She is still not fully recovered from her ordeal."

Joshua had seen Mary moving round the fort earlier in the day. He was not convinced.

"Good God," Faulkner ranted when his eyes beheld Joshua. "Who gave the cloddish colonial permission to sup with us?"

Officers cleared their throats, some shifted awkwardly looking over their shoulders.

"I did," said Captain Sunderland. "In appreciation for his heroic efforts in rescuing Lady Faulkner as I am sure you are so inclined with the gratitude we owe him."

Faulkner glowered. At the head of the table, he fluttered his flaccid fingers in unconcerned consent for Sunderland to sit opposite Juliet. Joshua gritted his teeth, his immediate contempt of Captain Sunderland filled him with loathing.

As an afterthought, the colonel signaled Joshua to the far end of the table next to the scarecrow sergeant, who smiled, making his cadaverous face seem thinner and longer.

To his other flank stood the lieutenant who performed his vocation wiping drool.

Colonel Faulkner was seated by his adjutant and the rest followed.

"Missives have come in across the lake? Any word of rebel attacks?" said the pox-faced scarecrow sergeant oblivious to his

190

breech. Joshua couldn't blame the man. Any news from home was prized.

The colonel flicked his eyes over his inferior's indiscretion. "My son will be coming for a visit."

"Edmund is coming?" Juliet's eyes shone. "When?"

"Any day now," said the colonel and his mouth tightened, his version of a sardonic smile. He shook out his napkin, leaned over the table to give a personal tone to the watchful eyes and said. "Of worthy note, War Chief Thayendanegea has sent strings of wampum to me."

Joshua tucked the information away. The woven shell beads signified a certificate of Thayendanegea's office, passing on the truth and importance of the message. The meaning was powerful and further declaration of the unification of the Iroquois in backing the British against the Patriots.

"As long as the sun shines upon the earth, as long as the water flows, as long as the grass grows, and as long as the Mother Earth is still in motion, the agreement shall be forever binding. Can't get any better assurances from the savages." The colonel laughed at his own joke, his tresses, powdered and glossed with flowery pomatum dusted the air. Joshua had read a tale of mice who ran up a man's back to eat the powder and pomatum off a man's hair.

"How will you deal with Washington if he dares to flounder into the wilderness with his troops?" Joshua goaded.

There was a faint trembling at the corners of the colonel's mouth followed by a flush of anger on his cheeks. "General Washington is a stupid, arrogant blunderer, trying to crush the proud spirit of a mighty people. He will fall beneath the boot heel of the empire."

Hubris hung in the air.

Joshua could remind him of the Patriot successes…Fort Ticonderoga, the retaking of Boston, Trenton, and Saratoga.

He said nothing, his attention caught by the expression on the captain's face. The man stared at Juliet, transfigured like a man in love or caught in a religious trance. Joshua's fingers gripped his flagon and if it were not metal might have broken.

The colonel hoisted his flagon, held it aloft where the lights shot beams of reflection off it. "As commander of Fort Oswego, I give a toast to my dear cousin, Juliet and to her safe return to civilization."

Joshua raised his flagon with the others, all eyes focused on the colonel. In the sudden stillness, the candlelight flickered by a breeze coming in the window and threw shadows across his flabby face.

There was an abortive movement of flagons toward mouths—stopped as the colonel lifted his flagon higher. "The die is cast. These inferior colonial traitors must submit, the criminal enterprise of their rebellion must be crushed. We cannot allow America to be ruled by the usurpers."

He threw back the contents of his flagon, and then slammed the vessel on the table to be refilled by an attentive soldier who stood against the side and doubled as a servant. The others at the table joined him.

At the colonel's nod, soldier-servants brought plates of food for the table. Succulent roast venison, crispy meat pies, baked beans with molasses, stuffed turkey, rounds of oatbread, even caviar taken from sturgeon of the Great Lake of Ontario.

"The gifts to the Indians are cultivating their favor," said

Joshua, leaning back in his chair—anything to feint a response from the colonel.

The colonel frowned as a bishop hearing a bawdy joke. "A mistaken philanthropy. The guns, knives, kettles, and food given them have created a never-ending demand for more. They have become lazy and do not hunt for their food or grow their corn. Like maggots they feast on their host."

Joshua lifted his hands, palms up. "But is it not a useful way to encourage an ally?"

There was a silence broken by the snuffling of a horse and the sharp song of a grackle strutting on the sill, a long-tailed version of an English blackbird, insolent and unconcerned.

"Whatever is necessary." The colonel's hard blue eyes peered across the table, as if studying his prey.

Necessary? Burning down the homes of innocent families and murdering them?

Joshua cultivated a pose of well-bred indifference and pinned his gaze on the colonel. "May I compliment you on securing the northern border and continuing the commerce of trading. No doubt your brilliant action will be recommended to His Majesty's favor," said Joshua, grudgingly politic and disgusted.

The colonel's conspiratorial grin seemed to spread over his body, and drawing in everyone to share the news. "Of course, greatness is an earned experience. For me, it appears to be consistent. I suppose it depends in part upon the myth-making creativity of humanity. The person who experiences greatness must have a feeling for the myth he is in. He must reflect what is thrust on him."

Joshua caught the exaggerated roll of Juliet's eyes before she pasted on a benign expression. "What are your reflections, dear cousin?"

All eyes turned upon her, and then to the colonel. No doubt, fired in her belly was the insult her cousin made to her upon arrival. Joshua's appraisal of Juliet raised another notch. The colonel had unwittingly released a cougar and the wildcat was setting her sharp claws into his arrogance.

The colonel waved to his servant to fill his glass with more wine. "My reflections? I bask in the knowledge people do not aspire to become extraordinary. Admittedly, happenstance and burning desire has made me extraordinary."

Juliet pressed her palm against her heart. "I remain overwhelmed, Cousin. To think fate has blessed you."

"With certainty." The colonel remained oblivious to her mockery.

She turned her attention to Sunderland. "Captain, how have you come to hold a military position in the Colonies?"

"I am the second son of Viscount Sunderland and serving His Majesty stretched before me. Of late, I have received word my older brother is quite ill and the doctors have said he will not make the summer." He looked at the colonel. "I will be returning to England as soon as possible."

Joshua tamped down a bark of laughter. So, he was to be a viscount. Joshua had gone to Oxford with the captain's older brother. Sad to hear he was ill. The Sunderlands were a wealthy and fine family. As the wife of a viscount, Juliet's status would increase. No wonder the colonel was pushing Juliet onto him. Faulkner himself would gain respectability by being a relative.

Joshua weighed the pros and cons. Sunderland was fair to

look upon. He overlooked her tragic history in the Colonies and would protect her from any spurning of his class. Juliet marrying Sunderland?

A vein throbbed in Joshua's neck. After seeing her bedecked in the alluring gown tonight, he decided he must encourage the relationship between Juliet and Sunderland. The frontier was no place for a woman of her stature. To make promises on his part would be selfish and too dangerous for her. She must be sent to live in England with all the refinements and good things life might afford her. Most importantly, she'd be protected, *safe*.

Joshua let the rum burn down his throat. Why was he not happy with the turn of events? He pictured her in fine silks and satins coming down the stairs at Belvior. His fantasy swung beneath the boughs of a great oak, on soft sweet grass to where he milked the essence of her feminine passion. More images emerged. Holding her naked in his arms and releasing a potent lovemaking this siren simmered with; her long hair loose and making a soft shawl over his shoulders, her breasts melting into him and a white leg flung over his thigh so that he did not know when his body ended and hers began.

She glanced at him, and she colored. Was it with the remembrance of what he did to her? He smiled. She straightened, quickly shifted her concentration to Sunderland.

A muscle ticked in his jaw. The gods were not inclined to let him be, leaving the red-haired witch to weave her enchantment.

No. Do not touch her again.

Juliet cleared her throat. "Captain Sunderland, have you read Locke or Spinoza?"

Like an overeager puppy, the captain was quite taken Juliet had singled him out. "I am acquainted with them, Lady Faulkner."

"Have you given any thought to the old idea where absolute authority is given to the King and his 'Divine Right' is an illusory power and will continually be in direct conflict to where men should be governed by officials they have chosen?"

The colonel pounded his fist on the table. The dinnerware jumped. "Such talk is treasonous and will not be heard."

Bestowing a demure expression on her cousin, she said, "I am only repeating the philosophers' claims. As Locke and Spinoza have purported, the age-old concepts of monarchy and aristocracy are to crack. The riveting tide sweeping across Europe will not be stopped."

Joshua's muscles tensed. *Hold your tongue,* Juliet. To argue with a man who likened himself to a heavenly body was useless. Yet he held her in secret admiration as she met her cousin's glare unflinchingly.

"Bah," Faulkner scoffed. "The promiscuous association between the classes must not once be tolerated. The nobility knows what is better for the lower classes and should rule over their ignorance."

Juliet pressed home her advantage. "What of Saratoga? The colonials won. Are not the Americans an example?"

"An accident. Rabble winning their rudderless war."

"There." She dabbed her linen napkin on her lip and glanced down the table. "For someone who usually has something usually to say, I'd say you are fairly quiet, Mr. Hansford. After living these years in the Colonies, do you have an opinion?"

Joshua inhaled. He avoided unwanted attention. He must not be suspect. Hanging existed the punishment of a spy. "If I may speak, Lady Juliet. Correcting legend is a very different and freakish pastime of making saints out of satyrs and satyrs out of saints, by which certain easy reputations have been won."

Juliet sniffed at his condescension. "I could point out your opinion could be viewed by both Patriot and Loyalists.

"Joshua is obviously loyal in his contention and his opinion is intelligent," the colonel said. "I agree with him. In time, the legend of General Washington will reveal the man's faults and frailties along with his mislead followers," said Colonel Faulkner, breathing heavily from the exertion of his speech.

Joshua smiled without mirth. "That is to flatter me beyond all I deserve."

"What does it mean that the French have entered the war?" Juliet asked.

An uneasy silence settled over the room. The yellow-faced scarecrow of a sergeant smacked his lips with Juliet's sacrilegious comment while the lieutenant gasped for air. The rest of the officers gave her a patronizing smirk.

The colonel brushed at a nonexistent piece of lint on his shoulder but his voice cut across the room like a whiplash. "Politics are not for your sex. Women are far too delicate."

The colonel used a roll to maneuver food on his plate to sop up the gravy. "Captain Sunderland, I think it would be gracious of you to invite my cousin for a tour of the fort, maybe even a picnic on the lake. She has gone through an ordeal, reducing her to feminine vapors. The exercise will help refresh rational thought."

Joshua shook his head to warn her to remain quiet. She tossed her head and sipped her wine. No doubt, it rolled sour over her tongue.

The colonel narrowed his eyes. "What do you think, Joshua? You have been with my…cousin."

Faulkner circled like a dog tormenting sheep, a master at casting doubt by endeavoring to entrap Joshua and besmirch Juliet. To place a well-aimed fist through the colonel's drooping face would satisfy immensely. The sooner he put Juliet out of harm's way the better. By Sunderland's veneration of her, she would live well with a devoted husband. The captain's fervor cemented Joshua's decision.

"Captain Sunderland, hosting a picnic for Lady Faulkner might be the thing to clarify her thoughts."

He didn't look at Juliet. He had to give up the greatest gift of his life. He'd stay with her forever if he could…wrapped in her arms. He dreamed his best when she slept with him, curling up to him close and dear. Sometimes he'd lie there watching her. She'd wake for the briefest moment, gaze at him, smile and go back to sleep…and he was home.

Maybe all that was a dream too. He was a man stuck with the nightmare of his Sarah Thacker. He didn't want to see the hurt or the fury in Juliet. He cursed. Never should he have touched her.

Whatever his feelings were toward Juliet he didn't not live up to the principles ingrained in him since birth—to protect those for whom he was responsible. His shameful neglect left him flawed and undeserving. If he'd been closer to Sarah, not left her alone and vulnerable, perhaps he might have prevented her death. And therein lay the problem…if he wasn't away at war.

Chapter 19

The next day, numb and emotionless, Juliet stopped beneath an alcove in the courtyard near the officers' quarters and pulled in her billowing skirts. How stiff and confining the dress felt compared to the soft doeskin. She placed her palm on the coarse hand-hewed log wall. Patches of splintery bark abraded her fingertips, and she shifted them across the cool rough chinking, still irked by Joshua's callous dismissal of her.

She watched him as he leaned indolently against the corner. A warm land breeze ruffled his dark hair and, for a moment the thick waves rippled as if tousled by the fingers of an invisible lover. How she yearned to run her fingers through his hair…to keep on touching him.

No. She couldn't afford to care or indulge herself in emotions that would lead to nowhere. Keep the relationship on an impersonal level. That was the best way to deal with matters.

Unaware of her presence, he stood alone looking up at the fort's parapets, the frontiersman whose fame and marksmanship garnered respect across the Colonies. How strange his observant activity. Things didn't add up. The questions he asked at dinner the evening before were carefully constructed. An offer in sympathy to the Loyalist cause? Or was it?

She tapped a finger on her lips. Was his friendly chatter and worthless information used to worm-out secrets under the guise of conversation? How his questions probed yet didn't probe and how he seemingly hung back in the shadows.

For encouraging Captain Sunderland, she took a step toward him to give him a piece of her mind, but stopped. Held herself back. Aphrodite, Joshua had called her, now that unfettered creature, imprisoned in a dark cell like a butterfly pinned under glass. It was pathetic, appalling—and she held thoughts of retaliation against the man who had reduced her to this dreadful feeling. He had made clear his intentions. Or had he? She saw how his eyes followed her during the dinner when he thought she wasn't looking. How his hands fisted and unfisted when other men paid attention.

A soldier came up to Joshua, bowed formally and addressed him, practically genuflecting. Why such reverence? Juliet did not hear what he had to say, but Joshua looked around worried. He placed his hand on the soldier's shoulder, and faintly she overheard him say, *"Keep quiet."*

Keep quiet? Regarding what? How peculiar.

Joshua stepped off the porch and joined Two Eagles where he had set up their furs amidst a knot of raw, uncouth traders, haggling over their pelts. She lifted her nose with the smell of them. How long had it been since they bathed? A month? A year?

A trader moved into a familiar bartering pose—shoulders hunched forward, hands held out, palms upward. Joshua shook his head and pushed the man's hand away. This was Joshua's means of support? This is what he lived for?

If she stayed with him, she'd live a life alone for many months in a log cabin while he was roaming the wilderness making a livelihood. Her musings scattered. Festering occurrences of the past tore open old wounds. She was alien, did not belong.

But wouldn't those seldom moments together yield a lifetime of happiness?

Joshua turned to the other dealers. "What price?"

A hatchet-faced trader crushed the brim on his hat in agitation. "I might go as high as four pounds for the whole lot."

Three pairs of eyes glinted their approval. The price was too low. The negotiating continued while Joshua pitched a higher price. The traders pitched a sigh which seemed to start in their boots.

"What a nice surprise, Lady Faulkner. Have you come to find me?"

Juliet turned sharply at Captain Sunderland's voice.

Young and handsome in his white wig and bright uniform with its polished brass buttons and bronze gorget, Captain Sunderland might have captured Juliet's fancy if she'd met him back in England. But now he seemed a mere boy compared to the big, brooding frontiersman.

At the sound of her name, Joshua looked up from what he was doing, his deep blue eyes flashed upon her, fierce and possessive. As if she were *his* property. Everyone followed his stare. A murmur of interest rippled through the fast-swelling crowd.

Recalling how Joshua had carelessly thrown her to Captain Sunderland the evening before, she smiled up at the captain, giving her full attention. Yes, she'd use her feminine wiles on the captain and seize the moment.

"Why-why, of course. You promised me a picnic and I wondered if now might be a good time." Juliet breathed a most captivating smile for Captain Sunderland's benefit, as if her approval were the most important mission he could attain in life.

Out of the corner of her eye, she glimpsed Joshua mutter a curse. A certain warmth radiated throughout her body that flirting with Captain Sunderland had produced.

But the effect lasted only a second. She tore her gaze from the captain's. Her heart clenched. *Oh, Joshua, it is as if I've known you all my life, and when I'm with you, I don't have to pretend to be anyone or anything.*

She knew Joshua Hansford.

Pushed behind a wall of painful emotions, trapped in the swirling waters of his subconscious, existed a fear of feeling…and being vulnerable.

Her heart ached for the highly intelligent frontiersman who was unable to see how his life made him into an island… untouched and…isolated.

He did not fool her. Not for one moment. He wanted to break free of that prison, thirsted for human contact. Teaching him to dip his toe into humanity's tumult was good for him…and she would teach him. Her maneuverings would be painful but would serve to annoy him enough to bring him to the light. Time was what she demanded.

Captain Sunderland held up his arm and she threaded her hand through it. "I'm on duty but have a few minutes to chat if you would do me the honor."

"That would be wonderful, Captain." She sashayed perfectly, having Joshua's attention.

Lost in her thoughts, she heard Captain Sunderland say something and nodded, not really hearing what he'd said.

"Then you will accompany me home to England?"

He looked surprised she had accepted and there was more depth in his meaning than she wanted to plumb at the moment. Captain Sunderland was gallant and handsome and would make any girl swoon. She liked him but not in the way he desired. "I-I can't surely say. Tell me of your ancestors."

Impressively, he went on, the entire lineage, back to Caesar's invasion of England, none of which she paid attention to as they circled the grounds, and then back to the bartering.

One trader shot forward, shaking his fist in Joshua's face. "You are a son of a whore to demand such price."

"I assure you my birthright is legitimate and should deck you for your disrespect. My furs are of excellent quality and will bring high profits in Albany."

Two Eagles stepped between them.

She said loudly, "This haggling is like two cockerels fluffing their feathers and shaking their wattles yet knowing they would not fight."

He stiffened from her insult, and then followed Two Eagles' gaze to where the doors of the fort opened. A well-dressed man entered.

Joshua left the traders, walked to the boardwalk where she and the captain stood and made an exaggerated bow. "Captain Sunderland, Lady Faulkner. I'll be leaving tomorrow."

Chapter 20

Leaving. Her stomach plummeted.

Juliet followed the scarlet-coated soldier to her cousin's office, irked by his haughty summons when she wanted to be alone in her room. How could her heart still be beating when surely it must be shattered to pieces?

Had Joshua left without saying farewell? Had he walked out of her life? To not see him ever again? She wiped her eyes, willing away a fresh wave of tears.

What did her cousin want and at a time like this? Where was Mary?

The door opened, and her jaw dropped. "Edmund!" She darted around the soldier and fell into her cousin's arms. "Is it truly you? I'm not dreaming?" She held him in a death-grip, refusing to let go and he swung her around.

"Fit as I'll ever be, Juliet. I've missed you."

His father harrumphed and nodded to the soldiers to leave. "Put Juliet down, Edmund. Such display of emotion is improper. You both forget your places."

Edmund pushed her at arm's length. "You are the last person I expected to see here. How are you here?"

"A long story but you are here and there will be time to share. You look wonderful. The years have been kind to you, Edmund."

The only relative who was ever considerate of her frowned. Conflicting shadows flashed across his face. She pressed her hand to her chest. A glimpse of that haunted look she'd seen in him as a child. What plagued her dearest, sweetest cousin?

"I see you have filled out from the scraggly, skinny boy I knew. If my sum is correct, you are at eight and twenty years. You are truly handsome and I'm sure, capable of causing any girl's heart to flutter." Juliet laughed and pulled him down on a chair next to hers. He'd grown tall and filled out his tailored breeches and frockcoat, so out of place on the frontier.

She raised her gaze up to his face and, looking at him, an odd familiarity struck her. How much he looked like someone she knew. How similar…almost identical…he bore an uncanny resemblance to Two Eagles.

"And you have grown into a fine young lady. We have so much to catch up on."

She could not take her eyes away from his face. The same angle to the jaw, high cheekbones, dark hair, dark eyes, alert. From head to toe, she examined him. Same broad shoulders, same build. Edmund's skin was lighter, his clothes English. Dressed in a breechclout the differences might be nonexistent.

Were their similarities a freak of nature? Was it possible that a cookie-cutter version of two people living on opposite ends of the world existed?

She shook her head, stopping her bizarre thoughts. No. It could not be. Impossible. Her mind was playing tricks.

"Edmund has recently graduated from Oxford as a barrister. I wanted him to remain home and begin his practice. You can imagine my surprise when I received his letter from Montreal and he was on his way," said Colonel Faulkner, his censorial tone severe.

"For some godforsaken reason, Father, I wanted to see this new world that beckoned me and kept you away from me for so many years. If I remember correctly, you've been home for only two weeks of my life."

The colonel clapped his hand on his son's shoulder. "It is good having you here, Edmund."

Juliet's heart swelled. It was the first time she'd seen the taciturn Colonel Faulkner show any kind of affection. He loved his son.

"You will have to suffer my company," Edmund said, looking to his father and smiling.

"Never will I suffer your company, Edmund." His voice hoarse, the colonel straightened his coat and returned to his chair behind his desk. "I've important dispatches to prepare to send on the ship you arrived on. We will have dinner this evening."

"Like true soldiers, we are dismissed," laughed Edmund rising and taking Juliet's hand. "Dear cousin, I will enjoy your company."

They moved inside the fort, passing the kitchens with meats roasting on a spit and the scent of warm bread drifting from the ovens. Sentries changed guards from their boxes atop the parapets. Curious onlookers took their fill of the two unusual newcomers.

"They are looking at you, Juliet. You were lovely as a child, but have grown into a stunning woman."

Juliet glanced at him again shocked by the similarities to her Indian friend. They strolled along a boardwalk to where Mary stood. She wanted her friend's opinion. "I want you to meet someone."

Mary turned and gasped. "Where did you get those clothes?"

Edmund glanced to Juliet, questions in his eyes.

"This is my cousin, Edmund, and this is Mary. You two never had the opportunity to make acquaintance in England."

Mary gaped.

"He has just arrived. What do you think, Mary?"

Mary's hand flew to her chest. "He is an exact replica. How can this be?"

Edmund narrowed his gaze, drew his hand up to his chin. "What are you up to, Juliet?"

Mary stared at Edmund in wonder and amazement.

Juliet swung her cousin around to face her. "Did you ever think of the possibility there could be someone who is similar to you in every detail?"

"You are talking riddles," Edmund said. "What are you talking about?"

"We must introduce them," Mary said.

"Introduce whom?"

Skin tingling, Juliet said, "Two Eagles. He is an Oneida Indian, part of the powerful Iroquois…" She looked Edmund in the eyes. "And an exact duplicate of you."

He snorted a laugh in dismissal. "You ladies are being silly, and I'm rather tired and prefer not to meet any savages."

Juliet tilted her head back. Oh, they may look alike, but there was a huge difference—Edmund's prejudice sizzled like acid in his condescending tone, bigotry stamped into him; inevitably bred from birth. "But you must. The resemblances are—"

He scratched his jaw, a chin relatively smooth, absent of facial hair just like the Indians.

"I am going to rest. Perhaps later you can show me this savage." He strode away, kicking up puffs of dust from his heels, leaving a dazed Juliet and Mary on the boardwalk.

Juliet pulled Mary away from two soldiers who seemed to linger. "I'm thinking about staying in America. I want to fight for my marriage, I haven't figured a way as yet, but I'm determined."

Chapter 21

$\mathscr{J}$oshua opened the door to his room, his eyes adjusted to the dim interior. He was not alone. He yanked a knife from his belt alert to an intruder.

"Joshua, I…"

He pressed the door closed. "Juliet, what are you doing here? We cannot meet anymore."

"You can't mean—"

"Shh." He stuck the blade back in the sheath. All of Joshua's instincts shouted to send her away, back to England where she belonged. "Your security is sealed with your cousin. If he finds you in here with me, he'll assume the foulest of conclusions. I'll be hanged and, worse, your reputation will be ruined."

"But the vows—"

He hungered for Juliet—and her alone. He had spent the past years teaching himself not to feel, and now in just a few short months Juliet had brought every bit back to him—the savage joy, the sweet torment, the lust, and the heat. "Our vows no longer exist. It was a ruse and one I at no time agreed to hold you to."

She said nothing and a long silence hung in the air, shattered by the sorrowful song of a whippoorwill.

Then he looked at her.

She searched his face, her pupils large, her eyes moist. God, it killed him to send her away like this. Then her tears released to fall on her cheeks.

His heart aching, he simply stared at her, the moonlight illuminating her beautiful tear-streaked face. He could lift her skirts, feel her feminine softness, let her warm musk pour over his hands. The bed yawned behind him. He could lay her down...kiss away her tears and release the throbbing ache in his loins...make her his. Spirit her away in the wilderness. She was his wife, after all.

She lifted her chin, brushed at her cheeks with her sleeve. "I suppose I have peculiarities that find your lack of advantages to be a major part of your charm. Each and every time, I was the one drawn to the lame cat or runt pig of the litter."

He deserved that, but it didn't take away the sting. "Your maidenhood is intact. No one need know anything passed between us. With encouragement on your part Captain Sunderland will provide you a good life. He has a fine pedigree. You will be coddled in England...a fine house...a perfect life."

"I don't want—"

He clamped both hands on her wrists. Perhaps too tight. "It is no concern to me what you want. You will be cherished and most importantly...protected."

Footsteps echoed down the hall. They stood like characters caught in an artist's mural rooted in the moonlight's dreamlike haze; time spinning by on flying wings. He had a sudden keen awareness of her lavender scent mixed with the woodsy smell of pine logs. And from the window, he felt the gentle breeze caress his face. It was as if they stood alone in the palm of the world, as if the beauty of the night existed only for them.

The world closed in on him, and he realized it was because he still held her wrists, his thumb moving in lazy circles across her skin. Outside a cloud passed, making a giant blur of the moon, like a distant lantern seen through threadbare curtains. The cloud was moving slightly to the northwest, and would soon disappear. She leaned into him, but he held her at a distance.

What a world of anguish and longing he saw in the glistening blue depths of her eyes. He thought of the slight melodious quality of her voice. He thought of her pealing laughter when she had pushed him in the river. He thought of her slim white thighs and pert breasts upon him, and the delightful moans when he had carried her to pleasure.

"It galls me how you can stand pious enough to make the decision for the both of us." She glared at him. "Why did you tell that soldier to keep quiet? Who is he? What are you hiding?"

He dropped her wrists. She must have listened to his conversation with John, his father's former tenant at Belvoir Castle. He had told John to keep secret his true identity. How much had she heard? "Do not allow your pretty head to mull on minor things that don't concern you."

"I could search him out. Ask questions—"

He took a step, towered over her. "That man wanted some furs for his wife, is all. Is it not right for a man to have a private discussion?"

"Perhaps you are a spy and are gathering secrets?"

A muscle flexed in his jaw. "You are a woman of the senses. I meant nothing by it. It is over. There is nothing between us."

"The lie rolls off your tongue slicker than water off a millwheel."

He lifted his hand to touch her but withdrew. "I made a mistake. I should have kept my urges in check. I will see to it our marriage is annulled."

Her voice trembled. "What made you forget what we shared?"

What could he give her? Death and destruction on a frontier amidst the pulse of revolution? An insecure future?

He could have none of it. He could not have Juliet, for his life was governed by dread. A bleeding, scheming dread that possessed a life of its own; in moments, it could render him powerless, infecting his body like poison.

He lived in hell. Loving Juliet would doom her to the same fate.

He had to let her go.

"We should have taken care not to complicate the problem. You're an appealing woman. It would be so easy to—" He compressed his lips in a grim line and glanced at the bed.

"Easy to what?"

"Easy to roll you like a whore. There is nothing lacking in your shameless offerings."

She drew up a hand to slap him but stopped. "Oh how you want me to hate you." Her voice softened. "What are you afraid of, Joshua?"

"Afraid? Your notion is laughable."

"You are afraid. You do want me."

"You have invented a far-fetched feminine whim." He stepped back, but she grabbed him to face her.

"Your façade is growing thin. I will not allow you to leave without me. I'll make sure of it."

She'd be happy as Lady Sunderland, the toast of society, fine clothes, bedecked in jewels, servants aplenty. Then why did acid bile rise in his throat at the thought?

"I see," she said at last. "Captain Sunderland is more of a man than you will ever be. Even his kisses—"

There was nothing more Joshua wanted to do but kiss her to teach her a lesson for taunting him. His body heated like wildfire as her soft curves melted into him. Hungrily his mouth covered hers, his tongue tracing the contours of her sweet mouth.

Her hands slid up his arms and linked around his neck, her fingers winding in the tendrils of his hair at his nap. Aroused now, he lowered one hand to the small of her back and kissed his way down her smooth throat, following the elegant curve to her collarbone, right where the edge of her gown met skin. He nudged it down, tasting one new inch of her, exploring the soft, salty sweetness, and shuddering with pleasure when he cupped the rounded swell of her breast with his hand, feeling her nipple under his touch.

God, he wanted her.

He took her mouth again and the minute she moaned, he thrust his tongue deeper to wield her passion. He breathed her, tasted the heady wine on her lips, and savored her. His mouth twisting, bruising, rousing, his tongue plunging through her like a brand, searing her, having her. The kiss was more than merely bending her to his will. He wanted total possession and to punish her for making him desire her.

He clasped the soft flesh of her bottom and pulled her against him, making her aware of his arousal. She pressed her soft body into him, driving him insane with need. He stood on the precipice of desire. Any longer and they'd both be lost.

Somehow, he managed to push her away, his breath bursting from him in ragged blows. "Does Sunderland kiss you that way?"

He opened the door, looked both ways.

"And what of me?" she hissed. "Isolation your master. Is that my punishment because you choose to wallow in mourning, personifying honor and duty to a woman who no longer exists? Oh, how you will wander around with your mantle of invisibility. Like a speck of dust floating in the air that will never be seen because it prevails to hide in darkness."

She twisted free and stumbled out into the hallway.

The door snapped shut behind her, the curtains rustled and stilled, and the room went quiet. He leaned his palms against the hard rough plank of the door as her steps faded away.

Juliet. Sweet, beautiful Juliet who'd captured his heart...and his soul. And he'd never see her again.

Chapter 22

A sergeant ushered Joshua into the colonel's office where Faulkner stood with his hands clasped behind his back. His pretense of calmness did not fool, Joshua. The colonel was tense. Warning bells clanged in Joshua's head.

"Meet Captain Snapes. He has shared some interesting information with me."

Joshua raised an eyebrow at the British captain sitting in the corner. The man who had incited Onontio's attack on the Hayes' household. Nothing to recommend...bulging cheeks, sloping chin, piggish mouth.

Yet his pig-like eyes flicked with keen interest, analytical, disciplined and something else he assigned to grasp—fanatical. Joshua's gut sunk with a leaden feeling. Had someone seen Juliet leave his quarters the night before?

Legs planted wide, the colonel said, "He has seen you going in and out of General Horatio Gates' tent at Saratoga. Guards, put him in irons."

As the guards fell on him, Joshua roared an awful warrior's cry, hoping to alert Two Eagles. He punched one guard in the nose, heard bones crunch, soaking him in a shower of blood. Joshua broke free and swerved his elbow into another guard's windpipe. The guard convulsed and fell back. The rest backed off. Not surprising. These were not seasoned frontiersmen.

The opened door was ten feet behind. Ten steps to freedom. Out the window, over the roof, a leap to the parapet and over. Once in the woods, they'd never find him.

Two guards down, six to go. Just as their bodies crashed together, Joshua grasped one flailing arm and broke it in two. He stopped and hit the next guard with a colossal right that came all the way up from his planted feet, and felt his fist drive right through and beyond. From his sinking body weight, he whipped his head from under his moving hand, allowing the momentum to carry him onward, shoulder first into the man behind him.

He booted a guard between the legs, and the man's head wrenched downward at the same time Joshua's elbow sailed upward, doubling the power of the blow. He targeted another savage blow at the head of another soldier, shattering his jaw with a high cracking sound.

He glanced at Snapes and Faulkner cowering together. Joshua danced, too shrewd to allow more to get behind him. He jerked his elbow, fracturing a man's ribs, the hammering force hurtling his assailant through a glass bookcase. Leaping to one side and then to another, Joshua outpaced them, owing his supremacy to his hard-bitten experience as a boxer.

"Guards!" Faulkner screamed out, and from nowhere, more guards piled in the office and fell on Joshua.

Before he could wrench free again, ten men seized him and

wrestled him to the floor, one of them giving him a short, hard jab in the stomach, and as he doubled over, another brought his fist down on the back of his neck. Joshua crumpled to the floor, his breath coming in short, painful gasps while the guards handcuffed, and then shackled to his legs, a two-foot metal bar to which a thirty-pound weight was attached. They stood him up, eye level with Faulkner who watched with a deep gratifying smile.

"There is a mistake. It must have been someone else," protested Joshua.

Joshua did not flinch when the colonel struck him.

"The main mistake was allowing an infiltrator under my nose performing firsthand exploration for days. Are you shallow of mind to forget your resistance speaks volumes?"

The colonel dropped in his chair behind his desk and steepled his fingers, examining Joshua like a rare insect. "You used my cousin, didn't you?"

A chill touched the base of his spine. His question implicated Juliet by association. She would be taken prisoner or hanged.

"I'm waiting, Mr. Hansford."

By acknowledging her innocence, he signed his own death sentence. "Yes. She was easy prey. She had told me she was related to you. When I saw her taken prisoner by Onontio, I used her desperate circumstances as an opportunity to gain entry to the fort to scrutinize your defenses."

Faulkner slammed his hand down with such force that it sounded like a gunshot and startled his aide so badly, he pinched his fingers in the desk drawer. "Get the Indian he came here with."

Joshua swore beneath his breath. Now Two Eagles was incriminated. Had his friend heard his warning?

Snapes chuckled and Joshua whipped his head to the captain who smirked. Nerves rattled down his spine. Had he met the pompous bastard before? No. He'd remember the closely spaced eyes—chips of glass, cold and lacking human quality. Was the captain's enmity more personal than the issue of spying?

"You cannot trust Snapes' word. He incited the Indian attack on Horace Hayes, a loyal subject to the King."

"He is a liar," sneered Snapes. "Rumors abound, it was you who led the attack with the Oneidas."

The colonel uncorked a bottle of ink.

"How crafty your manipulations, Mr. Hansford. I've found liars always the hottest to defend their veracity." He sharpened a fresh quill, took an empty page from his drawer. Slowly, he dipped his quill pen and in a furious but clear hand began to write.

Joshua hated using his only recourse, shaming his family. Damn his pride, he'd do anything to outmaneuver the orders signing his and Two Eagles' deaths. He had to do something to stall for time in the hopes of escape.

"I'm Lord Joshua Rutland. My father is a very powerful duke and is cousin to the King."

Faulkner stopped writing. "You Patriots will stop at nothing, lying to save your neck."

"Sir!" said Joshua haughtily. With heavy chains, and aching ribs, he drew himself up stiff as well as he could, befitting the part of the gentry whose word was being impugned. "I am the third inheritor of the Duke of Rutland, Baron Manners of Haddon and the Marquess of Granby. My father serves in the House of Lords. The Duke of Bedford, of St. Albans and York can vouch for me."

"Once a liar, always a liar. A Patriot born and bred. Do not fall victim to his contrivances," goaded Snapes.

Faulkner's eyes bulged. "Damn you. Have you ever heard of anything so fantastic? You will swing from the gallows as a spy."

It was done. There was nothing he could do to reverse events. The price he paid as a spy. "We will win this war."

The colonel blew on the paper to dry the ink. "While hanging from the gallows with the crows pecking your carcass, tell me of your Patriot successes then. Take him away."

Pushed, Joshua tumbled to the bottom of the stairs, the thirty-pound weight cutting into his ankles.

Mary came around the corner. "Dear God." She knelt next to him, put her hand on Joshua's shoulder, and then gave a scathing look at the guards. "Why is he treated like this? He has saved my life."

"Get moving, colonial swine!" said the scarecrow sergeant with the tip of his bayonet.

Another soldier kicked him. Joshua raised his fists and the rest kept their distance.

"He is the worst kind—a traitor and spy who used you to enter the fort for his nefarious deeds," spat the sergeant.

Mary's eyes widened. "A spy?"

Chains clinking, Joshua leaned on her to rise and in a breathless voice, whispered, "Warn Two Eagles."

"It is too late. They have taken him prisoner."

Chapter 23

*D*isaster clutched Juliet in its hideous dark claws…the icy breath of the gallows primed to inflict its gruesome vocation. She had to save him. He had saved her life and she owed him.

Her skirts swishing about her ankles, Juliet hustled into Colonel Faulkner's office. "You must stop the hanging."

His beady eyes glittered with the prospect of the execution. "I have been informed he is a spy and will hang for his crimes."

"That's ludicrous. I demand to know who would say such a thing."

"You don't demand anything, Juliet, but I will allow this one-time concession, and on good authority, Captain Milburn Snapes."

"Snapes is here?" She looked behind her, and then returned her gaze to her cousin. "His word is not to be trusted. He assaulted me, and led the attack on the Hayes' by Onontio. He is the traitor and should be hanged for his crimes."

Faulkner pulled up, squared his shoulders. His mouth flattened. "He is a respected officer of the Crown." He narrowed his eyes at her. "Interesting your rabid defense of the traitor.

220

Perhaps you are not as innocent as the rebel rascal said you were?"

Juliet practically laughed in his face. "After everything I've been through…now you accuse me of spying? Snapes is a liar and a monster. For you to believe the man is reprehensible."

"Anymore given to female hysterics, Juliet and your character and motivation will be readdressed. You are dismissed."

Teeth grinding, Juliet stalked to the door. "I am not one of your soldiers."

Juliet drew a breath, fought to think of a way out of this madness. She caught up with Mary, and with a knowing nod of the head, approached Edmund who stood in the center of the parade grounds watching drills. He blinked in surprise when both women flanked him, took arm in arm and steered through the inner yards. Beneath the shadow of the scaffolds, Juliet's stomach clenched, the macabre vision of Joshua swinging from the gallows appearing before her eyes.

Her heart hammering in her throat, Juliet peered up to her cousin, a half-formed plan spinning in her mind. "If you don't come with me now, you will be filled with regret. You must meet Two Eagles."

"I know what you are up to, Juliet, and I'm not going to interfere with my father's orders. Besides, you are talking of an untamed wild Indian. Why should I care?"

"Edmund, you must listen to me. I believe Two Eagles is your brother."

That stopped him. "Impossible. How could I be related to a savage? The idea is beneath me to even consider. Why are you saying such a thing?"

She placed shaky palms on the sides of his face. "No one is born hating another person because of the color of his skin, or his background. People learn to hate. Ignorance and narrow-mindedness are the handmaidens of intolerance. You must rise above the scorn and use your power to stop this atrocity."

Edmund, as tall as Two Eagles, stared down at her. "Just this one indulgence, Juliet, and then you must promise me to distance yourself from the frontiersman and the savage. There is talk—"

She grabbed his hand and dragged him to the stone house prison. Black clouds sprawled across the sky, billowing in from the north. The brassy glare drained color from the buildings, the walls and trees, tinting everything bronze in the faltering light.

Guards stood in front of the heavy oak door. Her chin held high, she postured with the haughtiness of the highborn, expecting to kindle a sense of inferiority in the sentries. "Edmund is the colonel's son and is on business here for his father. Let us pass."

The guards immediately stepped aside.

Edmund hissed, "If my father hears of this—"

"Worry later."

Keys jangling, the door swept wide, her eyes adjusted to the darkened interior of a small building cordoned off into two parts that included a barred cell. Juliet lifted her nose, the cell smelled of male sweat equaling the stench of ten privies. Joshua and Two Eagles rose from the filthy straw-strewn floor, dust motes floated through the air. Her throat closed up and her heart wrenched at the sight of Joshua weighed down with heavy chains and squinting at her though swollen eyelids.

With all the ferocity of a summer squall, Joshua rasped, "Juliet, you should not have come here."

She reached for Joshua's hand, warm and comforting and alive, heard Mary's gasp when she noticed Two Eagles' condition. He had been beaten as bad as Joshua. Edmund moved beside Mary. Juliet darted glances between the two men. Who was stunned more...Two Eagles or Edmund?

"Look and see the similarities," Juliet said, deeply moved by what was taking place. "Tell me it isn't so."

Edmund's mouth hung open, apparently dumbstruck by the physical likeness. He raised his hand, held it suspended. "My whole life, I've felt as if something was missing in me. I felt a void...yet I knew there was something else. But I had no idea what. It was like a sixth sense that felt a part of me was missing."

Two Eagles pushed his hand through the bars, clasped Edmund's. "I had dreams—of someone like me. Now I know it was you."

Edmund shook his head. "My dreams...you were there. I couldn't touch you and I thought it was just my wishful thinking for someone to fill the void. But those dreams helped me through the difficult times—"

"I suffered your pain," said Two Eagles. "You are home now. You can meet our mother."

"My mother? She is an Indian?" Edmund slowly released a deep breath.

Juliet's mouth went dry as ashes. Would his prejudice hold against his natural mother?

"Edmund," she spoke sharply, "you have been taught to hate. If you can learn to hate, you can be taught to love, for love comes more naturally to the human heart than its opposite."

"I know our mother will love you," said Two Eagles.

"Love me?" Edmund's voice choked.

Two Eagles gripped his hand tighter. "Like me, she has always somehow known you were alive even though she was told otherwise. She has always loved you."

Edmund set his jaw, his gaze wandering over Two Eagles' face, a face identical to his own. Finally, he said, his voice soft, "I feel you are my brother, Two Eagles. The connection is impossible to explain. I will do everything in my power to get you out of here. I don't know how, yet, but I will succeed." He eyes lit. Oh yes. I must meet my mother. I *need* to meet her." He turned. "Juliet, come with me." Edmund whipped open the door.

Through the bars, Joshua still held her hand, his breath warm upon her cheek. "I cannot bear being parted from you," she said, "but I've so much to do to try and stop the hanging, and if not, work somehow to help you escape. I know you have been accused as a spy and by that foul Snapes. I tried to tell my cousin the truth of him. He will not listen."

His fingers threaded through hers, and she drank in the feel of him.

She raised her head and he met her lips in a searing, demanding kiss.

"Do not get involved, Juliet," Joshua warned her.

"I'm already involved. I am your wife."

Chapter 24

$\mathcal{J}$uliet followed Edmund as he burst into his father's office, soldiers stumbling and murmuring apologies to their commander for allowing him to enter unannounced.

"Father," Edmund said, his voice deep and edged with deadly calm. I have come from the jail. There is an Indian...a mirror image of me. I demand an explanation and I want it now."

In an instant, Edmund loped to his father's desk and for a moment, she though he might jump over it to reach his father. But he stopped short, his thighs touching the wood, his hands clenching. Juliet glanced from man to the other.

Faulkner raised a flaccid hand and waved off his soldiers, waiting until the door clicked shut. "You've not been invited into my office, Edmund," said Faulkner, his expression passive...as uninterested in Edmund as he was in the half-eaten breakfast on his massive desk. He shoved aside the pewter plate. Studied his fingernails.

A tick vibrated in Edmund's jaw, his body rigid, as if holding back a rage so great it might explode if he allowed it. This was a side she had not once witnessed in her cousin before.

The air grew heavy and the humidity pressed down. The wool of her gown chafed and sweated against her breasts. A stillness fell over the office, and in the silence, came a low crackle of thunder, rolling across the rooftops.

"I'm not waiting for an invite. I want an answer."

The colonel stood, his chair scraped across the floor, smacked the wall behind him. "You are tired, and your mind is playing tricks on you."

"He is my brother. Do not deny it."

It was the first time Juliet had seen the colonel speechless. With his hands behind his back, Faulkner sauntered to the window, looked out, seemingly lost in thought.

The ominous clouds that had threatened crept in quickly. The atmosphere lay suffocating. The scent of rain wound dark and heady. Even the wind held its breath. A streak of hot silver split the sky and a downpour began.

Huge heavy raindrops pattered on the roof, then the wind picked up, slashing the rain against the windows and muddying the yard below, the storm spilling its wrath upon the earth.

"You are right, Edmund. I am not your real father although Emmaline and I are your parents in every sense of the word.

"Your mother was weak with the loss of several babes. I loved her. I had to bring her back from the madness taking hold of her. She delivered another stillborn and the doctor dosed her with laudanum. I dreaded her awakening to find she had lost another babe.

"To clear my head, I took a ride in the forests. I happened to come by an Oneida Indian woman who had given birth in the woods. As was their custom, they delivered babies away from the village.

"You were born on the cold ground from a savage woman. There were twins. One was dark and the other, peculiarly light. The savage woman lay unconscious from her ordeal. I rode back to the fort, took my dead child and replaced it with the whiter baby of the Indian woman's twins. I figured she had a son left to her, and my Emmaline would have a son."

Edmund rubbed the back of his neck. "All my life, I've known. I can't describe it...couldn't touch it...couldn't feel it, yet something tangible was there."

The colonel pivoted. "Stop your theatrics at once. You are not a savage."

Edmund stilled, a low hum of fury escaped his lips. He slammed his fist on the desk. The dishes, ink bottle and quill jumped. "You stole me from my mother?"

"It was a decision I made for you and your mother's benefit."

"You are confused, Father. Emmaline is not my real mother."

"How can you say that? She gave you great love. You were educated and given every advantage of a gentleman."

"I was denied my real mother and brother. And whatever your thoughts are of Emmaline, she was mad. The things she did to me. As a child, she locked me a dark closet for days, starving me, laughing when I begged her to let me out. How she lived to mock and ridicule me and make me cry because it was titillating for her."

Edmund tore his shirt from his waistband, lifted his shirt. Raised white leathery scars rioted across his back. Nausea rolled in Juliet's stomach and she turned away, her heart aching for her cousin. She thought back to when they were children. No wonder he wanted to hide in the garden with her. He was afraid of his mother.

"When the servants were not around, Mother tied me to the bed and burned me with a poker, and then threatened to kill me if I told anyone. I suffered in silence. The nanny had seen the burns and did her best to protect me from Emmaline, and wrote to you suggesting boarding school."

Outside, a dark, dense gray cloud cast them in a premature twilight, but inside it was darker, almost black. Though he did not move a muscle, the colonel turned pale. Juliet stood close enough to see the pulse leap at his temple. "I never knew—"

Edmund raked his long fingers through his hair, the same black hair of his twin. "Of course not. You abandoned us in the guise of duty. How could you have known from thousands of miles away? The one time you did come home, you were only there for two weeks. During your visit, Emmaline placed such fear in me that I dared not speak one word of her sins."

"I could not deal with your mother. She became worse and worse I was at a loss. England was the best answer for her and for you, I thought. I hope you can forgive me, Edmund and put this behind us." He glared at Juliet and moved to his desk.

"You will not execute my brother," Edmund said in clear, articulated words.

The rain lashed down, torrential and unforgiving. In the meager light, the colonel's dark blue eyes darted from Juliet to Edmund. Gone was any remorse, replaced by a smile that rattled the nerves up Juliet's back.

"Edmund, I should at no time allowed you to come here. You have been gently reared and do not understand the oath I've pledged. I'm a soldier of the Crown with sworn duty to the King. Two Eagles is a spy. I will act accordingly with the law. He will hang with the other traitor on the morrow. There will be no further discussion."

"Have you not neglected the weightier matters of law— justice and mercy? Do you not have a conscience?"

"My conscience?" The colonel's mouth curved into a cold sickle of amusement. His voice a whisper meant for Edmund alone. "My dear son, where on earth did you get the notion tI had one?"

"The greatest heresies in the world are not committed by people breaking the rules but by people blindly following the rules. Your dogmatism will be your undoing, Father."

"Are you threatening me for that savage and his traitor friend?"

Edmund drew his tall frame to his full height and glared at the man he had called his father all the years of his life. "The real issue is your prejudice. You cannot tolerate the fact my brother and mother are savages. You forget, I am a savage, too. Indian blood runs through me. I beg you once more to stop this madness."

The colonel's face flushed red and the veins in his thick neck protruded. "There will be no further discussion." He kicked his chair forward, flopped into it, and picked up his quill, writing furiously.

"You are not the father I thought I had. This is the end of our relationship. I'll return to England as soon as it can be arranged." Edmund turned, stalked across the room and slammed the door with such force it clanged the muskets hanging on the wall.

"Colonel," Juliet said, her voice composed in spite of her throat clogging. "Won't you reconsider?"

"Not all of life's lessons come wrapped in a shiny bow," said the colonel. He seemed as volatile and unpredictable as the winds racing across the Great Lake of Ontario. His craving for power and control equaled his lust for his rum.

"This is not about a suckling babe at his mother's breast. This concerns war, matters you as a woman cannot possibly understand. Regardless of the costs, I will remain in compliance with His Majesty."

The decision was set in stone. Nothing she might say or do would change the course of events. She balled her fists, her fingernails jammed into her palms, and the bloodletting of her soul began. He had the same disregard for women embraced by her own father. "I finally know the difference between pleasing and loving, obeying and respecting. It has taken me many years to be fine with being different. My father prejudiced me with being born, and now I see you, tethered with the same narrow-mindedness. Where will your waltz with pride and arrogance lead you?"

He pounded a meaty fist on his desk. "I am in charge here," he blustered. "The canny frontiersman you are championing used you to gain access to my fort to get information. The man is an accomplished liar. Do you know he claimed to be a nobleman to escape the noose?" He blew on the paper to dry the ink, and then peered up at her. "In time, Edmund will see the folly of his request and what is best for him. As for your opinion, I do not care. I have accepted Captain Sutherland's proposal in marriage for you."

"What!"

"Has it ever occurred to you that you might do better to bow to my wishes to join in matrimony with Captain Sunderland than try with my patience?"

He was her elder cousin and, with certainty, flaunting his control over her future. "Of course, wedding Captain Sunderland might raise your own misplaced standing in society. I refuse to marry him."

"A woman's path is not mapped, it is made. My decisions are for the best, and I will not discuss this further. Guards!"

Blood rushed to her head. She felt herself sway on unsteady legs as her last hope shattered.

The door opened and a guard stood at attention, waiting the colonel's further command. "Escort Lady Faulkner to her quarters and take this order to Captain Sunderland to commence the hanging of two spies on the morrow."

Chapter 11

$\mathcal{J}$oshua's hands gripped the iron bars over the small window of the cell he'd occupied for the past two days. Heavy fetters bit into his wrists and ankles, the iron cold and hard. The unending, ceaseless rain had stopped. Outside he scanned the slightly higher land to the east on the other side of the river. Beyond the forest, a hazy glow silhouetted the treetops, as if there were a distant fire behind them…like when the Indians burned the brush and forests to create new farmlands.

The glow, more golden than red, gradually spread as though worked by an artist's brush until he could see the upper edge of a full moon. Then with startling suddenness, the complete circle was above the trees, lighting the peaks of the distant hills.

"They look like teats on a sow's belly, not like they do in the daylight," commented Ghost. The man had been thrown unconscious in the cell an hour earlier and was now awake. "The nooses' glow in the moonlight."

Joshua ignored Ghost's morbid reminder of the last night of his life. Their cell was not much to recommend, hardly enough to hold three men and barely high enough for him to stand. Bars from floor to ceiling and beyond the anteroom was a six-inch oak door. Soldiers guarded the entry and elsewhere, the yard and fort walls were secured by more regulars. Joshua kicked at the two-inch bars. No recoil. No escape there.

Two Eagles slept against the wall, though he was always aware of his surroundings and never fully asleep. Could it be true? That Two Eagles and Edmund were twins? The idea was so fantastic, yet side by side, they were identical. Extraordinary how both had claimed they were aware of the other despite being raised a half a world away.

He had heard of the connection between twins but never so solid as between Edmund and Two Eagles. Was it possible two people could be so identical and not be blood related? Or had they somehow been separated at birth? Faulkner had been in the Colonies for a very long time and it wasn't uncommon for some men to take advantage of the Indian women.

He rubbed his hands together as much as the weighty chains allowed, the grime slipping over his fingers. A horrendous stench wound the air from a bucket in the corner that served their needs, far from the refinements of his ancestral home and the cleanliness he was accustomed to.

The moon illuminated Ghost's face. His friend who had warned him of Onontio's attack at West Point. The old trapper was legend. Could disappear in the wilderness with no trace of his footsteps. Even the finest of Mohawk trackers were incapable of trailing him. "Why are you locked up?"

The trader raised his shackled wrists and tapped a finger to his temple. "Accused of thievery which ended in a brawl. A sum of money was missing and it was that bastard Captain Snapes who took it and has me swinging from the gallows to cover his pilfering."

Joshua knew many men in the wilderness, and Ghost was one of the most honest trappers he'd met. Snapes had his hand in more people's lives than he cared to hear.

The fort settled into its slumber. Soldiers had retired to their barracks except for a few guards on the parapets calling an occasional "All is well".

Chains clinking, he slid down. The moldy uneven stone walls slicked his backsides. He cringed, his ribs and every muscle in his body sore where the guards had kicked him. He settled onto the filthy straw-strewn floor, lifted his head and gazed on the heavens. Death was the only star always lit. No matter where he traveled, he must ultimately turn toward it. Everything fades in the world, but death endures.

Colonel Putman and General Anthony Wayne would be wondering what happened to him. Certainly not enough time to get their help. Unfortunately, he'd be unable to report his findings of Fort Oswego.

He had not seen Juliet and prayed she'd not come to the lynching. As a spy against the Crown, soon he'd be damned in her eyes, a soulless wretch ready to be executed for the crimes he'd committed.

There was no need for her to remember him like that.

From the first moment he clapped eyes on her at the Hayes' farm, he had wanted her. Somehow, they were tangibly connected and he should have taken her from the Hayes' farm and hid her in the wilderness.

She awakened something that hadn't been touched in him for a long time.

His wife. She had determinedly called herself, *his wife.* He had dared to unwisely dream…of pushing the war aside…of finding a normal life…a life with her. Yet the vagaries of his existence were as wide as they were severe. In a bid for that elusive idea of freedom, his chosen path to navigate the wide frontier as a spy had earned him his sepulcher.

Though fatigued, emotionally as well as physically, sleep eluded him. He lowered his head against his chains, letting the roughness saw against his forehead.

Two Eagles' massive chains clanked as he shifted position.

"I'm sorry you were involved Two Eagles."

Beaten by the guards, Two Eagles rose with a moan. "I am responsible for my choices and accept the consequences. I understood my determination could lead to success or failure or death."

Joshua was envious of his friend, wishing he could accept his fate so peacefully.

Keys jangled in the outer room. There was the immediate scrape of a chair where the guard slept and no doubt stood at attention. The sounds of heavy footsteps pounded against the plank flooring. A lantern held high moved toward them, then hooked on the peg above the cell. Joshua's eyes adjusted to the piercing light. Snapes pushed his face against the bars, his piggish mouth grinning like a gargoyle.

"I thought I smelled the shit of a bull," Ghost spat.

"How does it feel to know you will not escape the rope round your neck, Joshua?"

"Come on in here, and I'll show you."

"I'll second that with a knife plunked in your black heart," said Ghost. Two Eagles snorted.

Snapes laughed and targeted his attention on Joshua. "I've come to gloat, enjoying every minute of your execution and feel cheated you were not disposed to suffer a thousand deaths, Lord Rutland."

Joshua blinked. His intuition was correct. It was personal between Snapes and him. Why? "You know me?"

A muscle in Snapes' cheek twitched. His hard bloodshot eyes bored into Joshua's like gimlets. "I know the Rutlands—especially your father."

"My father?" Joshua inched closer to the bars. *Keep him talking.* "So, what does it have to do with me?"

"Sarah Thacker. Does her name ring a bell?"

Cold crept up his spine. Dim presences gathered at the edges of his consciousness.

He knew.

Joshua moved a hair's breath from the bars, enough to reach through and grab him by the neck.

Snapes backed off beyond his reach, cackling. "An interesting evening I had with her. She put up a good fight. For hours, I toyed with her…kept her alive…her lush body, available to me over and over again, taking delight in my power over her…over you…over every single Rutland. Her last words was, 'Joshua' which I found touching. I dipped my letter in her blood as a memento for you."

Snapes.

Joshua roared, and lunged his arms through the bars. He clawed the air, anything to get his hands on the British captain.

Well out of his grasp, Snapes reclined against the opposite wall, his arms folded in front of him. "To extract my vengeance was worth the effort. I hunted you in the wilderness. Learned you had been at the Hayes' farm but lost your trail after that. On a fluke, I came upon you here. How convenient to point out your loyalties to the colonel and have you hanged as a spy. You must pay. All the Rutlands will pay if they haven't already."

If Joshua's heart still beat, he didn't know it. He was aware of one thing. The rage to kill Snapes inhabited every fiber of his being. Abby's and Nicholas' abduction. The explosion at Belvoir. All the horrible things that had befallen his family were connected. But how? He hauled in a deep breath. He had to keep a cool head...find out who had attacked the Rutlands. "What do you mean? Who put you up to my demise? Who is involved with the attacks on the Rutlands?"

"Some rich fellow. I took his money but he didn't have to pay me. The pleasure is mine."

Ghost said, "I'll scream your crimes to the world."

"I, too," said Two Eagles.

Snapes sneered. "And who is going to take the word of a thieving trapper or Indian who in the morn will have their necks stretched?" His sloping chin jutted from his bulging cheeks. "Juliet's interest in you is another matter. She will suffer the same fate as your Sarah Thacker. I listened to how she defended you to Colonel Faulkner. Of course, her defense fell on deaf ears given the fact that I reinforced my observations of your spying activities."

"You touch her and I'll squeeze the life out of you."

Arm still crossed, Snapes tapped his chin and laughed. "I thought to myself, why would she defend you so rabidly? Your weeks of journey together…there is more to the matter." Snapes lifted himself from his repose against the wall and laughing, strode out the door. A new guard entered.

Joshua gripped the bars, his knuckles white, a primal scream stuck in his craw.

Blood pounded in his ears. Juliet was in danger. He had to act. Had to do something. Anything. He couldn't again fail to protect the one he loved.

The guard unlocked the cell door. Rage pounded through Joshua's veins.

About to charge the man to get at Snapes, he stopped when the guard held up another key and said, "Hold up your wrists."

"What?"

"It is me, John. Juliet arranged for me to be on duty tonight."

Juliet? His father's tenant unlocked his chains, the massive weight plunked on the floor. He could still feel the chains pressing down on his wrists and ankles where they were bleeding, but it was the movement toward freedom that brought life to him.

John knelt to remove the fetters from Two Eagles, and said over his shoulder, "When I saw you the other day, I was incapable of believing my eyes and did as you requested—to keep silent. I'd do anything for you. I remember how you and your brother, Nicholas helped me rebuild my mother's home when it burned down. If it weren't for your family caring for us, we'd have had no place to go. Can't forget the boxing bouts either. You and your brothers were a force to be reckoned with."

Another person entered the cell. Joshua recoiled, ready to strike the man, but the cloaked man was so small he could push him over with a feather.

"Joshua," said Juliet pushing back the hood on her cloak and reached for his hands.

"Juliet! You shouldn't be here. You're in danger from Snapes. You must stay under the protection of your cousin."

John said, "I told you I pay my debts, Lord Rutland. Go over the east wall. I've put a sleeping draught in the guard's drink. Hurry."

Juliet whipped her head around at the use of his title, but before she could say anything, he took her in his arms, and kissed her soft hair. "Juliet, you must return to your room before you are discovered."

"I'm going with you."

He pushed her back. "No, you are not. If caught, you will be hanged for treason."

"It's too late for that."

Two more heads appeared with bundles. Mary and Edmund rushed to Two Eagles. "They are going too."

He swore. Time and numbers were against him. They were all mad.

"Hurry, your lordship. There isn't much time," said John as he unbolted Ghost's chains. "Give me your best to the jaw and then chain me up." John produced a piece of linen and Joshua gagged him with it.

"I won't forget you, John." Joshua chained him and then tapped him on the jaw, enough to leave a convincing bruise.

Joshua picked up John's rifle and tossed it to Two Eagles. He peered around the edge of the door, inhaling lungfuls of fresh night air. How vital to breathe the air of freedom, giving power and vigor when one had the chance to escape the hangman.

He ached from the blows and beatings. Couldn't think about that now. The suffocating damp atmosphere of the dungeon further weakened him. To have a bath to wash the grime and a bed of soft hemlock beneath his spine to rest upon had just moments ago seemed beyond his reach.

The way was clear. One at a time, he motioned for Juliet and the rest to follow. The hair lifted on the nape of his neck. Getting a large party through a well-fortified fort without capture would be miraculous.

He led them, keeping in the shadows of the buildings and wide yards. A guard was asleep next to a ladder set against the parapet. The sleeping draught John had given him had done its work. But farther down on the stockade walls, a guard was still at his post and alert. No doubt he'd not drunk his brew.

They stayed in the murkiness beneath the outcropping. Getting over the wall with this many people would be a problem. Two Eagles, Ghost and he could slip over the wall and disappear, but with three novices? He had to get rid of the guard first if they were going to make it happen.

He gestured to Two Eagles to stay with them. He looped back silently in the shadows, glancing apprehensively at the guard who was staring at the moon. It took Joshua more than ten seconds to climb the ladder. Beads of sweat gathered on his forehead. Two seconds to come up behind him. The soldier turned and met a hard right to the jaw. He tied and gagged the unconscious guard.

He ran down the parapet, helping Juliet up, her huge eyes bright in the gloom.

His pulse racing, he glanced over the stockade wall and to the ground below. A broken ankle on any one of them could spell delay, capture and death.

Two Eagles leapt to the ground. Edmund and Ghost followed. Joshua tossed their bundles to the men, and then picked up Mary, lowering her, he slipped his hands to her wrists and let go. Two Eagles caught her.

He faced Juliet. "Are you sure? You haven't been discovered. You can go back to your bed. No one would suspect—"

"You cannot get rid of me that easy."

He glimpsed the determination on her face and smiled. He lifted her, releasing her into Two Eagles' arms, and then he glided over the wall and dropped to the ground. A hundred yards away from the fort, under the canopy of trees, Ghost stopped, shook their hands and disappeared into the forest like a specter.

A cannon boomed from the fort. "We've been discovered."

Juliet said, "What now?"

"Luck favors those in motion." The moon was cloaked with clouds. Barely enough discernable light illuminated their way. Joshua pushed through a narrow trail, pulling Juliet and Mary behind him. Edmund kept up the rear.

Mary stopped, jerked them back. "Where is Two Eagles?"

Joshua hauled them ahead. "He's making a trail with Ghost to lead the colonel on a merry chase to the east, and covering our tracks west."

"I'm not leaving without him."

"He's an expert at this. He knows what to do and will catch up with us later," Joshua said as he led them on a winding path. They slipped in the mud from the torrential rains the day before, for a mile, in the dark. They stumbled on rocks and saved their breath for walking. The forest was dark and silent. Working around and beyond the fort, they came out of the trees by the river where Two Eagles had hidden their canoes. Two Eagles had planned in advance in case they needed to make a quick escape from the fort. He had obtained a second canoe just to be safe.

Joshua listened. No one approached. In silence, they cleared away the brush. More shots were fired to the east.

"Your dear cousin will not allow our flight. The woods will be crawling with redcoats. Move and quickly." He shoved both canoes in the water, turned to help Edmund and Mary. A shadow loomed.

"I have it from here." Two Eagles steadied the canoe while Edmund teetered to the bow nearly capsizing the craft. He lifted Mary, and she put her arms tight around his neck.

"I told you I'd never leave you," Two Eagles said. He lowered her into the canoe as if she were the most valuable cargo he held, and then pushed off.

Joshua lifted Juliet and she moved to the bow. She felt the glide of water as Joshua pushed off the stern into the current and both dug in their paddles.

Juliet glanced at Edmund flailing about, the paddle foreign to him. He paddled left and right, and not ever in accord with Two Eagles. The rain flooded the river, making the water high and fast. Two Eagles warned his brother to dig deep.

Juliet responded to the rocks and trees and overhanging limbs but Edmund struggled. Everything was moving too fast, flying down the river there was no time to think of anything but avoiding menacing rocks and tree limbs.

"Avoid the upcoming rock. Paddle hard right," Two Eagles spoke to his twin.

Juliet barely missed a rock.

Edmund slammed against a protruding rock, turning their craft sideways. Mary wailed.

"Rest easy," said Two Eagles. "I will turn us around."

Two Eagles had no sooner managed straightening the craft when Edmund steered them into a dangerous eddy between two enormous rocks. Like being scooped up by a giant hand, the canoe pitched heavenward. Juliet held her breath. The canoe slammed downward and flew forward, Edmund laughing in victory and ready to take on the river.

Edmund suddenly resumed paddling in perfect rhythm with his twin, zooming far ahead of them. Juliet couldn't help but note the uncanny and unspoken communication between the twins, moving as if one body, and as if they'd never been separated.

Huge logs swirled. Debris whirled in their wake. Hours passed and Juliet's arms ached. She kept glancing over her shoulder to see if they were followed. Joshua did too. Had Ghost been successful in leading the soldiers away from them?

The moon made its descent and the sun rose, a great gem in the sky. She worried about Joshua and his wounds. The purpling had gone down around his eye but he had cuts and other wounds. Still they paddled on with the sun dipping higher in the sky as the current rushed them along, and into a greater river of the Mohawk where the ride smoothed out.

She had taken a risk asking the soldier, John, who she had seen Joshua secretly talking to, for his help. Her hunch to have him aid with the escape had been a long shot but worked to their advantage as he had been more than willing to aid her. *Lord Rutland?* He had called Joshua Lord Rutland. Was Joshua an English lord and from one of the most powerful families in England? Had Joshua told her cousin the truth about his lineage?

Toward dusk, they steered the canoes to the deep-shaded shore of the swollen river. Joshua, Edmund, and Two Eagles jumped into knee-deep water, squishing through mud in the shallows and pulled the crafts up the embankment, concealing them beneath hemlock branches in case British soldiers happened by. Grateful, Juliet, with Joshua at her side, stumbled to steady ground. Joshua followed an animal trail away from the camp to check the area. Mary passed out food from the bundles they'd taken from the fort. Juliet ate heartily, and then collapsed on the furs Two Eagles had laid out.

She awoke two hours later and groggy, patted the fur beside her. Joshua was not there. She grabbed some bread and bandages and followed Joshua's trail through a copse of trees to a high clearing with a full view of the river glistening in the moonlight. He sat at the edge of the clearing overlooking the river, his back to her.

"Why didn't you sleep, Juliet?"

"I did for a short time." She moved toward him.

He turned.

"You must eat—for your strength." She offered him the bread. "Let me bandage your wounds."

He glanced down as if he'd forgotten his wounds existed. "Only a few bruises and scratches."

"I'll be the judge of that," she said, turning back his shirt on one side. Her stomach fluttered. A six-inch deep furrow ran across his shoulder still oozing blood "It looks terribly painful." She touched his shoulder lightly. "This must be dressed or it will fester."

Her eyes locked on to his lips. Heat flooded her face, the crush of his mouth, a lingering memory. Her finger itched to caress the smooth line of his lower lip and the firm curve of his jaw.

"You know of such things?"

"One Twelfth Night, I watched Moira sew up a man who had imbibed on enough spirits to sink a battalion of soldiers. He had attempted to carve a roasted goose. Instead, he performed a neat job of slicing his arm." She heaved a sigh. "Since there is a shortage of physicians, you'll have to suffer my needlepoint skills. If you would sit on the log, I can begin."

He nodded, straddled a beech log. Gingerly she blotted his wound and retreated into her shy and reticent self. His skin felt warm and he smelled of earth and river. How would she find the wherewithal to perform this task?

An English lord? Still reeling from the fact put starch in her knees. "Joshua Hansford? Lord Joshua Rutland? Who are you? Far from the atmosphere of wealth and respect, you present a mystery. None of it makes sense and you have a lot of answering to do."

She threaded a needle, wishing she had some rum to pour over the gash. Sinking her teeth into her lower lip, she pushed the needle through his flesh. She winced and looked at him to see if he'd felt the pain. "Why would one of English nobility carry a long rifle, dress like a frontiersman, live in the wilderness, and then pretend otherwise?"

"Does it matter?"

She narrowed her eyes. "I remember details…the dinner with the Hayes', and then at Fort Oswego…the refinements you revealed without realizing the civilities displayed. How you folded your napkin when done eating, holding your wine goblet just so, and slipping sometimes from your colonial vernacular. Every one of those instances spoke of polished manners ingrained from birth."

He was silent. He was good at keeping silent.

Aware of Joshua watching her every move, she gritted her teeth to quell her trembling, drew the thread through two layers of skin, pulling the cut together. She closed her eyes and swallowed. "I heard the soldier call you Lord Rutland and don't deny it. You can't fool me. I know nobility, yet you choose the occupation of a fur trader and spy. Why?"

Joshua lifted his brow, and next offered a slight bow of his head at her observations. "Lord Joshua Rutland at your service, Madam, the third son and third heir to the Duke of Rutland and very thankful you helped us escape."

"I couldn't let them execute you…for all that you had done for me." *Because I have feelings for you.* She pushed through his skin again. "I imagine you have family?"

"I have a sister, Abigail living in Boston and married to a shipbuilder."

Juliet frowned. The daughter of a duke would marry nobility

in England not a Boston shipbuilder. "She's in Boston married to a colonial?"

He scanned the river below and she followed his gaze. So far, no one had followed them.

"My family has been under attack by unseen enemies. The violence started at my sister's betrothal ball. There was an explosion and during that time, my sister was abducted, found herself in the bowels of a ship with her hair shorn, breasts bound, dressed as a boy, and the captain bent on her demise. She barely survived. An American privateer, Captain Jacob Thorne rescued her."

Joshua placed his foot on a fallen tree and laughed. "He thought her a male and kept her as his cabin boy."

"I can imagine his surprise when he discovered her to be a female."

"I don't know the details, but they fell in love and married. She has given birth to her first born by now."

Juliet inhaled. "What happened to the rest of your family?"

"My brother, Anthony remains in England. He's is a brilliant scientist who never surfaces from his laboratory…except for the miraculous fact both he and Father left the place seconds before someone blew it up to kill them," he said, his words laced with venom.

"My oldest brother, Nicholas was likewise abducted and no one knows what has happened to him. I've been out of touch so long, I don't know if he is alive or dead."

Joshua turned away. Juliet clasped his arm and continued working on his arm. No way would she allow him to retreat into himself.

"That's horrible. Who do you think is responsible?"

"Later, when Abby had landed in Boston, she was attacked again by a man named Percy Devol who admitted to kidnapping her back in England. We speculated there were two men involved, but now know there are more."

She took another stitch, felt his muscles harden beneath her fingers. "How do you know?" There was more to the story, she was sure.

He raked his fingers through his hair. "Not ever in a million years did I believe the hatred of the Rutlands might extend to the frontier. My war is on two fronts. Snapes wanted to get at me because of who I am."

Her pulse jumped at the mention of Snapes. She shook it off, tied off the last stitch, and surveyed her work. She wound bandages around his arm, then darting a glance at Joshua and took a step back from the ferocity of his glare.

"Snapes has a twisted score to settle with the Rutlands and I—have a score to settle with him."

"A score to settle?"

"If I knew..."

"When he came to the Hayes' farm and discovered you had recently been there, he asked many questions concerning you, and later he—" Her mouth went dry.

"He assaulted you?"

She shook her head. "No. Thankfully the cook came in and I was sent to attend Orpha."

Joshua bolted to his feet. "I'll get that bastard," he spat out, then took her hand and headed back to camp. "We are going back on the river."

"Tonight? I cannot—"

"I don't want to taste your cousin's hospitality again."

Reaching their site, Two Eagles alert, nodded to Joshua. The tall warrior touched his twin's shoulder to awaken him, and then gently picked up Mary, who slept soundly, carried her to the canoe and placed her gently upon the fur pack. Joshua steadied the birch bark vessel and taking Juliet's hand again, helped her alight. He plunked a fur pack behind her, hopped in, and shoved off with his oar. "Sleep, Juliet. I will paddle through the night. Until we come upon the safety of Two Eagles' tribe, I will not rest."

Facing him, she settled against the furs. Sleep eluding her, and her mind swirled with so many questions. "Why do you choose to go against your noble family?"

"I love my family. But I have opposition to a monarchial regime." Joshua dug deep with his paddle. "I left the feudal-aristocracy behind in England simply to be greeted with it again here in the Colonies. The status quo must end."

She trailed her fingers through the water, noticing how he studied her beneath his dark lashes.

"Look what happened to you, Juliet. Is not your own situation a demonstration of the ills of nobility? You were driven out of your home by a relative before your father was cold in his grave. Afterward, you fell helplessly into the abhorrent practice of indentured servitude with no retreat but submission and slavery. Where is the fairness?"

Joshua looked deeply into her eyes. "Of concern is the aristocracy. Is it fair everything goes to the hands of the few? That the rest sacrifice everything for the sake of nobility? What we are fighting for are new ideas where every man is equal."

"Noble but rare that rebels who revolt ever win. What if the Patriots lose this war? What then? Will you ever be able to return to England? If you stay in the Colonies, you will live in fear of being hunted down by British soldiers."

"Each time a man stands up for an ideal, or acts to better the lot of others, or strikes out against an injustice, he sends a ripple of hope. For every battle won, we cross a new threshold of daring, and create a powerful current that can sweep down the mightiest wall of oppression and resistance. This war will be won and succeeded by the exertions of men far better than myself. Losing is not an option."

They passed beneath a heavily canopied cover of overhanging branches, blotting out the light of the somber moon. As the canoe scraped over gloomy shallows, a slight breeze bowed the reeds growing near the bank. The magnitude of his conviction impressed her, and she admired his principles. Did she not believe the same? Did she not rail at the injustices she'd seen? His fervor was indeed infectious…and the deep timbre of his voice grew seductive to the point she wanted to reach out and touch him.

She folded her arms. To touch him anymore was a lie. Had he not pushed her away and told her to marry Sunderland?

He considered her a burden. She had helped him escape and now he felt responsible for her. With certainty, he was dedicated to his cause, and she was surrendered to the specter of intangible idealism. "Does your family know what you do?"

"My sister, I suspect, has eavesdropped on conversations I had with my uncle in Boston."

Juliet tapped her chin. "As a spy, why did you go to the fort when the risks were so great?"

"I had no idea I had been seen meeting with General Horatio Gates at Saratoga."

"You live a very dangerous life."

He shrugged. "All warfare is based on deception. The ruse of a Loyalist trapper and selling his furs was a believable trick. The best spies can make a very small shadow on the wall. Unfortunately, my ruse has been revealed by Snapes."

"I must say, I was almost convinced by your act, mumbling banalities despite your cloaked erudition, giving a calculated progression of disclosures with the right amount of praise to feed my cousin's vanity."

"You are a smart woman, Juliet. I should be wary of you." His mouth twitched at one end into a boyish grin. "Of course, the disclosures are already known to add credence to the deception. The flattery is to win easy favor. I thank you for your praise."

"It wasn't meant to praise you. Your foolishness nearly secured a rope around your neck."

He said nothing but she observed him consciously forcing his limbs to relax. "Juliet, thank you for saving my life."

She was overcome by his raw emotion. "I'm glad you escaped…I couldn't let them do anything to harm you."

She remained quiet for a while, and then asked, "When did you become a Patriot?"

"So many questions, *Lady Faulkner,* you make me dizzy." He inclined his handsome head meaningfully. "In England, I had attended a lecture by a passionate colonial, Benjamin Franklin.

As soon as I finished my schooling, I left for the Colonies, joining my uncle, Thomas Hansford, in Boston. He is an ardent Patriot and introduced me to many of the Sons of Liberty.

In Boston, there was great fervor against the Quartering Act and unfair taxation. I fought in Breed's Hill. Many of my companions died. A fire torched in my belly.

"From there, I traveled with Henry Knox, a bookseller and captured Fort Ticonderoga. We dragged sixty tons of artillery through forests and swamps, across the frozen Hudson and Connecticut Rivers, arrived in Cambridge in January and, afterward, set up the cannons on Dorchester Heights. Can you imagine the surprise of British General Howe waking up to the bombardment of Boston? As a result, General Howe was persuaded to evacuate Boston or have his troops and ships destroyed."

Juliet laughed.

"During the New York and New Jersey campaigns, General Washington asked me to scout the New York frontier. During this time, the British launched a major campaign to secure the Hudson River Valley. I did reconnaissance for General Horatio Gates at the headwaters where the British General 'Gentleman Johnny' was defeated."

Juliet pulled her loose hair back and braided it. "The Patriots have had remarkable successes. You are *dizzily* convincing, *Lord Faulkner.*" She gave a knowing smile, emphasizing his title, like he had hers, and pointing out how he had hidden the fact of his nobility.

Joshua dug his paddle where the current ran strong. "I have faith in the Colonies. We Patriots are like tiny bees that fly around the head of a great giant. We are but a little annoyance, even if we sting, at which time the hand of the giant might slap and crush us. But every now and then," he added, "the poison of the tiny bee's sting becomes deadlier than the bite of a rattlesnake and he who is stung dies."

Chapter 26

A week later they came to the mouth of a river branch, and they descended into an azure lake. In the distance, smoke curled to the sky, and a short break inland lay a settlement.

Two Eagles paddled harder, the pleasure and breathless haste of seeing his home spurring him on. Edmund's eyes rounded, suddenly alert, and Joshua, too sat in awe. Mary stayed reticent, looking to Two Eagles who beamed with pride and excitement.

"We will be protected here by the Oneidas who are loyal to the Patriots and also it being the home of Two Eagles," Joshua said.

Onuaga, was no insignificant Indian village. It sprawled at the edge of the forest, and like sentinels, tall trees of maple, ash, poplar and beech loomed up behind. Between the village and the lake were fields of rich black earth, cleared of underbrush, all worked and partially planted.

Bark canoes lined the shore. With dogs yapping at their heels, boys ran along the river's edge, hailing Two Eagles and Joshua, curious of the newcomers.

The boys helped them pull their canoes ashore, staring at Juliet and Mary. They gawked and pointed at Edmund, apparently noticing the similarity between Two Eagles and his twin.

Men dressed in breechclouts approached, followed by naked children. Women with necklaces and ear piercings festooned with shells, rushed forward topless, their breasts browned by the warm sun. Juliet colored fiercely at their blatant nudity.

They were led near a row of numerous longhouses, with sporadic holes in the roofs where streams of smoke rose. Over each door hung a carved head of a bear, symbolizing the magnitude of the famed Bear Clan.

Two Eagles was important in the village. No one entered his presence lightly. Here, Two Eagles had no time for trivial things. Even Mary was awed and subdued by the veneration poured on him by the villagers.

A hide was thrown back and they were led into a longhouse. Juliet blinked, her eyes adjusting to the darkness. Fantastic ceremonial masks suspended from bed poles along a series of fur-swathed bunks constructed against the walls. On shelves above, wooden bowls, ladles, dishes, spoons, baskets, and clay pots were placed. Snowshoes, hunting bows, quivers of arrows and braids of corn hung from rafters.

Two Eagles sat on the ground next to a fire. A bowl of corn mush was handed to him. He gestured for Juliet, Joshua, Mary and his brother to sit. Two Eagles gestured to Mary and spoke in his guttural language for the rest of the Indians to hear. They all nodded and smiled. Women patted Mary's hair. She blushed from the attention.

A woman handed him a pipe. He took tobacco and filled the

pipe. The woman took the pipe to the fire and laid a hot coal on top of the bowl, and then handed it back to Two Eagles.

Two Eagles puffed on the pipe, and then handed it to Joshua, who puffed, then handed it to the other braves. The room was quiet. After a period of waiting, Two Eagles spoke.

Joshua leaned over to Juliet and translated. "This is part of a returning ceremony where our story is told. He is telling of his long-lost brother returned and our escape from Fort Oswego. He is informing them that their continued support for the Patriots is good. The King's men do not keep their promises."

The crowd murmured and parted, allowing in, out of deference, an older woman who had many winters on her head, yet still beautiful with few wrinkles. She wore a blue skirt and bright red leggings made of broadcloth, embroidered with elaborate bead designs. A calico over-dress was fastened down the front with a row of shining silver brooches; silver earrings dangled from her ears, and her face gleamed with gentleness. The woman, an exact image of Ojistah moved through the throng with grace, her silver braids hanging down beside her cheeks.

For Juliet, Ojistah's prediction of seeing her twin came true.

The woman focused on Edmund.

Two Eagles stood. "This is our mother, Waneek."

Edmund staggered to his feet, stared at Waneek.

Juliet perceived his hesitation, his attempt to wring from the unknown where there were no assurances and no straight lines, and governed by fear of judgement and rejection. He had left his old world behind, banking on this one moment where there were no guarantees, and like a lost soul wandering in the dark, he sought confirmation and consolation.

A myriad of emotions crossed Edmund's face.

"You think a mother cannot recognize her own son," Waneek reproved Two Eagles in stilted English, her eyes not once leaving Edmund. "I, at all times, knew you were alive. Sensed it in my bones. I named you, 'Deganwida'."

"Deganwida," repeated Edmund. He glanced at Two Eagles, and then back to his mother, a look of yearning so deep, Juliet could feel the force of it in her heart.

"There is much power in your name," said Waneek. "It means two river currents flowing together."

Edmund took a tentative step toward his mother. The crowd stared, stirred by the tableau playing out in front of them.

Waneek moved closer. "Every morning, I woke and I told you how much I loved you. Many moons passed and the love I held for you grew and grew, nearer and dearer to my heart, each day, each year."

Waneek touched his face, his shoulder, his arm. "If I had to choose between loving you and breathing, I would use my last breath to tell you…I love you."

She lifted her trembling arms and Edmund fell into them.

Tears came to Juliet's eyes as Edmund wrapped his larger arms around his mother, absorbing the cruel and lonely years, of the longing to hear a mother's loving voice, to feel a mother's hand upon his hair, to see her sweet smile—tokens of a mother's love he'd been denied. Amidst the joyful shout of villagers with the reunion of Deganwida and his mother, Juliet could not help but be a little envious.

Edmund was home at last.

Chapter 27

There were three hundred Indians, including a number of Mohawks in Two Eagles' settlement. The difference between his village and Ojistah's Mohawk village emerged as a collection of smaller houses built of squared-up logs and stone chimneys. At the west end were larger, finely built log homes with glass window panes and ample furnishings that took on the structure of an upper middle-class family in Europe. The largest of these domiciles belonged to Two Eagles.

"It's a good house," Two Eagles said to Mary. "It doesn't shake when storms rage, and will not blow over with the slightest wind." He pounded the wall to emphasize his point and to call attention to the criticism Mary had made during their travels regarding his living in a primitive structure that trembled with the slightest breeze.

Mary turned a bright shade of red. "I hope you can forgive me for my rude comment."

A fine dinner was prepared by servants, and Juliet learned that in the Mohawk Valley, Two Eagles had grown up with

German, Scotch, English and Irish immigrants, making him comfortable with the European culture.

Waneek passed a bowl of squash. "As neighbors, we have to depend on each other for survival, resulting in a sharing of customs and traditions. Two Eagles and I speak three languages and have become Christians."

Mary set down her fork, staring at Two Eagles. "You are Christian?"

"You find it difficult to believe a savage can be Christian?" he replied.

A scarlet flush crept across her cheeks. "How could I have—"

"Assumptions grow firm as weeds among stones and are not so easily dislodged. We are not so different, Mary…you and I."

Juliet understood the deeper tones of Two Eagles' voice, where he'd existed in a world built of prejudices and arrogance. Mary had indeed outgrown her naïve childishness and preconception.

"Two Eagles is very educated," added Waneek proudly, her silver armbands tinkling. "My older daughter is married to Sir Jensen. He took an interest in Two Eagles and supported his English-style education at Moor's Indian Charity School and later at Kings College in New York City where he pursued an interest in law."

Mary gawked at Two Eagles. "What else have you been keeping from me?"

"I have studied law," said Edmund, marveling at his brother. "Strange how we both enjoy the same things. I want to learn everything of what you do and everything of the homeland of my ancestors."

After dinner, they retired to the coolness of the porch and Waneek brought out two rifles. "Now for the entertainment. Joshua and Two Eagles will have a competition."

A circular target of ten feathers was fastened to a tree.

Juliet stood on tiptoes to see over the villagers crowding to see the legendary Joshua. Two Eagles pointed at the bright red feather then aimed his gun and fired. The trunk exploded an inch above the target.

"I will knock the tip off the third feather." Joshua sighted down the barrel, took aim. The tip exploded off the feather.

Two Eagles hit the feather beneath. The villagers murmured their approval, oohing and pointing as each man took turns, demonstrating their prowess. Two Eagles' shots were close, but Joshua hit the tips off every feather. Breathless, Juliet bumped shoulders with Mary.

Joshua glanced to her and her pulse raced. "I'm going to hit the center of the target." He aimed and fired. A warrior took the target off and wiggled his finger through the hole in the exact center. Everyone hooted. Joshua and Two Eagles rejoined Juliet and Mary on the porch.

Two Eagles motioned to Mary. "Come with me. I wish to show you something."

The dong, dong sound of heavy blows repeated in quick succession boomed across the village. In front of one of the lodges, Two Eagles and Mary passed three Indian women pounding corn in hollowed out oak logs with heavy wooden pestles.

"Be careful of Big Beast," called Waneek, smiling.

Two Eagles held up his hand to silence his mother. To this, several women in the village within hearing distance giggled, their knowing gazes following the couple who vanished in the woods.

From beneath her shawl, Waneek handed two packets to Joshua. "These arrived for you weeks ago." She returned inside to talk with Edmund.

"What is Big Beast?" said Juliet.

"Big Beast is a mythical behemoth who gathers up two lovers and smothers them in his giant breasts," he said without looking at her.

Opening one of the letters, Joshua moved off the porch and out of sight. A private moment with news from home? No, she knew better. With each passing day since their escape from the fort, he'd grown more withdrawn. More distant. During the trip she had seen many of his moods—of anger, of heaving edginess, of festering disturbances and, yes, of great tenderness vibrating on the verge of something profound. Yet during the last days, he'd become pensive, his mood swings gone, as if he'd won a battle within and found some great resolve. What she saw now she had at no time seen before. Indifference. Cold, uncaring indifference.

Her insides trembling, she reached for the porch rail. Gulped for air. In loving him, she had vowed to tolerate anything he chose to be, but among his choices she had not counted indifference. Oh, God. She closed her eyes and drew her arms into her stomach. He truly did not care.

Her heart shattered, she fled, and like the walking dead, she meandered aimlessly through the village. Contrary to her despair, the sky was an extraordinary blue, giving way to a beautiful day. A group of boys shouted and cheered playing a game with a leather ball and scooping it up with wooden nets. The Indian women smiled and greeted her as she passed and suddenly the world faded away. She was in England, could smell the apple blossoms, roses, and lavender. She could sip tea, eat lemon tarts and marzipan and listen to sweet violin music. And yet a sour taste yielded in her mouth. There was nothing for her in England.

Infected by Joshua's enthusiasm for the Patriot cause made her rethink where she would go. Boston emerged a stronghold in Patriot hands and, at once, she entertained working there as a midwife.

She followed a path through the woods, her meager companions, gray mourning doves, their woeful cooing increasing her melancholy. Hearing voices, she peered through thick hemlock boughs into a bright green meadow. Two Eagles and Mary. She shouldn't spy on her friend but her legs were like stiff boards nailed together with iron hinges watching Mary's great delight in picking a bouquet of flowers.

"Are you happy, Mary?" asked Two Eagles.

"How can I not be? The sky is blue and there is the yellow of the buttercups and yarrow, the pink of the mallow, and brilliant black-eyed Susans are everywhere."

"The Great Spirit is happy, too. He made the beautiful world with his hands and took pleasure in its beauty," said Two Eagles, and then he stared at Mary with well-intended meaning.

The tall warrior plucked a cornflower from her bouquet and held it up to the side of her head. "The blue is like your eyes."

"Two Eagles, I would love to have children to run through this field of color. Your children," Mary said gazing up to him.

Two Eagles returned the same loving look with all the adoration of the world caught on his face.

He kneeled, dug through the loam and came up with a plucked root. He mashed the tuber, staining his palm a bright scarlet. He extended his hand to Mary. "When you shake the hand of a warrior whose hand is marked with the red stain of bloodroot, it means you will marry him."

Mary reached a trembling hand and placed it solidly in his. Two Eagles gathered her into his arms and with infinite gentleness, kissed her tenderly.

Juliet pivoted and shook her head. No. Mary couldn't desert her just like that, could she? They had come so far together. She had assumed Mary would be a permanent fixture in her life. But as much as she wanted Mary with her, she wanted Mary's happiness even more. In the white man's world, Mary would be scorned if her scandalous background was revealed. In Two Eagles' eyes, she stood revered. Mary would find happiness in her new world and Juliet would be happy for her friend...even though she herself would be alone.

Whether Juliet journeyed to Boston or to England, Mary would not be a part of her future. Her chest hitched. To be entirely alone? The grim reality slammed into her full force. Everyone made choices. She would not hold Mary accountable to her decision to accompany her. She loved her too much.

Still thinking, meandering, her feet leaden with her new reality, she plodded through the woods and back to the village. She came upon Waneek whom Juliet had learned was the tribe's Clan Mother, a significant ruling sovereign in the tribe, wielding great power. Her husband, the chief, had died of measles, or the white man's plague. In addition to treating both whites and Indians with her prodigious medical skills, she earned her living by collecting ginseng and selling the valuable medical herb to traders.

Waneek instructed a young girl who was making a clay pot, and did not look up when Juliet approached, yet she had a clear feeling the old *sachem* knew she was there the entire the time.

"The soil is black and rich. A plant is nourished by the soil it feeds on, by the winds that blow, the rains that fall and the sun that shines. Like a little white flower that has put her roots down deep, Mary is taking her nourishment and strength from the same sun, rain and wind that gives her life. To transplant her again, she would wither and die."

"Waneek, Mary has been my friend forever. I would not stand in the way of her happiness even if it means—losing her."

"Two Eagles has claimed Mary and she has claimed him. A wedding will be soon."

"You might be right," Juliet said, not wanting to reveal she had spied on Mary and Two Eagles.

"I am always right."

Waneek's remark struck Juliet as prophetically strange, like her twin sister, Ojistah.

Thinking of Ojistah's words, Juliet watched the girl's dark fingers work at clay coils, round and round she twisted slender ropes of clay, overlapping the ropes until the crude shape of a pot formed.

"It takes time to make a clay pot," said Waneek.

The Indian girl did not raise her head. She smoothed the unevenness away and scraped the sides smooth with a piece of broken gourd.

"It looks easy to make a pot." Juliet kept watching, fascinated with the girl's handiwork. A small girl with a faceless cornhusk doll clutched to her chest sat next to the girl making the pot.

"*Ohe!*" Waneek laughed. "Making a pot is not so easy. It takes time and patience. We pray over Mother Earth for permission to remove the clay from the banks of the river bed. The clay is spread on a stone slab and beat with hands and feet. When the clay is soft and smooth, it must be mixed with ground clam shells and mica and be beaten smooth again. All this before the coils are rolled. The pot will break if forbearance is not used."

Waneek's voice came as gentle as the south wind. "Like men with wounds, they are healed by degrees. Patience and perseverance have a miraculous effect before which difficulties disappear and obstacles vanish."

Juliet exhaled. Waneek spoke of Joshua. "I'm competing with a corpse."

The Indian girl turned and shaped the collar of her pot, making a scalloped design on the edge. She put the pot aside to dry.

Waneek kept her eyes on the girl's handiwork. "When the water has been drawn out of the clay by the sun, the pots will be ready for firing. It takes time. Patience is bitter, but the fruit is sweet."

"Ojistah compared me to the sacredness of Sky Woman. I do not understand."

"Like Sky Woman, you must accept the sacrifices made for her so that you can live life through the daughter which you will bear in the future in your new surroundings. This daughter and her daughter will be powerful to the world."

"What you say is improbable."

"The sun finds a way to shine each day, so will be your journey. Of this, I know."

Chapter 28

J oshua reread the contents for the fifth time, swearing at the delays in communication. A letter from Boston to the frontier took months and news from England took nearly a year.

Redcoats pulled their canoes on shore. He withdrew to a knot of trees to watch as Waneek greeted them. Sharp hand gestures and loud talk followed.

He moved to retrieve Juliet when she appeared at his side. He didn't have to look to know she was there, like the caress of sunshine over a flower, an innate quality stirred with her nearness. She put her hand on his arm, her scent beckoning him, the same woman he made a vow to banish from his life.

"Two Eagles and Mary have gone farther into the forests. One of the women brought me to you. Do you think the soldiers will cause trouble?"

The redcoats dared to move beyond Waneek. Several warriors moved in front of them. "The soldiers showed disrespect to Waneek," Joshua said. "But outnumbered, they dare not bring the wrath of the whole tribe on them. The Oneidas protect their own."

He folded the letter and placed it in his bag, keeping an eye on their visitors. He rotated his shoulders, feeling the weariness there, his stitches tight and sore. It had been a long journey, and he required rest to recoup, and still a longer journey lay ahead.

"Bad news from home?"

He cast his gaze out over the rippling lake. Wind torn clouds raced across the midday sky. Shadows loomed across the earth, encircling the impenetrable forest. Branches forming a solid arc overhead shook with a gust. "Good and bad. The missives postdate to last December from my sister, Abigail, in Boston. I have nephew."

"Congratulations." Her exuberant smile warmed him. "Joy is a net of love when a baby is brought into the world. My years as a midwife are proof, and for me, when a child is born, it is like the grace of millions of angels descending on the earth."

Thoughts of being an uncle flashed through his mind, thoughts about what it might be to be a father and hold his own child in his arms. That terrible, wonderful notion could make him happily elated and equally terrified.

Joshua assumed there'd be one great love in his life. Sarah. For ages, he reasoned she was the only one, yet this flame-haired beauty next him with her omnipresent smiles made him crawl out from beneath the fog of guilt and made him come alive, made him want more of which he had no right.

The flame-haired woman beside him had lifted long buried dreams. She released something inside him, made him pay attention to things he hadn't let himself feel or think about. Oh, how he wanted more, but that claim was lost to him.

She lowered a branch to peer at the soldiers. "Is my cousin among them?

"No. Neither is Snapes, the coward."

"Snapes is evil, and he must be stopped. I cannot believe my cousin took Snapes' word over mine. There must be justice."

Joshua lived in fear and rage. Fear for Juliet, his Achilles' heel—vulnerable, and how he hated that vulnerability. His rage had also emerged; the seething animal in him unable to rest until he exacted retribution from the British captain who'd wronged her.

Juliet frowned, and then glanced up at him, waiting for him to continue. But he could not tell Juliet about Sarah, or Snapes' vow to harm Juliet. No. He did not want her to worry. Before long, he'd have her far from here and out of harm's way.

"Abigail writes their shipbuilding trade is booming, having received numerous orders from the Continental Congress, to build a Navy. Rachel Thorne, Captain Thorne's cousin is in England at Belvoir as a guest of my family."

He stared at the letters. "Father says there has been no news of my brother, Nicholas." Joshua wanted to withdraw yet he wanted to retreat with Juliet, holding her in his arms and never letting go.

Why had he brought her here? God, he was weary. He should not have let her come. He should have tied her, or forced her back into her warm bed, anything to keep her at the fort. This trip was too dangerous. If only he had realized the biggest danger to her was him.

They stared into each other's eyes, neither speaking. His heart pounded against his ribs. Was her heart beating as hard? As fast?

She stood tall, assessing him, his Aphrodite, still and perfect, warm and pliant. A wind caressed the land, then lifted a tendril of her red hair to tease the bristles on his chin. All those days behind her in the canoe, all those nights she sighed next to him in her slumber, had wreaked an avalanche of havoc on his senses.

They had come so far. *Too far.*

Another gust crossed the land, cool and sweet. It did nothing to ease the fire ablaze throughout his loins. He could see the rise and fall of her breasts with the uneven whisper of her breath—and he could see the pulse beating at her throat, beating there in anger, or was it anguish?

His longing suddenly peaked and he pulled her to him, gathered her into his arms, his mouth covering hers with savage hunger. She cried out from the cruel ravishment of his mouth and pushed away, but he crushed her to him. Her skin was so hot and he craved the feel of her…free from all her clothing. His blood rushed at the thought of her naked beneath him. Just one more touch…

At her resistance, his mind cleared enough to understand he was ending his attraction to her. But the warmth of her pulsing body and her hand, stroking the back of his neck created a white-hot blaze of lust.

He slid her sleeves down her arms, exposing rosy nipples beneath the filmy fabric. He palmed the satiny skin of her breasts, their tender buds hardening to the graze of his thumb and forefinger. He shoved her back against a tree and her moan inflamed him. He lowered his mouth, suckled her breast. She tasted like wild honey. He pulled back, surveying the wet sheen on her nipple. He ran his hand down her abdomen, her skin searing hot as he came to rest on her hip, pressing her intimately to his arousal.

Stop. He had to stop. *Stop now.* Breathing raggedly, his lust still fierce, a blunt reality somehow snapped through his passion-ridden brain, he pushed away from her. Glared at her.

"Juliet," he rasped. "I'm taking you and Mary to Blackberry Valley where I will have you transported to Albany, and on to Boston. I must get you out of the frontier and back to England where you will be safe."

"Mary is staying with Two Eagles. They are to be married."

He stiffened. "I see."

"The soldiers have gone back toward Fort Oswego."

He breathed a sigh of relief.

"I will not be safe in England. Once Baron Bearsted learns of my return, he will seek a way to be rid of me again."

"Not this time. You will be under the protection of my father. He will see to it Baron Bearsted pays for his crimes."

"What about the fact I committed treason in helping you escape from Fort Oswego?"

"I will tell my father how to spin the story. How I kidnapped you at gunpoint. My father is powerful and will back up the account. No one would dare go against him."

"But what of us, Joshua? Doesn't our time together mean anything? Our vows?"

"Quit spinning girlish dreams that will go nowhere. An annulment will be designated by my barrister. You'll be free."

"But—"

He held up a hand to silence her, and it tore him apart to voice the words. "Enough, Juliet. We both agree our marriage was in name only, a temporary solution to a precarious difficulty." He reached out and cupped her chin in his hand, his thumb skimming over her bottom lip. Regret filled him with every word he spoke. "The pretense is up, Juliet. This forced marriage will be terminated. You will go to England, find a nobleman, be his wife and bear his children."

Though he'd said the words, the thought was like a knife to his heart. To think of Juliet in another's arms. A fat baron between her milky thighs.

He shook his head. *Do not think.*

He had to focus on her happiness. Her future. Not himself. "I will settle a sum of money for your use and make sure my father is aware you saved my life at risk to your own. Rutlands always pay their debts. He will be happy to launch you."

She jerked back as if he struck her in the face.

"I-I see," she said, her lip quivering. And then, her eyes riveted to his, she straightened. "You are not simply a liar, Joshua, you are a coward. You cannot face the fact that I love you. There I said it, may God forgive me, but I love you. If you do not wish to see me or speak to me again, I accept that too, however hurtful. What I will not accept, Joshua, is the denial, of your feelings for me. You lie to hide it. You do love me. As sure as the wind blows and I breathe, you love me, and before I leave, I will make you eat your remarks, every damned, lying one of them, I promise you that."

Guilt rolled through him like hot lava. "We are not meant to be together. It is over, Juliet."

Joshua met the rest of the day in torment. Part of him wanted to find Juliet and apologize. The other part faced reality. To protect her, he had to send her away.

He came upon Waneek as she worked at weaving a basket. Without looking up, she said, "British soldiers arrived and asked if we had seen any of you. I told them warriors returning from a hunting expedition had seen a group of their description traveling far to the southeast."

Joshua looked round for a glimpse of Juliet. "Thank you, Waneek."

The old woman wove a long reed, in and out, in and out. "You are leaving? What of your woman?"

"She will come with me. I will leave her with friends at Blackberry Valley until I can secure her passage to England."

Waneek was quiet, and then finally spoke. "The reed with which I weave is strong when woven. But if the reeds were not here, there would be no basket. You must learn how to weave them all together."

Joshua gazed into her upturned face. Two Eagles' mother was very wise. "I've promised to spy for General Washington...I have a duty to fulfill."

Waneek snorted. "What is duty compared to a woman's love? What is duty against the feel of a newborn son in your arms? Duty is what the Earth Mother Spirit has fashioned us for love. That is our greater glory."

Together, they watched Juliet stroll across the village and pick up a baby that had toddled too close to a fire. Smiling, she kissed the infant and placed the babe in the hands of the mother.

Waneek put her basket aside and stood majestic. "I will not

finish the basket today. Better to weave more slowly…and more surely. Then there will be no obligation to unravel what has been woven before."

Waneek cradled her warm palms on his face. "You are like a son to me, so I will speak. The Horned Serpent, the embodiment of conflicting impulses resides in your heart. Torments keep you away from your destiny. You hide behind wounds. Do not be afraid to be strong."

"I'm sorry. I must honor my commitments."

Waneek dropped her hands. "You will remember my words. I hope it won't be too late."

Chapter 29

$\mathcal{J}$uliet stayed for the Christian wedding of Mary and Two Eagles, happy for the two of them, yet saddened for she would never see Mary again. Her spirits sagged with the amount of energy used to convince herself, Mary, her "forever" friend, would not be near anymore. How hard it was to don the mask of emotional self-sufficiency at the ceremony when her own heart was hollow and her future in doubt.

Then afterward, for two weeks she trudged dispirited behind Joshua through the wilderness. *Joshua.* Even though he strode ahead of her, she could taste him with her eyes, hear the muted undulations of his breath and soft rustle of his deerskin. Even without touching, she could feel his pulse as if it were her own beneath the warmth of a skin she almost shared with him.

Juliet had started to include pain among her intimate and constant companions, but what she felt now, on the knife's edge of his apathy, was an incision in the core of her being and she almost cried out with the sharpness of it.

Joshua was setting her adrift. A wretched province of mind rose with those nearest to her, the ones the ones she had dedicated her heart to, and now abandoned her to wander a trail alone.

If she wasn't so distressed she would have better appreciated the wondrous town of Blackberry Valley nestled in the bosom of a primeval forest and caressed by murmuring hemlocks, oaks and maples. Her turmoil warred with the tranquil evening of summer's end when the sunset brightly gilded the sides of mountains, filling the air with a wistful and dreamlike light over a rich pastoral landscape.

In the middle of town was a bucket fastened with iron to a moss-grown well and near it a trough for horses. Juliet drew a bucket of water and from it, scooped a copper cup to drink. A bay-colored Morgan horse with a peculiar flowered bonnet ambled to the trough.

Juliet patted the animal. "You are beautiful," she crooned and tugged a rosy apple from her pocket and gave it to the horse. The horse nudged her as if it could feel her melancholy, and she leaned her cheek against the horse's withers, securing a bit of happiness from the animal's devotion.

"That's my Maybelle."

Juliet swung around.

"She sure took a shine to you," said an older man, his nose, long and pointed, and his face withered like an old apple with a tuft of beard on his chin. "She likes certain people and since she likes you, I like you.

"Good to see you, Crims," said Joshua, extending his hand.

"Are you staying long?" Crims scanned Juliet from head to toe.

"This is Juliet Farrow." Joshua said, using the alias they had agreed upon so as not to alert any Loyalists of her whereabouts in case her uncle or Snapes had lingering infiltrators that might report back to them. "She will be staying with the Bell family and is moving on to Albany as soon as arrangements can be made."

"Too bad," said Crims. "Blackberry Valley is obliged to have something fresh and pretty to look at. This old widower could dream a lit—"

"She is not available."

No doubt, Joshua cut him short to disallow the idea of bachelors to call once they received wind a new and available female was in town.

Not to be ignored, Maybelle extended her head over Crims' shoulder. He dipped in his pocket, retrieved a carrot for the horse who chomped noisily. "What do you think of General Washington and his plan for the Patriot's on the frontier? Do you think we have a chance?"

Joshua scratched the beard on his chin, as if weighing Crims' questions and angled his head to Juliet. "Crims is a die-hard Patriot…lost his leg in the Battle of Germantown and crawled away in a dense fog."

He turned to Crims. "General Washington thinks in terms of grand strategy. In the spring of 1777, I was there when Saratoga fell. The enemy was armed to the teeth like lairds out of Scottish tales. British agents were in touch with the vast numbers of Loyalist sympathizers and probably expected the rest to flock in numbers to the King's standard. But the British did not grasp the vast moral power animating the high-minded minority of the Continental command. Their folly was not realizing the war in northern New York was taken over by men who knew frontier and forest fighting, who were out to win a war, who would not delude themselves an army the size of Burgoyne's might be defeated."

Crims scratched his wooden calf with the toe of his boot. "I hate bowing and scraping to British law. This dratted notion where we must pay for the French and Indian War is ludicrous. It was the Colonists who fought in the war, including me. And then to think we are too far away from England to have representation?" Crims spat. "To hell with them." He lifted his tricorn and ducked his head. "Pardon me, Miss Juliet."

Juliet sobered. "Formerly, I stood as a bystander to this war. But my eyes have been opened and I've discovered, surprisingly, how the Loyalists hold their views as the moral absolute, refusing to recognize this is a war opposed to a tyrannical injustice."

Crims pulled on his beard. "The war is far-reaching and brewing a fever, a war to give victory to ideas of right and good, and carried on for an honest purpose.

"Aye," said Joshua. "Men seeking a new intangible premise where all men will possess the right to life, liberty and property."

"Amen. Nice meeting you, Miss Juliet. I reckon you are mighty tired from your journey. The Bells are good friends, and if you don't mind, I'll come to call."

"It would be and honor and pleasure," said Juliet smiling. Maybelle nickered and nosed her in response. Juliet laughed and smoothed the mane on the horse's head. "I hope to see you, again, too my friend."

Chapter 30

"I don't believe you…that you would send me away—"

Through the village they walked to the Bells', passing many homes, some large, some small, denoting the success of the town's inhabitants. Not once did he turn to look at her. Her heart ached at his withdrawal, his total lack of interest in her as a woman…as his wife…and she yearned to storm the citadels of his merciless apathy.

"My decision is for your own good."

Words died on her tongue. There was nothing she could say, nothing she could do. His mind was settled. He would leave her, and she would be alone. Again. The silence between them lay sepulchral and Juliet felt the entire load of his longing to be rid of her.

A little farther on, he stopped. When he spoke, it was with difficulty, as if he were having to prise every syllable out and it hurt him. "You have a place…in my heart. You must know that by now."

It was the closest he had ever come to telling her that he loved her. For a whole moment, the world stopped.

His blue eyes dimmed. If there was any identifiable emotion in his drawn features, it was sorrow. "You deserve so much better than I can give you, Juliet. I wish—"

"Don't!" She stepped into his space.

His eyes shuttered. "You are going back to England."

He turned and began walking again. She wanted to scream at him, tell him no, she wasn't going anywhere. But, truth was, what choice did she have…a woman alone in the wilds of the Colonies?

They climbed a high hill, five furlongs from the village, to a lovely farm with a large home possessing a broad view of the valley below and where every activity of the inhabitants of Blackberry Valley could be observed.

Shielding the house to the north from winter storms stood barns, bursting with hay. In the farmyard lay plows and harrows, folds of black-faced sheep and cows lowing in regular cadence, their udders full and waiting for evening milking. Under the sheltering eaves of a corn crib brimming with corn, a lordly turkey strutted and, secured in the lofts above, a cock crowed. Wheel ruts cut through the earth, marking a well-worn path up to the house with a horseblock. To the side were an overgrown garden, and a barrier of tall trees.

They paused on the threshold. Juliet stood behind Joshua, making a study of the tidy porch with carved seats, and farther to the end stood a colorful array of hollyhocks heavy with blossoms, like ladies waiting in line for a summer cotillion. Behind her followed the watchdog, patient, full of importance, waving his bushy tail and nudging her hand with his black nose. Juliet reached out and gave his ears a scratch. The dog whined in appreciation.

A sharp wind blew from the top of the mountain, wrestling

with the trees and chilling her to the bone. To be left with the Bell family…complete strangers? Would they accept her…or treat her like Orpha and Horace Hayes had? She shuddered, smoothed her mud-caked skirts, and then fidgeted with her cuffs, her breathing accelerating. Would the Bells scorn her ragamuffin appearance? She had brought little from the fort. Two dresses and the cross around her neck.

"Papa, there's someone on the porch," said a child from inside the plank house, creating an uproar and peals of laughter. At the click of a latch Juliet straightened. The door swung open on well-oiled hinges. Her stomach churned.

"Caroline," the man called over his shoulder. "Look who's here."

An attractive middle-aged woman very swollen with child, and with a two-year old toddler plastered on her hip scooted beside her husband. "Joshua! "This is a surprise for my sorry eyes. Come in."

She smiled at Juliet, and then frowned at Joshua for his lack of introduction. "Welcome, I'm Caroline Bell."

"I'm Juliet Farrow." She cringed from the lie.

She pulled Juliet inside to where she was ushered to a chair by a fire, surrounded by a clamoring host of light-haired children, red-cheeked, and smiling with a chorus of infectious enthusiasm, introducing themselves so quickly she lost count. Eight, wasn't it? She tried to remember their names from the youngest, Elias, then James, three years with his thumb stuck in his mouth, followed in age by Robin, Mary, Winnie, Suzanne, and Charity, up to the thirteen-year-old Thomas who stood proud like his father.

"What's your name?" asked Robin.

"Can you play Nine Men's Morris?" asked Thomas.

"Did you know Joshua is the best shot in the entire Colonies?" asked Suzanne.

"Where did you get your red hair?" asked Winnie, touching her hair.

Mary, a little brown-haired girl with crumbs on her face brought Juliet a half-eaten corn pone. "Thank you," she said, taking a piece.

"Children, give our visitors space. Pardon all the questions. They are still learning manners." Caroline grinned as she shooed her brood away.

"I hope you can stay and visit with us a spell."

Joshua spoke up. "That's why we're here. I've a favor to ask and want to know if Juliet could stay with you here at the farm until I return."

His words, so cold and callous…a chill ran up her spine.

The three-year-old boy, James, fell and bumped his head, delivering thunderous wails. Caroline dropped Elias in Juliet's arms and picked up the older sibling, kissing and crooning away his hurts.

Caroline smiled genuinely at Juliet. "We would love to have you. It has been a long time without visitors and news, and I crave female companionship."

Juliet's heart stopped. To be welcomed after her horrible treatment at the Hayes' home…and Joshua's cold indifference… sent a wave of relief through her. Caroline's immediate and friendly response laid her worst fears to rest. If she was to stay with someone, it would be the Bells. Their irresistible affection, acceptance and warmth overwhelmed Juliet. This precious family was love, smiles, joys, kisses and hugs.

Everything Juliet dreamed of.

A servant girl named Betsy served tankards of spiced cider. Warmed by the wide-mouthed fireplace, Juliet sat idly, Joshua next to her while the smaller Bell children regrouped and crawled up him, and rode on his knee.

Mr. Bell or James, she had learned sat in his elbow chair nonplussed by his brood's noisy commotion. Juliet tightened her hold and pressed her cheek against the two-year-old boy's soft blond curls. Sucking his thumb and making smacking noises, he peeked up at her with trusting eyes. He nestled his head against her neck until his head drooped with little pants of milk breath, asleep.

"Do you promise to go nutting with us tomorrow?" begged Suzanne.

"I'd be delighted," Juliet laughed. "Once I get some rest."

"Children, Mr. Hansford and Miss Farrow are tired. Off to bed with you." Beneath a myriad of moans and protests, the children climbed the stairs with assurances by Caroline to listen to their prayers and to tuck them in.

Joshua took off his boots and stretched his stockinged feet before the fire. Content while the men talked, she watched how the flames and smoke-wreaths struggled together like foes in a burning city. Behind her, the flickering light caught on pewter plates and reflected the flame as sunshine. She nuzzled her cheek to the snoring child's downy head filled with a rare serenity.

Joshua took a piece of corn pone from Caroline. "Juliet has had a tough time." And so, Joshua confided her story to the curious Bells from her kidnapping in England, the Hayes' and subsequent massacre, imprisoned by Onontio and delivering the chief's child. Of her forced marriage to Joshua, he said nothing, skipping to their flight down the rivers, and her helping them escape from Fort Oswego and saving their lives.

"You are a remarkable and brave woman," Caroline said and Juliet knew that Joshua had cemented the Bells' esteem, if not their affection, for her.

"Come," said Caroline, lifting the sleeping child from her and she escorted Juliet through the house. There were large well-appointed rooms, impressive chestnut beams, a secret staircase in full sight. Eight paintings of landscapes adorned the stark plank walls, Smollett in four volumes, six volumes Edward Gibbon's, *The History of the Decline and Fall of the Roman Empire* in bookcases with cheval glass. The house was filled with the finest of Queen Anne furniture, linen and drapes.

Exhausted, Juliet was led to an upper bedroom and cried out in glee. A copper tub filled with water and a fresh cake of rose-scented soap was laid out for her use. "How thankful—"

"Any friend of Joshua's is a friend of ours. He saved my husband's life at Saratoga…carried him two miles on his back, away from British troops after he'd been critically wounded."

Caroline shifted the babe on her other shoulder. "There's a clean muslin gown for you to wear. And in the morn, I'll lend you one of my dresses until we can clean your garments. Now I have to put this little one in his bed."

Caroline departed and her leaving left a void. Juliet couldn't help but think how this remarkable woman was the backbone of her family, and—how she envied her.

Chapter 31

*J*uliet slept deeply, a deliciously real bed pressed to her back. In the morning, she dressed in the gown Caroline had laid out for her, and gazed out the window of her room, taken with a commanding view of the town below. An isolated patch of blue mist floated lightly on the glare of the horizon, revealing the church but not yet its spire. A rooster crowed in tandem with the clangor of bells, heralding a new day. A horse and wagon filled with bags of grain rumbled.

Maybelle drank at the trough, lifted her head and whinnied when Crims approached. A woman dropped wooden milk pails and talked to another woman sweeping her porch. Cows followed a path up a hill to green pasture. A row of gabled roofs over square smug houses represented a tidy world of sincerity and progress.

The final button fastened on her dress, she smoothed the soft blue skirts and followed the pandemonium. She paused on the steps above a massive kitchen caught with the morning sun shining through glass windows, and brightening the dim interior. The radiance rested on a great spinning wheel and cantilevered loom in the corner, and then illuminated iron kettles dangling from rafters of oak. The beams lingered on somber homespun, dyed yellow with the bark of sassafras, and soft deerskin clothing slung on wooden pegs. It dawdled over the blue, green and red yarns hanging from the ceiling, and gleamed spotty patches on the polished wooden floor before mingling with the shooting flickers of the fire from a massive stone hearth.

But it was the light spread upon the deafening cacophony of family that drew her. She smiled as little Elias laughed and careened, arms out around the kitchen with his ability to totter; his older sisters, Robin and Mary, babes themselves, taking on the role of mother, following him and keeping him safe. James sat at the head of a long table, the rest of the children clamoring for his attention. The smell of fresh baked corn pone lay tilted up on a board and caused her stomach to gnaw with hunger. Betsy, the serving girl flipped the popping bacon onto a serving plate and the harried Caroline whipped eggs in a bowl.

Everything spoke of love and home. A real home.

Juliet stepped into the kitchen. "What can I do to help?"

"I'll take all the help I can get!" Caroline pointed to the hearth. "Scoop some porridge into the bowls and serve the children, please."

Joshua entered with a load of wood in his arms and she found herself facing him, her breath coming quickly and her heart in her eyes, she was sure. When he turned in her direction, Juliet quickly looked away. If he'd seen her watching him, he said nothing of it and stacked the wood by the fireplace. He picked up the squealing five-year-old, Mary, and sat her on his shoulders, the girl's skinny legs hooked beneath Joshua's arms, hands tangled in his hair.

As Joshua dipped forward to Juliet in an exaggerated courtly bow, Mary shrieked with delight. The three of them sat at the table, laughing, Juliet next to Joshua. He smelled clean…of warm spice. His arm brushed hers, Startled he gazed at her. The hunger darting out from his eyes devoured her from a whisper away. With the hunger, there remained the stubborn denial shouting through him, but deep inside she knew he cared for her.

When the fresh loaves of baked bread were sliced by Thomas, everyone grew quiet and bowed their heads in prayer.

A moment later, Crims knocked at the door and sauntered in. "I'm just in time."

"You old rascal. You know you are always welcome at our table," said Caroline. Through the open door, Juliet saw Maybelle, his horse, like a forlorn puppy, head down, ears flicked forward, stunned she had to be left outside.

"Children, eat well and after your chores and book learning, I'm sure we can convince Joshua, Juliet and Crims to play Nine Men's Morris," said Caroline and they all dug in.

Crims hooked his wooden leg over the bench and sat next to Suzanne. He reached for warm bread and lathered it with sweet butter. "There will be a cold and early winter. The fur is thick on the foxes, and the newts are already migrating to their hibernation grounds."

"I saw the first flock of geese heading south," said Charity.

A smile tipped up one corner of Joshua's mouth. "Soon Hó-thó will come."

"Who is Hó-thó?" asked the children, their eyes growing as wide as dinner plates.

"Hó-thó is the Iroquois god, Cold Weather. Every winter, he seizes his hatchet from his belt, flourishes it in the air and strikes the trees. That's what makes the trees crack with such a thunderous noise. The Indians have learned to outwit Hó-thó by building fires, sipping hot teas, and keeping warm under furs."

The "whoa" of a driver halting a team of horses and a dog's rousing barking came from the outside.

Caroline peeked out the window. "Oh, dear. It's Bethany Powers. I can count on one hand the times she's condescended to come here the past ten years."

Crims wiped his wrist across his face, smearing crumbs and gooseberry jam. "That ferocious, hatchet-faced dragon is here to hook Joshua for one of her girls. She got word of her red-haired competition."

Caroline pointed a ladle at Crims. "No doubt you fed the rumor."

"It gladdens my heart to see Bethany sweat in her stays. Makes Maybelle happy, too."

James and the children laughed.

"Silent, children," Caroline commanded them with a well-meaning glance. "We give our guests respect."

The children and her husband pasted on proper angelic expressions.

Crims did not. Rebellion shone in his sparkling blue eyes. "Mischief, thou are afoot. Take thou what course thou wilt."

Caroline plunked her hands on her hips. "Don't quote Shakespeare to me, Crims. Curb your tongue in my house."

"You have asked the impossible," Crims complained. "It is like curling the Mohawk River back to its source." He angled his head low and, confidingly, spoke to Juliet. "Bethany likes to throw herself around because her husband is rich. He's a swindler."

Joshua, chuckled accustomed to Crim's contentiousness. Juliet suppressed a smile, and straightened as Bethany Powers burst across the kitchen threshold. Mrs. Powers was a woman of robust frame, round-shouldered and stout; she had a large face with sharp angles, the under-jaw, much developed, her brow low. There was a spiteful attitude in her dark eyes flashing over Juliet.

A servant girl of approximately thirteen summers, head bent low, her brown hair tucked in her mob cap, shifted behind Bethany. Thin as a rail, looking starved and exhausted, she was with certainty, an indentured servant, and Juliet's heart went out to the child.

Bethany settled on a chair, fluffed out her skirts like a chicken ready to lay an egg.

"I shan't be long. Grace, you must stand behind me." Bethany ordered, her chin raised.

"I have an important announcement to make. As the matron of the town's leading family, I feel it incumbent upon me to host a dance for the harvest. And most importantly—" She smiled at Joshua, "—in honor of Mr. Hansford's return. My daughters are anxious to dance with you," she trilled.

"You see, I feel compelled—" she fluttered her deep blue-veined fingers over her massive chest, "even dictated by my esteemed lineage...Sir Eagleton, you must all know...is a distinguished knight in England."

Crims tilted his head back and scratched his neck. "I heard told Sir Eagleton was beheaded for posing as the King, shouting grand speeches, collecting crowds and huge amounts of taxes."

Bethany put her nose in the air and sniffed as if she were smelling the stink of a London sewer. "And your ancestry, Mr. Crims, probably comes from that horse you crow about."

Crims slapped his wooden leg and chortled. "Maybelle forgives your insult because she knows your condescending attitude comes from someone that has bad luck when it comes to thinking."

"How are you, Mr. Hansford?" Bethany crooned, darting a disapproving glance to Juliet.

Little Mary offered Grace fresh corn pone.

Bethany held her hand up. "Grace is not allowed to eat and should know better." She turned to the servant girl. "Wait 'til we get home."

Images of Orpha flashed through Juliet's mind. Poor Eldon Stevens whipped to death against the post. Hot blood rushed through Juliet's veins. She clenched her jaws. Only the flex in Joshua's arms beside her told his annoyance.

Bethany carried on. "You are all invited…that is, if you have proper dress. Do you Miss—?"

Juliet swallowed. Bethany's hubris was a developed art.

"Juliet Farrow," Joshua provided. "Everyone else will pale in comparison at the dance."

She fingered the humble linen dress Caroline had loaned her, nothing compared to the fineness of Bethany's day clothes, and certainly nothing to wear to such an occasion.

Thomas strode to the door. With a benevolent wink, he slipped corn pone into Grace's pocket. Oh, there was something between the two of them and hidden beneath Bethany's oblivious nose. Grace was so taken with his kindness when he went out the door, she stumbled and fell onto Bethany. The woman turned and slapped the girl across the face.

Grace cried out and held her hand to the swelling curve of an Irish cheekbone. A single tear rolled like a drop of quicksilver.

Juliet took two quick steps and stood to her full height in front of Bethany. Keeping her voice low and even, she said, "She is mere a girl. If I ever hear of you striking her again, you'll have me to deal with."

Juliet met icy eyes glittering with retribution, and then everything happened all at once. Caroline gasped. Chest lifting, Bethany sputtered and tromped to the door. James opened it. Crims applauded and whistled. Like a sheep dog marshaling sheep, Maybelle cut in front of Bethany, repeatedly blocking her passage to the carriage. The dog circled her, barking and nipping at her heels. In a flurry of skirts, Bethany screamed every time Maybelle pitched and turned, obstructing her path. She kicked at the dog but the canine was too swift.

The odd theatrics between horse, dog and harridan made the children laugh. And Juliet couldn't help but laugh, too. Had Crims trained the horse with his whistle?

"I'm sorry. I couldn't let her abuse the girl—" Juliet said.

"You've done a service that is long overdue," said Caroline. "I'm ashamed I didn't say something myself."

Joshua beamed with approval and, for one moment her breath halted and the rest of the world melted away. Naked hunger and longing swam in the depths of his brilliant blue eyes. He reached out...stroked her cheek.

Her heartbeat quickened even more. Had she uncovered a tiny crack in his armor? She would chisel it apart, chink by chink.

Chapter 32

A wind blew, kicking up her skirts. Scudding dark clouds strutted across the sky. Sheets flapped like seagull wings as Juliet pinned the last of the laundry to the line. An air of unreality choked Juliet, thinking on the wild, tumultuous events leading her from England. The life-altering nightmare blurred with the consequences of her recent impulsive actions, casting her in a direction she feared—irrevocably back to England.

Despite the moments of hope, the gulf between her and Joshua had grown as large as the ocean. Yet in the dark entrails of despair, the remembrance of what had been left unsaid between them, of distant echoes of emotion, of silent flashes in his tormented eyes, remained…a tenuous filament between them. A bond that couldn't be denied.

Juliet numbered the many startling contrasts of Lord Joshua Rutland, the highly intelligent, principled, and tenacious man. Honorable to a fault, he adhered to a code of ethics seeking out truth and knowledge beyond his advocacy of the Revolution. It would be a part of his legacy.

What others might find pushy or callous, Juliet viewed

through a different lens. She observed a man whose inner strength and integrity created trust and respect among his peers in the Colonies. Through discomfort and pain, he never gave up, assessing problems and coming up with solutions, taunting the face of impossibility that kept them safe during their escapes. And to Joshua, there was nothing more powerful than his promise. He would choose death before breaking his word.

A smile came to her face, how her warrior played with the Bell children, wrestling the entire brood to the ground. How every single one of them piled on top of him, and then booming with the mighty roar of a bear, he lifted, and they fled screaming to return moments later to start their play again.

Oh, how she understood his other side. Self-righteous? Relentless? Merciless? At the Hayes' farm he'd defended her...taken on Horace and Orpha at jeopardy to his trade. Hadn't he taken on Onontio, defeating the brave in front of the whole tribe? In a room full of British officers, and surrounded by the thick walls of his enemy at Fort Oswego, hadn't he gambled with the dangerous act of espionage?

Yet his need for control...to send her to England...that judgmental decision of his seemingly made for her safety. No. His decision came from a darker place—of fear and shame and it had to do with Sarah.

His pack had been carelessly deposited near a stump while he went up on the mountain to chop trees with James and Thomas. The question remained. What made Joshua so angry and cold? Why did he feel compelled to send her back to England?

Unchained ends dangled, mysteries shouted, contradictions swarmed and remained unanswered. She inched closer to

Joshua's pack, scanning to see if anyone was near. The younger Bell children were taking a nap and the older girls studied their lessons. The steady sounds of an ax echoing from the woods up above indicated the men were busy.

She bit her lip. Not once had she snooped in her life. Joshua was taking her to Albany. This was her one opportunity. She sat on the stump, rearranging her skirts. Opening the bag, she reached inside and drew out a handkerchief. She fingered the lace-edged handkerchief soiled from so much handling. How many times had she witnessed Joshua inhaling its scent when he was unaware of her watching him?

She drew out a letter and unfolded it. The number of wrinkles in the missive indicated how many times the note had been opened and reopened. Globules of red-brown stained the paper. She drew back. Blood?

A burning sensation rose in her chest and she pushed it away. Above the cloud cover remained. A fissure opened, and rays of sunlight poured from the sky. The letter was the key to healing Joshua's wounds. She bent her head and commenced reading.

Joshua hummed a tune. Two trees had been felled and five cords of wood chopped, putting the Bells well ahead of their winter labors. As he made his way down the mountain he thought of Juliet.

Juliet was different. Her wild heart saw blessings where most experienced millstones round the neck, and if one thing was for certain; her smile took on the same radiance as a whole tree of apple blossoms.

How brave she was when confronted with treachery. The

enslavement she suffered sold into indenture, and consequent cruelty of Orpha and Horace. Witnessing a massacre, she did not think of herself. She cared for Mary, helping her get through the punishing ordeal of Onontio.

He recalled her humiliation when he arrived at Tionnontigo, tied to a stake, suffering the cruel barbs and punishment of the village women. How she endangered her own life to bring the chief's son into the world. He remembered how hard he pushed her through the wilderness at a brutal pace. How she saved his life, helping him escape death from Fort Oswego. Without a doubt, she was loyal to those she cared about.

But most of all, he recalled her bravery the night she made solemn vows to become a complete stranger's wife—his wife.

He ceased humming. It was not the real reason for the twinge of guilt causing his chest to tighten, and that fact bothered him. She'd be leaving him soon. She'd be gone as soon as they traveled to Albany. He'd arrange reliable passage to Boston and authorize his uncle to secure her passage to England.

This was exactly what he had planned. He should be grateful. The whole ordeal would soon be over. She'd be protected. He'd have his life back. Just the way he wanted it.

Except he wasn't sure he wanted it anymore.

With his ax on his shoulder, he passed the last copse of trees, leading into the clearing of the Bells' home. He expected to see Juliet playing with the children. Instead, in her linen day dress, she sat on a stump...a letter in her hands. His heart stalled. His blood boiled. He stomped to her side and snatched the letter. "You dare to read my private correspondence?"

"I dare."

She shot to her feet, defiance thundering in every bone of her body. A second later, her eyes softened. "I know. I understand your fear and your shame."

"Do not say another word, Juliet." He closed the distance between them, stared down at her beautiful face...and he couldn't decide if he wanted to kiss her or wrap his hands around her slender white throat and throttle her. "You have no business."

"Concealment is a game we undertake, yet our secrets are surely revealed by what we want to seem to be as what we disguise. Sarah Thacker did not simply die, she was tortured to death."

He jerked back as if she'd slapped him. Then, eyes narrowing, hands clenched, he said, "Be quiet, Juliet!"

"There is fear and rage boiling in your soul, Joshua. It is infested, like gangrene, eating away at you."

He gripped the ax in his hands and closed his eyes. "I was responsible for her...she died because of me...of who I am."

"Should I fill myself with insidious poisons as you have? Sustain myself with fear as you do? To keep your Sarah on a sacrificial altar and pretend the rest of the world does not exist."

A furnace of rage roared up inside him, its destructive force verged on eruption. He beat it back, certain that once unleashed it would devour his sanity. And in the midst of this whirling, red-hot fury stood Juliet. He wished that numbness would overcome him. He wished he did not see and hear and feel so clearly, and yet he could not escape the riot of images before him. Sarah, bloody and tortured. Juliet and Sarah, alternating faces, both meeting the same fate.

He opened his eyes, glared at Juliet as if she were some bizarre creature, a curiosity, distorted and repulsive. "Get away from me, Juliet. I can't stand the sight of you. Get away from me before I do something I regret."

With a loud growl, he smashed the ax into the stump and cracked it in half.

Juliet froze. Her knees shook. Good Lord, what was she thinking, pushing him to his limits like that? How stupid.

Stupid. God, she'd been even more than stupid, believing her own fantasies. Bitterness rose in her throat. She turned and ran before she made a further fool of herself.

She ran and ran, tears flowing, arms thrashing at the air and the invisible visions of a life that would be out of her reach. It was her fault for having dared to dream, to be that susceptible, that vulnerable.

Not knowing or caring which way she went, she pushed through rough undergrowth. Trees, bushes and branches barred her path on every side. Thorn bushes snagged her hair and ripped her clothes. Rough branches tore at her hands and arms. A prison to hold her back. But she had to get away, far, far away and kept pushing on, farther and farther.

Out of breath, she leaned against a tree and wept. Collapsing to the ground, she wept for the mother she never knew, wept for the loveless life she had, wept for the all unfairnesses bestowed on her head. Even now in this alien land, she had come to love…again that love had been ripped from her.

Finally, her tears spent, she sat up. A clarity suddenly shone through the dark forests of her mind. No. she would not allow it. She would not be a pawn at someone else's whim. Never again. She would not go back to England. No, she would not. There was nothing for her there. Somehow, she would find a place in this New World.

The forest became silent around her, except for a few birds chirping. For a long time, she sat lost in sorrow for the way things were and for the way things were not meant to be. Her mind alternating between new resolve and her shattered dreams, the tears came again and with them, more sobs. That ugly loneliness swelled and heaved, then through the stillness, the regular beat of quiet footsteps. A bush stirred and Joshua knelt in front of her.

"Juliet."

He followed. *Why?* Why couldn't he let her alone to deal with her pain and misery? She wanted to beat his chest with all the wrongs incurred on her. Yet her arms lay leaden at her sides. She lifted her head. Faced him. Opened her mouth to tell him to go away, but the words clogged in her throat.

"Why are you here, Joshua?"

"Because you can't leave me alone."

In a half-haze, suddenly she was in his arm. He drew her closer, cushioned her against his warm chest, her mouth buried deep against musky, beloved flesh. His words had sounded like a cry for help, a beseechment.

"Why do you torture me like this?" He raised his head and stared wildly into her eyes.

Ignoring the burning ache in her throat, Juliet cleaved to him. Within her embrace his heavy frame twisted with spasms as he fought with his violent inner demons.

"Let it come," she murmured, cradling his head on her shoulder. "Let it come." Whispering comfort and love, she consoled him and waited, waited, waited patiently for the turbulence to subside, for the demons to retreat, for his body to still. Then she framed his tortured face between her palms and kissed him. Her eyes filled with tears. "I love you, Joshua."

"I couldn't keep her safe…if I couldn't protect her, how can I protect anyone else?" He shuddered. "I love you, Juliet. But do not love me."

He loved her. He had said it.

But his face contorted again. "How can I protect you? Snapes told me in the gaol at Fort Oswego he was going to kill you, do the same thing he did to Sarah."

Oh, God. The realization hit her like a punch to the stomach. Snapes? The signature on the letter was signed, *"MS"*. *Milburn Snapes.* Joshua had told her of his vendetta against the Rutland family. Her blood chilled.

No. "You will not push me away. I will not allow you to be driven into hiding by real or imagined fear, pinned there by a deluded acceptance you're helpless to do anything else but hide. Apathy survives solely on lies and can only be washed away by truth."

His fingers clutched the rumpled confusion of her hair, tightened. "It is proof you cannot stay with me."

"It is proof of what you deny. I see it in your eyes." She touched his lids with her fingertips and smiled.

"You see too many damned things in my eyes that are not real."

"They are real for me if not for you."

"With this war raging…I can give you nothing."

"You give without knowing, Joshua." Gently, she cleared his forehead of brown strand heavy with perspiration. "And what you cannot offer is perhaps not worth having."

"You are a child ignorant of tomorrow—and I am only a man, damn you, as flawed as the next."

"I am not fearful any more. I have been to hell and back. I want you, Joshua. I want to be by your side. To raise our children. I do not fear the future, but I would fear it without you." She looked directly into his eyes and said it again. "I love you."

Juliet sighed, too overwhelmed for debate, too paralyzed by the weight of love too long deprived of its natural fulfillment. She was no longer fooled by his assumed posturing. "Then prove your flaws, Joshua Rutland," she murmured dreamily into his ear as she leaned forward and kissed it. "Prove your flaws to me now!"

The last of his defenses crumbled. He swept her into his arms, growling curses and hoarse imprecations. He laid her back on the soft green moss, and swept aside her clothing, his hands wandering over her body, feeling licks of fire wherever they touched her skin. Gone were the doubts, the indecisions, the denials, and the uncertainties.

For an instant, one brief instant, he stilled. He sat up to drink in her wondrous body. She blushed, covered herself with her hands beneath his heated gaze.

"My God, you take my breath away. Yet this is madness," he said. "Tell me to stop, Juliet.

"Tell you to stop?" she whispered. Very purposefully, she freed her hair from its pins so that it flowed in waves beneath her. "That, my lord, would be madness."

His rich, alluring chuckle drifted over her. He stood to shed his buckskins letting them drop to the ground. She caught flashes of glistening flesh, hard and sinewy, damp with his day's exertion.

"You fill my whole world, Juliet." He kneeled next to her, hauled her into his arms, and held her tight in his embrace, as if shielding her with his body against all the torments, the fears and loneliness.

Cocooned within Joshua's arms, Juliet closed her eyes and drank it all in—the man, the millions of ways he moved her. He rose again, lifted her ever so gently and carried her beneath the shade of oaks, reverently laying her on soft moss. She buried her face against his throat, so conscious of where his warm flesh touched hers.

The air lay thick like the heat of day. She dared to glide her hand down his shoulders, chest, and midsection.

He seized her hands. "Slowly," he warned, perceiving her with hunger. He leaned down to kiss her. First his lips grazed hers, soft and fine as a breath of wind. She quivered at the brush of his lips against hers and the feeling swept downward, caressing the tips of her breast, the core of her belly, the place between her legs.

"Please," she said, pressing close, seeking release from the delicious ache inside her. "Promise me it won't be like before, when you made me rise to the sky and yet took none of your own pleasure."

A quirk of a smile tipped his lips as the length of his body pressed close to hers, their legs quickly entwined, their mouths inseparable as tongues intermingled on one shared breath.

"Juliet." He caressed and teased her flesh until her breasts budded and were full and heavy against his warm hand.

His hand splayed at the bottom of her spine holding her in intimate contact. She gasped as her bare breasts touched against the hairs of his chest, her cheek abraded into nettle stings, silken skin against stubbled maleness and the intimate contact of his arousal against her stomach. Suddenly, his hands were everywhere, her body aching for more.

Outlining the tips of her breasts with his fingers, Joshua brought their tips to crested peaks. Slowly, languorously, his hand moved downward, skimming either side of her body, exploring her thighs, then plunged down again searching the warmth that lay hidden intimately between.

"My Juliet. Do you know how hard it's been for me to stay away from you? Knowing you were my wife and not being able to have you?"

"Yes," she said, her fingers reaching down and caressing his manhood. "I think I might have a vague idea."

His mouth came down on hers, sapping her strength, her body boneless while he plied her intimately with his finger, withdrawing and sinking, pushing her over some unnamed edge. She could not get enough of him; her impatience grew to explosive proportions, his expert touch driving her to higher levels of ecstasy.

Dazed, she opened her eyes to meet his blue gaze, dark as lapis...and poised above her... Lord Joshua Rutland, a man who struck fear in the British and Indians alike, a man who had the lethal power to kill a man. Yet all he had yielded to her was an aching tenderness.

"There must be more," she beseeched, crying out in a frenzy of unendurable rapture, "please!"

For a fraction of a second Joshua's hand stayed. His face ravaged with uncertainties, he hesitated. Then with a helpless groan, he buried his face in her shoulder. "There will be pain, my Juliet. There is no way I can spare you of that."

She circled his neck with her arms and held him secure. "I love you, Joshua. I love you with all my heart."

"I love you, Juliet. You realize this moment will change everything between us."

"It had better." Her whisper came fierce with emotion, thick with feeling. She pressed her lips to the hollow of his throat, intoxicated by the taste of him.

The vow Joshua made not to touch her disintegrated like sand washed away in a river flood. She lay there soft…yielding, all for the taking, a fulfillment of every waking dream that had tormented him since the first time he clapped eyes on her at the Hayes' farm.

Her full ripe breasts thrust impudently like pink rose buds. Her trim waist melded down over rounded hips, revealing the dark red triangle of her womanhood where he eagerly explored.

He nudged her legs apart, fitting himself snugly in the cradle of her thighs. He groaned as she worked her dewy entrance over the tip of his shaft, digging her nails in his hips. Fully aroused, desire pulsed through his swollen rigid flesh.

His gut clenched tight, his reserve of willpower quickly dwindling. His head dipped toward her breast, he suckled and she moaned, and then he plunged into her, through her barrier, burying himself deep inside her as deeply as he could. He would not withdraw until he'd gotten his fill.

She gasped and he covered her mouth with his, whispering reassurances. He plunged into her again and again, smelling her excitement on the crest of an incredible flood into womanhood. Past and future were obliterated; there was only the here and now for each moment stretching into an eternity of timelessness.

Her whimpers, primeval, universal, wild…her body rose to meet his rhythmic thrusts and his control shattered. Nights of restraint, sleeping by her side, now unleashed, his ardor mounted as she rose to meet his scorching desire. Melding, merging, swaying with oneness, moving into rhythms as old and as enduring as time itself.

Her fingers dug into his shoulders and he buried his face on the side of her neck, the pressure building inside him unlike anything he'd experienced. Joshua thrust his fingers into the flaming silkiness of her hair as she abandoned herself to him, and with every forceful thrust, he claimed her in a raw act of total possession, mindless of everything except the indulgence of granting them both complete satisfaction.

As she peaked, she arched and vibrated with liquid fire. Joshua taut above her, emptied his seed into her. Breathing hard, he rolled her to the side, keeping her intimately joined to him, and reveling in the sensation of her wet warmth, and the brush of her lips against his chest. His chin nestled upon her head and his fingers buried in the fiery waves of her hair. For a moment, he abandoned the fears of the past and future, basking upon the wonder of the intimacy they had just shared.

She ran a fingernail across his cheek. "Joshua…was it…like this for you?"

He exhaled a long sigh of contentment, basking in male arrogance that she was shaken as much as he. He kissed her head, the scent of roses mixed with the musky scent of their lovemaking permeated the air.

"You are exquisite," he said. She was whirling through a haze of new feelings and desires, and she wanted him to explain what she was experiencing. "Rarely."

"I'm not going back to England."

"I suppose not."

"You're a clever man to have come to that conclusion."

"And you are a stubborn witch weaving her spells."

"Stubborn? You're the champion of mulish, pig-headedness."

"You might be right." He nuzzled his chin into her hair while she stroked down his back.

"I'm staying here in Blackberry Valley with you. My place is by your side. I'll take the risk."

"Did I ever have a chance?"

"No."

Latticed light penetrated the leafy bower high above, and rippled over her full ivory breasts. Her beauty was superb and regal, and in the glowing light of the forest glade, made her more ethereal than ever.

Joshua thought of the million ways he loved her. He was proud of how she pitched in with the Bells, never complaining. Her laughter and the way the children cleaved to her touched his heart. And yes, he endured her flaws. She sharpened her wit on him and kept him guessing at times. He wanted a woman who would challenge him. Her unassuming nature, he found awe-inspiring, not like spoiled aristocratic women he'd met in England. With her steadfast heart, he begrudgingly admired her persistence in rebuffing his detachment.

Juliet listened. To his dark moods, Juliet lifted him into her light. Her integrity, her spontaneity made him look forward to the magic of her every day. She trusted him.

Something sprang free in his chest. Its newness at first, painful, but the feeling resolutely exploded forth with a life and vigor of its own. Something marvelous, implausible, and all-consuming.

"I love you, Juliet."

"I know," she said, and then cleared her throat. "Is it possible for you to…again?"

She squirmed closer to him. The woman had no idea how much lust she kindled. "We must make love again to ward off the coming cold of Hó-thó," said Joshua.

"I'm all for that."

In answer, he grinned and rolled her onto her back.

They took their time returning to the Bells home, lingering on the mountain.

Once on lower ground, they hiked across a boggy shore as a blue jay called to its mate, then up on the drier hillside, where clumps of barberry, spikes of steeplebush, and sweet fern grew in a tangle of undergrowth that led to massive rocks clawed with tree roots. The wind whistled from breaches of stone, lifting a tent of grapevine.

"A cave." Juliet's eyes widened.

Joshua swept back the foliage, grabbed her hand, and pulled her through the concealing vegetation. A small animal skittered away in the darkness. Juliet reached out and felt moisture dripping down the wall, and the buffering softness of lichen and moss growing through the cracks. Twelve steps into the interior was the back wall of the cave. She turned around. "One can be completely concealed from the outside."

"You must remember this place, Juliet. You never know if your survival will necessitate its use."

She shivered from the dampness and heard the warning snort of a buck in the denser brush.

He guided her out and at a ridge was a wide impenetrable thicket of blackberries. Juliet clapped her hands and greedily partook of nature's bounty.

When she turned, she caught Joshua staring at her—intent, unblinking, hungry. He swung her up in his arms and carried her into the cool of the woods. There, on a bed of soft mosses, he made love to her again.

Afterward, Joshua picked up a colorful leaf that had floated down. Summer was fat on its eve and soon the seasons would be changing. He ran the leaf around her breasts and down her abdomen, then cradled her in his arms.

She gazed at the thick darkness of the surrounding trees, and the twinkling darkness where soundlessly, one by one, the vast fields of heaven flowered splendid stars, the forget-me-nots of the angels.

"You see that constellation?"

"Um-m. The Big Dipper." She snuggled closer to his warmth, the scent of their lovemaking permeating the air.

"There were seven brothers, one was fat and lazy. They set out to overtake the Great Bear. The slothful brother became incapacitated, forcing the group to cater to his demands. He was abandoned but found his redemption when he leaps and kills the Great Bear with the powers he absorbed from the rest of his brothers. The men consumed the bear's meat and rose into the sky where they remain to this day and can be seen any starlit night as the Big Dipper constellation."

Juliet stroked his chest. "Like the Greeks who believed Zeus changed Callisto back into a bear and making her the largest constellation in the sky."

"As the blood and oil drips down from the carcass, it stains the leaves that form the autumn landscape," he said. "The bear mysteriously reassembles itself, rises from the earth, and becomes the Great Bear in the night sky every fall—the seasonal bloodshed of the bear forever evident with the changing trees."

Juliet shuddered. Would there be more bloodshed with the changing of seasons?

Chapter 33

The Powers' had opened their home for a grand reception. Furniture had been removed and rearranged from the rooms, accommodating a wide space for dancers and guests. Two round-faced, grinning violinists tested their bows on their instruments and commenced to play.

Joshua had received a missive with orders from Colonel Putman at Fort Clinton and was in a quandary about leaving Juliet. He'd delayed long enough. As a going away gift, he'd given her satin he'd bought from Crims' late wife's bridal chest. He couldn't have been more pleased with Juliet's reaction, earning him a long slow day of lovemaking beneath a grove of maples on the mountain.

Juliet and Caroline had pored over an older issue of *The Ladies Magazine* and shooed him from the room, keeping everything secret. Now he couldn't wait to see Juliet.

Crims sidled up to him, the stump of his wooden leg making a thump against the polished cherry floors. He thrust a cup of punch into Joshua's hands. "The Powers' sure give out the best rum punch. Where's Juliet?"

"Since it was raining, the women packed their gowns and arrived earlier. They are upstairs dressing."

A violinist scraped his bow in accidental discord, and then stopped. Joshua's attention was half-focused on what Thomas Starring, a neighbor of the Bells, was saying to him on planting a late crop of wheat. He glanced left. Crims possessed a sappy expression on his face. He didn't have that kind of face for anyone but his horse.

Joshua glanced right. Thomas Starring gaped. Joshua followed the source of his friends' interests, looked higher, toward the oak staircase. He froze, eyes glued to the woman on the upper landing.

Above the gleam of tapers, Lady Juliet Faulkner stood at the top of the staircase and like a siren, ensnared every mortal man in the room. Even he might wreck upon the shoals to get to her.

Her striped blue satin gown matched her eyes, and the lace of the ruffles was as fine as any he'd seen in England. Her breasts rose and fell with every breath she took, and her red hair was caught up in an elegant coiffure, entwined with tiny dried white flowers. She was a breathtaking vision of beauty and breeding.

With grace, she started her descent and confidently glided to the bottom to greet the rush of young soldiers and local bachelors vying for her attention.

Joshua's eyes fastened on his quarry.

"Since you ain't moving, Joshua, I'll extract the poor girl from these idiots." Crims stumped ahead and offered his arm to Juliet.

Rudely dodging the eager Crims, Joshua pushed everyone aside and took Juliet's arm, sweeping her to the appetizer table where they could be alone.

She was his, not these wet behind the ears swains.

She laughed. "Captivating everyone with your company, I see. You look very patrician tonight, a scion of some aristocratic dynasty." Her gaze roved over his body inch by inch, from head to foot enough to harden his loins and roast his wits.

"Wait 'til I get you alone…" To repay her for the lingering glance she'd subjected him to, he whispered many wicked things he'd do. "I will caress and stroke and taste—" He was rewarded when her breaths rushed out of her in short pants.

Her fingers dug into his sleeves. Good. He quirked his mouth into a wolfish smile, dipping his gaze to linger on the rounded fullness of her breasts where they pushed up against her décolletage. "I'll strip you naked, suckle your breasts…ravish you with my mouth…until I stroke a hot fire in your loins and have it wrapped around my—"

Caught between a sigh and a moan, she said, "You are sinful, my lord. You will be punished." Her eyes lit with challenge and she ran her tongue across her upper lip with a soft sensual lick. "What if I repay you in kind?"

How he wanted to sweep her away, throw up her skirts and…she was far too knowledgeable for her own good. "A dangerous game you play, *Lady Faulkner Rutland.*"

She turned away from him, inspecting the table of delicacies, and delicately spooning a spiced peach on her plate. With dainty fingers, she picked up the slick confection and stared at him. She held it to her lips, hovering…drawing and nibbling between her perfect white teeth, and then sucking until nothing of the fruit remained. Her voice came full-throated and carnal. "Delicious."

He growled. "I warn you, Juliet. You are making a grave error."

"I hope so." Her laugh escaped low and seductive. "I hope I can keep you here and away from the war."

"It won't work, Juliet. I have my duty to perform."

"Fools and duty," she hissed. "You will get yourself killed."

Worry darkened the color of her eyes. His muscles tightened. They had engaged in many arguments regarding his leaving.

"We will discuss later—" He stopped when Crims and Thomas Starring joined came up to them.

"You are mighty fine on the eyes, Miss Juliet," said Crims. "I even shined my pewter buttons to impress you."

A blush stole across her cheeks matching her fiery hair. Their tentative game playing might have been witnessed. Joshua smiled, a jaunty, arrogant smile that never failed to disarm her. He wasn't going to let her get away from what she all but promised.

"The town sure has taken a shine to you, Miss Juliet," said Thomas Starring. We don't know what we have done without you all this time. Everyone talks of your kindness. Your help in delivering my neighbor's baby. And then my wife genuinely appreciated your help with the young ones while she was busy with her sick mother."

"The young ones loved playing with the Bell children. How is your wife's mother?" Juliet asked. "Did she use medicine for her legs that I boiled for her?"

"She did and her mother is so well-relieved she may be here tonight to dance," Starring laughed. "And that drawing salve you gave Mrs. Osterhout for her canker cured it up real fast. Folks say you are an angel of mercy."

"And Mr. Hansford," Starring continued, "we'd feel safer with your presence and your rifle skills. Rumors abound of Indian unrest. Blackberry Valley would be ripe for plunder."

"Unfortunately, I won't be here for long," Joshua said. "I received a message and must leave."

Juliet's hand worried the lace at her sleeve. "When?"

"Tomorrow." He had not told her. Tension tautened the delicate features of her face. He hated that fear.

"I don't know how you can leave a young beauty behind, Joshua. If that were me—" said Crims.

"You better watch your step," said Starring. "I don't think Joshua—"

"By the time a man is wise enough to watch his step, he's too old to go anywhere," winked Crims. "I had my wife and those were good years. All I have left is my horse."

"Look at Bethany Powers," said Crims. "Old Hatchet Face, the belle of the ball, eating up the attention she craves with that ridiculous pink confection she's wearing tonight. Not for an old woman. She crossed my path the other day and told me I must be drunk giving my time to my stupid horse. Nobody insults my horse. I told her she was ugly and when I woke up, I'd be sober."

Juliet laughed. How Joshua loved to hear her merriment.

Crims grabbed another glass of punch off a tray from Grace as she wove through the guests bearing a serving tray. "Bethany has sure taken a dislike to Miss Juliet. She has the tongue of a rattlesnake. And those girls of hers are as mean-spirited as their mother. Even Maybelle throws up her tail and races to the other end of town when they stroll by. Caught those demons throwing rocks at her."

Juliet leaned into Joshua, her rose scent beckoning. "Do you see how Thomas Bell's gaze follows Grace?"

Joshua peered at the lanky thirteen-year-old boy holding up the wall. A picture of misery. "Do you think Grace knows?"

"I'm sure she is very much aware but afraid to say or do anything that will provoke harsh reprimand." Juliet straightened. "And the deliverer of that punishment approaches."

Beating a wild tattoo on her silk fan, Bethany shoved Juliet aside. "Oh, Joshua dear, could you do me a favor and dance with Charity? She has had the megrims lately, and it would lift her spirits. And don't forget Comfort, Cornelia and Chastity."

Juliet looked heavenward and Crims spoke overloud. "Bethany named them all starting with a 'C'. I'm thinking Cuckoo or Crazy, the way those spoon-fed terrors carry on."

Bethany sneered at Crims whom she had chosen to ignore, and then, holding a hand over her heart, she gawked fawningly upon her brood. "I had the finest of satin brought in from Albany. Aren't they lovely flowers, Joshua?"

Joshua examined the primped, trussed-up, tittering girls with overlarge mouths. He shuddered. Nothing compared to the liveliness and loveliness of his Juliet with her red hair and, annoyingly, it was attracting the attention of every male in the room.

"Oh, Juliet, I'm so glad you came." Bethany's words dripped the opposite intention. "Someone said you were ill, even suggesting the pox. Of course, you would not have come to my party with an infliction?"

"I'm hale and healthy," replied Juliet. "Which begs me to ask of your servant girl, Grace. Caroline will be heavily involved in dyeing flax and wool and we require all possible hands. There is of course, some extra wool yarn that you might find given in return for services rendered."

"I've always admired Caroline's yarns. Grace will be there early tomorrow."

The dyeing took Caroline a matter of two hours. Grace would be free to spend the day with Thomas. Juliet looked to Joshua. Her eyes twinkled, and he held hers in frank approval. For a moment, he let play the slightest corners of his mouth, owning a secret camaraderie then hid it quickly to show perfect sincerity. The old harridan turned her back on Juliet and again placed her attention solely on Joshua.

Crims stumped his wooden leg. "Why Bethany, your complexion is perfectly pale. What is your secret? Leeches? The bloody flux?"

Bethany opened her mouth in an apoplectic rage. "How dare you, Crims!"

"Didn't know you knew I was here."

"An unfortunate circumstance. If you were my husband, I'd poison you."

Crims slapped his good knee and a cloud of dust motes rose like insects in the bright candlelight. "If you were my wife, I'd drink it."

Bethany stomped away in a huff of pink froth, Crims saluting her with his cup.

Starring jumped right in. "Joshua, the townspeople are very worried over Colonel Allerton, the new man to fortify the fort next to the town. I believe the Patriot commanders in Albany who appointed him have made a mistake. Did you see him riding his fine gelding, parading his regiment into town under gaily fluttering colors, smiling broadly with messianic self-importance? Everyone feels their worries are over, but for me, the glow of reassurance has melted like snow on horse's rear in July. I have my family to protect."

Crims pointed the stem of his pipe. "Allerton is a pompous ass who considers every single one of the townspeople his subordinates, in either rank or social position and doesn't fail to let us know he is a direct line descendent of John Allerton of Mayflower prominence. As if he were some fancy lordship. No one I've ever met has that kind of affiliation."

Joshua cleared his throat and Juliet peered meaningfully to him. If they were aware of his and Juliet's lineage.

"This afternoon he named the stockade Fort Allerton," griped Crims. "If that isn't a dunghill of conceit."

Joshua had heard enough. He had sent a missive to Albany earlier in the year, begging for a commander and reinforcements, not the buffoon, Allerton. If he was to leave Juliet, he wanted her safe and the colonel better see that the tumbledown stockade he called Fort Allerton was reinforced.

There was a commotion at the door and the object of his dislike entered with his officers in full regalia. Time and war had altered him. Of medium height, he possessed dark sandy hair, sparser now and an increased paunch.

Bethany Powers, not to miss her shining moment, swooped down on Joshua, hooked her arm and steered him to the town's newest celebrity.

"Joshua, this is our new commander from Albany, Colonel Ichabod Allerton," boasted Bethany.

Joshua slanted a scathing look at Bethany. With certainty, her rudeness and displeasure were because he did not give attention to her daughters. He nodded to the colonel.

He'd known of Allerton from the earlier part of the war although he was sure, the colonel didn't know him. An insignificant soldier, Allerton had risen through the ranks via the desperate requirement for roughly any kind of military leadership.

Bethany preened her layers of silk like an enormous pink crow. "We have felt defenseless, isolated, vulnerable…" she dipped her voice lower, "…even naked since the attacks to the south at Fort Fifty."

Charles Powers came up beside them. His face turned a bright red, and he shot his wife, Bethany an anxious glance with her bold words.

Unfazed, Bethany continued, "When General Lafayette was here in May, he had strongly recommended a proper fort be built to replace the clumsy and flimsy fortification that had been thrown up near our home."

Allerton peered down his nose like a benevolent King reviewing lower serfs. "I repaired at once with my regiment of two hundred and fifty men to Blackberry Valley. My purpose is to establish a strong military garrison. Mrs. Powers, you have been ever so pleasant since our arrival."

"You will be able to protect us and our belongings?" trilled Bethany.

"Have no fear," Allerton said as if he divined the secrets of the universe. "Your goods will not be plundered nor will your person be molested or damaged. My men will be on hand to protect you should the savages be foolish enough to threaten this valley. I must say I find it inconceivable Thayendanegea, Onontio and the British soldiers would ever consider attacking us. This isn't a unit of green militia. These are regular soldiers of the Continental Army seasoned and accustomed to fighting."

Allerton rocked up on his toes. "To prove my confidence in the strength of our position and unlikelihood of any sort of attack occurring, my men will arrange quarters for themselves within the stockade. My officers and I will take up lodging in the homes of the citizens. My lieutenant and I, for example, will lodge with Mr. and Mrs. Powers."

"I had no idea. You would live here?" Mr. Powers choked out. "I assume there will be added protection for my home and family?"

Bethany waved an airy hand. "Of course, dear."

"You think it wise not to be stationed at the fort?" said Joshua. He sensed Juliet come up beside him.

Allerton waved an uninterested hand in Joshua's direction. "Who are you to question a colonel of the Continental Army?"

Joshua said nothing.

"Joshua is a trapper," said Bethany in haughty tones.

Allerton's lips pressed into a thin smile. "A trapper?"

A vein pulsed at the base of Joshua's throat while Allerton's gaze made a drawn-out trail from Juliet's face down to her bodice. Hot blood shot through Joshua's veins. How long would it take to scalp Allerton? Two seconds? Three seconds?

"There were many a raised brow in Albany and the assumption was the promotion you received came from connections," said Joshua.

The colonel's jaw clenched tighter than a whore's fist over a coin. "You dare to question my qualifications?"

Joshua focused his gaze on Allerton. "I'm not questioning your qualifications. I'm refuting the existence or your abilities."

"Perhaps you are a spy to create havoc and doubt," snarled Allerton.

Joshua made a broad sweep of his arm. "The good people of Blackberry Valley should be aware that neither you nor your Massachusetts regulars have any experience in Indian warfare."

Allerton smirked as if he understood so much more. "I have won recognition from my superiors as early as the siege of Boston."

"The men underneath you deserved the credit. It was their creativity and bravery that saw the light of day. You took the glory."

Allerton leaned in to assign a confidential tone, his hard blue eyes locked on Joshua. "I could have you arrested for insubordination, thrown in chains."

Joshua stepped deliberately to within inches of Allerton. "You could try but it wouldn't work out for you."

The colonel's mouth opened and closed a couple of times before he sputtered, "You risk making such a contention?"

"How dare you speak to Colonel Allerton in such a shameful manner." Bethany sailed forward, mimicking the forward thrust of a fully rigged ship. "Perhaps you are a spy."

"He is not." Juliet's voice dripped with her ire. "He is as dedicated a Patriot as everyone else in this room. How easy it is to speak your mind, Bethany, when there is no one to hear you but the wind."

Joshua lifted an eyebrow. Juliet was quick; she had her answers ready.

Apparently, Bethany didn't have any answers ready.

Bethany sputtered.

Finally, the woman spat out, looking at Juliet, "Possibly, you are a spy, too!"

The ladies in the room gasped.

"I refuse to have a battle of wits with an unarmed opponent," Juliet said.

Joshua held back a smile. His Juliet didn't just bite, she took a chunk out of Bethany, and the fool woman strolled away smiling like an idiot, believing she'd been complimented.

The colonel took the liberty of eyeing Juliet's charms again.

A vein pulsed in Joshua's throat. "There are many invited guests...so you see, prudence suggests that we make amends, toughen our indulgent sympathies to recommend what is best for the town's defenses."

"I see." Allerton's gaze bored holes into Joshua. "What does a frontiersman know of engineering a fort's defenses and tactical military maneuvers?"

"What improvements have you decided upon?" asked Joshua. "Other than comfortable housing for yourself and your officers, there doesn't seem to be much thought given to anything else. Allow me to suggest—"

"You may suggest nothing. I find you tiresome."

"Then I'll be more tolerant," Joshua said as if instructing a child, "Your securing the fort is paramount. The stockade perimeter is strong enough but it is far from finished inside and though there are two small cannon, there are no raised embrasures through which to fire at the enemy, rendering them useless. There are three hundred civilian residents in the town, but they are ill-prepared to defend themselves and are dependent upon the military for that service. More reinforcements must to be requested."

Despite the visible tension in Allerton's shoulders, he said, "There is much vigor in what you say. The town of Blackberry Valley and its residents can be rest assured my men and I will look into the matter and make necessary reinforcements."

He turned his back to Joshua. "The backwoodsman dared to tell me what to do. He is an imbecile."

Joshua lurched toward the colonel, but Crims and Juliet held him back, but they couldn't stop his words. "Beware of the consequences if you don't heed my warnings, Allerton."

Chapter 34

Fall arrayed in robes of burnt umber, scarlet and yellow, and lent a blended rhythm of days where Juliet prayed for Joshua's return. Up came the golden sun, burning a slow fog off the land. She passed a cider press, veiled beneath the eaves of a shed, and past the beehives. With a basket brimming of hickory and black walnuts, Juliet paused with her morning chores to watch the children take turns swinging on an ancient grapevine.

Heat flew to her cheeks as she remembered the last days before Joshua's departure when they had made endless love, her body responding to his every touch.

She was stronger, wiser, more knowledgeable now. She'd met danger, fear, and pleasure beyond her imaginings, had done things she'd never dreamed she could do. She'd seen violence to freeze the marrow, had appreciated forests so limitless that they absorbed the soul, had glimpsed infinity in a star-filled night. But more than that, she now knew what it was to love and be loved.

The Bells' two giant russet-colored Percherons, Lancelot and Guinevere, pawed the ground in the dusty paddock, begging for an apple. Juliet produced two from her pocket, the mammoth equines distending their nostrils, inhaling the freshness of the fruit before scooping it between their teeth. Satisfied, they rested their necks on each other. Suzanne, the eight-year-old, stayed behind and doted on them as if they were royalty from a faraway land.

Georgie followed yapping at their heels, then would run off to chase an errant squirrel. Juliet kicked through the fallen leaves, sauntered into the house, her skirt hems skimming her shoetops and swirling round her ankles. She deposited the baskets of nuts on the kitchen floor to later crack, and hung her shawl on a peg. The aroma of a rich beef stew tantalized her senses. The three wheaten loaves she had helped knead earlier in the morning, a crock of honey, fragrant with wildflowers, fresh creamy butter and cheese brought in from the cold cellar…on the gleaming kitchen table.

With James' departure to Albany, Juliet had picked up the slack in chores. Caroline, her constant tutor, taught her more on running a farm. The children, animals, fields, orchards provided a place of magic, a dwelling separate from the rest of the world, and so enthralling that her heart caught. Juliet claimed it, and knew, deep down with hard work and initiative, she could manage Joshua's farm. He had told her it was a small log cabin and not so grand as the Bell home or anywhere near the Faulkner estate, her ancestral home in England. But with love and resourcefulness they could make it work and it would be home.

Juliet stood over little Elias sleeping in a cradle. Her hand pressed to her breast, clinging to the hope of someday having her own child. She couldn't help herself. She wanted that. She'd be a good mother.

They would be a family and the notion filled her with joy because, other than Moira, it meant for the first time in her life, she'd be a part of something wonderful. It meant she would love and be loved for the rest of her life no matter what. Would her dreams include a daughter and granddaughter as Waneek and Ojistah had predicted?

But what if Joshua never returned? What if he met up with a redcoat aware of his spying activities? What if he encountered Snapes? Two Eagles had stayed with his new bride, leaving Joshua to travel alone. What if he were injured and laying in the cold forests with no one to help him? The grim reality slammed into her full force. It wasn't the first time, and like the last, she forced down her negative thoughts and peeked out the window where red apples bobbed in the wide orchards and the children played hide-and-seek, falling to the earth in ear-splitting giggles.

Betsy spun flax for the loom, the whir of the spinning wheel made a gentle, pleasant hum in harmony with the clap of the loom where Caroline thrust the shuttle cock through. The woman's deft hands, wove a myriad of warp and weft threads into impressive fabric.

"We had sun on the Saint Eulalie's Feast Day promising plenty of apples and cider," said Caroline, over her shoulder. She pushed a fist in her back to ease the strain of her advanced pregnancy.

"Are you having contractions?" Juliet asked. Caroline had dropped and was due any day.

"I'm fine." She gazed at the great armchair where her husband idled when he was home. Charity read to Mary and Robin in his chair. "They miss their father."

Juliet was sure Caroline missed him the most.

"You and Joshua should get married," said Caroline. "The way you two look at each other and carry on…"

"We are married."

"Thought so," said Caroline, her feet clapping the foot pedals. "Made a bet with James, and it looks like I won." She smiled wide.

Hard thumping on the porch tore them from their conversation. Caroline crossed the kitchen, spied out the window, picked up a rifle and opened the door. A heavily-bearded, lean buckskinned man stood in the entry.

Crims hobbled up behind him, breathing hard. "He's my friend, Moses Bent and you better listen to what he has to say, Caroline."

Caroline nodded and gestured them to the table. Juliet scooped up plates of steaming stew and served the men.

Moses shoveled potatoes in his mouth, dripping gravy on the table and talked between mouthfuls. "Bad things happening all over. News of the build-up of Tory and Indian forces on the upper Susquehanna, especially at Unadilla and Onipua. They're also preparing to move against the outlying settlements. Blackberry Valley is a prime target. Despite what Colonel Allerton has done to reinforce your fort," he spat, "you are weakly defended. I would leave if I were you."

"My husband has gone to Albany to appeal to Brigadier General Edward Hand, begging for additional troops to protect us."

Moses pointed a hunk of cheese at her. "Thayendanegea is hot for destroying any Patriots. He holds all of 'em responsible for destroying Tionnontigo and Onaguaga, his villages. He will be swift and merciless and his numbers are growing."

Tionnontigo had been destroyed? Juliet hoped Ojistah's second sight warned her away before the attack. She cared for the old woman.

Caroline set a platter of warm rolls on the table, shooing away the children so the men could eat without being interrupted. "Brigadier General Hand said we would be well-protected by the garrison at Fort Stephens under Colonel Elijah Cummings. They are thirteen miles distant and could come quickly if trouble loomed."

The frontiersman blew a whistle between his two front missing teeth. "The logic is the same as setting your hair on fire and putting it out with a hammer. Ain't going to happen."

"What am I to do? The snows will soon be upon us. My husband is gone. I am a lone woman with eight children. Where would we go?"

"I would take my chances and leave if I were you."

Chapter 35

*I*n her dreams, Onontio came at her, his scalp plucked bald save for the stiff brush atop his head and his black eyes gleaming in murderous rage through his hideous war paint. He sneered at the sword she pointed at him, knocking it from her hand, before she could lift it to swing. He grabbed her arm, spun her around and pinned her back against his chest as, with his other hand, he drew his razor-sharp blade from left to right across her throat. He released her and she crumpled, the light of life fading from her eyes.

The next day, Juliet tugged her shawl tighter around her, unable to dispel the recurring nightmare. She and Caroline had stayed up late the night before debating what to do with Moses Bent's dire warnings.

Juliet strode with as long a step as her dress and petticoats would allow. Caroline kept in step beside her, their skirts swishing in unison across the frozen ground as they made their way to the Powers' home. The town, stood cheerless now that the freezing moon had come and the ground was frozen hard as a rock. The trees in the forest dropped the rest of their leaves with the sudden frost overnight.

How quickly the season had changed. Now the bare tree branches stood out starkly, silhouetted against dark evergreen pines and hemlocks. In the fields surrounding the Bells' house, dried-up cornstalks clattered like skeleton bones in the wind. Though it was not snowing, the early morning wind was kicking up snow crystals from the ground and they rattled cheerlessly against the glass panes of the homes they passed. Anger burned, blazing-hot, rendering her immune to the cold.

Where was Joshua? Her heart sank with still no news from him. She prayed he was safe.

She clenched and unclenched her hands, recalling the terrible events befalling the frontier over the recent months. Shocking news had come of the fall of Fort Benkins and Fort Halsey. Men cut to pieces in the most shocking manner. Men had holes from spears in their sides, their arms cut to pieces, tomahawked, scalped, and their throats cut. Two hundred and twenty-seven scalps had been taken, a handsome incentive of ten pounds for every scalp paid by the British. A few lucky women, now widowed, had escaped, and suffered terrible privations, fleeing through the unforgiving wilderness with their children.

By mid-September Caughmawaga destroyed the German Flats. Sixty-three homes and fifty-seven barns were burned to the ground. Grain and fodder, over a thousand horses, cattle, sheep and hogs were taken. Three people were killed. Too close.

If the rumors were true, with War Chiefs Onontio and Thayendanegea on the move, the entire area might flow red with blood. The enormity of reality piled on top of her like a million invisible blankets, suffocating her under the weight.

Concern grew in Blackberry Valley. But Allerton, the buffoon, remained unmoved. Juliet prayed his foolishness wouldn't be their demise. She shuddered as hideous images flared through her mind.

Grace smiled when they entered the Powers' home, and then took their wraps. "They are in the dining room having breakfast, but you will have to wait until they are done. The Powers' do not like their meals disturbed."

Boots dripping snow, Juliet marched into the dining room with Caroline on her heels.

The men stood. Charity sneered. Comfort harrumphed. Cornelia and Chastity tittered between one another.

Bethany narrowed her eyes on Grace and said, "How many times have I told you not to disturb us during meals. There will be repercussions."

"It isn't Grace's fault," said Juliet. "I chose to interrupt."

Charles Powers jerked his tight waistcoat over his girth and with stentorian imperiousness, intoned, "What do we owe the honor, Miss Farrow and Mrs. Bell?"

"We've come to complain concerning the lack of protection there is for Blackberry Valley," said Juliet, impatient with the forced smiles and sneering glances sent her way.

The men took their seats again.

Colonel Ichabod Allerton held up his glass in a toast. The wine was deep red and the glow from the candles reflected off the glass. "To the continued safety of Blackberry Valley."

"Hear! Hear!" murmured an echo of followers and they drank the toast with obvious pleasure.

Allerton set the glass down on the polished oak table and delicately brushed at his lips with the knuckle of his index finger. "I'm available to hear complaints from the local citizenry, especially one so lovely as you, Miss Farrow."

A vein pulsed in Juliet's neck. Her spine went ramrod straight. *You patronizing fool.* "Not good enough, especially with you camped in luxury. Don't you feel any responsibility to those who are vulnerable and under your protection?"

Allerton expelled a long drawn-out sigh. "I know when I first came here, the backwoodsman had some concerns, but I have rectified the situation. I hope you see I was right in my assessment of the state of affairs. And I'll point out there has been no attack by War Chiefs Onontio and Thayendanegea, and there will be none. The Indians are obviously cowed by the military strength we have here."

"I agree," said Lieutenant Johnson nodded like a woodpecker ready to strike. Of course, the lieutenant's concurrence with his superior meant nothing. If Allerton told him the sun would spin and pitch into the earth, Lieutenant Johnson would concur.

Charles Powers leaned indolently in his chair. "Female hysterics will create an unnecessary disturbance, Miss Farrow, promoting worry and a waste of time."

Bethany patted her lips with her napkin. "Charles is right, Juliet. You mustn't yield to excitement. It is so unladylike."

Juliet pinned her glare over every one of them. "There is every justification for Blackberry Valley residents to be fearful. Look what has happened around us this year—destruction at Fort Benkins and Summermute, Cobleskill, Wyoming, Andrustown, Schoharie, the German Flats."

Charles tapped his finger on the table. "Blackberry Valley might have fallen as well, but with our pleas for troops granted, and the winter period upon us, we are no longer at risk."

"The danger has not passed," hissed Juliet.

Charles pulled at his beard and shook his head. "Well now, I wouldn't say that. Perhaps the danger's not passed, but it should be concluded for this year, don't you agree, Colonel Allerton?" He eyeballed the fort commander.

"Of course, of course! I assure you, gentlemen and—ladies, Blackberry Valley can breathe freely. The season is much too advanced for any sort of attack to be launched against us. This is especially true since Onontio's and Thayendanegea's bases of operations at Tionnontigo and Onaguaga have been destroyed. As for the next spring—" he shrugged. "That's another matter."

Colonel Allerton chuckled and added, "Maybe Onontio and Thayendanegea will die of pneumonia during the winter, now that we've burned his wigwam."

"I am not so heartened," said Juliet. "You have done nothing to improve the safety of Blackberry Valley. There are little or no improvements to the fort. You have not added more troops. We are at the mercy of Onontio and Thayendanegea if they attack."

Charles picked up his knife, cut off a piece of steak and swirled it through his egg yolk. "Everyone knows Indians do not attack in the winter. They are hunting to get through the starving period."

Lieutenant Johnson chuckled. "The Indians don't like the cold any more than we do. They'd much rather be sitting around warm fires in their longhouses, snuggled beneath their blankets.

"Agreed." Allerton raised his glass again. "I'll drink to that!"

"Hear, hear!" said the others, all laughing and they drank, too.

Juliet balled her fists in her skirts. "I have witnessed what horrors Onontio is capable of. Your indolence, arrogance and recklessness will be our deaths."

Colonel Allerton narrowed his eyes on Juliet. "Rest your pretty head. The savages are the greatest of fools. To initiate a major onslaught in the winter is beyond their stupidity."

His comment again was met with uproarious laughter.

How they made her feel like an old woman she had seen roaming the streets of Leicestershire, screaming that the rats in her hair told her Judgement Day was upon them. How she itched to tear the rich paintings off the wall, to take the candelabra off the table and bludgeon sense in every one of their skulls. "The greatest fools are often times cleverer than the men who laugh at them. While you continue your journey of hubris, remember to dig your graves."

As paralyzing and upsetting as it was to think of another Indian attack, Juliet vowed to be ready. Never again would she be unprepared. She had walked through fire and wasn't the scared naïve girl anymore. She was stronger, organizing and planning an escape with the logistical deliberation of a general. With Thomas, time was set aside to practice shooting. Guns were cleaned and ammunition readied. Mink oil was smeared on everyone's boots to make them waterproof. Dried food, extra socks, scarves, a tinder box, candles, a knife, bundles of clothes and quilts were hauled up to the cave with countless trips. Backpacks were sewn with strong straps to carry the loads on their backs for last-minute items.

She worried about Caroline. Heavy with child, could she make the difficult climb to the cave if the need arose? With so many young children to care for, the odds were against them, but Juliet refused to give in to defeat. On guard, she looked out the windows constantly, drilling the children in the eventuality of an attack. She laughed. Oh, yes, they'd leave at the first wind of attack and escape Onontio.

Chapter 36

*M*enacing gray clouds scudded across the sky, spitting stinging snow crystals on Joshua's face. Over the past two months, fears involving New York and Pennsylvania's frontiers were growing. From the Indian villages of the upper Susquehanna in the southwest—especially the large village of Oquaga to the upper Mohawk Valley—and of paramount concern lay the principal Indian trail running directly through Blackberry Valley. The few Mohawks remaining at Canajoharie under Chief Steyawa were keeping strictly to themselves and had promised neutrality, but the Indians of the villages southward had not. The news from Fort Niagara alarmed him the most. General Butler and his Rangers along with numerous Senecas, had made their way to the Genesee River, traveling down the Chemung River to Tioga and up the Susquehanna inching closer to Blackberry Valley. Something fearful yielded in every footfall, the hills boiling with greed and violence.

Joshua had traveled to Fort Clinton to meet up with Colonel Putnam and had been ordered to scout north, and then west, careful to stay away from British troops, now that it was confirmed he was a spy. During the two months, he'd written Juliet, regretting his delays and every second he was away from her. He needed news of the east and the south and moved down the valley onto the farm of trusted Patriot and courier, Jacob Smith.

"Scalping parties have been sent out," said Jacob. "Thayendanegea and Onontio are boasting how Butler and Snapes will unite forces to be in the march to Fort Stephen and Blackberry Valley. John Butler's father is mustering more Rangers by the beat of the drum."

Joshua's muscles went rigid. Why did he waste time in the west? "What else?"

"In Cobleskill, a small party of Iroquois drew the local defenders into a trap, set by a much larger party of Iroquois and Loyalists headed by Thayendanegea. Militia members took cover in a house and Thayendanegea burned it. Twenty-two settlers were killed, eight wounded. The seven captives that were taken had to run the gauntlet, and then were forced to build their own funeral pyre. The savages celebrated as they burned those poor men at the stake. They killed the militia and destroyed the village."

"Damn!" Joshua spat out.

The courier shook his head. "The massacre at Wyoming was worse. Colonel Butler and his Senecas raided the valley across the border into Pennsylvania. They took five prisoners, burned a thousand homes, taking two hundred and twenty-seven scalps.

"Fort Peterson fell badly. The commander escaped on horseback with his wife. Only sixty Patriot militia made it out alive. The rest were tortured, slain and scalped. The countryside has been laid to waste, homes burned, settlers burned in their beds, children abducted. Now the War Chief Thayendanegea has congregated larger numbers of his Mohawks along the Susquehanna near Windsor to attack frontier settlements in retaliation to the Continental Army attacking and destroying Onaguaga and Tionnontigo."

"What are their numbers?" Joshua asked.

"Like the leaves. There are nearly two hundred and fifty Tory Rangers, three hundred and fifty Hanau chasseurs."

Joshua gazed off over the mountain. Hanau chasseurs were German light infantry troops trained for rapid maneuvering. "What else?"

"They have forty experienced artillerists equipped with a pair of six-pounder cannon, two three-pounders and four cohorns. With the thousand Indians assembled under the principled command of Thayendanegea of the Mohawks, Cornplanter, Onontio of the Onondagas and Gucinge of the Senecas, you have a combined force of approximately two thousand men under St. Leagear."

Joshua had met Brigadier General Robert St. Leagear in London, a King's man, not an expert strategist nor a daring or imaginative commander, more a pompous ass. Yet he was probably smart enough to listen to Butler and his experiences battling in the wilderness.

A stripe of fear rattled up his spine. Fort Stephens was closest to the march and ill-prepared for the coming onslaught. What lay next in the path of the British legion was the vulnerable treasure trove of Blackberry Valley. How could he be in two places at once? If he ever needed Two Eagles by his side, it was now. But wishing wasn't going to make it happen.

"Captain Milburn Snapes has brought troops from the north adding to the numbers. It will be a slaughter."

Damn! Joshua had spent long hours trailing Snapes to discover the man was on his doorstep! Juliet was at risk. He raked his fingers through his hair. Every contingency unforeseen.

"I'm packing up my family and heading out," said Jacob. "There's an extra horse in the barn."

Joshua rode through the woods, hightailing it down an old Indian trail, making it to Fort Stephens. Covered with mud and exhausted from his hard ride, he slid off his horse, and approached Colonel Elijah Cummings, taking stock of ammunition and rifle supplies.

Joshua saluted. "Bad news. You are about to have several British visitors and their companions camp on your doorstep."

Cummings blew out his cheeks. "Thank you, Joshua. We have made fortifications in the past months expecting a visit of this nature and have received as of yesterday, a good supply of gunpowder by Colonel Mellen's detachment, but our supply of lead remains low. We have fourteen pieces of artillery in the fort, although small and without the range or effectiveness of the artillery your intelligence indicates the enemy is bringing with them. Ours will not be able to reach them in their positions, but if the enemy tries to carry us by storm, they will receive great benefit of our cannon."

"With numerous miles and hours before dawn, I must travel the distance to warn the people of Blackberry Valley." Joshua cinched the saddle tighter on his stallion and mounted.

Colonel Cummings pivoted, his clear blue eyes, glacial now, focused on his men, and shouted out orders. "Man the parapets. Shoot only when a sure target is in sight. Nine shots per riflemen each day. Recover any enemy lead that is shot into this place and melt it down into new balls for us. By the grace of God, we are going to defend this place."

"Colonel Cummings, if you can send any men to Blackberry Valley—"

The gates closed behind Joshua and a rousing cheer followed him down the road from men on the parapet. He spurred his horse, doubting that Cummings would have any men available to send to the valley. Two miles to the west, he jerked back on the reins. The horse reared, then settled on all fours. Joshua stood up on the stirrups, alerted to the spirited notes of bugles and fifes, and the stirring, cadenced rattling of marching drums, joined by the piercing squeal of bagpipes, and the unnerving cries of Indians. Joshua pushed his mount higher up the mountain, leaning low over the saddle to avoid tree limbs, finally breaking through thick undergrowth at the top.

Below St. Leagear's army marched toward Fort Stephens in precise ranks and files, the regulars clad in scarlet, Johnson's Royals in green and the Germans in blue, with the early sunlight glittering off the swords and blackened gun barrels, and all the while, moving from cover to cover on each flank were war-painted Indians with tomahawks, knives, war clubs and muskets. Like maggots in rotten meat, the countryside crawled with men. Hope was all he possessed—yet that was an act of desperate defiance against monstrous odds.

With probing gaze, Joshua swept a hand across his forehead

to get rid of sweat and estimated the numbers. Only five hundred warriors, half as much from what the messenger had indicated. A stripe of fear ran up his back. Where were the rest? Damn! They had divided their offense.

Blackberry Valley.

His blood ran cold. He had to get to her.

He had promised to protect Juliet.

Waneek's words haunted him. *"What is duty compared to a woman's love? What is duty against the feel of a newborn son in your arms? Duty is what the Earth Mother Spirit has fashioned us for love. That is our greater glory."*

Joshua hoped he wasn't too late.

Chapter 37

Elias' stirrings roused her to awareness. Juliet pushed beneath the covers, wallowing in the delicious disinclination to move out of a womblike comfort. Thomas touched her shoulder. He'd done the night watch.

Shots. A whole barrage of shots. She bolted from the bed. At the window, she stood paralyzed. Warriors charged from the marsh toward the Powers' home their skins shining like flashing copper, their faces painted with grotesque streaks. Indians and red-coated British soldiers swarmed from every direction.

A half-dozen of colonial soldiers on the Powers' porch fell at the first firing and the others ran around in chaos like ants kicked from an anthill. Colonel Ichabod Allerton, still in his slippers and shirtsleeves ran from the home, pistol in his hand, his tunic flapping and heading north toward the fort. Lieutenant Johnson followed.

Reigning tall in their midst stood Onontio. He pursued them across the field. A warrior threw a spear that penetrated the lieutenant's back and he tumbled to the ground. Indians were upon him, knives plunged into his body and one held his scalp held high above his head.

Cannons fired from the fort but were useless. The embrasures Joshua had suggested weren't made. Several yards from the fort, Allerton turned to fire a shot. His final act of stupidity. If he hadn't broken stride he would have made it. Onontio threw his tomahawk. End over end it twirled and into the colonel's forehead. Due to the unfinished parapets, soldiers in the fort were unable to fire their guns due to the risk of exposing themselves. Onontio ran up to Allerton, jerked the tomahawk out of the colonel's head and scalped him. Onontio tracked back to the town.

Thomas pulled on her arm. *Run! Move your feet now!*

Across the hall Juliet flew and shook Caroline awake, and then prodded the servant girl, Betsy to get dressed. Quilts were thrown back and bare feet thudded the floor. Jerked awake, the older children sobered with the cries in the valley and stared out the window.

"Do not look," Juliet whispered.

Unaware of the ongoing massacre, the smaller children sleepily protested as they were urged into their boots and warm coats.

Juliet stashed bread and a ham in a burlap bag, upending the Nine Men's Morris game, lying unfinished from the night before. Suzanne cried out, cheated from her certain victory and started picking up the pieces.

"No time for that Suzanne, put on your coat. Remember the drills we practiced?" ordered Juliet. She hooked the food bag and blankets on Thomas' back.

She checked out the window. Shots were fired from Powers' upstairs parlor window, and afterwards stopped. Bethany, Charles and the four girls were pushed out of their home by warriors and British soldiers. The family knelt, forming a circle, their hands pressed in supplication to their deliverer. The girls were ripped from their mother and tied to a tree. Charles was tomahawked first, then Bethany. Juliet put her hands over her ears to shut out the girls' screaming. Their parents and three domestics were hacked and stabbed, and scalped.

Juliet swung a musket and powder horn over her shoulder, picked up Elias and bolted out the back door, her homespun skirts flying behind her. She passed the grindstone and shuddered, like a bleached bone it lay against the well in the meager light. Circling the barn, she stared at the unchinked log outbuildings as if she'd never seen them before. The ancient vine rope dangled like a darkened tendril.

"Can we swing on the rope?" Mary pleaded.

How many seconds before the Indians discovered the Bell home? How many minutes until they caught the murderous cries of Indians on their heels? Guinevere and Lancelot, the two draft horses galloped up to the side of the corral, their eyes rolled wildly white, their ears thrown back. Juliet unhinged the gate, slapping their flanks, and shooed them out. No way would she allow the Indians to a make a meal of them.

Single file, hands linked to one another like a human rosary, Caroline, Betsy, the children, and Juliet plunged into the shelter of the woods. Georgie, the dog, followed at their heels. Juliet worried the dog would commence barking at any moment but the canine must have sensed danger, and padded along quietly. Juliet followed and with a huge spruce branch swished the snow to cover their tracks.

Underneath the shadowy oaks and dusky hemlocks, the air pitched black and gray. The trunks of many trees crowded close and pressed upon them.

A scrabbling of claws against tree bark sounded as an animal raced to the top. Juliet lifted her head to catch a glimpse of bushy tail tucked into the hole of a tree. Even the squirrel had hidden.

Overhanging spear-like branches lacerated her skin. With a trembling hand, she held one back for Caroline and the children to pass. Her breath came out in tenuous white billows shredded by the wind. Rotting wood and the scent of a dead animal permeated the air. She tripped across uneven ground pitted with rocks and roots, righted, grappling Elias close to her chest. The forest had changed from a world of beauty to a world of fear.

The shouts and whoops of the Indians and the screams of women echoed over the mountains. Juliet cringed, imagining what was happening to the townspeople. Then rose the moans of Caroline, her children and Betsy. Juliet regarded Caroline, her face unrecognizable, and twisted with fear. Her hood had fallen and her long brown braid matted to her shoulder with sleet. She bent over, grabbing her abdomen. A gush of water soaked the ground beneath her. She looked at Juliet with terror in her eyes.

Dear God. Not now.

"I'll help you through this, Caroline. We just need to get to the cave."

Robin, the four-year-old, took Juliet's hand and curled into her leg. "Please stop that noise."

Juliet led the way up the steep path. Smoke filtered through the air mixed with the dampness of leaf mold. From time to time, Juliet glanced behind to see if anyone was following. At the top of the mountain, there was a break in the trees giving them a clear view. "Do not look," Juliet insisted. "Betsy, Thomas, take the children into the forest."

It was the Hayes' massacre again, only worse. In the distance, half a hundred columns of dark smoke rose from homes, barns and outbuildings that had been set afire. Skittish horses, mist pluming from their distended nostrils and snow flying from beneath their hooves, were dragged with other livestock from the barns.

From the homes that were not torched, Indians ran in and out, carrying chairs, bread, paintings, whatever suited their desires. Fights broke out with British soldiers over prisoners and valuables. Occasional shots were fired from the fort.

Was that Mr. Clyde laying across his porch's railing, his head circumcised? Was it Mr. Starring who had laughed so pleasantly at the Powers' dance, lying dead next to his two sons, wife and mother-in-law? No. He was safe, with his family in his home, having breakfast. Wasn't he? Juliet bit on her knuckles to stifle a scream. Was that Crims and his horse who lay dead beside the trough? No. But there on the ground lay Maybelle's flowered hat.

Mr. Leppers and Mr. Hoyers spurred their horses into the village at a full gallop. Leppers made it to the front of his home before numerous Indians fell upon him and tomahawked him. A ball entered the back of Mr. Hoyers' back and exited from his chest, leaving a gaping hole. Blood spurted, splashing over the saddle and his horse's mane and neck. He stayed in the saddle for twenty yards then plummeted to the ground. He rose and drew his sword. His movements were sluggish. Before he could get to his knees, a warrior raced up and buried his tomahawk in Hoyers' temple.

"Dear God," said Caroline. "I hope James doesn't return and is provoked to the same madness to save us."

"A useless endeavor earning Hoyers' and Leppers' their deaths," Juliet whispered and turned Caroline into the forest, praying Joshua wouldn't return and risk his life.

Juliet forced her feet to move yet could not feel the earth beneath her shoes. The journey was like a pendulum of the clock in her father's library—the brass disc swinging relentlessly back and forth, back and forth, heedless of anything going on in the world around it.

Juliet caught up with Betsy, Thomas and the children. Juliet veered a sharp left and pushed through the bracken, thorns tearing at their clothes. Juliet stumbled with the weight of Elias on her hip. Betsy took the rifle from her, relieving her. Some of the children were crying. Caroline bent over with another spasm. Elias wailed for his mother and Juliet came abreast of her to silence him.

"Let's play hide-and-seek. We must be very quiet and move quickly to our hiding spot where no one will find us," Juliet instructed the children. She paused and took a breath. The cracked branches and foot falls in the sleet would lead the Indians right to them. "We must travel down the mountain."

She slipped and slid down the sharp incline, holding Suzanne's small hand in hers, and descending to where a small creek gurgled. Georgie plunged down ahead of them where he waited. The shoreline had ice crystals on the rocks. "I know it's cold but we have to cover our tracks so the Indians won't find us. Thomas and Betsy carry the younger children. The older children will follow." Juliet tied up her skirts.

Little James sucked his thumb. Juliet picked him up, too, and stepped into the freezing creek. She inhaled, the bone-chilling cold wrapped around her legs.

Betsy held a child on each hip when she strode into the stream, a yelp of surprise at the cold. They moved over slippery rocks and, twice, Juliet leaned in to give support to Caroline and Betsy before they were swept away in the current. Elias sobbed and burrowed his face into the hollow of her neck. She ducked her chin on top of the little boy's soft, blond curls and he peeked at her, his little mouth puckering, his big eyes watery with tears.

"Don't worry. Aunt Juliet is going to find a safe place."

For a half of a mile, they traveled downstream. Juliet pointed for Caroline to climb up on the rocks to the left and handed James and Elias off to Caroline. Joshua had trained her to walk on the rocks which would show no sign of their passing.

Juliet crossed to the opposite bank, creating numerous tracks to confuse the attackers in case they trailed them, and then retraced her steps. She held her breath, again wading through the freezing waters and returned to the group waiting for her.

"Keep going forward." With a stick Juliet brushed leaves across their footsteps. Like frightened, uncertain sheep they shuffled through the forest. An awful stitch in her side turned to a burning numbness. Around enormous rocks covered with massive tree roots, they advanced. Nothing seemed familiar with the newly fallen snow. What if she couldn't find the cave?

Georgie growled. A nighthawk brushed over their heads, the wind from its flapping wings fanning their hair. It swooped again, startling with its nearness, then plunged down the hill before settling on the iron-clad branches of a stark oak.

"Rarely does a nighthawk feed in the day," whispered Caroline, panting short breaths.

Her contractions were coming more readily, and Juliet needed to get her to the cave before it was too late.

Animals assist us and act as potent spirit guides.

Two Eagles' words were tattooed on Juliet's brain and his imaginative story of animal helpers, aiding his escape from his foes. Maybe his story wasn't whimsy. She scanned the terrain, scrutinized where the nighthawk settled. Waiting? Waiting for her? A sensation tingled over her skin in a wash of fevered heat.

Juliet tingled with awareness. "Follow me." She made an abrupt turn down the mountain. Under fallen trees, they crawled, slipping and sliding on wet leaves down the steep slope and through tangled underbrush. She kept an eye on the unwavering nighthawk. An indescribable link resonated between them. The bird shifted. She lowered her gaze to a grapevine tent.

The cave.

She lifted a veil of vine and ushered Caroline, Betsy and the children inside. She glanced up to the looming oak to mouth a thank you to the animal spirit. The nighthawk had vanished.

Allowing their eyes to adjust to the dim light, they moved far into the recesses protected from the sleet and icy wind. Shivering, the children wailed, wishing to be home by the warmth of the hearth. Juliet took turns relieving the harried Caroline of her frightened brood, glad to have stocked the cave. Thomas found a dry spot, unrolled the blankets and put the exhausted children to sleep. Georgie curled up protectively beside them.

Juliet assisted Caroline, helping her to a blanket and covering her with the furs they had stored. The contractions came quicker and quicker. Juliet calmed Caroline, giving her a bite stick to suppress her cries.

"I've done this a hundred times, Caroline," Juliet assured her and despite the horror in the valley, a baby fought its way into the world.

Chapter 38

Three days and three nights passed. "I'm going back to see if they've gone."

"What if they haven't departed? You could lead the Indians back to us," Caroline said, nursing her infant at her breast.

"There has been silence. I believe they have left. Your husband and Joshua might have returned and we must let them know we are alive. I'll use another route to keep you and the children safe."

"I'm coming too," said Thomas.

Juliet let loose her hold on Mary and tousled Thomas' blond hair and nodded.

With a rifle in her arms, Juliet moved deeper into the woods, moving through the bracken and entered the creek going north until she was opposite the town, and then moved eastward to where the woods gave way to a little marsh. Keeping concealed at all times, she climbed Blackberry Mountain where Joshua and she had made love on the last nights of summer. At the spot cloaked with moss, she touched her heart and felt Joshua near.

She slid down a ravine, briars and sticks poking into her. She rested, and idly observed a remaining leaf drop gently to the earth in a hushed whisper immune to the chaos. The ground lay a ghostly white beneath the straight shaggy hickory trunks, covered with nuts, freed from their shells that the squirrels hadn't taken. With Thomas beside her, they climbed the other side. She understood his vested interest was Grace and couldn't bear to tell him the servant girl's body was one of the charred remains.

The sun was at its zenith, yet remained hidden behind a heavy mantle of leaden clouds. The day remained blustery cold, when she came to the crest of the town. She tugged her shawl around her to ward off the endless dismal sleet. What was left of Blackberry Valley lay in smoldering ruins. Almost every building was gone except the stockade walls of the fort.

Was the town safe? Had the British soldiers and warriors departed? Gunfire from the fort was infrequent and sporadic. Had anyone made it to the outlying fort or communities for help or were they destroyed as well?

Juliet inched closer, keeping hidden in the bushes just in case any Indians or redcoats remained. She thought she saw Crims and his beloved horse had been thrown on burning timbers that still smoked. Their scorched bodies drew up in the characteristically pugilistic attitude of death by fire. Juliet put her fist in her mouth to stop a sob, saying a prayer for the grizzled old widower who was now with his wife.

Colonel Allerton's body had been dragged away from the fort, stripped of his clothes, scalped and dismembered.

At the Powers' home, she counted seven bodies. Two domestics and Charles and Bethany lay near what had been their front porch. Under a tree, their daughters, Charity, Chastity,

Comfort and Cornelia had been brutally scalped and mutilated and no doubt raped.

Dozens of bodies lay scattered. Many must have been taken prisoner unless they made it to the fort or escaped. She prayed for the latter and that help would arrive to free them of their bondage.

Through the gloom, the Bell household and barns remained untouched. Odd. Perhaps the Indians had not cared. At least, Caroline would have a home to return to with her children.

A twig cracked. Bushes rustled. She and Thomas backed farther into the shrubs. A wraithlike figure crawled from the hollow of a log.

"Grace," Thomas squeezed the shaking girl in a tight hug. "I feared you were dead."

"I took refuge in the pantry, slipped a window open, dropped to the ground and ran. There were so many of them. With the glow of fires, Indians passed back and forth from where I hid, but never detected me."

Sheltered in Thomas' arms, Grace whimpered. "So many mercilessly killed, beggin' for their lives. They lined up many prisoners, stripping the men naked where they suffered fiercely from the cold and forcing them to carry heavy loads of the stolen goods. There was no sympathy for the infirmed or weak, hurried along at the points of jabbing spears."

"Old Mrs. Leppers," Grace shook her head. "Could not keep up and stumbled. A warrior whipped out his tomahawk and chopped the elderly woman across the back of the neck, severing her spine. He scalped her and left her lying where she had fallen."

"Then they herded the horses, cattle and sheep that could be herded."

"Do you think they have left for good?"

"I saw them all leave, but was too afraid to come out until I saw you."

A cannon boomed from the fort and they flinched. "Soldiers continue to defend the fort but I'm too afraid to make a run for it after what happened to Colonel Allerton. If only they had listened to you, Miss Juliet," she cried and turned into Thomas' chest while he consoled her.

So much for the folly of men and the misfortunes they reaped. "Stay here. I'm going to scout the Bells' home."

Grace grabbed her. "No, don't. What if they return?"

"I doubt if they will return. Three days have passed and they would be fearful that word had gotten out to surrounding areas and a counterattack mounted against them. I'll be back. I promise." Juliet picked up her gun, less sure of what she'd encounter.

On the hill above the Bell home, Juliet crouched and listened. Nothing stirred except for the horses whinnying for food. Thank God, she had released them so the Indians didn't slaughter them. Lancelot and Guinevere must have been smart enough to run off and now had returned home for food.

Probing her surroundings, she waited, head cocked for any sound. Nothing. She rubbed her mud-caked hands to get the circulation going. Senses heightened, she edged with slow, cautious movements to the back of the barn.

The grim sleet gave way to a dense enshrouding fog. Her garments were soaked, and she yearned for the comfort of the house. The seductive force to start a fire and snuggle deeply beneath a cozy feather tick waxed before her. She shivered. To be warm again. So close.

She leaned against the barn, clutching the growing spasm in her stomach and peered through the layers of thick fog obscuring the house. Silent. Empty? Strewn across the yard was a broken spinning wheel, books, paintings and kettles, everything the Indians decided not to take with them apparently satisfied with the booty from the town. No movement in the house. Oh, she could run to the house. Yes. She could savor the warmth and security, and hadn't Grace said she'd seen them all leave?

Lancelot and Guinevere whickered. Were the horses warning her? They were hungry, her wary mind rationalized. Suddenly their nostrils flared, tails flagged, heads elevated, ears flicked forward and backward, and then ran from the paddock. Her heart thudded wildly.

Seized by her hair, she was jerked viciously upward. Above her, Onontio's lips stretched in a cruel smile. The red and black stripes painted on his face ran together in a ghoulish mishmash. Cold, dark fear jagged up her spine. Onontio wrenched her arm.

"I will have her," shouted Snapes, stepping off the porch.

Juliet shot daggers at Snapes. The man who had brutally tortured Sarah. She did not shake with fear but with anger at herself.

"No," said Onontio. His braves crowded around him. "The woman is mine."

Snapes stepped in front of the gigantic Indian. "We are taking her to Fort Niagara with the other captives. The commander will pay money for her."

"No." Onontio threw her to the ground and lifted his breechclout.

In one swift move, Juliet kicked with all her might, struck him in the groin, rolled over, scrambled to her feet and ran into the woods. Branches slashed at her skin, tore at her gown. Roots hidden by treefall tripped her and she went sprawling, her hands skidding across sharp rocks. Palms smarting, she picked herself up and ran across a meadow until her heart exploded, until her legs were made of lead, until her breath came out in whimpers. Stumbling, tripping, someone grabbed her hair again and slammed her to the ground. Her breath whooshed out of her. Her head swirling, she rolled.

Onontio, on top of her, suddenly jerked up. His eyes hardened.

Clutching her mother's golden cross around her neck, she twisted her head to see what distracted him.

"Joshua!"

Sitting on his stallion, rage and relief surged through Joshua's veins. Onontio dared to raise his breechclout. The War Chief would die.

Then suddenly, like a plague of ravenous locusts, Onontio's men swarmed across the hilltop. Their footsteps thundered across hoary frozen ground. Ferocious war screams like a million teeming banshees.

Joshua lifted his rifle, primed and loaded, and at full gallop he fired, hit the closest Indian square in the chest. Grabbing a pistol from his belt, he put a bullet through another's head. No time to reload. Joshua dropped his guns, and shrieking a war cry of his own, he leapt from the stallion and ran at them, a tomahawk in one hand and a knife in the other.

With a sweep of his tomahawk he arced down on a warrior's head, cracking and crunching his skull. Joshua pirouetted, slashed his knife across the throat of his next assailant. A geyser of blood soaked his face, tasting vinegary. In zealous numbers, they came at him, a tempest of knives and tomahawks, rasping and keening under the leaden sky. Joshua slashed and pummeled, whirled and twisted a macabre dance of death. His foes, choking in blood fell to the ground, groaning and yowling, the sodden earth beneath oily with gore.

He saw Juliet crawl from the War Chief. And seeing Joshua, Onontio stood, twitching and throbbing with rage. He looked deranged, eyes buried deep. Bared teeth, chiseled to points. His meaty left hand bunched in a fist over his tomahawk.

A trickle of blood ran from the top of Joshua's head. Dizzy from the blows he'd received, he struggled to stay upright, his legs barely cooperating. He winced at the ragged wound a knife had left behind. Pain. Pain was good, it meant he was alive.

Onontio was six inches taller. And six inches wider. He was all bone and muscle, stronger, swollen up like a mountain. Pulse jumping in his neck. The Mohawk War Chief expected him to fear.

Joshua smiled, and then his lips drew back in a snarl. In the Haudenosaunee tongue, he bit out, "This day, you will enter the spirit world."

Onontio beat his massive chest. "You think you will defeat me. Look at Blackberry Valley. I am invincible."

"Onontio, the great warrior, slaughterer of old men, helpless women and children. Cowardice will be your infamy," Joshua taunted.

"It will be a pleasure to take your scalp and your woman."

"I defeated you. I shall do so again."

Onontio shifted his weight from one foot to the other. His prancing less sure of victory.

Joshua waited.

Juliet screamed. "Snapes!"

Joshua looked over the mammoth's shoulder. *Snapes*. The madman had a struggling and screaming Juliet in his grasp. Images of Sarah flashed.

Snapes dragged Juliet away by the hair. Onontio used the distraction to move first. Joshua hit him in the face, a colossal right, all the way up from his planted feet, as hard as he could. He caught Onontio dead on the nose, a big target, and felt his fist drive through it, and beyond it, and then his falling body weight whipped his head out from under his moving hand. Onontio went down, swung his leg out, tripped Joshua, and raised his tomahawk. On his back, Joshua clinked his tomahawk against Onontio's, his red and black striped face glaring down at him and dripping sweat in Joshua's face.

A wink of metal flashed and Onontio ripped their tomahawks away. With no weapon but his bare hands, Joshua crushed the warrior's throat, his fingertips right behind his larynx, squeezing and tearing. Onontio's face reddened, his eyes slits of rage…his right hand grasped a knife…raised it…aimed at Joshua's heart.

Joshua kicked, threw his assailant off balance, enough for him to roll and get out from under him. Onontio rose, his knife high.

A gun blasted from behind, lighting Onontio's face with surprise as a ball had entered from the back of his head and exited the front. Eyes wide open, blood spurting, he plummeted face first to the ground, flinging up columns of caked earth.

"I told him I would kill him." Two Eagles kicked the War Chief, and then reached down to pull Joshua up.

Breathing hard, Joshua said. "Good to see you my friend."

Two Eagles spat on Onontio and, handing Joshua's rifle over, said, "Go get your wife."

Rifle in hand, Joshua sprinted. He saw Snapes slap Juliet across the face, then planted his pistol on the side of her head, forcing her forward.

"You'll breathe your last," Joshua roared. A ball whizzed past his ear. Joshua halted. It was a long distance, too long. But Snapes headed to the tree line and, from there, he'd melt into the forests. No time.

Calling on his innate skills as a crack shot, Joshua raised his rifle. Eyes narrowed down the barrel, taking in all the precise silvery details. The speed of the wind and what direction it hailed from. The arc of the ball at this distance. The coward, clutched Juliet in front of his chest. Juliet, his dear sweet Juliet. What if he missed and hit her? Joshua clutched and unclutched his finger.

She stomped on Snape's foot, twisted, dropped to the ground.

He squeezed the trigger.

Snapes crumbled. Joshua ran and ran, scooping Juliet into his arms as he reached her.

"Joshua, I thought I'd never see you again," she said, collapsing against his chest.

Snapes breathed through a fine red mist oozing from his mouth. The whistling noise came from a hole in his chest.

"You are dying, you deserve to die." Joshua knelt. He had to get answers. "Why did you kill Sarah? Why the feud against my family? What have we ever done to you, Snapes?"

"An eye for an eye."

"But Sarah?"

"I had to make you suffer by killing her."

Snapes stared at his wound with wild red eyes, fearful eyes, eyes that recognized the beat of his heart pumped out and added to a pool of blood coagulating on the white hoar frost, scarlet on white.

"Suffered financial ruin and humiliation when an investment deal done with the Rutlands went sour. The Rutlands have everything. I have nothing."

Each word was punctuated with a deeply drawn-out burble as Snapes dug for one more breath. Joshua knew Snapes' lungs were filling with liquid and, in a few more seconds, he'd drown in his own blood.

"I loved my brother. He was all I had, but he was a coward... took his life. Not me. You had to pay. The Rutlands will be sorry they crossed me...all the Rutlands must pay if they haven't already."

"What do you mean? Who put you up to this?"

Snapes bubbled through a harsh laugh. "The Duke of Westbrook. I took his money, but he didn't have to pay me. The pleasure was mine."

Pleasure? Only the vilest, evilest person would take pleasure in someone else's suffering. But right now, he wanted more than anything to make Snapes suffer even more.

Snapes gurgled out a laugh. "Too bad I didn't get to tell the duke all the details."

Joshua gritted his teeth. "You're crazy. The Duke of Westbrook is a good friend of the family."

"Is he?" Snapes coughed out, then his eyes flicked from side to side and he stared into nothingness, his pig-mouth slackened and his head drooped to the side.

Joshua stared. Then shook his head. Just another bloodied corpse the devil had called home.

He stood, took Juliet again into his arms. I saw British troops heading toward Fort Stephens and guessed too late that they had divided their offenses. I hurried to Blackberry Valley as fast as I could."

Joshua smoothed a hand down Juliet's back to ease her trembling. "Did Onontio or Snapes hurt you?"

"No. I kicked Onontio to get away from him."

Within the next few minutes, while he was still holding Juliet, a dozen men from the town surrounded them, including Grace, Thomas, his father and Two Eagles.

"Crims, Maybelle!" Juliet shouted with tears of gladness, kissing the old reprobate and hugging his horse. "I thought the Indians had killed you. I saw Maybelle's hat—"

"Maybelle and I galloped out of town, dodging those demons. Her hat flew off. I wasn't fool enough to risk going back for it. She'll have a new one made for her."

To James, Juliet said, "Caroline and the children are safe. You have a new son. They are safe in a cave."

"I know, Thomas told me everything you have done. We are going to fetch them. Thank you for saving my family and bringing my new child into the world. I'll always be indebted to you, Juliet." James said and turned to Joshua. "Fort Stephens is safe, thanks to your warning. Colonel Cummings sends his best along with reinforcements."

Joshua picked his wife up in his arms and carried her to the Bell home. "When you were in those madmen's grasps, I thought I'd lost the sun, the moon and the stars. I despaired and feared of losing you. Not two sentiments I want to repeat."

"In my heart, I'd knew you'd come."

Joshua gazed down at her, nestled up against him, her tousled head resting trustingly against his chest. "How I love you."

Yet peace would not come to Joshua. Not yet. Not when he surveyed the catastrophic ruins of Blackberry Valley, innocent civilians slaughtered for nothing. The remainder of the war yawned before him. If he survived.

She pulled his face to look at her. "Joshua, I love you." The smile she gave him contained the pride of a legion of conquerors and the love of a chorus of angels.

Unexpectedly, he found himself grateful. Grateful for all the darkness, the misery and the sorrow because it allowed him to know love when he found it again. And he understood without reservation that all the ruined, broken, disregarded fragments of his soul were worth placing back together again, because, in Juliet, he discovered love and new light.

Epilogue

 $\mathcal{J}$ oshua clicked his tongue and flicked the reins, their wagon wheeling along a grassy road and Juliet's heartbeat quickened with each rhythmic thud of the horse's hooves. One step then another, closer to their little log cabin. She imagined every descriptive image Joshua had once told her.

The soil is fat and lusty and everywhere a man spits, plants grow. Cherry trees that fruit like clusters of grapes. All sorts of fowls, to take at our pleasure. Nuts as big as eggs. The river flows with lush green grass with the shelter of a mountain.

Having learned how to farm and run a household in the frontier while at both the Hayes' and the Bells' homes, she was well prepared to take on everything as a frontiersman's wife. The art of plowing, baking bread over a fire, skinning rabbits to make a stew, smoking and preserving, she could do it all. Yes, she could, and she'd be very good at it.

The last leg of the journey seemed to last forever. Her gaze drifted to her husband's handsome profile. Every time she looked at him she fell in love all over again.

A year and a half had passed since leaving the massacre of Blackberry Valley behind and subsequently moving to the safety of Fort Sullivan. There she waited, waited for Joshua, waited for the war to conclude.

The attack and destruction on Blackberry Valley and other communities created a hue and cry throughout the Colonies; that the Indians and Tories had hit vulnerable targets, taking advantage of insufficient troop weaknesses of the Colonists unable to defend themselves had brought the people together.

General George Washington vowed never to allow such carnage to happen again. So long as there were Indians in western New York and Pennsylvania who lent support to the British, such attacks as those that had occurred to Blackberry Valley, Cobleskill and German Flats and Andrustown would continue. To prevent further outrages, the perpetrators had to be rendered incapable of mounting attacks. The Iroquois Confederacy had to be destroyed.

Ojistah's prophecy whirled. *The ice this winter is thin and where once we walked upon it boldly, we must now feel our way with care, lest it collapse beneath us. We have walked into the lair of the great panther and have slapped him in the face with our hard hand. The Iroquois have brought tears to his eyes with the blow, but we have not killed him! His claws are still long and his teeth are still strong. And now, for what has been done to him, he must be very angry and we must tremble as he growls with rage.*

Behold my vision. I see many villages destroyed, hunger pinching the bellies of our children, the crying of women and children, diseases and the losing of wisdom of our elders for they will die.

But no one had listened to Ojistah. They believed the lies they had been fed. Had not good food and liquor in abundance been provided by the British? Does not their father, the King, continue to give them weapons and men to support them? They shared in the bounty of plunder that had been taken and the prisoners. They had been paid well for scalps. Why then should they be begging the Americans for peace?

Raid after raid continued, led by Thayendanegea, Sayenqueraghta, Cornplanter, Redeye, and Gucinge, who took up the hatchet against the Americans in a time of unparalleled terror. All Iroquois except the Tuscaroras and the Oneidas stayed militant. In addition, the Mingoes supported by the British attacked in the upper Ohio and Detroit, the Shawnees in Kentucky.

There had been no surcease. No relief from the horror. As promised, General Washington ordered General Sullivan and General Clinton to take the enemy to their ground and break their morale. The expedition destroyed forty Iroquois villages, demolishing stores of winter crops and breaking the power of the Six Nations in New York all the way to the Great Lakes.

Of comfort during her long months at Fort Sullivan was a letter she received from Mary. Her motherless friend basked in Waneek's care, her mother-in-law, predicting Two Eagles would be surprised upon his return to be greeted by two sons. Mary was to have twins.

After long and lonely tension-filled nights where Juliet had prayed solidly, she was rewarded with Two Eagles' and Joshua's safe return.

There were so many incidents in the aftermath, some good, some bad. Edmund Faulkner, her cousin, had set up a law practice in Albany, partnering with his brother, Two Eagles.

Edmund traveled the Mohawk Valley to meet with clients and using every opportunity to visit his mother Waneek who welcomed him with open arms. Of Tionnontigo's fall, Juliet learned Ojistah had made it safely to her twin sister's home with her grandson, Morning Sun, and Father Devereux. Never reaching the coasts of his beloved England, Colonel Thomas Faulkner had died from alcoholism, his bones interred on the shores of Lake Ontario. Crims, James and Caroline Bell and their nine children, Betsy, Grace and several other Blackberry Valley surviving citizens left the town and had resettled closer to Albany. Of the eighty prisoners the warriors took hostage that fateful day, only forty returned.

With the war ebbing, communications flowed back and forth across the Atlantic. A letter had arrived from the Duke of Rutland, Joshua's father, comforted with the news of Snapes' death and Joshua's safety. The duke detailed the demise of Duke Cornelius Westbrook, answering the mystery of who had been the mastermind behind the plot to ruining the Rutland family. Vicar Abrams passed away from a violent heart attack during a Sunday sermon never knowing his only child, Mary, was happily married to a savage. Juliet's uncle who had taken her ancestral home in England had lost all to gambling debts and died in a duel. Reports of Baron John Bearsted's prosecution for his crimes against Juliet and Mary was followed by his imprisonment at Newgate. This news was met favorably by Two Eagles, Joshua, Mary and her.

Of most significance was the safe return of Joshua's older brother, Nicholas, and then the surprising and joyful arrival of two subsequent nephews, one born to Rachel and Anthony, and another to Nicholas and his wife, Alexandra—both born on the same day!

Juliet turned and patted the wedding wheel Ojistah had given her, a fine gift she'd hang in her home. She adjusted the blanket around her sleeping infant daughter, held securely in her arms, and decided now was the time to share the foretelling with Joshua.

"Waneek and Ojistah prophesized our daughter, and her daughter will be of great importance."

The glowing adoration in Joshua's eyes as he gazed upon his daughter warmed Juliet. "I take their visions as gold. Who knows what our daughter and granddaughter's destinies will be? All the events these past months have opened up the vast Ohio country, the Great Lakes region, Pennsylvania, West Virginia and Kentucky."

"Our daughter is an infant," she continued, "—and I pray she doesn't have your wanderlust, at least not yet…which brings me to question…how are we going to house your father, Rachel and Anthony, Nicholas and Alexandra, your Uncle Thomas, Abigail and Captain Thorne and their children in our tiny log cabin when they come to visit? Joshua, you must think this out."

He clicked the reins, urging the stallions forward. "I'll think of something."

"You better think fast. Chances are they will appear on our doorstep the same time we arrive."

Juliet sighed. The forests they traveled through were struck with the colors of fire, the leaves had turned to magma-reds, hot-oranges and fever-yellows. Wild turkeys clucked beneath the bushes and hard nuts thunked to the ground while squirrels scuttled across crackly leaves, eager to seize one final reward. A wind gusted, swirling the branches of the trees surrounding them. Leaves soared to life by brusque autumnal notes that stirred them from slumber, inviting a final waltz before a wintry embrace would claim them.

Ahead, the undulating path gave way to an aperture of blazing saffron-yellow light and opened to a clearing. Juliet blinked. Dazzling sunrays streamed over a three-story mansion of blunted gray stonework with huge white columns; stretching its rousing length with undeniable luxuriant confidence, before surrendering itself to wide green meadows where cattle and sheep grazed. The owner had strategically placed it on a high bluff above the glittering, jewel-blue Mohawk River. She gazed in awe so taken with the beauty of the home.

Joshua hauled back on the reins at the entrance, and Juliet leaned into him, reminded of her worn appearance. "We cannot possibly stop here. I'd rather travel farther…to our home."

Joshua leapt from the wagon and swooped Juliet and their daughter up in his arms. Disturbed, the baby cried from the movement.

"You've woken, Rebekah," Juliet chastised, knowing the babe wanted to feed. "Put me down. What will the owners think?"

Joshua laughed, holding her tight in his embrace. "How else am I to carry my bride over our threshold?"

Juliet widened her eyes. "Ours?"

"I had the home built the past few months. I wanted it to be a surprise."

Juliet's mouth worked up and down. "I thought we were

going to live in a log cabin. I thought we were going to work your little patch of earth."

"Oh, that." He swept her into the house and she estimated, more than a dozen rooms on the first floor.

"Our little farm," he laughed, "has in excess of five thousand acres. And you will have little work to do with hired servants."

He did not let her exclaim as she struggled to take in every single thing. Moira's words came back to her. *Sometimes, the bad things that happen to us in our lives put us directly on the path to the best things that will ever happen to us.* How right she had been.

Joshua glided into a dining room and stood her in front of a tapestry. "A belated wedding gift from my father. I remember how you were immersed in the tapestry at the Hayes'. This is of finer quality and has hung in Belvoir Castle for centuries."

Juliet sat in a chair her frontiersman husband had pulled up, transfixed by the beautiful tapestry. Pulling out her breast, she let her baby greedily suckle while gazing upon the story of her Achilles and the lovely maiden.

She considered the tapestry, discovering how every aspiration, purpose, struggle, every hue, every character, every deed and consequence, every part of worldly realism and the conclusions that it produced, every connection made, every delicate instant of history and possibility, every emotion and birth and vow was intertwined into that endless, magnanimous web.

Her real life Achilles knelt beside her, nuzzling his chin into their daughter's downy red hair. "I am so blessed to have you in my life, Juliet."

She would always remember this time, this instant, this memory stamped forever on her mind. Joshua, their daughter, Rebekah, and she were each a thread woven together to make a tapestry of elaborate texture. And the tapestry told their story...the story was their past soaring to their future.

Author's Note

This is a novel, and to construe it as anything else would be an error. The frontier during the American Revolution was a place of beauty and violence. For the sake of storytelling, time was compressed of fictionalized events, places and people. Real components of New York and Pennsylvania personages and history are woven and mirror events of the Cherry Valley Massacre, Wyoming Valley Massacre and the brutal annihilation of Fort Forty and Fort Wintermute by Tories and the Iroquois.

Thayendanegea, or Joseph Brant, was a Mohawk War Chief and educated at Moor's Indian Charity School, a forerunner of Dartmouth College. He had traveled to England where he met the King and had great celebrity.

During General Sullivan's campaign, the homelands and foundation of Iroquois life had been shattered. Breaking the Iroquois Confederacy's power to maintain their crops and use their villages caused famine and dispersion of the Iroquois. Many relocated to Canada, Oklahoma and Wisconsin, leaving their homelands in New York, Pennsylvania and Ohio open for the white man's westward expansion.

White slavery under the guise of the "Indentured Servant" is a forgotten story of the thousands of Britons who lived and died in bondage in the American Colonies—a cruelty that spanned a hundred and seventy years. During the seventeenth and eighteenth centuries, more than three hundred thousand white people were shipped as slaves to work in the tobacco fields of Virginia, and on farms throughout the emerging Colonies. Because of the brutal conditions, life expectancy was no more than two years. Street urchins in London were swept off the streets, and parents of large families too poor to maintain all their young were duped into selling their children for what they thought yielded opportunity. Brothels were raided to provide "breeders" and prisons were purged of convicts and paraded like livestock. George Washington abhorred the trade and abolished the practice with American Independence.

The Haudenosaunee, or Iroquois, people recognize animals and spirits with deep reverence, believing they possess potent "orenda" or great power and can aid one to achieve success through particular gifts. By understanding the religion of the People of the Longhouse, one can perceive the mystical connection with the animal world which produces great feelings of affection, wonder, awe, and—fear. The combination of these sentiments encourages great animal beings to establish themselves as productive and good, or unearths monstrosities that use "otgont" or destructive power endangering humans.

I always say that I'm a storyteller, not a historian, and as a storyteller, I'm more concerned with the what-ifs than the why-nots. I so enjoy taking a bit of artistic license in order to bring you the most exciting, sensual, love story that my what-if imagination can create.

Acknowledgments

Most books wouldn't be written without the help of some special people. I would like to acknowledge Caroline Tolley, my developmental editor and Linda Styles, my copy editor and Scott Moreland, my line editor. Their insight and expertise were indispensable. Hugs also to my spouse, Edward, five children, eight grandchildren, Eugene Dollard, Dr. Marcianna Dollard, and posthumously, Loretta Bysiek—your love and comfort surround me.

Many thanks to the gracious support of Nancy Crawford, Brenda Kosinski, Paula Ursoy and Western New York Romance Writers Group.

Also, many thanks to Mr. James Crane, Director of Seneca Language and Custom School for his infinite knowledge of the Senecas, posthumously to Chief Corbett Sundown of Tonawanda who inspired my love of the Iroquois. Men of his ilk walk the earth but seldom am I glad to have shared the same path. Special thanks to the late Seneca medicine woman, Myrtle Petersen, who inspired my love of wild plants and medicine. Also, special thanks to the late Princess Morning Dove for her diligent and delightful descriptions of the Iroquois.

About the Author

Elizabeth St. Michel, the best-selling author of the *Duke of Rutland Series* has received multiple awards for her work.

Her first book, *The Winds of Fate*, was a number-one hit on Amazon's list of best sellers and a quarterfinalist for the Amazon Breakthrough Novel Award.

Sweet Vengeance: Duke of Rutland Series I received the International Book Award.

Surrender the Wind received the Holt medallion and the Reader's Choice Award and was a finalist for the National Rone Award, which honors literary excellence in romance writing.

St. Michel lives in New York and the Bahamas.

Dear Readers,

It has given me great pleasure to write *Lord of the Wilderness* for you. There is no greater compliment to me as an author than for my readers to become so involved with the characters that you want me to write more. That said, I'm happily returning to the Civil War era and the Rourke family.

As you know, my first installment, *Surrender the Wind,* detailed the journey of Catherine Fitzgerald, a wealthy New York heiress and legendary Rebel General John Daniel Rourke. My second installment will acquaint us with General Rourke's brother, Colonel Lucas Rourke, head of Civilian Spying for the North. Colonel Lucas Rourke is honor bound to uphold the Union and responsible for a vast network of spies. When Confederates abduct him, his only hope is the enigmatic spy who surrenders her heart and soul to save him.

Rachel Pierce is the notorious Saint. Witnessing her father's brutal murder by slaveholders, she emerges disciplined in the high art of spying, moving through southern latitudes like a ghost with no trace of her footsteps and defying every one of her enemies without the slightest hint of their knowledge. Caught in a dangerous web of intrigue, they uncover secrets that will prolong the war and cast them both in danger.

Although I can't tell you much more I can promise you this: like my last novels, it is written with one goal in mind—to make you experience the laughter, the love, and all the other myriad emotions of its characters. And when it's over to leave you smiling...

Warmly,
Elizabeth St. Michel

P.S. If you would like to receive an emailed newsletter from me, which will keep you informed about my books-in-progress, please contact me on Facebook or my webpage at elizabethstmichel.com. The greatest gift you can give an author is a review for her work. I would be thrilled to hear from you!

Made in the USA
Middletown, DE
24 June 2019